THE LAST
BROOMSQUIRE

MARTIN HESP

THE LAST BROOMSQUIRE

FLAGON PRESS

SOMERSET
2010

First Published in 2010
Flagon Press
Forge House, Fore St, Winsham,
Chard, Somerset TA20 4DY
www.james-crowden.co.uk

ISBN : 978-0-9562778-1-7

Cover image of the Quantocks © Sue Onley 2010
from an original painting commissioned
specifically for the book.

Design by Andrew Crane
www.axisweb.org/artist/andrewcrane

Printed by Remous Ltd, Milborne Port,
Dorset DT9 5EP
www.remous.co.uk

Typeset in 11pt Monotype Bembo

AUTHOR'S PREFACE
HOW THE BROOMSQUIRE CAME TO BE

If you grow up in the shadow of an exceedingly beautiful upland like the Quantock Hills there is a strong likelihood that the great eminence will in some way affect your development. Such a large physical feature in the landscape maintains a constant presence simply because of its size and scale, but there's more to it than that: the mere curvature of the hills seems to echo thoughts and memories, and the distant winding coombes that disappear into the red sandstone bowels of those hills never fail to inspire thoughts of mystery and excitement.

For the imaginative child growing up in the vale nearby, the hills become that "other place". They are a realm of the subconscious. They are a constant, and yet their secrets remain aloof and unknown. They are with you always - but, for the most part, only as an idea or whim.

Over time, this idea evolves and grows. As a tiny child you might be taken up to the ridge by your parents to see the views, later you will explore their forests with boyhood friends after long wearying walks up from the vale. Then the legends and tales of the hills begin to have their role. But strongest and most formative of all, there's the influence real stories have, because they've been told to you by real people.

My first Quantock memories are, somewhat inevitably, linked with food. My grandmother would serve delicious whortleberry pie and tell of how she and her sisters would, as children, pick the tiny fruit up on the heaths above Crowcombe. If the unique flavour and colour of that pie live long with me, more powerful still is her tale of the broomsquire. He had come stalking up to where the sisters were kneeling at their labours in his long blue cloak and caused such fright that they took to their heels and didn't stop running until they passed the Carew Arms way down in the village. My grandmother's fear of this strange, almost supernatural person called a broomsquire has haunted me ever since, just as it haunted her. I shall forever hold in my mind an image of those sisters running down that white dusty road outside the pub, where the old men laughed and jeered with delight as the panicking girls passed in a blur of skirts and screams.

Years after she told me the story my old editor, Jack Hurley, at the West Somerset Free Press, would tell me more about broomsquires. He said very little was known about them, but that his predecessor - a man called Herbert Kille - had done some investigations in the early 1900s. Jack's favourite story concerning them was that one of their number had achieved a notoriety unusual for a broomsquire by killing his wife.

I can still see old Jack, with his 60-a-day rasp of a voice describing the scene when Johnny Walford is taken into The George for a final meal, with the great press of now silent villagers peering through the windows. I imagined that dark room and that hush as Jack sat there wreathed in cigarette smoke in his own dark room, with a single beam of light coming through the window to illuminate the blue billows emanating from his "gasper". Never before had I heard a real story about a real person that was so filled with the terror of the inevitable – a yarn so incredibly pregnant with the sense of unavoidable doom.

And never before had I heard a story that seemed to provoke so much visual imagery. The tale of Johnny Walford's last journey being halted at Nether Stowey by a wild and angry throng seemed to me to be an English version of something you'd see in some exotic Italian or French movie. As a young reporter, I knew that village, I knew that pub, and I knew the place which to this day is called Walford's Oak.

Then there were the tales of the Romantic Poets, told to me by my own journalist father who loved nothing better than to explore the hills and write about their crop of famous poets. Since he told me about them I've loved the idea of these extraordinary men who, as far as I can make out, invented the concept of walking in untamed countryside simply for pleasure and inspiration. How strange was it that Coleridge and Wordsworth should have lived in the very same parish as the doomed broomsquire?

It was my father who took me to Fyne Court and showed me the lightning rods erected in the trees by the Wizard of the Quantocks -copper rods that that still remain aloft there to this day.

You can imagine how powerful the story became when my father told me it was thought that Andrew Crosse had been the main inspiration for Mary Shelley's Frankenstein story. Later I took a television camera down the pot-hole near Fyne Court where The Thunder and Lightning Man collected the pure water for his experiments and saw his rusting implements lying amid the stalagmites. As far as I know, I am one of the few living people to have gone down there, and so spooky and cramped was it I'd never dream of returning again.

As a newspaper journalist I have spent years writing features about the mud-horse fishermen of Bridgwater Bay and their strange sledge contraptions. I've waxed lyrical about the smugglers of Kilve who had a revenue-dodging horse who was trained to bolt when told to stop, and stop when told to run…

And so I suppose it is hardly surprising that, since I was a child on my grandmother's knee hearing about the broomsquire, the rich seam of yarns and anecdotes have been building in me. Over half a century those hills of my youth – those near-yet-far, beautiful, mystical eminences – became in some ways more tangible, in others more ethereal.

For me the tale of the Quantocks has become a romantic weft and weave - a mental tapestry draped across a very real backdrop. Which is what this book is. A series of fairly real pictures based on authentic situations and occurrences, weaved together to form a whole that I am the first to admit is far from being historically correct. If you are a stickler for accuracy, best read no further. If you demand hard-and-fast dates to run in a genuine chronological order, then this will be a yarn you can shoot down in flames.

But if you are fascinated by the idea that just a small handful parishes huddled around some scenic hills could play host to so much that was amazingly romantic, thrilling and intriguing - then read on…

MARTIN HESP

DEDICATION

For Chris Flewitt – a Quantock boy
whose early death
helped inspire this book

THE LAST BROOMSQUIRE

WITH A FRONTISPIECE PURPORTED TO HAVE
BEEN WRITTEN BY THOMAS POOLE

It is with a heavy heart that I write these words. I do so because I have become the recipient of the following narrative in which my friend Johnny Walford has written down the story of his life: a life which, as the result of the murder of his wife, is to be concluded at the end of a rope tomorrow.

I have visited Johnny one last time today and it was his final request to me that I should keep these writings safe and, after one year and a day, hand them to the woman that he loved. This I shall do, just as I fully intend fulfilling his other request: that I describe the events that surround his final hours in order to provide the postscript that he cannot write himself.

I do not know whether any person other than his beloved Anne Rice shall ever read the manuscript, but if it is to be seen by people who did not know the man then I feel it is my duty to furnish some details as to what sort of person he was.

Johnny Walford had more vitality, more spirit and life flowing through his veins than any person I have known. He was generally cheerful and always generous. Added to these qualities, he was handsome - so much so that there were times when one found oneself querying if he was indeed of this world. I have heard others mention this unearthly quality, but perhaps they, and I, have it wrong: he was more earthly, more as Mother Nature intended man to be, than anything else I have seen in the general run of human-kind. This beauty was not only related to his physical appearance; it was also produced by a gentle radiance that seemed to emanate from him.

His good humour, his cheerfulness and intelligence made him by far the most popular denizen of these hills. Morally speaking he was not a saint and, latterly, he succumbed to all manner of temptation that came his way. With his yellow-tinged chestnut locks and his brown, handsome face; his laughing eyes and the smile that was never far from his lips - it would be an understatement to say that the opposite sex were drawn to him. Indeed, his charm went further than that; for men too, found it easy to fall under his spell.

I first knew him when he was but a small boy. His late father was a man for whom I held a high regard and he too enjoyed elements of this natural charm which seemed to be a thing handed down from generation to generation among their clan. It is an interesting story, the account of those people collectively known as Broomsquires, for it is said that they represent the last vestiges of an ancient race whose territory has declined over many centuries. The few remaining members of this old Westcountry tribe are now to be found living in just one place, and that is on the ridge and in the coombes of the Quantock Hills.

In some ways Johnny became the son I never had. Consequently, I have been a close witness to much that he recalls in his narrative and can vouch for almost every word of it. It is my hope that his writings will convey some of the happiness and joy that was inherent in his life. If I know him as I believe I do, Johnny Walford will die with the same sense of courage and grace that has, throughout, been such a central part of his character. I have wondered long and hard these past few weeks how different his lot may have been if certain things had, or had not, occurred. But there is no point in us gnawing at the unchangeable. Johnny Walford knows he must die, and God in His Mercy will deal with my young friend as He sees fit.

THE LIFE AND TIMES OF JOHNNY WALFORD

PART 1

EARLY DAYS

My name is John Walford and that is all I have left in this world. A name. And even that is illusory, for rarely have I been hailed as either John or Walford. Johnny is what people have called me since the days when I first crawled and stumbled in the coombes and cups of the hills. My Quantock Hills. The soft curving mountain that runs south from the Bristol Channel, betwixt the flatness of The Levels and the remote sea-borne vastness of Exmoor.

I call it a mountain, knowing that it is but a tiny ridge in the greater scheme of God's geography, but to me Quantock is the stuff of eminence and elevation. From the great bare tops you can see half the world. You can see the country of Wales across the sea: you can see the Mendip Hills, unlovely and stark to the east and between them and you lies the wide flooded void of the flatlands. Sweeping west they rise to the landlocked, patchwork Vale of the Tone and beyond, to the south, stand the flat-topped Blackdown Hills. And so the great vista rolls on into the county of Devon and to the south and west there is a glimpse of distant Dartmoor while close by, in the direction of the setting sun, the Brendon Hills begin their march to Exmoor's lonely heights.

I tell you all this because I am setting out the story of my life and, if anyone is to understand it, then they must have some concept of the Elevated Sense of Being enjoyed by the folk of the hills. Few are born up there on Quantock's lofty ridge. Even fewer remain to eke a living there. And none but the Walfords stay to die.

My friend Sam Coleridge put it like this:
"Dim coasts, and cloud-like hills, and shoreless ocean -
It seemed like omnipresence! God, me thought,
Had built him there a temple: the whole world
Seemed imaged in its vast circumference."
The Quantocks: with their bosomly cleft of combe, their sylvan,

shapely, contours and their high, heath-clad moors where the breeze soughs without end. Who, and what I am, is but clay formed in this crucible of sandstone and heather and my life-blood is naught but the clear cold water of a Quantock stream.

Johnny: that is how the people in the hill-side villages and farms have known me. From Porlock in the west and the Parrett in the east, Johnny the Broomsquire has enjoyed his own humble fame among the vales. It is strange, now that I come to think of it in my final days: the idea that all his life a man is attached to a thing as abstract and whimsical as a name. A sound, and that is him: Johnny the Broomsquire. That sound is me. But soon there will be no flesh to give substance to the name. It will have to survive by itself, as a memory, as a thought - as a little murmur of sadness passing the lips of an old Quantock friend. And then, when the people who knew me are gone, the name that was mine will be the stuff of hand-me-down whispers. That is why I have asked for pen and paper. In these few remaining days I will write the name Johnny Walford, and I will furnish it with the story of its companion in flesh.

This then, is my tale: an explanation of what I did and why. I had hoped to see more in my years, but at least I can rejoice that for quarter of a century I have sauntered as free as a buzzard across my beloved hills.

I may as well begin the story by telling you why I am about to die. I will not hide from you what I did - or at least am supposed to have done - in a single moment of madness. I took the life of the woman to whom it was my great misfortune to have been wed. As far as I can remember, it was a single blow lashed out in anger and frustration. But it seems some evil must have overtaken me in my sleep and urged me to finish the job. Having felled her by the side of the road, I cut her throat. Perhaps I did but, though I recall knocking her down, I swear I know nothing of the terrible, final act. That it occurred I have no doubt, for I awoke on the moor to find her lying next to me, cold and dead. The blood on my clasp-knife proved my undoing, though how the blood got there, I shall never know.

Poor, unhappy Jane: I cannot think that her judge, the Lord God Almighty, will have had much leniency on her when she came before him. He must surely have sent her to the dark domain that is her rightful abode. Soon I too shall stand before Him and no doubt

He will treat me much the same. All I can ask is that the two children that we leave on this Earth will not be tainted by the sorry debacle of their parents. I am beyond compassion, Lord Kenyon knew that when he sentenced me. He did what he had to do, though he did it in tears. Already, I am told, the people of the county are calling him the Weeping Judge.

There is an oak in a Quantock coombe that I love. In my mind I can see it now; a magnificent thing that's cast its mighty shadow over that secret glade for many a long century. Often have I sheltered under its boughs, yet soon its soughing majesty will be defiled by my corpse.

So how did I come to this brutal, untimely end? Temptation is the answer. The base enticement of man. It was the lust which lies in all our bosoms that had the beating of me.

To tell my story properly I must return to the sunlit days of my childhood, for I would wish you to know something of the way in which my character was wrought. You see, they say that we Walfords come from a different stock; that we are the last of an ancient race - a people that, long ago, lived in peace from the low moors of the Parrett to the granite hills of the west. Centuries and centuries ago, before even the Romans came, great tribes moved across the country and began to clear the forests and farm the valleys. Our people - my people - called the Dumnonii, were driven from the land, but a few survived in remote parts.

To be honest, I have no knowledge as to whether this is some fancy, or if it may be true - but I do know that the Walfords were always hill people through and through. My father, his father, and his father's father - Walfords way back beyond memory have only ever lived high on the moors. From Lydeard in the south, to the great headland at West Quantoxhead in the north - those uplands have been our domain.

My father did what his father did, and his before him. He made charcoal and he cut broom to make the brushes which he sold down in the villages of the vales. That is why, long ago, we came to be known as Broomsquires. Famous from hamlet to town were we, dressed in our great blue capes, carrying our bundles of brooms.

Famous but few. When I was born you could count the number of broomsquires on one hand. Now, I believe, my passing will see the end of us. In my short lifetime this traditional existence of ours has been eroded by the promise of comfort. Life is hard up there on the hill and, one by one, my compatriots have taken the lure of cottages and paid work. The Quantock broomsquires are now, or soon will be, a race of the past.

My father was a great broomsquire. A man whose doings were renown from Bridgwater to Barnstaple. A man, it is said, who could knock down a stag with a single blow. A man who knew more country-lore by the time he was a dozen years of age than most wiseacres do in three-score years and ten.

Much of his time was spent in the woods at the shrouded and unseen job of charcoal burning, which is endless and wearisome work unless you are born to it and then, somehow, the slow rhythm of the moil marks time deep within your soul. Although we are known as broomsquires, it is the charcoal that brings us in a large part of our meagre income. Somehow it is easy to put down in words the basics of our existence, but it is more than a story of work; it is a way of life, and to do it, to understand it, you must live it. The charcoal burner must tend his kiln day and night for weeks at a time and often my father would not venture from the forest for a month. But he was never lonely, for we lived there with him in the woods. It is a world of green darkness smeared with smoke and steam. A world of ceaseless toil made bearable, at least it seems to me now, by the fragrance of the smoke mixed with the leafy, lush, verdant, fungal smell of the woods. There's many, I am sure, who would dislike that aroma, but for me it was the essence of home.

It is strange how, when you miss something, you think of its scents and smells. Sound too, is evocative and ours was a life eased by the gentleness of birdsong, yaffle-call, fox-bark, stag-bulving, axe-fall and the music of the lark.

Apart from the charcoal burning, there is the gathering of oak bark for the tanning works owned by a man we shall hear more of in my narrative. This is a springtime job when the bark is stripped as the sap is rising. The bark is levered off then stacked to dry before being taken down to the tannery.

But the work that gives us our name is the wild harvest of the broom out on the sunlit, windblown heath. That is a lonely and yet invigorating time. A life of vista and clean air, followed by weeks of manufacture which would see the whole family sitting around the camp tying the brooms. Once they were made, my father – like all broomsquires – would be off on his travels to sell the brushes and we would not see him for weeks as he collected, and spent, his coins. When I say we, I mean mother, my three sisters Sylvestra and Avice and Petronilla, my brother William, and me – the youngest.

First memories. There's a thing to bring tears to a man consigned to die. Essences – dreamy, misty glimpses of babyhood – flood and choke a battered soul. The darkness of the hut. Sheepskin. The oily scent and touch of lamb's wool. First impressions of the warm void of the smoke filled hut. The soft, creamy, unforgettable smell of mother. My mother's perpetual presence, somehow indeterminate – she came and went with her gentle grace and I knew not why she should ever put me down. I craved her soft arms, her milky breast. Even now I can recall the longing.

Other details begin to crowd. Always the rank breath of dog and the friendly warm slipperiness of their tongues. My sisters falling out with each other and shouting, or laughing, or playing with me as if I were some kind of an inanimate doll. The sound of metal upon metal associated with the aroma of food – utensils stirring whatever was in the big pot. And music. There was always music in the Walford camp. The violin would haunt the place and somehow dictate its very mood.

William pinching me to make me cry. Flies, moths, lamps and then outside – birds, butterflies, the dogs chasing each other, my sisters' laughter, the muffled echoey sounds from the woods, ant-bites, ants, bees, flutterbies. The hot earth under my naked back while I gazed up at white drifting clouds. Clouds that stayed still while the earth shot past on its way to a world of childish reverie. The minutiae of intense fascination in the vast blank of eternity: that is the lot of the small, watchful child.

And then there was the great presence. The man. Strong, a little fearsome, and always somehow thrilling. The enormous blue cape of my father darkening the door. The first memories of being borne aloft in his strong arms. The feel of his beard upon my face. His soft crooning voice, sometimes whispering to me – often singing his strange meaningless songs as he played the violin. For him, selecting notes on that instrument was something akin to breathing. It was as effortless as the soughing of wind in the trees.

My father would come and go, seemingly without reason, at any time of the day or night. But when he returned it was always me that he caressed with his beaming affection. From those early days until the moment he died, there was no-one on earth I looked up to more. And until much later there was no-one I loved more, but that was to change, as you shall hear. Of course I loved my mother dearly too, but I was a boy, living far out in the depths of the hills, a father is an all-powerful thing. What knowledge, what strength and courage he must have, to come and go as if there was nothing to it. To step beyond the forest.

One of earliest memories is of him coming into the clearing carrying a dead stag on his shoulders. I must have been about three or four years of age and I recall mother fretting because my father had taken a terrible risk in killing the beast. Within minutes the noble, stinking animal was being butchered; its once powerful limbs, cut asunder. The fartings and stench of its guts. The dogs going mad, ripping the foul innards apart in a frenzy. Father's hands would carry the sharp acrid smell of dear-meat for days. But the venison kept us in food for a midwinter month and even now in this dank cell I can smell the savoury roasting of its flesh. Other times it would be a sheep or a lamb, more often there were rabbits, hares or wild birds. My father made sure that his family had flesh to eat and in later years he taught me to steal, quietly, stealthily, for the pot.

We cooked over an open fire, outside if it was fine weather, inside if there was rain or snow. Then the hut would fill with smoke even though there was a flap in the roof. We had one enormous pot and so most of our meals would be served as stew or broth, though sometimes good meat was spit-roasted over the fire. Both mother and father knew of herbs and mushrooms that would add a luxuriance and interest to the meals. That same old pot still hangs above my fire. Or maybe it doesn't anymore. Anyway, by the age of six I had learned many of these culinary tricks and I have used them to help me enjoy my food ever since.

Indeed the hunt for food afforded me my first adventure away from the camp. I was taken by father to a fish-weir down on the coast while my mother and sisters prepared for our annual move. Every year we moved from one small coombe to another so that father could begin coppicing fresh woodland. These were always fraught periods and as a small boy I disliked the disruption of it all. Our meagre family belongings had to be packed in groundsheets and tarpaulins which my father told me were sails of ships that had wrecked along the coast. He liked the sea and its shore, and was forever going down there for fish, prawns, shrimps, limpets, cockles, mussels, laver and the like. As I grew older I discovered that he did more besides collect the harvest of the sea, but on this day mother had made up her mind that he should take me with him. They fell into a dispute, but I had noticed that she often got the best of the great man when it came to the domestic side of things. I was plucked from a corner and hoisted to the lofty ramparts of father's wide shoulders, and so began my first journey beyond the woods.

Within a dozen minutes we had gone farther than I'd ever ventured before. We were climbing out of the coombe through the low, thick hoar oak that covers so much of the Quantocks' eastern flanks. Suddenly we were out on the high heath and I had never seen such space before. I did not know the sky could be so big. The great hill seemed to curve away forever.

"Look around you Johnny, for this is your home," said my father as we topped the ridge. "This is the kingdom of the Walfords. It was the kingdom of the ancient people from whom our seed has sprung. Look at it son, and remember."

I do remember. There, across the valley from which we had just emerged, was the circular rampart of Dowsborough with its ancient fort, now just an earthy bank. Father told me our people had once fought great battles there. Below us, on the same ridge, was Lower Hare Knap and beyond were fields stretching across smaller hills to the sea.

The sea. Blue and grey and vast. Beyond it you could see the black hills of Wales. My father pointed to the villages far below and said we'd be passing through them on our way to the shore. I could see why we'd come to the ridge which cut down through the maze of coombes and by following it we could make good ground. So began my education in the little known art of travelling fast in hill country. No-one can cross moors and heaths, valleys and coombes quicker than a broomsquire. We know the secret ways - how to use each dip and tuck to advance us on our way. On foot, I have beaten a horseman crossing the length of the Quantocks. Only a broomsquire could cover such ground in such time, and I did it barely breaking into a sweat.

At Kilve we saw buildings and I was taken aback to learn that people dwelt in such places. To me they looked like upright caves. Windows, glass, chimneys, thatch, the smells of cooking, the chatter of men together, men on horseback, oxen ploughing, donkeys braying, the screech of the pump, the ring of the blacksmith's hammer - all were new to the little boy from the hills. Father spoke to various people, who all seemed to know him and there was a good deal of banter and laughter. It wasn't long before we entered one of the buildings. Inside I recognised the beery, cidery smells because they had often come home on father's breath. The people in the room made a great fuss of me and I was given an apple and a hunk of cheese.

Then we were on the beach. The great, grey, endless, rocky beach that reveals itself at Kilve Pill when the tide goes out. There was the smell of salt and mud, seaweed and ooze. My father was talking to an old man dressed in rags - to this day I have never seen anyone adorned more filthily than Montague Chidgey. The word unkempt does not do justice to his wild appearance. Nor have I ever seen the face of a man more creased and pitted with lines and grooves. This visage was black-brown in colour and it had the texture of a rock that has been scraped by barnacles for a thousand years. Montague was a mud-horse fisherman and a glatsman -and it seemed father had some sort of understanding with him over the fishing. My presence though, seemed to be causing Monty some concern.

"Leave 'un up 'ere on the grass," the old fisherman was saying. "There'll be a good haul of pilchard and herring if I know ort about it and us'll 'ave our 'and's full enuff as tis."

But my father was having none of it. And I was placed on the top of Montague's 'horse'. This was a wooden sledge with a trestle that carried the big basket in which the fish would be thrown. It was all a mystery to me that first day, but the basis of the business was that the fisherman employed the services of the tide to help him catch his haul, rather than set to sea in a boat.

"You'll never catch I in one o' they boats," he once told me. "They'm dangerous things. What do ee wan' 'em fur when the sea will bring the fish to thee?"

He had two ways of trapping fish. The first we came across that day was an enormous 'V' shaped wall made from loose stones. The point of the 'V' was nearest the sea so, as the tide went out, fish would be caught in the narrowest end where a wattle gate let out the water, but not the catch.

Then, even further down the beach, there were the long, sock-like nets hung between poles. The mud-horse gave Monty an easy way out to these and I soon saw the beauty of the thing as he pushed it effortlessly across the sea of ooze. The two men busied themselves at the nets while great flocks of birds wheeled about hoping for a morsel. Indeed, a use was soon found for me and I spent a happy hour chasing the crows and gulls.

Later, in Monty's dark, aromatic home I had my second memorable meal that day. He boiled shrimps in a cauldron and put still flapping flat fish into a huge spitting skillet.

The old man's bright eyes seemed to gleam from the darkness and I had the feeling some distant thought had stirred a wave far out on the salty horizon of his life.

"Mind the bones boy," he sighed, and the three of us sat there in darkness of the hut and ate in a silence that was broken only by cracks from the fire and the sound of the two men swigging from their flasks. Eventually they talked of the glat-hunt where men go out with small dogs to hunt conger eels that lie in crevices in the tide pools, it is the favourite sport of the poor men of the coast. And the herring. They talked of the herring season when vast shoals of fish would be caught and put in barrels to be sent across to what they called plantations somewhere across the ocean.

After that first outing father would often take me along on his travels. We liked each other's company and somehow I knew when to be silent and when to chat and laugh. We often returned to the beach and I do believe old Monty grew fond of me. Indeed I know he did because, when he died years later, he bequeathed me his mudhorse, glatting hooks and nets.

But I recall other characters from those early days. There was mad Marmaduke who crossed and recrossed the hills driving a herd of imaginary cattle. He spent his entire days ranting and raving at the cows that never were – but, so real were his words and actions that my father swore he could see the flies around the heads of the phantom beasts.

Then there were the Greenslades whose peculiar abode we'd often visit on our travels. Mr Greenslade had been a broomsquire until the rheumatics made life on the hill unbearable for him. After that the Parish wanted to put the old couple in the Poor-House, but no broomsquire could survive that, so Fenwick and Mercy Greenslade had finally settled under the buttress of a disused church tower. The main body of the church had been ruined in some violent storm of old so only the tower remained, but it was in a quiet dell out of the wind and rain, and few people ever passed that way. The old couple were quite content with their eccentric home. We'd call in occasionally and take them a rabbit, or whatever, and father and I would listen as they talked of the old ways of the broomsquires before the numbers died away.

When the Parson tried to evict them from their home, my father went to see a wonderful man - a great man - who, I am proud to say, was to become a true friend of mine. Mr Thomas Poole was the finest kind of friend a man could ever have and father knew him because he was the gentleman who owned the tannery that bought in the bark we stripped. We had walked down off the hill to the village of Stowey to see if there was anything he could do to help the Greenslades keep their home. Knocking at the door of the largest house, father gave his name and we were shown to the back where we found ourselves in an area the likes of which I'd never seen before. "Tis a garden Johnny," said father in a whisper. Even he seemed daunted by the intricate, domesticated arrangement of the place. Any amount of flowers and shrubs grew in rows and we walked down a path made up of thousands of beach pebbles laid on end. This entered a kind of tunnel that was ablaze with roses and, after a few yards, there was a bend that gave out upon a wonderful spot which the servant had called Mr Poole's lime tree bower.

There the great man sat. It was the first time I'd seen anyone wearing spectacles and, for that matter, it was the first time I'd seen paper or writing. For that was what he was doing - writing with a quill pen. He looked up and asked if we would mind if he continued for just a moment and so I was able to study this person - his hair was close-cropped on the sides, but the top of his head shone bald. He had a large nose that stretched down between two squinting eyes and a ruddy face that looked as if it had been out in all weathers. I must say he frightened me a bit, for he had about him a rough, tough air that spoke of indefatigable determination.

At last Mr Poole looked up and nodded to my father, then gazed down through the small half-lenses at me: "So you are Johnny," he said, "I have been looking forward to the honour of meeting you."

He continued: "If I cognise anything about it, I should say that you, young man, could become the last of the broomsquires. And the world will be a sadder place."

Father ran his fingers through my hair and said: "You are right Mr Poole. He is my joy and yet he stands for the sadness of my ancient race."

I had never heard my father talk in that way before. The gravity with which he addressed the gentleman was not his usual patter - as a rule he swore a lot and joked even more - but now he chose his words carefully and there was a thoughtful softness in his voice.

My father told Mr Poole about the plight of the old couple and the great man listened with his chin buried in his hand. It seemed he held some sway in church matters and he promised he'd see to it that Fenwick and Mercy would be left undisturbed.

"I am sure that God in His charitable wisdom would make the redundant temple open to them - for fresh air is the only other occupant the place shall ever have, save for a bat or two."

When it came time for us to leave he saw me gazing at his books and said: "Writing Johnny. Writing and reading. Tis a thing that you shall learn one day by the look of you."

"Not with the name Walford he won't," replied my father. "Not one of us ever has."

"Then I shall wager that Johnny here will be the first," laughed Mr Poole.

There were many other folk who, I am proud to say, I came to know during those early years, but there were no children save for the three sisters and my strange older brother William. It is with great regret that I have to write of the rift that has always existed between we two brothers. I do not know what started it or why it grew from bad to worse, but his dislike of me certainly became more obvious as the years went by. He showed no desire to be in father's company, and yet William hated me for being our parent's son and friend.

As I say, for the first part of my life there were no other children I could play with up there in the hills, but the day did come when I found a companion. She was called Anne Rice.

Anne Rice. I repeat the name because thoughts of Anne lie heavy upon me. And because of such thoughts, I shall go to my grave laden with regret.

I must have been six or seven years of age and we had finished making one of our seasonal moves and were now situated in Ladies Combe, high above the village of Holford. One fine spring morning my father seemed to be in a frame of mind that matched the weather – there came a moment when he caught my eye and jerked his head in the direction of the woods. Within a minute we were halfway down the coombe and father was telling me that we were off to visit a place he was certain I'd like to see.

It wasn't a long journey. Just ten minutes later were entering the orchards and gardens that surrounded the huge clanking, groaning darkness of Harold Rice's mill. As we walked down the side of the leat father was explaining the basic workings of the place and he showed me where the runnel spilt over a wooden shute to turn the gigantic wheel.

Gaze at a water wheel – watch its continuous motion – and you can experience a kind of mesmerising trance. That's what happened to me that morning as we stood there surrounded by barking dogs and scratching fowl. So entranced was I by the hypnotic motion of the wheel, that I started to fall.

Father had me hold in a trice and he laughed and said that the same had happened to him when he was a boy. I was shocked by the effect, and it was a second or two before I realised that we were not alone. There, above the roar of the water and clank of the wheel, was a tiny bell-like laugh, and I looked around to see a small girl sitting on a wall. She was dressed in white and never before had I seen anyone so perfect and clean and untarnished by the general muck of the countryside. It was like looking at a creature from a different world. My mother often spoke about the folk she called 'gentry' and I could only think that this creature was a small example of that race. It was her hair that struck me most. Where my sisters had wild locks that flew this way and that, this child's golden mane was groomed to perfection. It gleamed and shone in the sunlight. So amazed was I by the look of her, that I forgot to consider my own pride. I'd certainly have given her short shrift had I realised she was laughing at me.

"Morning ma'am," said my father taking off his hat and bowing towards the girl in what I could only think was a gesture of mock grandeur. "I have brought my son Johnny here to look at the splendour of your father's mill."

The girl stopped laughing and suddenly she was gone – over the other side of the wall she disappeared from view, but after a moment I could see her running up across the big orchard towards some barns.

We went into the mill and father spoke to a couple of white dusty men. Soon they were showing us how the corn was ground to make flour when another man entered – a big man with a rolling chin and a large moustache – and he grunted at the men to get back to their work. From that moment, I took a dislike to Harold Rice. He had a sneering, aloof way about him. Perhaps I'd become over-accustomed to being made a fuss of and was unused to people who paid me no heed, for wherever I went people seemed to take to me – I don't know why. But Rice took no notice of me. I caught his eye for a fleeting second and then I was dismissed from his mind and father told me to go outside and play as he had business to attend to.

I dared not go back to study the wheel. There was something about its suppressed power that frightened me. Instead I found a gate that led through the wall into the orchard. I probably had some idea of seeing the girl again, for she certainly fascinated me, but the orchard seemed empty save for half a dozen sheep and some swine that were snorting in a pen. I leaned on the fence and the pigs made such a fuss of my arrival that I was glad there was a barrier between us. For some minutes I stood there, fascinated by the antics of the porkers, and suppose I must have been some kind of reverie because I didn't hear the girl come up beside me.

"Did your father tell you about the Sprite of the Wheel?" she asked.

"What d'you mean?" I stammered, startled by her sudden appearance.

"Did he tell you? He must have," she insisted. "That's why you were gazing into the wheel."

"Sorry Miss," I stuttered. "But I really don't know what you're sayin'."

"Well, your knees gave way didn't they?" she laughed. "I saw you falling and your father had to catch you. Why did that happen? You must have asked your father - he must have explained what made you fall."

"He didn't. Father only said the same 'appened to him."

"Then what do you think it was that started to pull you down?" she asked. "It would have done, you know, had your father not been there to catch you."

I could only shrug.

"It was the sprite of course," she laughed. "The sprite of the wheel is the most powerful thing in this valley. He doesn't have to say anything, he doesn't have to reach out to pull you in. Down there, in that great wheel, all he has to do is think hard and in you'll go."

My face may have shown fear because the girl seemed delighted by the effect her tale was having. I'd heard my parents talking of the elfin folk, and they told stories about the gribbins who'd steal children away at night. But in those moments in the orchard, this sprite of the wheel was far more awesome, if only because I'd felt his power.

"Never mind about him now," she smiled the girl. "The sprite's only dangerous when you stare at the wheel. He doesn't like it."

With that she span away to march off through the fruit trees and, without turning, she beckoned me to follow. When I caught up with her and asked where we were going she whispered something about knowing where the apples were stored. Through another gate we came to a yard where we climbed a flight of outdoor stone steps to a huge dusty loft. In the darkest corner, wooden racks were stacked one on top of another, and each was filled with a single layer of apples. The girl grabbed a fruit in each hand, and we were off again, through a door and into another loft which was stuffed to the eaves with hay. Crawling through the sweet smelling store I followed her to the front end of the barn where an open door gave out upon the yard. In the warm gloom just inside this vantage point, the girl and I disposed of our stolen fruit. From somewhere she produced a small, pearl-handled knife and peeled the soft wrinkled skin of the apples and handed bits to me.

"These are last year's," she said. "They look horrible with those old skins but bite and see - they're sweet and juicy as if they were new."

They were, and I swear I can taste the fragrant tang of those fruit now.

We talked of our lives and I painted a proud picture of life on the hill. She spoke of the many people who visited the mill and how she attended them at tea. It seemed that I was supposed to be impressed by the high standing of these people, but I'd never heard of any of them, until she mentioned Mr Thomas Poole and I told her I knew him, and that he was my father's friend.

That hour, lying there in the hay looking down upon the sunlit yard with was one of the happiest of my life. I was intoxicated by Anne Rice, and I think she liked me well enough. At any rate, she told me a good deal about herself - how her mother had died giving birth to her and that ever since her father said she was an angel sent from God.

"Will you come to see me again Johnny?" she asked when we heard my father shouting my name and were scurrying back through the hay.

"I hope so," I replied. And she smiled and turned to pull some of the hay off my clothes as we walked out into the sunshine.

"Don't tell anyone where we've been," she grinned. "I'd be in terrible trouble with father if he knew about the apples, and the hayloft is my secret place."

Some months later Mr Poole came to our camp and had words with my father. The two men went off to the edge of the clearing to talk and I was surprised to see father become agitated. But Mr Poole kept pressing his point and eventually father was reduced to shrugging his massive shoulders and shaking his head. I thought it must be some fuss over Mr and Mrs Greenslade's sacred home, but the talk, it transpired, was about me.

Eventually they both came over to where I was sitting carving a stick near the fire. Father said: "There's to be a new school down in the village and Mr Poole has offered, very kindly, to pay for you to attend. It's a handsome offer indeed Johnny, and you must thank him with all your heart. The learning will provide you with great opportunities."

I could hardly understand the words my father had said. A school? What was a school? When the gentleman had gone and my sisters had exploded from their unaccustomed hush, father started to explain the thing to mother. But I said: "If it is such a good thing, this school, why were you so cross when you were talking about it with Mr Poole?"

He picked me up just like he used to do when I was younger (I was about eight by now and he hadn't done it for a time) and he whispered: "Because, my lad, you are your father's dear friend, and I shall miss our journeyings and adventures together."

I was unhappy for days. Never did a son love his father more than I. The life of the hill was all I knew and I was none too keen on the idea of this thing called a school. But the day came and father took me down to the house on the edge of the village which had been opened as an establishment for elementary education, and I went in biting my lip.

There are several things I wish to say about my experiences there. The first is that I never felt entirely comfortable being pent-up inside the classroom and there were times when my old carefree life on the hills came back to haunt me. Added to that I initially had problems with the village boys, who thought it fine sport to bait an outcast like me. For that is what I realised I was, perhaps it is what I have always been. They had already sorted themselves into some sort of pecking order and Johnny Walford entered at the bottom of the pile. Perhaps there was something different about me - they knew it, and I knew it - I was not of their kind and at first they were determined to make me pay dearly for entering their preserve. I was bullied, but that didn't last long. Although I was younger than many of the lads and not as large as some, I beat each and every one of them soundly until they thought better of picking on a young broomsquire. It wasn't long before their dislike of me turned to grudging respect, and one or two of the boys began to regard me as a friend.

I have always been of a cheerful frame of mind and I have noticed over the years that people never dislike a spirited person for long. It is not a thing I have worked at, I was simply born of a cheerful disposition and the few large clouds that have darkened my horizons have rarely managed to wipe away my smile. Which is ironic in a way, because the complete reverse of this rule could be applied to my brother William. By the time I started attending the school he, being a few years older, had moved to the village of East Quantoxhead to work for a blacksmith, for he had never taken to the ways of the broomsquires. When I occasionally saw him he would only scowl, and never speak. William was never happy. Not once did I ever see him laugh.

After a month or two I'd either won round my enemies or clubbed them sufficiently so they wouldn't bother me any more. As for the school work I took to it with all the ease of a young stag taking to the woods. I learned reading and writing at a gallop and I could twist or turn this way or that without so much as a slip or stumble as we changed from one subject to another. I never really knew if the Master, Mr Barker, liked me or not, to begin with he seemed to regard me with suspicion and I was often caned for scrapping with the village lads, but as time went on he began to soften in his regards for me. After a year or so he'd get me to help the others with their learning.

There was another reason why I took to school: Anne Rice joined at much the same time as me and she, of course, was my special friend. We would walk to and from school together, which was a natural thing to do as I had to pass her father's mill on my way from the hill. We would have been inseparable had Anne not insisted that her father should never see us together. So we would meet in a glade of trees just down from the mill. I recall one occasion when my father came with me on some errand of his own – and when I said I had to wait in the trees it seemed to irk him in some way and he asked me if I thought I wasn't good enough for the miller's daughter. Even in those early days father probably saw the writing on the wall, but he left well alone and not a word more did he say on the matter. Anne arrived and he swept off his hat and bowed in the same mock fashion that he'd done months before by the water wheel, and then the three of us walked to the village and father made us laugh telling us some tall story or other.

There was something which drew me to Anne. It was inexplicable. Magnetic. Like the sprite that bided in her father's water wheel. Having lost her mother, and as daughter to the second wealthiest man in the parish, she could easily have been a haughty, unbearable child, spoilt beyond redemption. But she was not. Anne was the warmest, most loving human being I have ever known, and loved. For that was what was to become of it. So close was this childhood friendship between us, that I suppose it was bound to blossom into something greater and more perilous one fateful day.

But that day was not yet. We were still children and we were happy as the day was long. Throughout that autumn and long cold winter, those school-bound journeys gladdened my heart. Just seeing Anne was enough to put a smile upon my face and I believe I had the same affect her. A shared joke would have us helpless with mirth and more than once we fell into a hedge weakened by great gusts of mutual laughter. But in those early days Anne was the wise leader of our little pack of two. I did what she bid, it was as simple as that. Her imagination left mine standing and sometimes she'd scold me for being a dullard. Once, and once only, she made a fool of me. It was one autumn evening when we had arranged to meet after school. I was supposed to have gone straight off home to help mother with the chores, but was easily persuaded to forget this promise and soon we were climbing the steep wooded bank above the mill to where Anne had another of her little dens. After a while she must have noticed some look of concern shadowing my face because she asked what was troubling me. I told her how my mother had been unwell for some days and how I ought to be on my way home to help her with the fire.

"I'll come," said Anne. "I'll come and help. It's only ten minutes up the coombe you say, and I would like to see this camp of yours."

I was hesitant to say the least, but soon we were being licked by the dogs as we entered our camp. The visit, as I had feared, was not a success. Mother was overcome by what I can only describe as panic – I had never seen her in such a state. The appearance of Anne seemed to alarm her and she kept repeating: "Oh Miss Rice, you never should have come. What will your father say? He won't want you visiting a broomsquire's camp, I know that for sure."

Anne was upset: "Don't you want me to be here Mrs Walford?"

"That's not it my dear," said mother wiping her long hair from her smoked smeared face. "That's not it at all. It's a great honour to have you here, but I'm afraid that Mr Rice would think our camp beneath you. We don't want to get you into any trouble. You better take Miss Rice home Johnny and, if her visit's not mentioned, no harm can come of it."

I asked who would do my chores, but she shooed us away - past my sisters (at least the two who were left at home, Sylvestra was married to Jeremia Luck by then) who had been standing with their mouths agape at the site of Anne.

"I'm sorry Anne," I said perplexed, "I have never seen mother like that before and I can't think what she means by it."

"Your mother is probably right. My father can get angry sometimes." Then she added: "But tell me. Do you really all live and sleep in that awful little hut?"

Her question stung me and, after I had said goodbye to her, I walked home feeling very much out of sorts. That night I heard mother and father quarrelling about what had happened. But worst of all for me was the aftermath which was to occur the next day.

In the yard at school a group of girls took delight in ridiculing me so that tears began to sting my eyes. I wasn't used to this and couldn't remember the last time I'd cried, and I ran home without going to the afternoon lessons. They taunted me as I ran: "Johnny lives in the wo-ods, A gypsy, a gypsy, a gypsy."

Anne had obviously told them about our camp and the next morning I was still so angry I didn't wait for her in the glade below the mill but marched on to school alone. I heard Anne calling for me to stop, but I didn't. I tramped on so that she had to run to catch me up.

Only when she manoeuvred herself in front to bar my way did I stop. "Johnny I am sorry. So, so sorry. I have been crying all night and father said he wasn't going to let me come to school because he thought I was ill. You are my very, very best friend Johnny Walford and I shouldn't have told those stupid girls about the place where you live. I will never, ever, do anything to hurt you again."

With that she lifted her hand and passed it through my long curly brown hair and smiled her beautiful sad smile. "Are we friends?" she asked, and I smiled back and said we were, but had to try very hard to keep back yet more of my unaccustomed tears.

Anne Rice was good to her word. She never did me a disservice again, although her loveliness, her very being, has inspired the main strata of grief that has run through the bedrock of my life.

A year or more went by and we moved once or twice from one copse to another, but always in the same system of valleys so the mill remained on my route to school. Consequently I was happy to set out in the mornings no matter what the weather. Not even the winter snows prevented me from making that journey down the coombe. I was growing bigger and stronger, which was just as well because there was a week just before Christmas-tide when the drifts were waist deep and took some striding through. But each morning I'd be waiting for Anne in the glade where there was one mighty old beech that was so voluminous its tangled roots made a small cave. In the worse weather I'd huddle up in there where it was always dry and comparatively warm out of the wind. I used to enjoy that cosy nook where you could listen in comfort to the soughing of the great trees above. Anne would often bring some morsel in her bag and she seemed to enjoy feeding me with the wonders of her father's pantry. I'd never had food like it. A piece of pie, or wedge of cake, a bit of pudding wrapped in muslin, fresh bread with jam, strong cheese tucked into a small, nutty roll. All these made a handsome change for a broomsquire's boy.

There were other delights in this new life of mine. Once a month I had to report to Mr Poole who'd quiz me over what I'd learned at school. And here too I'd enjoy the bounties of that mysterious domestic treasure house called the pantry. Mr Poole would instruct his cook to "give Johnny a dainty or two" if, and when, I provided him with enough satisfactory answers to convince him my schooling was progressing at an acceptable rate. It always was. My Saturday afternoon visits to the great man's house grew longer as time went by.

"You are a bright lad, Johnny," he used to say. "Undoubtedly a shade or two above the rest. I always knew it would be so, from that first moment I set eyes upon you. Your father is an intelligent fellow, though he'd never admit to such a charge – and I believe that your mother is too. I am not sure why they insist upon banishing themselves to the discomforts of the hill, but I suppose your father has some notion of ancestral leanings and feels it is his place."

On that occasion I answered him thus: "But it is a wonderful life Mr Poole. There is no life better and cleaner than that of the broomsquire. That is what my father says, and I believe him."

"You surely cannot think that," he replied, waving his hand at the vast, dark, oak panelled room that we were in. "Not now you have tasted learning and wisdom and seen the life that it can bring."

"I believe that I shall always be proud to be a broomsquire, Sir. I am glad of the learning you have given me, but father has taught me to love the hill and I'd find it difficult to live down in a village like my brother William."

Mr Poole then said something that caused a shadow to pass across my cloudless horizon. He said: "I wonder Johnny, how long you will feel like that. Times are changing. People and their expectations are changing. Take your friend Anne Rice for example. Can you imagine what she would think of a man who lived in a simple hut with a face black from charcoal smoke?"

My face wasn't black, but it must have turned bright red, because dear Mr Poole suddenly seemed to regret what he'd said. "Never mind Johnny," he laughed. "You have some growing up to do yet and things and ideas will change for you, just as they do for everybody else."

He rang a bell and when the cook materialised, asked to her to supply me with a handkerchief full of morsels. But I was bothered to the extent that I couldn't look at the food. I suppose, now that I think of it, I'd never had occasion to look into the future before that moment - and, without knowing it, Mr Poole had installed in me a conundrum that I'd puzzle over for the rest of my life. It boiled down to what Andrew Crosse would later call the juxtaposition within me. My education and my love of Anne Rice, both lured me away from the hills. But my own nature, my sweet shadow-free upbringing, the way father nurtured my wild soul up on those great empty moors… All these things pulled me back to the high places.

Midwinter came with a vengeance that year. Great snows fell and settled for months turning Quantocks' coombes crisp and white. Not that the cold ever put me off going to school which, by that time, was teaching me a lot more than letters and numbers. For example: I'd never been to church and so services, hymns and prayers were all foreign to me. We'd never paid much heed to religion, so the great fuss and excitement that seemed to overtake the school at Christmastide took me by surprise. The enigma of it started on the morning of December 21st when Mr Baker told us we could take the afternoon off so that we could enjoy what he called "the usual nonsensities". When I asked the other boys what he meant by this they told me it was Mumping Day. Mumping meant going around the village and banging on the doors of wealthier folk to demand a small gift of some sort. It was the one day of the year when the poorer children were given free licence to beg. And so my classroom compatriots were in a frenzy of excitement as the afternoon drew closer and Mr Baker had his work cut out keeping the school in check.

Anne though, who was usually in the midst of such revelries, remained gloomily aloof. Later, as the children exploded from the schoolroom in a frenzy of excitement, she gathered her things and, looking up at me, said: "Go on Johnny - you must go with them. I shall walk home by myself."

"Why? Why aren't you joining the others in the mumping?"

"It is for the poorer children Johnny," she replied. "And father has forbidden me to go. But you must join in. You might enjoy it - who knows what treats you might collect."

I didn't go, but walked home with Anne, crunching the frozen puddles in the lane and wondering what I was to do with the rest of this unexpected free afternoon. For her part Anne was filled with guilt, although I tried to assure her that I had not really been taken the idea of mumping anyway. She was determined to make it up to me and soon devised a plan that saw us sneaking up to the hay loft that was the venue for our first meeting. This time though, we had with us an entire feast of excellent foodstuffs that she'd managed to glean from the cook. We lay close to each other for warmth in the hay and talked in whispers and watched our plumes of breath rise into the darkness of the barn. It was dark because now the big end door was closed except for a crack where we could watch to see if anyone might be coming our way.

"This is better than mumping," whispered Anne. "I'm so glad you didn't go Johnny. I hate to be alone when I know that everyone else is having a time of it. And I'd forgotten that father is away for the day, and so we should be quite safe up here for the afternoon."

We lay there in the warm hay and I could feel the electric closeness of her as we whispered and laughed and talked of this and that. We were not yet twelve years of age, so we were quite innocent, but for me it was pleasant and soothing to feel Anne's fingers slowly passing through my hair.

"I love your hair Johnny," she whispered at one point. "It's so thick and yet fine. You are by far the most handsome boy in the whole of Somersetshire."

There was a thing that made me smile for many a long cold winter day. No mumping gift could beat that. Anne though, never stayed on a subject for long and soon she was hatching another scheme. This one was aimed at the night of Christmas Eve when, she'd heard, all the animals in a farmer's manger would bow in honour of the Lord. We had to see it for ourselves, she said, and it would be easy as there was going to be a midnight service in the church and we could sneak out to her uncle's farm next door to witness this holy mystery. I, of course, was none too sure. The Walford family, I knew, would not be making plans to attend a midnight mass.

I have just one other memory of that Mumping Day and that is my meeting with Anne's father shortly after I had left the mill. It was in the gloaming and new snow had just started to fall. I was making my way back to the hill with only the slight hiss that snow makes when it falls for company, and I realised it was just as well I'd taken my leave when I had because here was old man Rice coming up the lane, swaying precariously on his big cob horse.

"Whoa - who goes there!" he shouted like some old soldier on patrol. "Come on boy, show me your face."

"Tis Johnny Walford Sir," said I, trembling in my boots.

"Ah Walford. Bin out a-mumpin I suppose. Seein' what you can scrounge from the hard workin' folk have you?"

I didn't answer, and to my surprise he reached in his pocked and threw down a silver sixpence which I managed to catch.

"There. That'll round off what I take has been a profitable day. And now away with you back to your hill. You've no need to come to my house a-mumpin' now. I don't want my daughter embarrassed by such things."

There was something within me that wanted to fling the coin straight back in his fat unpleasant face, but I bowed my head and mumbled some sort of thanks.

I knew little of my mother's history, for it was never discussed.

My father could be a domineering man in many respects and, when it came to the past and ancestry, all we heard was the tale of the broomsquires. But it began to dawn upon me, around about that time, that my mother was not of the ancient stock and that there seemed to be a blanket of silence laid over her past.

"You are a true broomsquire Johnny," father used to say. "A man of the hills. We are different from the valley folk, never forget that. We come from a prouder, older people."

Perhaps it was this aloof pride of his that made him angry when I mentioned I was planning to go to the Midnight Mass. But things soon got worse - he was rendered almost speechless with rage when mother announced that she would like to join me. The battle lasted two whole days but, for once, father's will faltered and we found ourselves preparing for our first ever family outing to the church. When I say family, I mean mother, myself, Avice and Petronilla. When the night of Christmas Eve grew dark, father was nowhere to be found. We learned later that he was entrenched with a half a dozen unholy ne'er-do-wells in the Castle of Comfort Inn.

Mother never looked more splendid. For hours she and the girls had banished me to a corner of the hut while they prepared themselves for the great outing. Where mother found the clothes I had no idea, normally she wore layer upon layer of rags, but here she was in a proper dress and coat along with something that she rather majestically described as a hat. I had never seen an object like it in our home or anywhere else for that matter, and begged her not to wear the thing for fear that my classmates might see. But she insisted that it was a very good hat and that she had owned it for years.

"You are the man of the house tonight," she said as she handed me the lantern. Then we were off down the coombe, crunching the brittle, frosted grass beneath our feet; my hands stinging with cold as I held the lamp aloft. A cosy sight we must have made, making our way along in our pool of yellow light, through the trees with everything else glinting silver under the great full moon. We didn't need the lantern, you could have read a book in the moonlight, but mother insisted on keeping it lit and soon we were passing Anne's home and the great, dark, silent mill. A few minutes later we heard the clatter of hooves and the grinding of metalled wheels and had to press ourselves into the hedge as Mr Rice, his daughter and their housekeeper clattered by in a governess cart.

"Make way," shouted the miller, although we already had. As they flew past I caught Anne's eye in the light of my lantern and glimpsed the flash of her smile.

At church a great crowd had congregated outside the door. People were in a festive mood and most of them, I imagine, had been at the punch. As soon as we entered the churchyard I handed the lantern to one my sisters and was off among the graves to the far wall where I was to meet Anne under the yews. She was already there and the moment she saw me she turned to open a gate that led through to a farmyard. It belonged to her uncle and she obviously knew her way well. Without saying a word, she led me across to the byre where the stock was kept, and we could hear the deep huffing and snorting of the cattle. Anne lit a candle and we stood in silence looking at a scene. It could have been the manger where Jesus was born.

"What's meant to happen next?" I whispered.

"When the clock strikes midnight the master bullock - probably that one there," said Anne pointing at a particularly large beast, "Will low three times. At least, that's what the legend says - and he should kneel with his front legs bowed towards the manger."

We waited and after a while the clock chimed the midnight hour. Anne held her breath and so did I. The big bullock slowly took another mouthful of hay and continued his slow methodical chewing as if this second was like any other in his life. But we heard a lowing. And then another and another. Three times some animal bellowed into the night, but it was not any beast in our stall, so we never did get to see if the master bullock knelt to Christ. It was enough for the fanciful Anne though.

"Did you hear it Johnny?" she cried as we ran back across the yard. "It's true, it's true. Even the cattle know that there is a Lord."

I was less convinced, but happy to enter into the spirit of it for her sake. We were nearly caught on our return, as most people had entered the church where the old Parson was beginning the Mass. The clergyman, according to my father, was an old rogue who would probably be nine-tenths-to-the-wind on the punch he had been drinking, which may have been why the service was starting late. There were one or two stragglers still lingering in the porch, so we parted and were able to melt into the throng. Anne knew exactly where she was going, while I didn't have a clue where to find my mother and sisters. It was the hat that came to my rescue. I was able to slip to mother's side unnoticed since she was close to the rear of the church. She scolded me in a whisper, but I was happy enough – I had accomplished yet another mission with my dearest friend.

An hour into the endless speeches and prayers I was beginning to wonder why anyone ever attended church at all and I was tired and keen to go. But, as the service ended, mother struck up a conversation with some old friend and, as she didn't see many people, was talking away ten to the dozen. Being at the back of the church meant that people had to pass us as they made their way out and I looked up to see Anne and her father just a few feet away in the company of Mr Thomas Poole. As they drew near Mr Poole called out to me and bade me good tidings of the season. What a splendid and magnanimous man was dear old Tom Poole: to speak to a broomsquire's urchin in such friendly tones in full view of all the village dignitaries. Anne was obviously surprised and impressed to see the great man speak so kindly to me and in an instant she did something that both she and I were to regret.

She smiled at me and said: "Happy Christmas Johnny."

It was like seeing old man Rice being shot not once, but twice. I could see the suspicious weaselish expression cross his ugly face. It probably seemed bad enough to him that Mr Poole should go out of his way to speak to me, but when the apple-of-his-eye did the same, it was too much. He grabbed Anne's arm and was about to pull her firmly away when something else happened. Harold Rice caught sight of my mother and stopped dead in his tracks. His angry expression was instantly replaced by another – he made as if to speak, but his mouth opened and no sound came from it. For her part, my mother did not speak a word all the way home.

The next day, Christmas Day, my father took me poaching. "It is a good day to hunt," he explained. "It is the one day when you can be sure the lowland folk are safely tucked up by their firesides."

With the help of our dogs we took a small hind and that night, after a day out on the freezing hills, the family enjoyed our stolen

Christmas dinner which I'll wager was better fare than many were having. The haunch of venison sizzled above the fire and my father performed an endless stream of songs from his vast repertoire, and all should have been jolly in our little camp. Except that a small shadow lurked within my heart. I knew that those enigmatic few seconds in front of the miller at the midnight mass would bode badly for the broomsquire's boy.

My notions proved correct. A few days later when we returned to school Anne was absent. For a while I tried to convince myself that she was perhaps unwell with a winter cold and that she'd be back before the week's end, but that is not how things turned out.

So desperate and lonely was I that one evening on my way home I decided to enter the beech wood - just in case. Just in case of what, I wasn't sure, but I knew Anne would never simply drop me without some good reason. She would make an effort to contact me, no matter what the problem was. And I was right. I found her missive among the roots of the beech. A stinging sleet was falling and so, forlorn and melancholy on my lonely way home, I thought I'd sit for a while among the dry leaves in the hopes of meeting my friend. No sooner had I entered the little arbour than I found the note. You wouldn't have seen it unless you had entered the cave and sat down among the leaves. Just above the entrance a tortured root made a sort of shelf and on this was propped the note.

This is the message she had written:

"To my dearest friend, Johnny Walford,

I will put this letter in our trysting place in the hopes that you might find it there. It is my only chance, the only way I can think of. I have to tell you what has happened since Christmas Eve. It was my own stupid fault and I have no-one to blame but myself, I always knew if father found out we were friends he would stop it. Outside the church he turned to Mr Poole and I heard him mention your name. "Yes'" says Mr Poole, "he's a bright lad and I have made it my business to help him through his schooling." "You mean," says my father, "that my daughter is sharing a schoolroom with a broomsquire's boy?" "That is the way of it," says Mr Poole, "and there is nought wrong with that if the boy is right-headed, and I most certainly can vouch that he is."

My father says no more of it, although he has been in an ill temper all through Christmastide. And then, three days after Boxing Day, he calls me to his private room and tells me the thing which has upset me so deeply, dear Johnny. He told me that our school is no longer good enough for me and that now I must attend a special establishment for young ladies over Bagborough way. And, Johnny, I fear to say that the news gets worse still. It is the sort of school attended by girls from the more well-to-do families, and it is run so that each pupil must stay there throughout the week and sleep in a thing called a dormitory. I begged. I wept. I pleaded and pleaded, but father would not be moved. The day you start school I shall already be gone to Bagborough. I cannot imagine how we shall see each other again. I am thinking and thinking about how it can be done and I WILL find a way. Of that you can be sure. All I can think in the meantime is for you to call at this trysting place of ours as often as you can and I will endeavour to leave notes here for you.

You are my best friend Johnny Walford. My only friend. I love you like a brother and pledge that I will not, for a single moment, forget you. I hope that you will also think of me and maybe, if we try hard enough, we can meet one another in our dreams.

Your dear friend,

Anne Rice."

These were her exact words. I still have that note tucked away in a special place and have read it until it has nearly worn away. So there it was. One brief greeting in the church had split us asunder, cast my own happiness into a pit. I sat there until it grew dark, brooding on all these thoughts. It was the first time I'd ever felt truly sorry for myself. Not the most fitting emotion for a man or a boy. One gleam of light came through the whole sad cloud, though, and that was Anne's note. I read, and reread, that last paragraph a thousand times.

I didn't see, or hear, from her until the Spring and then one day there was another note placed upon the shelf among the roots. It was brief and to the point. It told me that she would be waiting for me in our old den in the wood high above the mill on Saturday afternoon.

It was Monday when I found the note. Anne had obviously been home, just as she had been every Saturday and Sunday since she'd been going to her new school. I knew this and had become increasingly vexed by her silence. I couldn't understand why she had let it go on for so long. Surely, I'd thought time and again, she could flit down to the glade to leave me a note?

I had seen her once, but in a rather odd circumstance and at a distance. It was just two weeks before I found the second note and a sort of desperation had developed within me. To catch a glimpse of her I went all the way to Bagborough. It was father's doing - he had some business or other over there, and I begged him to let me go along. We were there sooner than I'd thought after a brisk walk and I was enjoying myself. It was a fine day and I had never been so far south along the hills. I say it was a fine day, and that was true of the morning, but beyond noon it came on to rain. We called in at the Rest and Be Thankful to wait for the weather to clear, which father said it would. Of course, he took the opportunity to sustain himself with a glass or two of cider and soon he was talking to the people in the bar as if it had only been a few hours since he'd seen them last.

Sitting by the fire drying off as best I could, I wasn't paying much heed to the general banter until I heard a name mentioned that brought me instantly from my reverie.

"Old Rice can afford it right enough," were the words that grasped my attention.

An old man was holding forth. "Ee's been short changing and cheating with 'is weights ever since I can remember. I'll tell you 'ow rich the beggar is - ee sends that daughter of 'is to the school over yer - and that ain't cheap, that I can tell thee..."

My father looked across at me and later, back out in the rain, he said: "We'll walk past that school shall we?" I didn't say a word, but within a minute or two were passing a grand house set back across a wide open lawn bordered by trees, when he stopped and pointed: "Your friend Anne attends the school in there. I suppose that father of hers thought she was too good to go to be in a class with the likes of you."

At that moment a group of girls came out of a side door and hurried around the front of the house in the rain, which was still falling despite my father's predictions. In their midst I spotted Anne and, at the same moment, she caught sight of us and stopped in her tracks. The poor girl looked confused. She told me later that she was thinking of running over to see us, but she knew she'd be in awful trouble if she did. She just stood there in the rain, staring across the lawn until two other girls came back for her a woman poked her head out of the big door and called out. Then Anne waved and was gone.

Not a word did my father say until we were up on the ridge and halfway home.

"So, you saw your friend today then Johnny - is that what you had in mind when you came to Bagborough?"

I shrugged and told him it wasn't, but he went on: "You worry me, boy, I can tell you that. You're young now but soon, in the next year or two, you'll be reaching the age when a young man's heart begins to rule his roost. It rides rough shod over everything. You fall in love and it is a terrible thing. A wonderful thing too, if all is right. But terrible and painful if things are wrong. Like, if you were to fall in love with young Miss Rice - that would be wrong and there would be pain in it for you. Of that I am quite sure. The miller is never going to let that precious daughter of his marry a broomsquire's boy. Not in a thousand years. Then there's the fact that young lady is used to a different life, not the rough way we live on the hills."

He put his hand on my shoulder as we marched along the old ridge track: "The world is an unfair place Johnny. If ever I manage to teach you anything - it must be that one cast-iron fact. It is an unfair world. You might like Anne Rice well enough, and she might like you - but I promise you this: it will be a case of the twain never being able to meet. You might as well get used to it now, for that is how it will be. Forget her, son. Forget her and you can be as free as that hawk hovering there above the ridge. Keep some idea of Anne locked up in that heart of yours, and you will never find true happiness."

My father was a wise man, but I was young. "It's not like that father," I said. "Anne is just a friend of mine, that is all."

I was right in a way. It wasn't like that then, for we could only have been twelve years of age at the time. But that is what became of it. The seed of my love for Anne Rice had been planted too deep within me for father, or anyone else, to pluck it out.

I knew that for a fact when I next saw her. It was several months later and through our note leaving we conspired to go for a long walk in the afternoon. Out over the loneliest of the hills towards West Quantoxhead, we went, where we knew we'd never meet a soul. She told me that at school she had been reading books and that her favourite ones described people like us. People who loved each other, but were forced apart by circumstances. She said that she had learned the real meaning of words like 'determination' and phrases like 'loyalty in adversity'. And she said if we could believe in – and learn to live by – those words, then we would win out in the end. One day we would be free to be together as often, and for as long, as we wished.

"Do you wish it so Johnny?" she asked. "Am I just a silly girl suffering some childish notion? Or do you think there's more between us?"

I told her that I didn't need to learn all those words or read those books. I told her I ached to see her when she was away, that it was like having a part of me wrenched asunder.

Such high and rosy thoughts...You must remember though, we were but children speaking our excited, muddled, minds. It seemed easy to do out there in the warm spring breeze that sighed fresh across that high purple heath.

That one golden afternoon bolstered me for many a month to come, and several other secret meetings between us allowed the year to pass easily enough. Autumn came and I suppose by then I would have been 13 years of age. Another cold winter closed in and I recall the darkening days bringing frosts so crisp that we had to break the stream to fetch water. As Christmas approached I was so busy helping mother and father keep up a supply of wood and food, as well as attending school, that thoughts of Anne dwindled as the days grew shorter. Never altogether though. Always Anne was at the back of my mind and I only had to walk past the mill, or look at the desk that was once hers at school, or jump down the bank to the roots of big beech tree, to think of her again. Indeed the coming of Christmastide itself was enough to remind me that it had been almost a year since our happy days were so abruptly ended.

It was in December that something of profound importance occurred in my life, and again, it was Mr Poole who was the making of it. He came into the classroom one day and asked me to call upon him on my way home. By then I had become a sort of unpaid locum for Mr Baker, our teacher. A door linked the classroom and the schoolhouse, and through it he would disappear for increasingly long intervals.

"Walford," he would say, "See to the class will you? I have something to attend to. I'll just be a few minutes so take them through the six-times-table..."

Poor old Baker. I knew half of what he was up to, for I had often smelled the odour of alcohol upon my father's breath. The other half I didn't know, but I was to find out soon enough, thanks to Thomas Poole's visit to the school.

"Where is Mr Baker?" says he when he enters the class, and seemed quite annoyed when I told him the teacher was indisposed.

Later, when I called at his house, Mr Poole quizzed me about the teacher, but I covered for the man as best I could. You see, when he'd returned to the classroom I told him about Mr Poole's visit and he seemed most put out. Later he asked me to follow him through to his schoolhouse and a snug little place it was.

"What did you tell Mr Poole and why didn't you call me?" he asks as we enter his den, out of earshot of the other children.

When I told him I'd made some small excuse for his absence, he clapped his arm around me and thanked me warmly. I added that I felt Mr Poole would be sure to smell the alcohol on his breath and be cross about it: for a moment old Baker looked as though he would explode, and then I nodded to the bottle on his desk and told him I knew the meaning of it because of my father's liking for a drink. The old fellow seemed to relent. He said I was wise beyond my years and, because of it, he felt I deserved to see what was really keeping him out of class. There was indeed a half-filled bottle on his little desk, but his main occupation seemed to be involved with the massive ledger that lay next to it.

"Early Man, Walford," he said with glee. "That is what I study and what I write about when I take my little excursions out here. You might say that I am becoming obsessed by the subject. That wretched classroom will be the death of me, boy, can you understand that? There are far more important things to work on than helping a gang of village dolts through their three-times-three.

It is a fact that you can run the class just as well as I. You are a good lad Walford, I will tell you that, for I have no fear that it will go to your head. You are not of that ilk. I will tell you another thing. I have studied the ancient peoples of these hills and I have interviewed your friends Mr and Mrs Greenslade up at the old church tower. Very interesting, Walford. Certainly as far as you are concerned. Have you any notion that you are from an ancient stock? The blood that runs through your veins, is far older than most. You and your father, and the Greenslades, are among the last of an antediluvian tribe that has been fading from existence for a long, long time. It is all here in this ledger, and if you maintain your good work at this school I will endeavour to present you with the story of your clan..."

He went on about Bronze Age and Iron Age peoples, and some folk he called the Dumnonii, and it took some insistence on my part to extricate myself from his enthusiastic grasp. Poor old Mr Baker. The conversation I was about to have with Thomas Poole would result in my not taking any further part in helping the alcoholic anthropologist in his studies.

For, as soon as I reached Mr Poole's house, he uttered this singular remark: "I hear you are 13 years of age Johnny Walford. That means you are no longer a child but a young man. A clever young man, to boot. A young man who must now take seriously the proposition of work."

I suppose I must have looked little nonplussed. Such a thought had never struck me before, I regarded myself as being nothing more than a boy who, slowly but surely, was taking up the work of a broomsquire.

"No Johnny, I watched you through the window today taking the class, and I listened as you spun some yarn for me about Mr Baker, knowing that you were quite aware that I should be cross if I were to discover that the man was in his cups. That showed a maturity beyond your years. Now, young man, I believe it is time you took your next step in life. No good looking perplexed – for I have found you a position. A good job, with a fine employer. None could ask for better, in fact. If your father agrees then we shall go together tomorrow – indeed, tell him to come here this evening and we will have it out then. It is far too cold for me to shift my old bones this afternoon. Your father will have to come here if he has anything to say on the matter, is that clear? Otherwise you and I will be on our way to see Mr Andrew Crosse in the morning. Remember to bring your few belongings Johnny, for tomorrow night you will be installed at Broomfield."

I suppose I was so taken aback I forgot to ask Mr Poole what sort of work he'd found me, and my father boxed my ears for the oversight. He was furious about what he called "Tom Poole's meddling" and out he went into the cold night saying he was blowed if he was going to have anyone else taking over his son. I don't think I ever saw father more angry and we remained silent for some minutes after he left. Normally he was such a cheerful man.

He came back very late and very drunk and after a few minutes stumbled to my bed and smoothed my cheeks with his big rough hands. "Johnny," he whispered. "My dear, dear little broomsquire. You are the son I always dreamt of and now I am to lose you..."

I sat up and said: "Don't worry father, I'll not leave you. I'm not interested in the learning I've been doing, I'm happy to collect the broom and bark and make the charcoal. I will always be here with you and mother."

Deep inside, some part of me knew that this was not wholly true. But I loved my father and, if he had demanded I stay on the hill with him, then that is what I'd have done. Instead he muttered this one remarkable thing before going to his bed:

"You will not be staying here my laddie. I have agreed with Mr Poole that what he has suggested is for the best. You are going to work for the Thunder and Lightning Man..."

PART 2

TO WORK–
THE WIZARD OF THE
QUANTOCKS

Mr Poole rode his old mare and kindly carried my small bag of belongings behind his saddle while father and I walked along beside him. I was as nervous as a hare, thinking all the while about what my own immediate future held, it still remained a mystery to me. The fact that I was to work for a person they called the Thunder and Lightning man hardly filled me with joy. The only thing that lifted my spirits was that I noticed we were heading in the same direction as Bagborough. For an hour we walked in silence but eventually, as we crested the ridge and the cold wind from the west cut into us, Mr Poole spoke thus:

"I suppose young Johnny," says he, "that I should furnish you with some idea of the lay of the land. Your future, I mean. First let me tell you that Mr Crosse is a fine Christian gentleman. He is Squire of Broomfield and he will, I can assure you, be a fair and kind master to you. It is important you understand that because what I have to tell you next might disturb someone with less intelligence."

"Mr Crosse experiments with something called Electricity. I doubt that you've heard of such a thing at school Johnny, but this electricity is a thing of the future. It is a clever, invisible power that will change everything that we do. Mr Crosse says that one day the stuff will help us to manufacture all sorts of goods and allow us to communicate with the ends of earth. Can you imagine such a thing? No. Well, neither can I, to tell the truth. But Mr Crosse can and he is working day and night to bring these predictions to life. He has shown me the way it can work and I have been impressed. The Squire is a very learned man – not a fool, and don't you let anyone tell you he is. You may hear him being called the Wizard of the Quantocks, but that is a lot of idle chatter. Ignorance. That is what men like Crosse are up against – and that, my boy, is where you come in."

"You see, these experiments of his have manifested themselves, at times, in a lot of flashings and bangings and goodness knows what else, and I am told that the explosions are enough to keep the innocent from their sleep. The staff at Fyne Court have got themselves into a real old pickle about it all. The long and the short of it is that Mr Crosse can find no-one to assist him in his laboratory. Being ignorant country souls, they've all managed to scare themselves and he has become quite desperate. A short while ago he told me of his wish to find an intelligent young man who could do his bidding without running off in blind panic - and that is when I told him about you Johnny. Top of the school, and the brightest boy I know. I had no hesitation in recommending you to Mr Crosse and, though he felt you were a little on the youngish side, he agreed to take you on. You will like him, for he is a courteous and kind-hearted gentleman. And, if I know you and the stock you come from, I am sure that you will not let him, or me, or your father, down. Mr Crosse can bang and crash all he likes with his infernal electricity, and I know that you will stand your ground."

I must admit to feeling daunted by talk of such crashings and bangings. I couldn't really imagine what Mr Poole meant. Little did I know that the worthy Squire Crosse really did collect lightning from storms and that, within two weeks, I would be helping him do so...

Over Bagborough Hill we went and I looked down at the village far below with a slight hastening of my heart and a lump in my throat. I asked if Broomfield was much further and was delighted to hear it wasn't - which, at least, meant that I would be living closer to Anne.

In under an hour we were standing in front of the grandest house I'd ever seen. Fyne Court was huge. The great frontage with its pillared porch backed onto an even greater house with magnificent wings. To say I was nervous would have been to understate things - I was trembling as we approached the place and even father looked cowed. It seemed beyond the realms of possibility that I should become a part of all this after a lifetime spent in a broomsquire's hut.

As we approached through the rolling grounds, Mr Poole was explaining that he would go to the front door to make our arrival known to the staff, while we should make our way around to the rear of the building where people of our standing were received. In the event there was no need for any of this because we were stopped in our tracks by a shout from across the neat green swathe which I later learned was a lawn. We looked around and saw a dark haired, clean-shaven, gentleman approaching us at a rapid pace across the clipped grass. My first impression of Andrew Crosse was that he was far younger than I'd imagined. To me a Squire was a grey-haired autocrat of the Tom Poole mode, but the Wizard of the Quantocks was far more youthful than anything I would have imagined calling Master.

Moreover he was not dressed in the formal way of the gentry. He had a workmanlike rough hewn suit of thick tweed and across his shoulder was slung a large leather bag in which you could see all manner of tools such as sieves and hammers. His brown hair was as dishevelled as a workman's and his handsome face was tanned from much time spent out of doors.

"My dear Tom," he beams trotting towards us. "So you have come as promised - and have brought young Walford with you, if I am not mistaken. And this, I take it, is Mr Walford senior, come to see that his son is to be left in good hands. Come in then gentlemen, come inside, and I will order something hot to thaw your bones after such a cold journey from Stowey."

With that he ushered us through the main front door which old Tom had told us was the entrance reserved only for gentlefolk. Later I would learn that Andrew Crosse, although strenuous in undertaking his many duties as Squire and magistrate, was not a person to stand on social ceremony and nicety. He was a logician, a man of action; he had little time for hierarchical nonsense, as he called it. But for us this helter-skelter introduction to such a grand establishment was a shock indeed. The smell of the place - oak-smoke tinged with citrus fruit and wax polish, as I recall - was enough to make us sniff with wonder, and the grand sweep of rooms and splendid furniture caused my father look very uncomfortable. He was a humble countryman who'd spent his entire life out of doors and he was not used to interior splendours. He held his hat in his hands and I do believe that if we'd been in this residential quarter for a minute or two longer he would have wrung that sorry object into rags. However, we were whisked along at a great speed with Mr Crosse talking all of the way:

"Come through, come through," he says, hardly stopping for an instant as he instructed a man-servant to bring food and warm beverages into what he called the Laboratory. "We may as well start where we mean to carry on, for this will be young Johnny's home should, of course, he prove to be the sort of lad that I so desperately need."

With that he flung open a huge, dark, double door and there, before us, was the vast, church-like interior of his workplace. There were no pews of course, or anything of the sort - the only thing that prompted me to liken it to a church was the size of the place and the fact that an enormous organ, perched high in a gallery, dominated the great room. As for the rest of it - well, at that time I had no clue as to what any part of it could be. Like my father, I stood there in wonder while Mr Crosse, who'd already divested himself of the heavy leather bag and his overcoat, was pacing about examining this strange object and tinkering with that.

"Now then Johnny Walford," he says as he goes. "Mr Poole has been telling me that you are a bright and clever lad. Is it true? Can you read and can you write? Can you do your maths?"

"Yes Sir," says I.

"Well then, read out to me what I have written on that paper," says the Squire, pointing at a manuscript on a large desk surrounded by a clutter of mysterious objects. I bent down to study the meaningless drawings and marks, and found some scrawny text written there.

"A. Iron rod penetrating into the ground. B. brass knob for escape of super abundant fluid. C. insulated funnel. D. Incoming wire...." and so on. That was the sort of thing, though I will admit I stuttered and faltered a good deal because the handwriting was difficult to follow. Added to that, of course, I'd never heard of half the words before.

"Excellent, excellent," says Mr Crosse. "Now, before we have some refreshment, I wish you carry out one small experiment that should prove to me whether or not you are of the mettle to help me in my work..."

With that he ushers me to a weird and wonderful piece of apparatus where the only thing in any way recognisable to an ordinary mortal was a handle. Apart from that there were numerous belts and pulleys and, dominating all, was a large brass ball suspended over what Mr Crosse later told me was a capacitor. He instructed me to wind the handle and said that I'd need all my strength to turn it some 230 times - after that we'd see something that might make us jump. I did as he bid, and to begin with it was heavy going, but once the brass ball was spinning at speed, the work became easier.

My head could only have been a couple of feet from the ball as I bobbed up and down winding the handle with all the might I could muster. I tell you this because suddenly there was a blinding flash of light that seemed to explode from the spinning sphere. I jumped for fear of my life and, as I did, an ear-splitting crack boomed so that I thought that I was bound to be injured - more probably killed. However, I found myself still standing on my feet, although several paces from the handle, and when I looked around I saw that my father was cowering behind a bench while Mr Poole was sitting on the floor with his arms up as if to protect his head. They looked a comic sight, those two heroes of mine, and I turned to the Thunder and Lightning Man and couldn't help myself but laugh, though I knew I shouldn't.

That laugh brought me five years of happiness. I suppose it proved to Mr Crosse that I wasn't likely to take to my heels – and he took me on as his laboratory assistant there and then. At the time I didn't know what a privileged position it was to be. Some of the other staff at Fyne Court did though, and it was a while before my easy going nature began to put them at their ease.

I can see what the problem was if I use the wonderful microscope of hindsight: there was me, a 13-year-old broomsquire's boy, coming into an important household and immediately taking up the honoured role as the Squire's right-hand man. Not in all respects of course, the butler Beale ruled the roost in the house itself, the head gardener ran everything in the extensive grounds and Giles Buncombe the factotum oversaw just about everything else around the estate. None of these fellows, though, held any jurisdiction in the laboratory, and nor did they want it. It was Mr Crosse's hallowed domain and, being his one and only assistant in a way elevated me in the pecking order. Of course, I knew none of this when I began my work there.

That cold grey morning I bade farewell to Mr Poole who shook me by the hand and wished me all the best, laughing over his shoulder as he climbed on his horse, that he knew I'd learn as quick as grease-lightning. I turned to my father and still recall the long searching look we gave each other through tear-clouded eyes. I have known few fathers and sons to be as close as we, and it was a wrench for us both to part. Neither of us had anything to fear though. Squire Crosse was a generous and understanding man who allowed me freedom to visit my mother and father at the other end of the hills regularly.

Perhaps I had better explain that Broomfield is at the southern extremity of the Quantocks. It seems to hang above the Vale of the Tone and from its sylvan edges you can see the county town of Taunton far below. A town, by-the-way, which I have always loathed. It is a place where insidious people seem to dwell, unlike Bridgwater, which can be seen from Broomfield's eastern limits. Yes, the folk in Bridgie are a scrappy lot too keen to use their fists, but at least you know where you stand with them. Indeed, one of my favourite days of the year was the one that brought us the Bridgwater Pony Fair, an event at which the broomsquires have been wheeling and dealing for more centuries than anyone can remember.

Anyway, there is Broomfield - a hamlet with a pretty church crowning the first high ridge as the hills begin their journey north to the sea. As I mentioned, it is not far from the parish of Bagborough and of course, this was not lost on me. More of that later. First I must explain my duties and describe something of my life at Fyne Court. I was given a small room above the stables, which I was supposed to share with one of the grooms, but his mother lived in the village and at night he would sneak off through the grounds to go home where the old widow would spoil him with food and drink. I ate my meals in the servants' kitchen at the rear of the big house and can honestly say that I have never fared better before or since. Good food and plenty of it - seemed to be the modus-operandi - which, of course, was a phrase I learned from my new Master.

Duties began before breakfast when I was expected to light the laboratory fire (at least in winter) and then see to the batteries. So important were these that they deserve special mention. There were hundreds of them all of different forms and sizes. They were mostly voltaic batteries but they varied considerably - some were in porcelain troughs, others were in pairs of glass vessels and yet more were in double metal cylinders and some were in glass jars with strips of copper and zinc. The basic Volta's Pile consisted of paired discs of silver and zinc sandwiched between paper strips soaked in salt water. These discs, or cells, were supported by glass rods and between each disc ran a metal strip which, at the bottom of the pile, passed into a vessel filled with an acidic solution. The electric current would run down this metal strip into the vessel. Caring for these cells was an endless task, and that is what I would be about every morning before Mr Crosse came to the laboratory. The metal plates required constant cleaning because of the acidic solutions that washed across them, and for me this maintenance work became a labour of love. At first though, I was anxious to say the least. The garden and stable boys didn't help matters. In the evenings they would taunt me insisting I would most certainly perish in my new job.

"You wait until the lightning comes," said one of the older lads. "Then you will rue the day you ever set eyes upon Fyne Court. If you are in that laboratory when the explosions are going off, you'll not stand a chance."

Well, within a week or two, I was in there when explosions seemed to be bursting all around me and I can put my hand on my heart and say that, after I'd acclimatised to the madness of it, I'd never had such good fun. This is how it went. All this particular day we worked outside in the grounds where Mr Crosse had me shinning up trees with ropes to haul up what he called his lightning conductors. At first one or two of the gardeners were detailed to do this work, but both of them were clumsy in the high tree tops and neither fancied the job much.

"Let go the branch you fool, and tie the damned thing on," shouts up Mr Crosse to Alfred Marks, one of the garden lads. But Alfred was none too keen on the idea of letting go, even though he was well tied on. You cannot lash a tall copper strip to a tree without using both hands and, as the other fellow proved even worse at altitude, so Mr Crosse began to despair. "I've got to get them up today," he says, "for I would wager my father's watch that there'll be a storm tonight."

Now, I had been climbing trees since learning how to walk, so (still being shy and uncertain of myself at the time) I muttered that perhaps I should have a go.

"You?" answers Mr Crosse patting me on the back. "You are far too young to go up there and, anyway, I promised your father and Mr Poole that no harm would come of you."

I told him I was certain I could do the job and he looked at me for a time before nodding towards the ladder. "I have no choice, I s'pose, but the moment you feel unsafe or scared, you come straight down."

Up I went, passing poor Alfred who was still clutching for dear life in the main bole of the mighty tree. He had more-or-less secured the base of the copper pole but there was no way he was going any further up to tie the higher end. Indeed it was trickier than I'd imagined and at one point I found myself swinging out on a branch to hook my feet over a higher one. It took some strength and agility to pull myself up to that next bough and by the time I got there the backs of my knees were sore.

Far below I could hear the Squire shouting up at me, but the rest of the climb was easier. I must say, when I looked down the world seemed a smaller place than I had thought. Even the big house was dwarfed by the height of the thing and I realised that my tree climbing experiences had never taken me as far aloft as this. I lashed a length of sturdy cord around the top of the copper conductor and used a knot my father had taught me. I knew it had to be good and fast because the only way for me to get back down to the bole where Alfred sat was to shin down the pole itself. Climbing up a thing is always a lot easier than climbing down...

Looking back, it was all a bit of a lark, but Mr Crosse seemed mightily impressed. He put his arm around me when I reached the ground and said he was glad indeed that Tom Poole had recommended the broomsquire's son.

"I have a feeling that you and I are going to be friends," he said as we went inside, and he was right. We did become friends and all these years later I can tell you that Andrew Crosse has stood by me through thick and thin.

Several of these lightning conductors were placed in the trees and all were linked by copper wire to a large brass ball just inside the window of the organ gallery high in the laboratory. That night the storm duly arrived and Mr Crosse called for me to join him as the first rumble of thunder was heard crashing somewhere to the west out over the wilderness of Exmoor.

"Turn the handle now Johnny," he smiled. "It took you 230 turns to generate enough electricity to create the spark when you arrived the other day. Now see how long it takes..."

Within a few turns the ball flashed a big cracking spark to the conductor. Soon though, as the great storm gathered around the Quantock Hills, the larger brass ball up in the gallery was generating violent sparks all by itself. The massive, gloomy interior of the laboratory was lit by intense light and the resulting claps and bangs were so loud they hurt my ears. I shall never forget the scene as the storm passed overhead. Outside, lightning bolts were hitting the conductors in the trees - when I looked out I could see brilliant yellow-blue snakes of electricity dancing along the copper wires as bolts from the heavens hit the conductors in the trees time and again. For seconds on end it was day out there in the blackest night - but if the scene outside was dramatic, inside there was mayhem. Each bolt seemed to break loose yet more equipment and the general impression of havoc was personified by the Squire himself as he ran here and there like a madman checking on the various experiments that were being subjected to violent voltages every few seconds. Each was connected to that mad glowing ball in the organ gallery via a giant conductor. The ball cracked and blasted out its blinding electricity like something that had been wrought by the Devil himself. Indeed, the laboratory looked like a place for gods rather than men and soon we were forced to don the thick black spectacles that the squire had made especially for these occasions.

In this devil's kitchen the blinding flashes and ear-shattering explosions had nothing whatsoever to do with human flesh and blood. But weirdest and strangest of all was the groaning, surging, bellowing, wailing and trumpeting of the mighty organ. Whatever caused it, I am not entirely sure - some build up of pressure, perhaps the vibrations of the giant frenzied ball that flashed and flickered next to it - but the massive pipes played an eerie dirge of their own. It was the music of hell and heaven and everything in between.

Andrew Crosse said to me later: "Did you hear the music of it

Johnny? If eternity could sing or speak, that would be its sound."

I heard it all right and was frightened by the eerie caterwaul. However, as the mayhem came to its astounding crescendo, I did a thing that may seem strange, a thing which I have done a few times in the face of absolute black fear. I laughed. I laughed until tears ran down my cheeks and streaked my vision.

Then came a point at the very height of the storm when the Squire cried out: "Enough. My God that is enough – we must stop it before we are killed..."

With that, like some necromancer from ancient times, he leapt to a large lever and struggled with it with such energy you'd have thought it was the very switch of life and death. I could see that he needed help so I ran over and, while he hauled with all his weight, I pushed and grunted until suddenly the thing lurched sideways and the mad lightning ball in the galley fell silent.

The cacophony of the organ faded in a series of eerie wheezings and sneezes. At last there was silence, save for the diminishing rumblings of the storm outside.

"It is the insulating lever," he puffed, out of breath, sitting on the floor where the sudden lurch of the lever had deposited him. "If we had been unable to throw it Johnny, I think you can safely say we'd have blown ourselves and the rest of the house to pieces."

With that he roared with laughter too, and I joined him until we were both helpless with mirth. Now, my laughter was born from a sense of relief, but let me say this about the panic of that mad night: no boy has ever had such fun.

Looking around, as the excitement ebbed, I surveyed a scene of smoking batteries, scorch marks and one or two flames, harmlessly playing on cables and benches. The great ball above was humming and hissing with heat and moisture. If there is such a thing as the Devil – and I believe there is – then a visit from him would surely result in a scene such as this.

"That will be all for tonight I think Master Walford," sobbed my master as his laughter also died away. "You have seen the very stuff of which our universe was formed, and few in the world have witnessed that. To bed with you boy – you truly are the Wizard's apprentice now."

He smiled and walked over to pat me on the shoulder and I left that mad magnificent room a happy lad. The storm was still groaning outside and as I made my way through the big house I began to wonder what had become of the other denizens of the place. I came across them huddled in the kitchen with Mr Beale the butler reading out loud from the Holy Bible under the light of a single lantern. He stopped as I entered and in the sudden quiet of that gloomy room, all eyes were fixed upon me. There must have been a dozen members of the household and garden staff gathered there, and all at once I was the centre of their attention. I think I rather liked the sensation, it had certainly never happened to me before.

"Are you unharmed?" shouted Beale. "And the Master, is he alive?"

"Mr Crosse is very happy with his experiments this evening," I replied, perhaps a little pompously. And then I grinned: "You should have seen it! It was like Old Nick his-self had come to call..."

The next day Mr Crosse reprimanded me for that. Gently of course, for never did that good man utter an angry word: "I would appreciate it if you did not speak of our experiments, Johnny," he said as we were cleaning up the next morning. "Beale is in a bad enough state as it is, but whatever it was that you reported to the staff last evening, it seems to have put the fear of God into him. Something about the Devil coming to call, I believe. It almost had the poor man packing his bags and, believe me, I wish to avoid such domestic annoyances. Best not say a word in future Johnny - we'll keep our experiments to ourselves and the less well informed can rely upon their prayers. Unfortunately, ignorance is the most dangerous of mankind's many sorry traits"

Little did I know then how real his words would ring years later, but I'll be coming to that. Old Beale though, did eventually go. He couldn't stand being in such close vicinity to what he called the Devil's work, and found a position in an altogether holier household. I, on the other hand, took to my work - and to my master - more happily and thoroughly than I dreamed was possible for a boy brought up in a broomsquire's hut.

And so the weeks turned into months, and the months into years, and the pattern of my life settled into a relatively even-keeled existence – if working for the Wizard of the Quantocks could be described in such rational terms. I will record the events of these years at a gallop to save myself time, for I do not know how much grace I shall be allowed in which to finish this work.

Firstly, it may be asked why Johnny's old sense of freedom did not rebel against the settled routine of a gentleman's household. To this I can reply in simple terms: there was no settled routine. My Master and I would work through the night if we found it necessary. At other times we would do very little experimental work at all, but go on long marches to gather minerals and crystals in the hills. Also, I was enjoying what might be termed as an academic freedom – one in which I could pit my wits, alongside my Master's – against the many problems that forever faced us in our mission to learn more of the mysterious ways of electricity.

Needless to say, I became a valuable servant. Indeed, it was more than that: in a few years, I can safely state that we were friends. Companions in adversity – as he once called it.

But I am getting ahead of myself. I am sure that the kind person who may one day read this will be wondering about my slowly evolving relationship with Miss Anne Rice, and to that end I can happily relay the following. In short I was able, through another servant of the Crosse household, to communicate with Anne. She was as delighted as I at the news of my new-found position. It was Alfred Marks, whose bacon – to use his term – I had saved by scaling the tree with the lightning conductor, who I turned into a conductor of my own. Only the innocent Alfred was conducting the electricity of love rather than the electricity of the firmament. I had thought that he might turn belligerent towards me after I had somewhat eclipsed him at the top of that tree, but it turned out to be quite the reverse. So terrified had he been, the burly Alfred took a sort of shine to me for coming to his rescue. That one act of high altitude heroics stood me well in that particular corner of the household – which was just as well, for I was soon learning that my favoured status with Mr Crosse was the cause annoyance among other staff.

"You saved my bacon up there Walford," Alfred said later that afternoon before the great storm, "And I'll not forget it, you can count on that."

This friendliness of his came to manifest itself during my first few months at the Court when some of the men took it upon themselves to bully me. Alfred, I am glad to say, would not allow it, and none were brave or big enough to take him on. But my friend's goodwill towards me was to bear fruit in an altogether unexpected direction. It happened one day in the staff kitchen when the under-cooks were chiding him over his connection with a maid who worked at the school at Bagborough. Without saying a word I went to my room above the stables and wrote Anne a letter, which was duly delivered - via Alfred - the very next day. He passed it to his sweetheart and soon a reply from Anne was handed to me, and so a line of communications was established.

As I have said, Anne was delighted by my rise in rank. To her, my promotion from broomsquire's urchin to squire's right-hand-man could only mean promise and good fortune. In that very first note, handed to me by a furtive but smiling Alfred, she extolled the virtues of my new found luck.

"Do you see what it could mean to us Johnny," she wrote. "My father might be unforgiving in his ideas about people who live out on the hills, but he cannot possibly decry a young man who holds a position of importance in such an establishment. You wait and see, if you do well in your work and become an invaluable servant to Mr Crosse, then my father cannot possibly object to our friendship."

This thought had not fully occurred to me before, but I could see that she was right. My being the valued servant of one of the area's leading gentlemen would surely be the making of me. Indeed, I was already beginning to behave and speak like a gentleman and my Quantock burr was being subdued as I endeavoured to echo the speech of my Master. The Squire had insisted on providing me with apparel more becoming of a laboratory assistant than the fustian rags that had seen me through scrubbet and heath for so many years. After all, the place was constantly visited by all manner of people, from a gang of leather workers who walked all the way from Bristol to find out more about one of Mr Crosse's patent processes, to high and mighty scientists such as Sir Humphrey Davy.

For these new clothes I had to make a lonely journey down to the county town of Taunton. It was my first visit and to this day I remain unimpressed by such places. Towns, with their filth and stench, remain an anathema to me and I cannot understand why anyone should chose to live in one when there is so much countryside to soothe and prettify and add colour to a man's existence. I entered the streets of Taunton with nervous trepidation, and I left heartily glad to be rid of the place. I experienced abuse from drunken scoundrels, and I experienced the odium of the crawling tradesman keen to take my master's money. The town was but a compendium of mercenary grasping and human misery and I was mightily glad to leave the banks of the River Tone and ascend through the meadows to the slopes of my beloved hills.

Anyway, my new appearance was startlingly different from the old. The girls of the staff made quite a thing of me when I entered the kitchen for dinner that evening.

In the laboratory my appearance was dominated by the large leather apron that I wore at all times because of the many acidic substances in the place. But for dinner with the servants, and for Sundays, Mr Crosse had ordered me a fine suit which really did make me look quite the gentleman.

It was this suit I wore on my first visit home to my parents. Neither of them could believe the sight of me and the one sister who'd remained at home was rendered quite speechless by my grand demeanour. I cannot pretend that I did not enjoy such attention. My mother spent the entire day preening me and brushing the shoulders of my suit. My father sat on a log smoking his pipe, and I could tell by his expression that he was proud of his son. At the end of my visit nothing would prevent him from escorting me all the way home to Fyne Court, and he must have returned to his hut long after dark.

But, if their surprise at my appearance was remarkable, then the expression upon the face of Anne Rice was one that I shall never forget. By then she had turned fourteen years and, for her birthday, had received from her father a fine young mare so that she could travel more easily between her school and her home on the other side of the hills. It was a journey only made once a fortnight, and to facilitate her visits the miller would send a man over to Bagborough on one of the carthorses so that she could be escorted in safety. But the fellow was an old retainer, a man Anne knew well, and so it was all too easy for her to dupe him into plodding sedately along the ridgeway while she enjoyed a gallop over the heaths for the pure pleasure of the thing. All she had to do was to promise to meet him before he entered the woods above Ladies Coombe. Anne arranged all this and communicated the plan to me by note - and that next Sunday I was out on the hill high above the parish of Aisholt, which has to be one of the loveliest places on Earth. To all intense and purposes I was on my way home to visit with my parents, but of course I tarried up there in the bracken waiting for Anne.

I found myself a little hollow out of the cool sea breeze where I could lie in the furze and enjoy the weak winter sun. Life was an enormous joy to me in those heady days and I lay there dreaming dreams of my own fame and fortune and how proud my beloved would one day be of me. I worked with electricity every day, and yet I could somehow, illogically, feel the stuff at work deep inside my veins. Everything was a thrill. And when I heard the distant thud of hooves I jumped up and almost gave Anne a fright. Or at least, her little mare which shied away and it took a second or two to calm the beast. Then Anne looked at me for the first time in many months. For a while she did not speak and I could see her looking up and down scrutinising everything from my new boots to my smart new hat.

"Johnny," she whispered in an uncertain voice. "You have changed. You are... I don't know... It is like you have become a man."

Full of delight I ran across and held up my arms to help her down. When her feet touched the ground our faces were brought close together and we stood there for a long time staring into one another's eyes. I suppose that, had we been just a few months older, then we should have kissed. I do know that, for the first time, the idea of a physical desire for her was borne upon me. But I certainly didn't have the courage to do anything about it. I didn't even know how to begin.

"I've missed you something terrible Anne." I said and for half-an-hour we walked side-by-side across the heath towards Will's Neck.

The next time we met, about two months later, we did embrace and we did kiss one another. It is a moment engraved deeply in my soul. If I could take one thought with me to my death, and keep it for eternity, it would be the thought of that first kiss. Even now my hand shakes and my eyes water at the memory of it.

The next thing to happen was that Anne's school was holding a spring garden fete followed by an evening dance, and Squire Crosse was to be guest of honour. Somehow, from somewhere, that good man had gained some inkling of my desires concerning a certain young lady at the school and, once or twice, he had teased me upon the subject. But on this occasion he suggested that I might like to wait upon him during his long day out.

"You can ride with me and enjoy the fun of the fete Johnny – and why not...? Who knows, you might even catch sight of that young lady of yours."

I blushed deep red, I am sure, but managed to mumble something about being only too pleased to do my duty by him. It was a grand affair - far too grand for the likes of me. I was uncertain of my place, of my social standing, and so joined the stable lads and others who had driven their masters and mistresses in carriages and the like. Several times I saw Anne at a distance - in the thick of the crowd, all dressed up in finery. She looked regal and stunning, far beyond the reach of a broomsquire's boy. I began to wish that I had stayed at Fyne Court. Perhaps on this occasion I noticed it more than any other: the fact that there were of two worlds and that I was placed firmly in one, while she inhabited quite another. Towards evening as the gloaming closed in, Mr Crosse came to look for me, which was thoughtful of him as the great and the good were at that moment all entering the main house for a grand dinner. The servants and working people of the village were being entertained in one of the stable yards that had been decked out with flowers and bunting for the great occasion. Wonderful smells of hot food were emanating from the place and normally I should have joined in cheerfully, as I enjoy good company and have a healthy appetite. But on this evening I felt miserable and out-of-sorts. My sole purpose that day had been to see Anne - and of course, I had only half-achieved that - but to no avail at all. Her remoteness - the impossibility of our situation - served only to frustrate and depress me.

Mr Crosse found me sitting on a wall by the school's stables, looking sorry for myself. He told me to cheer up and announced that he was having the time of his life, but, when he saw the extent of my dejection, he said I should ride home to the Court and he would see himself back later. I think he realised how impossible my position was. In his own, unusual, eccentric house, I could come and go almost as if I were a member of his own family. Here, in Society proper, I was a broomsquire's lad out of place between the pillar of the gentry and the post of the working men. A curiosity in an expensive suit.

"You'd better go on home Johnny," he said gently and then, as he turned to walk off across the cobbled yard, he added. "Tell me the truth, is there a particular young lady to whom you'd like me to pass a message? She might appreciate it, you know."

I realise now that the dear man was slightly the worse for alcohol. And in the next few days I was to realise exactly why he had worked himself into a state of excitement that afternoon. For it was the school spring fair that brought him together with the woman who would become Mrs Crosse. Of course, I dared not say a word about Anne to him - and off he went to his ball, and me to the lonely black hills. It is not a long journey, especially by horse, and I was riding one of my master's fine hunters that day, so I didn't expect it to take long before I was lying in my loft above the stables. As it happened, it took an hour or so longer than I'd anticipated.

I was climbing the steep hill towards the ridge high above Cothelstone and had come to a place where the vista opens out to reveal the vast swathe of the Vale of the Tone. The lights of Taunton and all the other towns and villages of the great valley were beginning to twinkle in the darkening night and I slowed my mount to gaze at the fine view. I recall falling into a mood of deep melancholy as I gazed forlornly down at all those lights - each one illuminating some cosy family life where children laughed and mothers and fathers loved and wept and lived and died in the peaceful heartlands of our ancient shire.

But I was born and raised an outsider. A man cast in the mould of the outlander will always be apart from the crowd. For some years I had been aware that there was something different about the blood trickling through my veins and, I think, I felt it more acutely in those moments than at any other time of my life. This sense of remoteness that we hill-folk feel, compared with the snug lives of the men and women of the valleys and villages, has for the most part been something of a joy to me. But there, on that ridge in the last gloaming, as I looked down on Bagborough far below - hearing the revelries and music wafting up through the coombe - I felt the full weight of a young man who is far removed from his fellows. The loneliness that is the lot of the broomsquire distracted me for the first time in my life. The burden of solitude weighed heavy and a sense of foreboding carried me into the falling darkness of night.

It was during this gloomy reverie that the sound of clattering hooves startled me. My horse stirred and I looked down the lane to see who could be making such haste with so little light to see by. When the black, fast moving shape materialised through the last wisps of dusk, the instant rush of joy that coursed through my body was so absolute, the onslaught so indescribable, that I could only sit there on the horse like some gawping fool. For it was Anne Rice, cantering bare-back up over the hill. When she saw me, she pulled up short and wheeled her mare towards my great hunter. We didn't say anything. I wanted to, but was still overcome with a sort of thrilled panic, and anyway, it was a moment when words could be of no use at all. Instead we looked into one another's eyes and then I recall - to this day I recall - shifting my gaze from her eyes to her lips. Suddenly our lips were meeting for that very first sweet time and the long, soft, passionate moment was more powerful than any lightning bolt collected by Wizard Crosse.

So began the full-fledged liaison between Anne Rice and myself. That night, as we walked along the lane hand in hand with our horses following behind, we made great promises and plans, stopping often to embrace. Two souls - two beacons of light - that have found each other in the cold, lonely, starless void of eternity. That is how I see it now in my time of sadness and remorse. We agreed with a great passion that sooner or later we should be man and wife. Nothing would prevent us, nothing could succeed in keeping us apart: we were, we decided, bonded for endless time, from the moment we first met that sunlit day by the dizzying waterwheel. And Anne - if you are ever to read these words - I still believe that and will take the sentiment with me beyond the grave.

For days I moped about like a person in a dream, as if some sickness had overtaken me. A poet I knew later called it the terrible, powerful, miasma of first love. There's no doubt that my Master observed all this peevish youthful moodiness, but I think he was in much the same state himself. However, after the passing of a couple of days he said to me:

"Johnny," he says, "When I left you t'other night you looked most frightfully cast-down. And yet, since then, you have moped about the place with a sickly looking smile upon your face. What ails the boy? That is what I have been wondering. Is he ill or is there some other devil playing within his soul."

I replied that I was in rude health, but Mr Crosse was not to be put off. "Hmmm, I am sure that your physical being is as hail as a spring stag's. It is your mental demeanour that seems adrift. I was wondering..." says the Master rubbing his chin. "No, no - surely not? It couldn't possibly have any connection with something I heard in Bagborough the other night..."

We were at our work in the laboratory and I was busy cleaning the surfaces of some battery plates. But these last words caused me to cease so that he could see that he had caught my interest. The squire continued thus: "Nothing really Johnny. It was just that someone at the fete ball was asking for you. A pretty little thing. Quite fetching. A Miss Rice, I was later told. She comes up to me as bold as you like, and says: 'Mr Crosse, I am most sorry to bother you, but I wish to know what has become of your assistant Johnny Walford?' And then she adds: 'I thought I saw him escorting you earlier and, you see, he is a family friend from my own village and I would dearly like to pass on some message to him.' Well, I was about to offer to pass on this communication to you when she span on her heel and was gone. At least, she was away once I'd muttered that you'd already returned home. In fact, so abrupt was she that it was remarked upon by my friend Miss Hamilton. And so, you see, I have been wondering whether this small incident might not have some bearing upon your strange mood of late?"

You must understand that I had what could only be described as a special relationship with my Master. He was a kind and learned man who had become a model and mentor to me. If my own real father was lord of the wild things and places, then Mr Crosse was, for me, master of the world of man and learning. But it was more than that, for there was an easy atmosphere between us. And for that reason I opened my heart to him:

"Her name is Anne Rice," said I. "She is Rice the miller's daughter and she and I have been comrades since we were small children. But Sir, I must tell you that there is more to it than that. I am in love with her, and she with me. It always has been so, but now we have grown older we have come to realise it. I am sorry - you probably think it wrong that a broomsquire's son should swagger about having such longings for someone of a superior class. But there is nothing to be done about it. We have been drawn together as surely as the lightning must strike your copper poles."

"On the contrary, I am most pleased to hear of it Johnny," beamed Mr Crosse. "I am very happy for you - though I happen to believe that, at sixteen years of age, you are hardly old enough to know such a thing with any certainty. However, you could not have found a finer looking girl and she obviously has courage and spirit judging by her determination the other night. What did she do - come after you?"

"She did," says I shamefacedly.

"Ah, young love. What a splendid, splendid thing," he replied, putting a fatherly arm around me. "I wish you the very best my young friend. And know this: after a decent period of courtship when I can see that you know, for sure, what is in your own mind - I will support you to the hilt. In a couple of years, if you wish to marry, then I will make sure that there is a proper home for you both on the estate. You know that you will always have a place here Johnny."

Well, you can imagine the bitter-sweet effect that my master's speech had upon me. It was some moments before I was able to stammer: "Thank you Mr Crosse. You have already been more kind to me than I can ever repay. But I'm afraid that no good fortune on my part will ever dissolve the dark cloud that hangs over us. It is her father: he regards me as being beneath the lowest of the low and will not have Anne passing so much as the time of day with me. Indeed, it is why she was packed off to the school at Bagborough in the first place. He learned that she and I had developed a friendship at the village school, and he had her taken away so that she should have no further dealings with me."

"Hmm," mutters the squire. "Rice might be a bigot of the true rural mould, but he is not an idiot. You carry on working here with me in the excellent manner that you have been doing, and you shall be rewarded. Perhaps we shall make a gentleman of you, and if I can ever get around to concentrating on the business side of our work, I promise to ensure that you shall benefit greatly from the financial gains which our researches will produce. I had a letter from George Singer in London just yesterday, in which he opines that electricity will in some future time be the power that fuels the commerce and business of human endeavour, not to mention facilitate the comforts of our lives. I tell you Johnny, it will be employed in a vast variety of manufactures throughout the world. And if I am astute - which I have to admit I am not when it comes to business - we should be able to harness some of the resulting wealth to make our lives more comfortable so that we can continue with our experiments. Not that wealth has anything to do with my own fascination for the subject. But I am trying to paint for you a rosy picture. You shall share in this future fortune of ours - and I promise you: the day shall arrive when you shall travel to Rice's Mill in your own carriage and the old rogue will be beside himself with eagerness for you to marry his beautiful daughter."

It was indeed a rosy picture. Some days later I related it to Anne who laughed at the idea of me travelling in my own carriage. I thought it way beyond the bounds of the possible too. However, after that I began to detect a difference in Anne's attitude toward me. Where once she had been the leader, now we were equals. For the first time I began to feel that the strange effluvium, that occurs between childhood and adulthood, was tipping towards the latter. I was still young certainly, but I was beginning to feel the gravity of manhood.

All this occurred during a time of change that was the start of a new and happy period. Several threads seemed to evolve during this era and I must hasten through them, for I wish to complete this narrative betimes.

Mr Crosse was about twelve years older than I, and it seemed that for the first time in his life he was taking an interest in the opposite sex. To be exact, he was taking an interest in Miss Mary Ann Hamilton, whom he had met at the summer fair. The result of this was that there were occasions when I would see less of him than before. As I was happy in my work and becoming more and more intrigued with the studies and experiments, this in no way perturbed me. I had settled in to our academic regime and, as I had never felt particularly comfortable within the domestic side of the house, I was happy to spend more time in the laboratory. As the visits of Mr Crosse's fiancée Miss Hamilton became more regular, so I felt even more at ease confining myself to these regions. She seemed to regard me with some small degree of misgiving which resulted in her being somewhat aloof. She no doubt thought this befitting of my lowly standing.

The staff, for the most part, were also uneasy with me - indeed they were suspicious, not to say alarmed, when it came to anything related to the strange experimental work we carried out. My increasing solitude in no way upset me and in truth gave me more freedom than I'd enjoyed before. Often I was able to take to the hill in order to seek out some mineral or rock for our experiments. In particular, I was regularly required to visit Holwell Cavern some two miles distant, in order to collect the pure water that dripped from the stalagmites there. The cavern had only recently been exposed by a small quarry working and, as it lay on the Master's land, he was quick to become fascinated by the possibilities inherent in a place that had never seen daylight since time began. The walls contained every possible type of arragonite and the water that dripped from them was of a particularly pure quality and consistence. Time and again I would be sent for more and on these occasions I'd take a pony and trap. The journey out would, for me, be filled with some dread. The deep, black hole was not a place I enjoyed. To enter the cavern it was necessary to descend a steep bank of scree caused by waste from the quarry, and this took you some 60 feet down an ever-narrowing pit to the entrance of the actual tunnel. This aperture in the bedrock ran horizontal for some way before terminating in what seemed to be a dead-end - but behind a fold in the rock was a tiny hole through which we would wriggle and writhe until we came to a point where we had to turnover to negotiate a tight, upward bend. This was the most unpleasant part of the work as it required a difficult turn of the body in order to reach upwards to some handholds above. Only by grabbing these could you haul yourself up out of that wretched, body-gripping bend, and I can tell you it took a good deal of struggling – especially for me as I was already by this age fairly broad in the shoulder. I never came away from that pit without a bruise or a gash. Often, at this point, I would utter an oath or two. A broomsquire is a man of the outdoors, a creature of hill and sky – to me this claustrophobic black sump was the epitome of hell.

After the bend, the tunnel grew larger until it passed downwards through yet another narrow aperture into a cavern, similar in size to one of the largest rooms at Fyne Court. This place was altogether more bearable than what had been passed before, save for the depressing knowledge that you'd have to return via the pot-hole. In the lantern light the weird shapes of the stalagmites and stalactites were quite fantastic. Between these strange edifices – which were anything between 15 or 20 feet in height - lay quiet pools of clear cold water, and it was their ice cold contents that I was required to collect in straw-wrapped stone jars which I would pull through the tunnel on a rope.

As I say, I found this underground work unpleasant and in truth I was downright scared. The first time we crawled in there I thought my master must be mad - left to my own resorts I wouldn't have entered more than a single inch into the place. But once we were in the cavern proper he became so excited and animated by what he found, that it was hard not to be caught up by his enthusiasm. Later, when we started carrying out experiments, I too became thrilled by the discovery of the numerous crystals that could be found existing in the clear water.

"Look Johnny," said the Wizard of the Quantocks in a reverent whisper that echoed around the cavern as he stroked a rock icicle that hung down twenty feet from the roof. "The water has built this smooth pillar, that is obvious. But how?"

I must say, in that moment in that strange place in the eerie light of the lantern, Mr Crosse lived up to the name the local people had given him.

Back at the laboratory we laid a length of platinum wire in a large glass jar of cavern water and passed a permanent but extremely weak electric current through it. In a week or two we began to see crystals sparkling on this wire which excited Mr Crosse beyond measure. The cellars beneath the house were opened up and more jars were filled with more of the water, and more wires with different degrees of weak electrical current were put into place. Within a year or two we had, through the process Mr Crosse called electro-crystallisation, created over a hundred types of crystal including quartz and malachite. Once, in hushed tones of great reverence, my master whispered to me that he felt it would even be possible to manufacture diamonds using such a method. But in this, as in many things, he swore me to secrecy.

Secrecy was central to the ethos of Squire Crosse. Not that he was in the least bit jealous of his findings. It was simply that he was not a public man; he did not want his experiments and results crowed from the rooftop. Nor was he a man who required wealth and fortune in return for his endeavours. He honestly and quietly wanted to research and discover – in his own time, at his own pace. In his quest for the scientific answers to the vast conundrums which face mankind, he was completely and utterly genuine. A man humbled, he said, by the greatness of nature.

Anyway, the narrative seems to have left poor Johnny alone in Holwell Cavern, which will never do. Suffice to say that as soon as my jars were filled I would whistle to the boy who escorted me on these trips and, lowering them gently to the level part of that narrow bend in the sandy-bottomed tunnel, would watch them disappear toward the distant daylight on the pulley system that we had set up especially for the work. When the last jar had been despatched, I would gladly join them and deliver myself from the darkness with the desperation of an eel fleeing a trap.

My Master knew of my fears and to a certain extent seemed to sympathise, but said that there was only one way to overcome such a fear or "phobia" as he put it – and that was to meet it head on. "You are the only one I can trust Johnny," he sighed slapping me on the back. "If I were to send young Harris he'd go as far as the nearest stream to fill the jars."

His compassion was such that he rewarded each of my visits to the cavern by allowing me to take the rest of the day off. Harris, the boy, would return to Fyne Court with the pony and trap and its watery load, while I was free to wander. And so the monthly trip to Holwell Cavern was a double-edged sword. The dark dread of the morning would be transformed to the pure light and delight of the afternoon. Sometimes I would hit lucky and be able, through much arrangement, to meet with Anne. At other times she would be engaged with her duties at the school where she was rapidly turning from student to assistant teacher, and then I would stride across the hills to visit my mother and father.

At Fyne Court our experiments seemed to be attracting an interest in the world of science. How word got around I do not know because, as I have said, Mr Crosse was most fastidious when it came to the concealment of our work. But, just as the flashings and bangings of our nightly experiments could sometimes clear the entire southern end of the Quantock Hills of their human and probably animal populations, so conversely we had an increasing number of academic visitors flowing in the opposite direction. What an odd lot they were. Some were grandees of pomp and fame. Others were eccentric doe-eyed poets who drank a great deal of my master's wine and spoke of things I could hardly understand. Then there were rough hewn fellows who Mr Crosse described as "industrialists", alongside nervous pale-faced fellows whom he called "academics".

Occasionally there were even ladies and I always felt rather nervous when these strange birdlike creatures arrived. Why? Because, with the one exception of Miss Hamilton, they would always make a terrible fuss of me.

"Your assistant grows more handsome each time I visit," said one lady to my master, knowing that I could hear and enjoying the awkward reddening of my face. Another even stroked my hair and said that I was the most handsome examples of male youth that she'd ever set eyes upon.

I tell you this because one of these female visitors was to afford me an experience that, much later, helped shape a change in my life. I will call her Lady L. so as not to give any clue as to her true identity, for she is still very much alive and married to man of importance. Lady L was I should think half a dozen years older than myself and, I will not deny it, quite lovely to behold. But that was not the thing that attracted Mr Crosse to her: he was impressed by the way in which she took a true academic interest in our work. Indeed, she was such a mathematician that he would sometimes turn to her for advice. To tell the truth I could never understand why a more permanent relationship did not exist between them, for she certainly shared his love for science, where, I think, Miss Hamilton did not.

At first Lady L remained aloof with the boy that she obviously regarded as some under-servant in the household, but as time went by - and as my own standing as Mr Crosse's assistant undoubtedly increased - she began to take more of an interest in me. In the beginning she addressed me only as 'Walford'. By my second year it was 'Johnny'. By the third...Well, I will tell you just how close Lady L and I came to an intimacy of a surprising nature. Mr Crosse was away from the laboratory seeing to the onerous estate duties that always caused in him bouts of nervous indigestion. He was never comfortable in this drudgery, as he called it, and complained about it all the years I knew him. I was at work as usual in the laboratory and Lady L was sitting at my Master's desk having undertaken to work out a number of complex formulas for him. As the morning wore on, so the heat of the summer's day increased and I, forgetting her silent presence, undid the buttons of the dust-coat that was my usual working garb. Normally this state of semi-undress would not have mattered in the least as few, if any, servants ever dared to enter the laboratories.

Sometimes a man has a sixth sense that he is being watched, and so it was now. I glanced over at Lady L, surprised in a way that she was there for, as I say, I had forgotten. The good Lady was staring straight at me. She made no effort to glance away and at once I stammered some sort of apology and pulled the open coat across my bare chest.

"No please don't," she gasped, getting up from the desk. "I should hate for your master to return to find you had expired from the heat."

Slowly she glided toward me and, for some reason I cannot completely fathom, I stood there as if held by her gaze. When she reached me she lifted her hands and ran them gently up and down the lapels of my dustcoat, which I was still holding closed. Then her hands were softly placed upon my own. Without force she pushed them apart so that the lapels of the coat fell open again. With no hesitation her hands moved to slowly stroke their way across my chest. My breath had become shallow and I could feel my heart pounding under her touch, but still I stood there transfixed. I looked at her and saw that her own breath was coming in short pants. I watched the magical movement of her bosom and then looked away from it because the very appearance of it drove some inexplicable desire deep within me. Lady L was, and no doubt still is, a beautiful woman.

She looked up at me and at the same time moved her hands inside my clothes around my naked back, pulling me towards her. She slowly moved up the inch or two it required for her lips to reach mine and was suddenly kissing me with a passion. I will admit that to this day I do not know whether I was kissing her back or not.

"I have watched you for months," she gasped taking her lips away from mine for a moment. "I have watched you grow from a boy into a man – and I will tell you that you are the most beautiful man I have ever seen. The thoughts I have for you sometimes become an obsession so that I wonder I'm not mad."

She placed her lips upon my own again… Alas, what is the point in my telling untruths now? If a servant had not rapped on the door of the laboratory to announce her Ladyship's lunch was served, I know we should have regretted the next minutes for years. But our honour was saved. The knock on the door caused Lady L to jump away, and the moment of madness was over. She turned and walked across the laboratory rearranging her blouse as she went, and turned just once at the door to shoot a parting glance at me. Then, without a word, she was gone. For my part I leaned against that bench for an age with my mind racing through what had occurred. Then I buttoned my coat and marched out of the house, across the lawns, deep into the hills. I didn't return until after dark when I discovered from a member of staff that Lady L was gone. Only the next morning did I find a note secreted in the small desk where I kept my own notebooks, pencils and things. It read:

"Dear Johnny,

I am sorry for what happened earlier, and yet I am not. I will be frank with you: I desire you and it is a desire that distresses me greatly because today for the first time in my life I lost my self control. You have some kind of native grace and elegance that is both profound and beautiful, and yet deeply disturbing.

Of course it is wrong that I should even be penning you this note. Such a thing could never be. Though I class myself as a scientist, I am aware of the impossible difference in our standing. I fear I must now leave this place, for I could never allow such an occurrence to happen again. The terrible truth is that I fear it might. If our embrace has caused a similar stirring within you, then I am sorry. It is unfair – everything is unfair. But it is I who should have known better, who should have had the fortitude to ignore temptation.

Yours with much affection

Lady L."

Two weeks later Mr Crosse handed me a sealed letter addressed to Mr Walford that he said came from Lady L inside a letter from her that he had received. He muttered something about her sending him a note explaining that, while he was away, we had embarked upon some interesting discussion on the subject of mathematics. The idea that she had failed to explain the particular issue properly had irked her and now she was hoping to make good by setting it down on paper. By now I was almost seventeen years of age and I stood much taller than my master – which was just as well as nothing would have pleased him more than to look over my shoulder to read Lady L's answer to the mathematical conundrum. I believe he had no suspicion whatsoever of the real matter, and later I 'accidentally' burned the note so that he could never ask to read it. Her Ladyship wrote:

"Dear Johnny,

In a covering letter I have explained to Mr Crosse that I am writing to spell out some complex formula to you. In reality I want to ask you to come to me. I will find you a situation similar to the one you hold at Fyne Court, on my father's estate. Then, if we are careful, we can see one another. Each hour I think of you, and I know that you must think of me. Please come.

L."

Armed as I was, with naught but sorry inexperience in matters of the heart, I suspected that she was mad. I was even angry with her: she had no idea of my own affairs, she had not bothered to ask, nor did she consider I may not feel the same way about her. Looking back, of course, I realise that this anger was directed at none other than myself. It was pure and simple guilt. Had her

Ladyship's luncheon not been announced with such excellent timing… Well, I think I know what would have occurred. But in those head-high days when my world was filled with optimism and idealism, such a loss of my own self respect would have been intolerable to me. Later, things would change with me but I will be coming to that. For now, allow me the say that this strange interlude with Lady L taught me a salutary lesson. I had discovered, with startling clarity, that Anne Rice was not the only woman to find the broomsquire's son attractive. Through no doing of my own, it seemed that women were drawn to me and, although flattering, I learned that such a thing could be dangerous.

I told no-one but Anne of the incident, and to her I only sketched the vaguest detail. You see, I had to clear my conscience. She, of course, was outraged and at first forbade me to write back to the woman, but then agreed that I should do so explaining that I was more than content at Squire Crosse's establishment and that hoped soon to become engaged to the love of my life. Anne, wisely I think, felt that her Ladyship could make trouble if I were to shun her advances with sullen silence. I think the episode took her by surprise. I swear from that moment she looked at me through slightly different eyes.

"I know it won't be of your doing Johnny," she told me, "For I trust youmy darling, but I fear that you have something about you which appeals to the feminine mind. It is not only that you are handsome, it is something else. Something I cannot explain, but something that I love."

Thinking about it I had noticed how the girls of the domestic staff often tittered and reacted to me in a peculiar way. They never approached me, though, for I was the Master's assistant and, to them, anyone who went into that laboratory at night was either mad or bad, or both. But enough of my sorry vainness – I hope the reader will forgive me for mentioning this draw that I seemed to have over women – but there is good reason why I tell it. I sent my short note to Lady L and, in consequence, did not see her for over five years.

Let us return to the great work of Andrew Crosse. For a period it became even more frenetic than usual, and that was as a result of a visit from Mr George Singer of London, who was an old friend of my Master's. Mr Singer was a quick, darting, little man of enormous energy – and he seemed to have as much knowledge in the science of electricity as the Wizard of the Quantocks himself. Mr Crosse even used to joke that he was Singer's apprentice. Our guest stayed for a few weeks and we worked long hours into the night with him on many diverse experiments using our Leyden Jars, our Gold Leaf Electroscope and in the developing of the great batteries that we called Volta's Piles. There were nights when we got no sleep at all, and I don't think that I saw Anne Rice during the entire duration of Mr Singer's stay. To remark that these two men were enthusiasts would be to understate their profound love of science in general and electricity in particular. Somehow, with some energy that seemed to come from the illusive stuff itself, they sparked in each other an extreme desire for further discovery. There was no sense of competition between them: indeed, close to the end of his stay, Singer did his utmost to persuade my Master to remove himself, his laboratory and his entire household to London where they could continue their experiments together.

"We both know that the future of mankind lies in this extraordinary thing that we call electricity, Andrew," Singer ranted on one occasion. "One day it will be employed in all the manufacturing that occurs throughout the world. It will be the life blood of industry. It will propel us from one place to another. It will allow us to create almost anything that man could wish for. And yet what I cannot understand, is how you moulder away down here in these hills. Fine work Andrew, no one could deny that your experiments are of the highest quality and exactitude. But London, my dear man – London is where the brains are and we must feed off each other's knowledge if we are to truly reach for the stars. You must come to London and we shall work together. The fruits of our labours will afford us the very finest instruments and laboratories and we shall go forth into the mysterious world of electricity together..."

My Master smiled: "I agree with you. You are correct in every single thing you state. And yet I cannot. You see, when I was up at Oxford I yearned for these hills and, when I eventually returned, swore that I should never leave them for any length of time. I have a stake through my body that nails me to Quantock."

He was right there. On our long journeyings together across the hills where we would hunt for this geological sample or that, I have seen Andrew Crosse with tears streaming down his cheeks at the mere sight of a sunset. He would put his arm around my shoulder and say: "There Johnny, is a little part of Paradise. This is our own Arcadia and we two are lucky men indeed to know what Heaven looks like upon Earth."

Moreover he took his duties as Squire very seriously, and no workers or parishioners in Somerset were better looked after than the people of the Fyne Court Estate (although there was a dirty business going on there for some time which I shall come to later). Suffice to say that when it came to thoughts of our removing ourselves to London, there was no possible chance this should ever occur. Mr Singer went away disappointed, but at least he obtained a promise from Mr Crosse that he would soon travel to the metropolis to deliver a series of lectures. These were to be addressed to such august bodies as the British Association for the Advancement of Science. And, in a way, they were to be the beginning of our undoing.

But again, I jump ahead of myself. First, in preparation for the lectures, we worked more furiously than ever and I believe several people left the village during this period because of the explosions that boomed, and the eerie flashes that flickered through the place at night.

You could hardly blame the local folk, for we had miles of wire placed through the trees of the surrounding estate and sometimes at night the copper would gleam with electrical power. In human terms, this generated all manner of freakish theories which ran unabated through the hills. For example, the rumour went about that devils and sprites could be seen dancing along the lines. And even I will admit that sometimes, when there was a good deal of static in the atmosphere, you could see what the villagers meant. There was an unhappy mood in the parish and many people complained that the Thunder and Lightning Man – to give Andrew Crosse one of his other names - was putting the population in danger.

"T'aint never natural," said one farmer to me as I was passing his yard. "They explosions last night was enough to wake the dead. You casn't go near Broomfield on such a night wi'out bein' in danger of yer life. Tis Devil worship if you ask me, and ee should know better."

I laughed and told him not to be such an old fool. But he, like many other local farmers, blamed the squire for attracting electric storms to the hills and ruining their crops. One of the most vociferous fellows in the village stopped me one day by the green where he was loitering with a gang of his mates:

"'Ere comes the Wizard's apprentice. They says Squire Crosse couldn't get no-one else to 'elp un - so ee 'ad to rely on a stupid broomsquire's boy. 'Ere Walford," he shouted to me. "Is it true yer the only idiot who steps foot in thic labreetory save for the Wizard unself? And they says you only does it cos yer too daft in the 'ead to be frightened of the devils in there."

It may seem hard to believe, given my present predicament, but I have always shunned violence, despite my superior size and strength. By that time I had grown into a burly youth - I was a good four to five inches taller than most full grown men when I was 18 and I had the breadth of shoulder to go with it. Anyway, I walked up to this yokel and I says: "You would be wise to watch your tongue Arnie Takle. If there are such things as Devils as you say, then 'tis true that I am not afeared of them. Indeed 'twould be nothing for me to persuade them to dance their dangerous dances with a fool like you."

Then, picking him up by the throat with a single hand, I added: "But believe me Arnie, those Devils aren't as terrible and vengeful as me. If I ever here you decrying the Squire or myself again, I will beat you to within an inch of your life."

Arnie Takle had a reputation for being a local tough but when I threw him to the ground he lay there coughing and spluttering, no longer the fighting cock that he so loudly professed to be. From that moment, few of the lads of that parish took the trouble to bait me - in dealing with the miserable Arnie I believe I earned their grudging respect.

The experiments continued and so desperate were we for more battery power that Mr Crosse made the perhaps eccentric decision to melt the family silver. His fiancée Miss Hamilton was horrified and gave the squire a piece of her mind when she found out, but by then it was too late - we had been down to the estate forge with a cart load of salvers, tureens and bowls and the whole lot went into the cauldron.

"I never liked the stuff anyway," laughed Mr Crosse as the last ladle slowly submerged in the bubbling silver soup. "Far too ornate for my tastes, and difficult to clean I am told."

Beale the butler did not speak for days and was said to have wept when we returned with the exotic silverware turned into thin rectangular battery plates. Even Mr Crosse's brother Mr Richard was enraged; he came storming into the laboratory the day after the forging and cried: "You have gone too far this time Andrew! What the devil do you think you are playing at? It's not as if you've money to burn - quite the contrary in fact!"

But he was soon mollified. There was a great deal of understanding between those two brothers, and in truth Mr Richard had one or two strange ways of his own. He had been in France at the time of the Revolution and on his return was jeered by the miserable people of Taunton as a Jacobin. He was a great believer in what he called the "decimal" system of mathematics and had designed and built for himself a house based on a cube. He hadn't been to the laboratory for some months and was amazed by what he saw there that morning. Seven or eight tables groaned under the weight of extensive voltaic batteries of all shapes and sizes; some were in porcelain troughs, some in pairs of glass vessels with double metal cylinders beside them, others were in glass jars fitted with strips of copper or zinc. Altogether there more than one thousand five hundred voltaic pairs at work in the room and you could almost feel the latent power humming in the place. Soon the family silver was forgotten between the brothers and the two of them were in hot debate over some matter of mathematical theory...

It was around about this time that a singular and dramatic occurrence was to shake my otherwise pleasant workaday life. The adventure began as my Master and I were in the laboratory when Beale the butler rapped at the door. He would never enter unbidden and only ever came to the laboratory under duress.

"There is a girl at the tradesman's door insisting that she speak with Walford," he snuffled in obvious high dudgeon. "I have told her that he is busy with his Master, but she has become quite angry and insists she will make a scene if I have her removed. She says she is Walford's sister."

Without even asking leave from my Master I ran - with his voice booming after me: "Bring her here Johnny. If there is some misfortune then I shall want to hear of it..."

It was Petronilla. She stood leaning against a wall in the back yard, obviously upset and exhausted. I held her and this is what she told me between sobs and gasps: "Tis father. He's in trouble John, very bad trouble. The Excise-men have got him down at Kilve Pill. Tis brandy and Hollands and more besides - and he's down there with Montague Chidgey and they're waiting for the Captain of the Guard to come so they can take 'em to prison."

I marched her through the house to the laboratory where Mr Crosse was waiting and that good man ordered food and drink for my sister. She, it seems, had been at home in the hills above Hodders Combe, when a friend of father's from Kilve had run up from the shore with the news. Smuggling was a serious crime: my sister and I were just about to find out how serious.

"Did you know that your father was involved in this business?" the Squire asked me, before hastily adding: "No, no - do not answer that, for perhaps it would be best if I did not know. You are aware Johnny, aren't you - that I am a magistrate and so take a very dim view of those who break the laws of this land. Those laws are there for a reason and, if your father has broken them, then he must be punished. However, punishment, in my opinion, should be made to fit the crime. Importing a little French brandy doesn't seem to me to warrant a punishment of deportation. For that is what will happen to your father if he is taken to prison and tried."

"There is though, maybe - and I say just maybe - one way out. You must ride to Kilve as fast as you can, and you must take the money I shall give you. Once there you will ask the Excise-men to calculate the amount of duty owing on the brandy; you must say there has been some administrative oversight as to its payment - and you must say that you have come to pay the sum so that there need be no further action. Oh, and bring the brandy back with you, or at least arrange for it to be transported here."

No man has ever crossed the length of the Quantock Hills more rapidly than I did that day astride one of Mr Crosse's great hunters.

The squire rarely rode this particular brute as he was a frisky, temperamental beast, but when you let him know who was in charge he generally did as bid, and at great and terrifying speed. By the time we reached Kilve Pill that horse had very little mischief left in him. He almost disappeared in a cloud of his own steam that sunny afternoon as I leapt off and confronted a couple of the uniformed men. They told me they were still awaiting the Captain of the Guard and his militia, who were said to be coming from Bridgwater to collect the prisoners.

Three smugglers had been seized and, through the crowd of villagers that had congregated to gawp. I could just about make them out languishing in the village stocks by the churchyard wall. Never had I seen my father look more dejected, which was hardly surprising given what was in store for him. To a man of the great open spaces, a prison cell would have meant death – a fact which I, alas, can reluctantly vouch for. But, if my father appeared dejected, poor old Montague looked utterly demolished in spirit. He lay there crumpled on the floor with his feet and hands bound by the wooden stocks, openly sobbing with pity for himself. But by far the most noticeable of the three was the third man, whom I most certainly had never set eyes on before. He sat peering grimly at the far blue horizon of the sea, and while he did so, most of the eyes of the village gazed down upon him. For not only was he a huge, giant of a man, but his skin was as tawny as tanned leather. Something deep in my memory stirred at the sight of him – when Father and Monty had spoken of the herring trade they'd talked often of a tall black mate from the Caribbean whose business interests stretched far beyond the world of fish.

The crowd stood around, eagerly awaiting each and every development, for rarely did Kilve ever in its long history witness such a commotion as there had been that day. A hum of expectation went abroad at my arrival. You must remember I had not been to the village for some years and that, though many of the villagers probably recognised me, I had changed a good deal from the urchin who used to occasionally pass here to go mud-horse fishing with his father. Remember too, that now I was dressed to some degree as a gentleman, and that I had arrived upon a gentleman's expensive steed. So that when I asked to speak to the officer in charge I was duly taken to the nearby ivy covered building that in some previous age had been a Priory. The place had for many years been linked with the dubious business of smuggling but, ironically on this occasion, the law had borrowed it to store the booty they had so recently seized. Inside the old chapel I found a bespectacled wizened little man taking stock of the smugglers' haul, which was more extensive than I had imagined. I introduced myself as a representative of the local magistrate Squire Crosse who wished to know of the extraordinary developments that had taken place that day upon Quantock's shore. The officer seemed to be in a jolly frame of mind and was quite happy to tell me how the smugglers had been apprehended.

"For years we have known that smuggling occurs along this coast with outrageous regularity, but never have we caught a single soul. Until today!" he gleamed triumphantly. "Today we have the rascals good and proper and they will be made an example of, you mark my words..."

This didn't bode well for my negotiations, so I decided to skirt the subject of punishment. I feigned admiration for his wiles and asked how he had masterminded the capture of the rogues.

"Well, it is something that I have been pushing for in my own humble way: money with which to lure informants. Only with the help of local knowledge can we ever achieve a realistic patrolling of these remote coasts. It is surprising how far a sovereign or two will go in persuading someone to come forward with information. Although, in this case, I am not sure whether our informant was interested in the reward so much as gaining revenge for some personal difficulty which I'm told he may have suffered at the hands of one of the smugglers. He seemed to take a particular pleasure in the idea that this particular prisoner would be sure to lose his freedom.

"Anyway, this informant duly came forward and so we were able to set a trap. I have to admit that it didn't go entirely to plan, owing to the fact that the scoundrels played clever with the tides and took us almost completely by surprise. But we got them in the end," he chuckled, before adding, in explanation: "You see, I - like any other sane person of sane mind - would have expected the ship to have landed at high-tide, which was at dawn this morning. You must surely know what a laborious task it would be to drag any cargo across the muddy, rocky terrain that stretches for miles below the high-water mark? But it seems these villains, by some madness that I do not yet understand, managed to land the booty at low-tide in the dark hours around midnight. I am still trying to work out how they did it. Anyway, we were here at dawn and the "Mavis" - the Cornish yawl that brought the contraband - was still at anchor someway offshore. A Cornish gig boat, presumably belonging to her, was pulled up on the beach and so we knew that something was afoot.

"I must say that I have never known smugglers to take such a relaxed attitude to their hazardous work and can only imagine that they are either complete fools or that they have become overly confident after years of being unmolested. More likely still is that they were drunk. Intoxicated on their own spoils. For we were surprised to hear uproarious laughter booming from the fisherman's hovel some hundreds of yards along the shore and, when we entered the place guns at the ready, the three men that you have seen in the stocks guffawed even more merrily. The fact that their good humour had been supplied by a small cask of smuggled French spirit that sat between them on the floor - incriminating them beyond all doubts - seemed to have escaped their concern. They even had the temerity to offer me and my men a tipple!

"One of them, the old rogue of a broomsquire, even whistled a merry tune which had the others in convulsions of mirth. But within a minute or two, one of my men came running into the hut and he told me that the informant, who had remained outside in the interests of anonymity, wished to speak with me urgently. I found the man in a state of great excitement: 'That tune, that whistling,' says he, 'don't you realise, it's a signal to his pony! I heard it rattle off with the cart, up the lane on the other side of the copse. The brute will be halfway between here and the village by now'."

"With that we started running, with me shouting orders for the three occupants of the hut to be restrained. And sure enough, after five or ten minutes of furious endeavour, we gained upon the pony and trap. That intelligent little horse was heading for the hills at a trot - with several hundred pounds worth of French brandy and Hollands gin sloshing about in its bouncing cart. So we had them, and we had their booty. My only regret is that we didn't get that scoundrel of a Cornish skipper - Abraham Hicks. But his days are numbered now that we have his foreign mate. They say it has only been that scoundrel's nerve and cunning that has allowed Hicks to keep his freedom this long while."

I sat on a barrel and rubbed my chin (a habit that I must admit to having picked up from my Master). It seemed my father was in an impossible fix, and yet I was bound to try my damnedest to help him. For a start, I pondered, it bode well for me that this officer had no clue as to my real identity. I had been introduced to him as an assistant to Squire Crosse, the magistrate and, although I had no official powers of reference in any way, the man seemed to regard me as somebody to be reckoned with.

"May I speak with the prisoners for a minute?" I asked.

"You may speak with them all you wish - until the Captain of the Guard arrives. And then they are his and I shall be rid of all responsibility for them. My duties lie with the booty which is why we are waiting for the militia. I have no intention of leaving this much French and Hollands under the guard of just one or two of my men in a lawless place like Kilve."

Outside I walked quickly across to my father and knelt by his side: "It looks like this new form of mud-horse fishing is more lucrative than collecting broom, depending on how you look at it," I said.

The old man gazed back at me with a forlorn look, and said: "Tis good to 'ave you 'ere Johnny. For a whiles there, I thought per'aps I'd never see my sweet boy agin."

"Sshhh," I raised a finger to my lips, and whispered, "The Revenue do not know I am your son and tis better that they do not. Just tell me this. You haven't admitted having anything to do with the contraband have you - to the officer in charge?"

"Course not - do ee think I be daft? We told 'em we found the firkin of French we was drinkin' bobbin' 'long the shore."

"And the pony and cart - do they know it is yours?"

"They says they do. They says some scapegrace from the village 'ave told 'em. But I don't know a soul in the 'ills who wouldsn't let on 'twas my kit. Just about every feller I do know gets a snifter o' this brandy. Not one o' 'em uld gi' the game away."

"Someone has. I don't suppose they've told you who?"

"No, course not. But I'll tell ee this much. I've been a–puzzlin' it all day. There ain't many folks that know little Eskie'll trot to a whistle. Not many at all."

"Leave it with me then - I think there may be a chance that I can get the three of you out of this."

Montague sighed a pitiful whimper. And for the first time the big foreigner took his eyes from the sea. He said to me: "You get us off this hook, boy, and I shall never forget my debt to you. That is my pledge, and one day, I swear, you shall be glad of it."

Looking at him, I had the feeling that this strange man would only bother to utter words if there was some profound, portentous reason to do so. I nodded to him and slapped father on the back before making my way back over to the Priory where the chief of the revenue–men was telling someone else of the wonders of his night's work. I asked to speak with him privately and when the other had gone, struck out on what seemed like a daring tack...

"I must say, I am a little concerned over what I have witnessed here. As you know, Mr Andrew Crosse is Magistrate for this area and he has instructed me to come down to Kilve in order that I should be able to report to him that all is in order. Several cases to have reached the Assizes in recent months have been thrown out because the upholders of the law failed to provide full and thorough evidence (I had only recently overheard Mr Crosse complaining of this to Mr Poole and so had some vague notion of it). I must tell you Sir that, having looked into the matter briefly, I am worried such an unfortunate state of affairs might be the case here today. After all, not you, or any of your men, actually witnessed the disembarking of the contraband."

He looked askance, but I went on before he could interrupt. "Your prisoners tell me the brandy they were drinking was found floating in the tide and, although it is an offence in itself not to turn over such booty (I had once heard my father argue over this legality with Montague), it does not seem to me to be a matter for the Assizes. Furthermore, you seem certain that the pony and cart belongs to one of the prisoners. He swears that it does not and, moreover, states there is not a single man or woman in this village who would place it so – save, that is, for your informant who, as you suggest, may have some personal feud with him and so cannot be counted as a reliable witness.

"My concern Sir, is that you are preparing to turn these men over to a court of law without as much as a single strand of hard evidence against them. Any lawyer worth his salt will say as much and of course it is up to you to provide the burden of proof (again, I had picked up on such goings on by listening to my Master who often liked to talk of the problems he faced as Magistrate). Would three smugglers really sit back and allow their valuable cargo to be delivered to heaven-knows-where by an Exmoor pony? I think not, and nor would a judge."

"So what exactly am I to report to Squire Crosse?" I concluded with an air of exasperation. "Believe me, I am as keen as you sir, to put the rogues behind bars. The Magistrate dearly wishes to see an end to the embarrassment of smuggling occurring along the Quantock coast. But in this case the best I can come up with is that you are assuming the guilt of these men because they happened to be close to the place where the contraband was brought ashore – and because they were drinking from one single small barrel of the brandy. Believe me, Squire Crosse will not be impressed by that."

The man looked visibly shaken. "But who else?" he stammered. "I mean, I know they were at the bottom of it – they were drinking the damned stuff."

"Smugglers do not risk life and limb so that they can drink their booty as soon as it comes ashore. Their intention is to profit from it. Do you know for sure," I continued, again, without allowing him to draw breath, "that the foreigner is mate of this infamous Cornish yawl you mention?"

"Well, I've heard about him. Who hasn't? He is not a man who fades easily into the background."

"But do you know for sure that it is him? I presume there are a few other foreign fellows serving in the Westcountry fleet?"

The Excise-man looked down and, for the first time, began to bear an expression of doubt. "No, I do not know for certain. But it is common knowledge that a foreign man by the name of Laversha is mate upon the 'Mavis'."

"But has he admitted it? Is there someone here who can testify that he is Laversha? Is he the outlandish mate of the 'Mavis', or might he be another? Indeed, could you make out from the shore that the boat anchored off the Pill was really the Cornish yawl?"

The man groaned: "But it is ludicrous - surely it is too much of a coincidence that this man was here while a yawl, that I'd wager was the 'Mavis', was moored a mile offshore? I could not see her figurehead or name, I admit, but she was Hicks's ship all right."

"Wagers are no good in a court of law, sir," I replied a little haughtily. "Facts are what you need, and if I may be so bold, you seem to be armed with precious few. You have the word of one dubious informant who remains unnamed and who, it seems, has some desperate reason for seeking revenge upon one of your prisoners. And you seized half a firkin of brandy from the three without any tenable link being made between them and the hundred gallons that were disappearing into the night as you made the arrests. You cannot possibly think that this will ever reach the Assizes?"

Now the officer seemed genuinely concerned: "Well, what do you propose? I have made arrests - we have the contraband. The militia are coming and are expecting prisoners. I cannot just drop the thing now. And there's the indisputable fact that they were drinking illegal liquor which should have been handed over to the authorities."

"I see your point," says I. "But I can also see how this could very well turn out to be a most embarrassing situation - just the kind of situation, in fact, that my Master was so keen to avoid. So keen in fact, that he requested me to take any action possible to avoid the law falling into disrepute. In that light there is perhaps one legal way out of our dilemma. Tell me if I am right when I say that contraband is only contraband because no tax of duty has been paid on it?"

"Of course," says my friend gloomily.

"Now, say for the sake of argument, that some wealthy party wished to import some best quality French quite legally, but somehow - through an oversight - he forgot to forward the required duties to the excise authority. The brandy duly arrives upon our shores but, of course, is deemed illegal because no tax has been paid. But now, say that our gentleman is reminded of his oversight and comes forward with the necessary payment. Then, surely, that contraband would be contraband no more, and would instantly attain legal status?"

"I suppose it would," says the man, now with a flicker of interest in his bespectacled eye.

"And do you know how much duty is owing on the goods that you have seized?"

"I have calculated the exact amount."

He handed me a piece of paper which I studied for a minute or two before reaching into my pocket for the purse that Mr Crosse had given me. It was a far larger amount than I could ever have dreamed of, but I knew the contents of the purse would cover it. I counted the money and slapped it down onto a barrel of best French spirit.

"I think that we can draw the matter to a close," I said. "I will take the three prisoners who will be set before Squire Crosse tomorrow morning on the charge that they neglected to report the firkin found upon the shore. I will also take charge of the cargo and use the pony and cart to transport it to the careless gentleman - who shall remain nameless - who so recklessly overlooked the payment of the duty. Good day to you..."

And so that is how an honest, upright, gentleman magistrate came to help set free three of the busiest smugglers the county of Somerset has ever seen. As soon as we were out of sight of the revenue-men my father wept tears of joy and pride. "My boy," he said shaking me by the shoulders. "To think that the son o' a broomsquire should ever 'ave become a gen'leman - and outwit those knaves from the Revenue. Never 'as a father been more proud than I be this day."

I must admit, I felt rather proud of myself. The ploy had been an artifice and I had been lucky to get away with it, but the excise officer had struck me as a weak, self-important soul who could see trouble facing him in the eye. A more determined individual would have sent me on my way, but this man was a gullible nervous little fellow who'd spent his life in a backwater. I'd seen that, and had acted accordingly.

Father though, was not quite so overjoyed when I told him that he would indeed be appearing before Mr Crosse the next day. Nor was he particularly pleased when I informed him that all the liquor was to be transported to Fyne Court. Monty was even more aghast and said he'd never left the shores of the sea in all his life, and was not about to do so now. But the big dark mate stepped in and, grabbing them both by the collar, he says: "You are couple of worthless swine. This boy has made some sort of a promise to this Squire of 'is and, thanks to it, 'as got us out o' a pretty jam. The least we can do to repay him is do as ee bids, otherwise the lad may land in some trouble 'imself. And, my old friends, there is plenty more brandy in France, gin in the Flatlands and rum in the West for us. At least this evening, we are free men and may look forward to drinking a noggin in the future."

I had the feeling that when this big man spoke, other men were in the habit of doing his bidding. Monty and my father were no exception and a strange throng did we make crossing the hills in the evening light. Indeed, father soon rallied and, feeling guilty perhaps, once more became proud of his son's work that day.

"To think it," he kept saying. "That a son of mine should outwit the law by fine words and legal tricks. And all those years I was a thinkin' e'd become nothin' more than a burly dull-wit of a broomsquire like meself..."

We stopped to let the pony rest when we reached the top of Ladies Combe and I had not the heart to prevent them broaching a small barrel for what my father described as "medicinal" purposes.

"Tis for Montague really," he explained. "Poor fellow'll expire if us takes un any further from the sea. Our only 'ope is that this French'll fortify the poor old begger."

We sat there in the gloaming watching the very last rays of sun disappear behind the great bastions of Exmoor to the west. The beauty of the scene perhaps, or maybe the mountain air, seemed to make a shift in my father's mood. Until then he had been as jocular and as proud as a boy who has survived some hilarious mischief unscathed. But now he became thoughtful and exhaled several long sighs before, eventually, seeming to come to some kind of decision. He motioned for me to follow him a few yards from the cart, and when we were out of earshot of the others he said:

"Friend Laversha over there 'as said that us do owe you a debt of gratitude for what you 'ave done this day. And I, as yer disrep'table father, owes you far more than they. I understand, from the money that you handed the Excise-men, that we also owe thanks to Squire Crosse unself. For t'was ee, no doubt, who funded yer mission to Kilve."

"Well then, I will go some way to repayin' that debt 'ere and now – though what I am about to tell ee must never be linked in any way with me. Understand that: I will never stand in any witness box to repeat it. You must do wha'ever you wish wi' the facts, but you must never let on from whence they came. If you did my life may be in danger and, though I am not afeared for meself, we must 'ave some thought for yer mother and sister – and per'aps, for yerself."

"Any'ow, t'is like this," my father now drew close to me and breathed the following into my ear. "This yer liquor… Sure I smuggled the stuff and 'ave been doing so for many a long year. For me t'is just part of the great game that I 'ave played at since I were a boy. I calls it a game, some people call it life – t'is but the same thing. For Monty the smuggling is a way of life. And for him with the foreign tongue…? Well, I do not know what wildness there be in that dark heart of 'is – all I can say about 'im is that when ee is yer friend – then er is a true friend indeed. And when er is yer enemy – then woe betide!"

"But Johnny, think this: me and Monty are poor men. When it comes to the smuggling, we are just like those actors you see in the shows that come round the villages. We carry out the play, but someone else 'ave written the story. You know we couldns't afford the payment on a 'aul like that. Us do get a few shillings out o'it, and we gets a small share of the liquor. But someone else does the ordering and the payin' – and makes the fat profit at t'end o' the day. They'm the clever ones, the men who never faces the Revenue or the goal. They'm the crooked men of the piece Johnny. Every village 'as one – and Squire Crosse's parish 'as a bad one in 'ticular. This is where I come to my debt o' gra'itude to you, boy. Or really, I be thanking Mr Crosse I s'pose – which will do you no 'arm I am sure. You see, there's two men behind our little game – and one of 'em is none other than your Squire's facto'um, Giles Buncombe. If 'twas just the liquor involved, I'd not 'ave said a word about un. But I do knows that er funds this trade of ours from money that er swindles from your Master's estate. I suppose the funny thing is, thick Master of yours has now paid for this lot twice! Buncombe's been at it for years and 'tis nothin' less than staggerin' that Mr Crosse 'ave never noticed the shortcomings o' 'is affairs. But there 'tis – too busy with those 'speriments of yours as I understand it. Let me tell ee though, 'tis Giles Buncombe who'll really lose from what 'as 'appened this day – and if I know the man, ee'll set about recoupin' 'is losses at a cost to Mr Crosse."

"But you say there are two men. What about his partner?" I asked. "Surely he too will be short from the loss of the liquor?"

Father grunted laconically: "Uhh. That greedy toad can afford it – and I for one 'ud dearly like to be there to see 'is fat face when the news reaches un."

"Who is he – will you tell me?" I asked, with a feeling of ominous foreboding.

"Ee is the black-hearted father of that sweetheart of you'rn, my boy," was the reply.

With that he laughed and slapped me on the shoulder: "Watch this for a trick!" he cried: "Whoa Eskie! Whoa!"

Upon that last word the little Exmoor pony bolted, throwing Monty and Laversha on their backs and disappearing along the ridge track with her cart bouncing about behind her. Running to my horse I heard my father shout: "There's only one way to stop her Johnny. You must cry 'Giddi-up, giddi-up...'"

That night the three men were bedded down in the stables at Fyne Court, while I went in to see the Master who had stayed up waiting for my return. I found him tinkering with a large Volta's Pile, but he soon stopped all pretence of work as I began to report my account of the day.

When I finished he said: "You have done well young friend. I am not so sure about the pretence that you were acting on my behalf, but no harm has come of it and I must commend you for the way in which you have thought quickly and acted upon your deliberations."

"You came here as a country boy knowing nothing but the lore of the hills. Now you are beginning to be a young man of the world. An impressive and intelligent young man, if I may say so. Not once, since the day you arrived, have I had a single reason to regret taking you on. I even hear that you defended my honour in the village the other day – employing your physical strength rather than your obvious mental capacity. Don't concern yourself how I know – I do."

I supposed that he was referring to my tussle with Arnie Takle. Anyway, he continued with a warning concerning my father and his comrades: "No matter how highly I regard you though Johnny, you understand that duty must be done. Tomorrow I must punish your father and his companions on the smaller matter of the firkin of French. I shall do so just as if he were any other man. As to his obvious guilt on the larger charge of smuggling the entire contraband, well... I am forced, I suppose, to turn a blind eye to the fact that it was he, for I am not a fool. The truth of the matter is quite plain, but we shall have to leave it to God to be the judge. However, on the lesser charge justice must be seen to be done."

"I agree Sir," I replied. "The three men now in your stables are quite prepared to take their punishment and I have told them they must stand before you tomorrow. However, there are circumstances behind this entire affair that might be of interest when you are making your deliberations..."

I then revealed to Squire Crosse the intelligence that my father had confided in me. I had never seen the man more shaken: upon hearing of Buncombe's involvement and the accusation that the funds for smuggling came from no place but his own estate, Mr Crosse turned an ashen white. Within minutes he was bent double with the stomach cramps that so often attacked him when he became agitated. As I helped him to bed he instructed me that first thing in the morning I was to ride to Mr Poole's house to ask him, as a fellow magistrate, to kindly attend Fyne Court without delay. In the meantime one of the servants was to go to Goathurst to bring his brother Richard Crosse.

It was a frightful morning of driving rain, but that stalwart fellow Mr Poole came straight away. He had already heard of the goings on in Kilve and laughed merrily when I recounted to him the tale. "At least my journey today shall be rewarded by a glass or two of best Hollands," he chuckled. "I shall hold Andrew Crosse to that, at least. But why, tell me, is he requiring my presence? Surely he will fine your father and these other fellows a few shillings and that will be that?"

I told him there was a good deal more to the intrigue. More than that, I dared not say and Mr Poole was judicious enough not to pursue the matter further. Instead he asked: "The informant who cooked your father's goose? Does father - do you - have any idea of who it could be?"

"None at all Sir," I replied. "Indeed my father is most perplexed as he cannot believe that any man in Quantock would do a thing to harm him. Of course, there's no good in my hiding from you that it was his pony and trap; I am sure that you know it. But - as father says - very few people know that little Eskie will take off at a particular whistle. Very few. And none would volunteer the information to the Revenue-men."

"Someone did," mused Tom Poole as he bounced up and down on the huge old cob that forever conveyed him about his business. "Someone in these hills has it in for the old broomsquire, that is for sure. But I wonder why? Your father might be a bit of a rogue, but he is one of the most popular men in the hills..."

At Fyne Court Squire Crosse and his brother were waiting for us in the front hall, and upon our arrival old Beale was called and told to ensure that the meeting would be held in the greatest privacy. No one was to come near the hall until otherwise instructed. Then Andrew Crosse bade me repeat to his guests the information that I had put to him the night before.

Without mentioning that the intelligence came from my father I did so and, never before or since, have I held an audience of such important men in such attention. When I finished there was a short silence as they digested the gravity of the situation. It was Mr Poole who eventually spoke and, being an astute businessman, he suggested that the three of them go through the estate books and accounts that very day.

"Buncombe must be removed from office with immediate effect, that is for sure," he said. "But we must find some evidence of his doings and, if we can reveal some criminal activity, then he must be arrested."

"As for Rice," he went on, turning to face me as he did, "The person who laid this information before you will not repeat it in a court of law then? In that case there is no way we can touch the cunning devil. I can't pretend that I haven't had some inkling of such goings-on - few people could have failed to realise it. Like many, I have turned a blind eye to it, but have often wondered who was funding the conspiracy."

"Rice, of course!" he exclaimed, slamming his fist down upon the table. "The man would steal the milk from a baby if he thought he could get away with it. He has been in trouble before for his weights and measures and it is rotten to think that he will get clean away with this, but there is not a thing we can do to touch him. As for Buncombe, there must be evidence of misdoing in your accounts Andrew and, if we have to devote the whole day to it, we'll weasel the stoat out of his nest."

They did just that. But not before passing a fine of a sovereign apiece on the three miscreants. My father winced at the amount, but the man called Laversha put his hand in his pocket and paid for all three. Mr Crosse gave them a lecture on the evils of smuggling and afterwards my father spoke to me as he made his leave.

"Tread carefully my son," he whispered as we hugged. "Buncombe and Rice are not men to meddle with. In some ways, I regret 'avin' mentioned 'em."

The person who had been treading carefully, it seemed, was Giles Buncombe. He had covered his tracks very cleverly indeed, and Messrs Crosse and Poole in pouring over the estate accounts were hard pressed to find examples of his importuning. That money was missing was clear enough, but exactly how it was taken, and where it had gone was not. Eventually the two brothers aided by Mr Poole were able to uncover enough to warrant sacking the man. But they never got close to unearthing sufficient to have him arrested.

I was there that evening when the three of them confronted him. He was a burly, thick-set, red-faced man, and now he fairly glowed with incandescent rage. After a minute of listening to Mr Crosse's quietly spoken accusations Buncombe stormed out of the great hall brimming with indignation. As he went, he pointed over at me and threatened revenge for my meddling.

"This is your doing Walford, and you'll pay for it. You think you're so high and mighty lording it with the gentry, but you're nothing but a filthy gypsy and I'll make it my business to bring you down to where you belong."

It did not occur to me while all this was going on, but our actions had ruined a profitable enterprise run not only by Buncombe, but also by the father of my beloved Anne. Asking Rice for his daughter's hand in marriage was going to be an even more unpleasant mission than it had been before.

Not that I had much time to think of such vexations during the next few weeks. Mr Crosse, in an attempt to rid himself of his bout of nervous indigestion, threw himself at his work in the laboratory with renewed vigour, and I was expected to be there morning, noon and night. He was, of course, working up to his forthcoming lecture tour which would take him both to Bristol and to the capital, but he admitted to me that the Buncombe affair had upset his natural disposition to trust in his fellow men.

During this period another creature was to walk into our lives: one that, though infinitesimally small, would have a far reaching effect on both the squire's future and mine. One of Mr Crosse's great obsessions was with the formation of various crystals and in one particular experiment we were trying to form silicate crystals from a dilute solution of powdered flint and potassium carbonate. This was dropped onto a piece of volcanic stone saturated with hydrochloric acid and subjected to a low electric current. In a matter of a few weeks we expected to see tiny crystals growing on the surface of the volcanic stone, but on this occasion something altogether stranger occurred. Something that Mr Crosse himself was never able to explain and something which, in time, not only shocked the two of us but the rest of the English speaking world.

It was some fifteen days after we had set up the experiment that I was woken in the grey hours of dawn by my Master who was shaking me for all he was worth. I couldn't remember him ever visiting my garret above the stables before, so you can imagine my surprise.

"Johnny, get up and be quick about it," he whispered. "I need your excellent eyesight to assure me that I am not going mad." He stood there and waited for me to throw on a few clothes, and then the two of us marched across the yard to the house where the servants were only just beginning to stir. "Look!" he whispered loudly, pointing at the volcanic stone which sat in an enamelled dish in the centre of the laboratory. "Look very carefully and tell me what you see there."

I bent down to study the damp surface of the rock and was surprised to observe what I can only describe as a number of white filaments stretching across the surface. The odd thing was that in places these filaments had what appeared to be tiny legs. I reached for a magnifying glass, but could not really see anything more than I have described. Perhaps the Master was irritated by my nonchalant shrug, at any rate, for the rest of the day he paced about the place muttering about the darkness of science and the hazards of mystery. I, for my part, thought no more of the excrescence on the rock and supposed it to be nothing more than some natural slime or fungal growth.

But, if I had been surprised by the nervous disposition that had led the Squire to my room that first morning, imagine my alarm when he came dashing into the servant's dining room some four weeks later. He had, to the knowledge of the household staff, never before entered that room. If he had, he'd certainly not appeared in the deathly white guise that he wore this day. Such was his state of shock, you could see him shaking.

"Johnny," he shouted. "With me. Immediately!"

The others staff were shocked. They told me afterwards that they thought that I must be in some great trouble, or that something truly cataclysmic must have happened in the laboratory. I ran after Mr Crosse and found him standing by the side of the volcanic slab with an almost triumphant look upon his face; at least it would have been had it not been tinged with pure horror. Pointing at the rock he cried:

"Now tell me what you see...."

In a moment I was sharing his agitation. The white filaments were there, but their form had changed. They seemed to have divided themselves into short sections. Each of these had the tiny leg-like projections jutting out on either side. And then I saw a thing that made me jump for the magnifying glass. One of the sections of filament moved. At first I thought I was hallucinating, but when I got the glass on it I was able to see without any shadow of a doubt. What I was looking at was an eight-legged mite. Each of its legs was moving. The damned thing was walking across the stone!

Andrew Crosse spun me around and, with an effort to speak calmly, spluttered: "You helped me set this experiment up Johnny - you remember that don't you? You recall how we studied the surface of the stone very closely for imperfections? And you know that when we started dropping the powdered flint and the potassium carbonate there was not a thing there. Now, tell me what you have just seen!"

"It... It was a sort of mite," I stammered.

"Exactly! And what is a mite?"

"I'm not following you..." I began to reply, wondering what he meant by the question.

"It is life, that's what it is!" he shouted. "Life! Where there was no life before - now there is life. Powdered flint, potassium carbonate, volcanic stone and hydrochloric acid — these things contain no life - and yet pass an electric current through them and they do! Or so it would seem by what we have here."

He shook his head and held his chin in his hand, as was his custom when deep in thought. "But I do not know how, or why. In all these years of experimentation, I have never been so utterly bewildered. There is no scientific reason to support what we have witnessed. No reason at all!"

Later that day he spoke about the mites again: "I have been thinking long and hard Johnny, and have come no closer to finding an answer. What I do know is this: we have discovered something profoundly important. But we have discovered it without having the means to explain how or why. That is why secrecy is to be of the uttermost importance. I mean that young man. Silence in this matter is crucial. Some sixth sense tells me that if this were to become public knowledge - this discovery of life where there was no life before - then we would find ourselves in some kind of trouble. So you will swear to me here and now that you will never mention this matter to anyone. Is that clear?"

What he said was clear enough, though at the time I couldn't fully understand my Master's foreboding. I was too naive to comprehend why the strange tiny creatures that moved across the surface of our piece of volcanic rock should make any kind of trouble, but I of course agreed to his demand for secrecy. In the end though, it was Mr Crosse himself who let the world know about our mysterious discovery...

For weeks the scientist remained silent and morose and I knew that he was brooding about those damned mites. I avoided the subject because, whenever it was mentioned, he seemed to find new depths to his anguish. Then, one warm summer's day, Mr Crosse and I set off at the crack of dawn so that we could walk the fourteen long miles to the bay at Blue Anchor, west of the port of Watchet on the West Somerset coast. I had suggested that we might make such a trip as we were running low on some of the minerals upon which several of our experiments depended. Close to an old inn at this seaside hamlet is one of the most remarkable geological areas to found anywhere in our Westcountry world. Specimens of great diversity abound thanks to the fact that twice a day the sea smashes against the soft blue lias that constitutes the greater part of the cliffs there. The resultant rock falls uncover an endless supply of treasures. Perhaps most noticeable is the alabaster which lies about the beach in a thousand different hues of pink, orange and white.

We had taken a pony to use as a pack animal for our samples and, after a long day spent with hammer and chisel, were at last making our way back along the cliff-path to Watchet. It would be a long trudge home, and it was our intention to have some sort of early supper at the ancient port before continuing on our way. The coast path between Blue Anchor and Watchet dips up and down as it follows the undulations of the coastal hills, and is as lonely a stretch of bye-way as any in the county. So we were surprised when, on reaching the top of one of the little hills, we spied two men in the dip before us. They were obviously heading in the same direction – toward Watchet – but seemed in no particular hurry and appeared to be taking an interest in the red sunset that was growing in grandeur over our shoulders. It wasn't long before we were overtaking them.

Suddenly Mr Crosse lets out a cry of surprise: "My-my – if it isn't my old friend Southey!"

At this the Southey fellow started to speak, but was smothered as Mr Crosse fell upon him like a long lost brother. After a moment, during which I thought they were going to break one another's necks with such heart-felt embraces, the other man was introduced. I shall never forget him, for he was to become my friend. His name was Mr Samuel Taylor Coleridge.

"My dear Southey, my assistant Walford and I were hurrying to sup at Watchet before proceeding on to my home at Broomfield.

You and Mr Coleridge, I hope, will be good enough to join us?"

They needed no second invitation and within the minute the three of them were marching apace, arms linked, while I brought up the rear pulling our pack horse behind me. I have never heard three men talk like it. Not once was there a second's silence – and Mr Crosse was like a new man. Within minutes of meeting Mr Southey he had lost the sullen pallor that had darkened his demeanour since the dismissal of Giles Buncombe, and which had become even more noticeable since the appearance of the mites.

As for our new found friends, they were two of the most remarkable men that I have ever met – before or since. Robert Southey was a fine featured fellow with a handsome, well structured face and piercing, intelligent eyes. His dark curly hair was short and well groomed and he looked a gentleman in his fine attire. My Master and he, it transpired, at been at college in Oxford together and Mr Crosse said all evening that he could not believe his luck in coming across – in the very heart of the wilderness – the very man he would wish to see most.

Mr Coleridge, on the other hand, was a young man of an altogether different bearing. Where Mr Southey was smart, he was unkempt: indeed, his clothes looked older and more disreputable than my own. And where Mr Southey had fine facial features, poor old Sam Coleridge had sagging jowls that somehow added to his generally dishevelled appearance. His lips were unusually large and he was forever moistening them, just as he was forever pushing back the great mop of dark brown hair that fell across his face. But most remarkable of all were eyes: where Mr Southey had intelligent orbs that seemed to look out upon the world with some understanding of what they saw, Coleridge's were dreamy, melancholic things that were like great pools filtering through to another world. If he looked at you with those eyes, then you somehow seemed to feel their gaze upon you. There was something sensual about the way he appeared to gaze deep into one's soul, and I could imagine that women would be bound to feel some shimmer of electricity in his visual caress.

He looked at me often, I don't know why. Indeed I was almost embarrassed by his constant interest in me. In a while we arrived at Watchet's harbourside and at once repaired to The Bell Inn. Mr

Crosse ordered supper for the four of us and Mr Coleridge decreed that he was delighted that I would be joining the party. "It is refreshing to see a Master adopt an attitude of equality with his servant," he observed, and Mr Southey agreed.

Mr Crosse replied with a comment that I shall never forget: "We are not so much Master and servant," said he. "More - how would you put it Johnny? More companions in the pursuit of science. Johnny has been with me for the best part of five years and I can count on his loyalty, his good humour and, perhaps most important of all in my somewhat unusual case, his courage. While all about him have fled in horror from my house during those times when my experiments have been, how shall we say, at their most dramatic, Johnny Walford has remained by my side acting as the most able of assistants. We have been through a good deal together, and it has made him a valuable friend to me. That is why he sits at our table: this splendid youth is worth ten of your average Oxford graduates."

At that they all drank to my health, and never did a servant turn a deeper red and yet at the same time feel more pride and more love for his Master than I did that evening in the smoke-filled bar of the Bell Inn.

In the next hour I was to hear more of the ideals of the two young poets, for that was their declared calling, and yet I felt they'd both sit happily as politicians for all of their far-fetched and high-minded principles. It seemed that they were touring the Westcountry together on a sort of extended holiday so that they could, without interruption, discuss their basic plans for formulating what they called a "Pantisocracy". This was to be a communal, utopian settlement - probably situated in Northern America - where folk could live in harmony and brotherhood. Mr Crosse was most intrigued and plied them with questions until the two began to argue. And I mean argue. I have never seen two men enter a more spirited debate without coming to blows, although what lay at the centre of their dispute I cannot say, for I found it difficult to follow their extraordinary language.

I suppose the venom of their outbursts may have been something to do with the drink consumed. They were great quaffers, these fellows. Mr Crosse, who never was much of a drinker, soon showed signs of inebriation too. We were finishing the sea trout that the landlord had served us, and they were still sinking pints of ale, when my Master seemed to come to some hard fought decision. It was after Mr Southey had quizzed him about his experimental work: "Tell me the latest Andrew. Surprise friend Coleridge here with talk of your mysterious electricity..."

Putting his arms around the two young gentlemen, Mr Crosse huddled them together and, a little slurred I thought, exclaimed: "Surprise Mr Coleridge? I can do more than surprise. I can astonish him. In fact, we can shock if you wish. Isn't that so Johnny?"

I muttered something, for I knew what was coming.

"Secrecy – that's what the boy has been sworn to and that is why he seems uncertain. But there should be no secrets between fellow thinkers. Not to men who, in their own way, spend their lives seeking truth." For a moment my Master looked in doubt. "On the other hand, he is correct, gentlemen. If I confide in you this night, then I shall expect from you a blanket of silence in the matter."

They laughed and asked what could possibly be of such import that they should be sworn to secrecy. I think the two of them believed Mr Crosse was about to deliver some sort of joke for their amusement, but in a while his earnest attitude convinced them and they promised to keep what they were about to hear to themselves. He then told them the story of the mites.

"Let me see if I have understood the full gravity of what you have said," enjoined Southey when my Master came to a finish. "Are you claiming that life now exists where there was no life before? Are you saying, indeed, that you – through this experiment – have actually created life?"

"If I have done, then I am ignorant as to how or why it came about," sighed the Squire of Broomfield.

"But this is momentous!" cried the poet. "They may only be mites, but this must go down as the most important thing to have ever been done by the hand of man. To manufacture life! It is unbelievable."

The head of Andrew Crosse sank wearily in to the palms of his hands. "I know full well Robert," he bleated. "Do not think that I haven't considered the outcome of the thing. What will be said and by whom… Can you imagine, for instance, what the Church will have to say about the man who claims to have created life? It will not be tolerated. I will be reviled, tormented and driven from the country."

"Not a bit of it," countered Mr Southey. "On the contrary, you will be lionised. You will become the king of science. The emperor of experimentation. You will be courted by the good and the great. For, if what you have told us is true, there is but one place for Andrew Crosse, and that is in the Pantheon of the Gods. To create life! You really are a veritable alchemist. You have succeeded in finding the Holy Grail!"

"Maybe, if I had done so with full understanding of what had occurred. But I do not have a single clue as to what those mites are doing there on that stone. Did I create them by that low current of electricity? Or were they there all along? Microscopic, invisible to the human eye? That is the more probable answer, though for the life of me, I cannot imagine how their growth became so accelerated."

"There is nothing for it but we must see," says Mr Coleridge, who had been listening attentively. "You say it is another nine or ten miles to your home? Then let us drink up and go. These mites may be the most important creatures to have walked upon the surface of the Earth for a million years and I, for one, do not intend to miss the patter of their little feet!"

It was a long walk in the dark. The worst of it was climbing from the old port through the lanes to the most northerly part of the hills at West Quantockhead. Above the hamlet, the old ridgeway begins and the going from there along the wide and level track is easy. It was a fine late summer's night and, now we were walking at a pace, I was impressed to find that our two new friends had no troubles in keeping up with us. We made good time, arriving at Fyne Court just after midnight. Beale made a fuss and provided a great bowl of hot toddy before going off to bed and then Mr Crosse was keen to show the two poets the experiment. We went through to the laboratory and both Southey and Coleridge were in awe at what they found there.

"This is quite incredible Andrew," murmured Mr Southey. "I cannot remember anything as impressive as this at Oxford. Indeed, I have never seen a laboratory like it."

"I can assure you, Robert," says the Squire, "that neither have you seen anything such as this either..."

He was standing by the volcanic stone with magnifying glass in hand. Sam Coleridge took it from him and, upon being shown where to look, studied the surface of our volcanic stone so that he could view the celebrated mites.

"Good Lord," he cried. "They are nothing much to look at. Are they - I wonder - the denizens of a new-born universe? Was there an Adam and Eve, or were mites such as these fellows, present at the very beginning of it all?"

The three men began to talk of theology and I took myself to my bed. I was tired and couldn't keep up with their fancy words and theories. I believe they went at it until dawn, certainly Mr Crosse did not make an appearance in the laboratory until after ten in the morning. Messrs. Southey and Coleridge went to stay with Mr Poole the next day, promising that they would return to Fyne Court before leaving the country to set up their Pantisocracy. They were concluding their Westcountry perambulations by repairing to Bristol with the intention of meeting two sisters by the name of Edith and Sara Fricker. Later Mr Southey would marry the former, while the latter was to be Mr Coleridge's bride - and in this, at least, his ambitions were successful. I was to meet Sara Coleridge a year or so after, but I shall be coming to that part of my tale. Neither poet went to America to live communally either in a Pantisocracy or in any other kind of way - which is a shame as far as I am concerned, as they made me promise that I would join them there. Had I done so, my life may have taken a more fortunate path.

Their visit was a highlight in what otherwise was a late summer of naught but solid work and endeavour. My Master was most desirous that certain results should be achieved before he embarked upon his winter lecture tour. "The biggest and best names in Science will be there Johnny and, though I am reluctant to put myself before the crowd, I am vain enough to want to do it in style."

Such were the Squire's comments during this period of intense activity.

"What about the mites Sir?" I once asked. "If you really wanted to knock their hats off, you'd tell them about the mites."

"I doubt I shall ever mention those wretched creatures to anyone again," he replied. "To tell the truth, it was only the ale from the Bell Inn that persuaded me to confide in the two poets. Frankly, I regret doing so now, for there are times when I wake in the night fearing that Southey or Coleridge will talk of the matter when oiled with drink."

He was right to worry. And he was wrong when he said that he would not be mentioning the mites.

PART 3

FATE OVERTURNS US ALL

For some time I had hoped that Mr Crosse would take me to the great cities with him, for I would have liked to have visited them just once. But, as the time drew near, he bade me stay and look after things at Fyne Court. His brother and Mr Poole were to oversee the estate during his absence, and I was to be left in charge of the laboratory and all the experiments that continued to develop there. If I was disappointed not to be escorting my Master, then I was proud to be left as proprietor in charge of such exacting responsibility.

The original plan was for Mr Crosse to be gone for a period of just over one month. In the end, he was absent for more than three. At first I was delighted by a sense of newfound freedom. As master of my own work it meant, of course, that I could come and go from the house as I pleased, and this allowed me the pleasure of seeing my dear Anne on a far more regular footing. What she told the mistress at her school (where she was now working as an assistant teacher) I do not know, but she never seemed to have much difficulty in meeting with me.

We were about a week and-a-half into Mr Crosse's absence when, one cold November day, Mr Poole comes riding up on his old cob. Beale would have announced him to me, for it was I that he'd come to see, but I had caught a glimpse of the old countryman out of the window and thought I could see some expression of consternation upon his normally placid face.

"Johnny, how glad I am that you are here," he says as I brushed past the butler at the front door. "Let us go to the laboratory for I wish to speak with you privately, and urgently!"

Inside, Tom Poole bade me check that no servant was lurking outside the huge oak door before he would continue. After that he took a broad-sheet newspaper from his venerable leather bag and slammed it down upon the bench before me.

"Read that," he says, "and when you have finished you must tell me what you know."

I cannot remember the exact words that I found printed across several columns of that broadsheet, but suffice to say that within seconds my legs were weak with shock. The emboldened line at the top of the page said something like:

"Scientist Claims He Has Created Life In Electrical Experiment".

That was enough to set my knees quivering but, reading further, I was to discover that matters were worse than Squire Crosse could ever have imagined. It seemed that, at the third lecture in Bristol, a gentleman had taken my Master to task during a period of questions at the end of the evening. The person described our experiment and the resulting mites with all the accuracy of someone who had actually been to Fyne Court and witnessed things at first hand.

"Is this true Sir?" the newspaper report quoted the gentleman's demand. "If it is, will you tell us if this experiment of yours has indeed given life to creatures that were not present previously?"

The newspaper went on to describe how Mr Crosse appeared to be stricken down with some pain, and how he was unable to answer the question that had been put to him. The gentleman continued regardless: "For, if what I have heard is true Sir, then you are either a conjurer and a fool - or you are in league with the Devil. Which is it?"

Poor Mr Crosse, I could just imagine him there in front of the crowd, smitten with the stomach cramps that so often afflicted him in moments of nervous strain. Somehow he managed to reply that it was true some tiny creatures had appeared during an experiment. He was, no doubt, attempting to continue with his answer but - with his voice weakened by the cramps and the crowd now in uproar, his statement was never heard. Lecture notes were thrown at him and people in the audience took to jeering until he was forced to leave the auditorium.

I let the newspaper drop to my knees and gazed across at the volcanic stone. So Mr Crosse had been right to be wary of the power of those infinitesimal creatures. He knew what harm they could do. Acres of column inches in the newspaper spoke of such things as the Arrogance of Science, the madness of men who spent their lives experimenting with unnatural substances such as electricity, and the ungodliness of dabbling with matter invisible to the eye. Apparently, even a bishop had joined in the fray and had threatened to ex-communicate him. Another priest had offered to come to Fyne Court so that he could exorcise the Devils that undoubtedly occupied the place.

It must have been the poets; I had no doubt of that. Apart from Mr Crosse and myself they were the only people to have ever seen the mites or to have heard mention of the experiment. And they had been on their way to Bristol, the scene of this great debacle. Either one, or both of them, had spoken about what they had seen at Fyne Court, and word had got around. Mr Poole brought me out of my reverie by tapping me impatiently on the hand.

"This broadsheet is three days old Johnny – do I take it that you have received no missive from your Master concerning this calamity? Well then," continued the solid old businessman, "There is much to be done. First we must address the servants. They will assuredly get news of this and, if I know anything about it, will take to their heels taking their superstitious fears with them. But first, tell me, what is the truth behind this whole affair? Are there really creatures and did you and your Master create them as is claimed?"

I nodded and took him over to the stone slab where he peered through the magnifying glass. "The Lord preserve us!" he whispered. Looking about him, he spied a wooden mallet over in the corner of the room and dashed over to get it.

"What are you doing?" I cried.

"We must destroy them," shouted he, smashing the hammer down upon the stone with tremendous force. "It is the Devil's work Johnny. There is something evil and unnatural here and it must be destroyed."

I grabbed his arm to restrain him and was surprised to find just how strong he was. We tussled, and I said: "Surely we must await the Squire's instructions. He will not thank us if he returns and finds months of work smashed. Indeed, he may well be relying on the mites as proof of what he has said."

He ceased struggling and looked at me. "You may have a point there," he said eventually. "I had not thought of that. But Johnny, are these things safe without your Master to oversee them? Not that I am doubting your judgement, but if these unholy bugs were really created by some mystical force, then who knows what could become of them? Do you?"

I did not, in truth, but told him not to worry and explained that they had remained in much the same state for weeks. The old worthy seemed mollified and announced he was going through to address the servants. I escorted him to the great hall and we sent Beale to collect as many staff as he could from the house, the grounds and the estate. There must have been a score of them congregated when Mr Poole made his speech, and a well honed and comforting address it was too. He waved the newspaper in front of them, and told them that journalists were in the habit of making a drama out of mundane things and there was barely a word of truth in any of it. Afterwards he and I sat down to a glass or two of smuggled brandy and he apologised for his actions in the laboratory.

"You were probably right Johnny, for I suspect Andrew will want evidence to corroborate his findings. But I will say this: between you and me this is bound to cause trouble. Trouble all around, with his business affairs and with his planned marriage. I know the Hamilton family and, being church people, they will not be impressed by the thought of their daughter marrying some mad ungodly scientist. Even if there isn't truth in it, it is high time the Squire set aside his experiments for a while and took his responsibilities as a gentleman more seriously."

To tell the truth, I was only half-listening to all this. Something Tom Poole had said had sparked off in me some absurd neurosis, and as a result I was itching to get back to the laboratory. It was what he had said about the mites being the Devil's creatures. When he had smashed that mallet down into their midst I had, just for a second, peered down in horror at what he had done. Thinking about it over that glass of brandy, I could swear that I had seen them milling about as if nothing had occurred. At last the dear old fellow took his leave, and I was able to return to the stone slab. It was as I had feared, as if no momentous blow had been struck among the mites. The force of Mr Poole's rap would have been enough to kill a donkey, let alone a creature no thicker than an eyelash, and yet there they were - tramping about the surface of the stone in what looked like rude health. Not one mite seemed in any way injured or flattened by the blow. I took a spatula and lifted four of the little creatures off the slab and put them on the floor. I stamped on them, I hit them with the mallet and, lastly, I took them over to a vice and crushed them. Imagine my horror when all these attempts to kill the creatures proved useless. What freakish devilry could be at work in their tiny frames? I could feel the sweat collecting cold upon the palms of my hands. What else could slaughter them? The indestructibility of these dreadful things… Were they were indeed the Devil's work?

How I wished my Master was with me during those moments, but he was far away in Bristol where the mites were already destroying his name. Had I been a year or two younger, I believe I should have slumped down in tears. Instead I sat there looking about me in anguish, desperately searching for some sort of solution. For a while nothing would present itself and I took to remembering all the happy times I'd spent in this vast room. More than five years it had been since the day Tom Poole and my father brought me here – the day they'd both ended up on the floor after I had wound the handle of the big electric conductor. All those years, all that work – was it all for nothing? Were we really to be ruined by these wretched mites?

But wait a minute – I thought, staring down the dusky vale of memory. Wait just one minute Johnny – surely there is something there that could help? Something powerful. Something that produces enormous violence in one awesome moment... The conductor. A thousand volts in one gigantic, extreme and vicious jolt...

I grabbed the spatula again and picked up the tiny creatures. In the years since that first visit to the laboratory, we had developed the big conductor so that now its electricity could be channelled to several different benches where various experiments took place. It was to one of these that I transported my sinister cargo. Carefully, I clamped the metal tool to wires that connected with the conductor, and then crossed the room to begin the laborious task of winding the handle. After a couple of hundred turns it would produce a massive voltage that was the laboratory's own humble version of a lightning strike. Only, this time, there would be no crash and flash from the spinning cylinder: as the apparatus built up friction I would lean across and throw a switch sending a thousand or more volts straight through the metal spatula.

There have been few occasions in my life when I have found it necessary to pray to God, but that period of winding was one of them. As I laboured, so I prayed – and believe me, I meant it. Within a minute I reached for the switch and heard a sharp crack explode across the spatula. Before I even managed to get to the bench I could see smoke ascending from my now contorted tool. Upon closer study, I was overjoyed to see four petrified mites. Not one of their collective thirty two legs moved. They were dead beyond doubt. And yet, astonishingly, their forms remained perfectly preserved.

After a good night's sleep, I awoke to find a special messenger was waiting for me at the Court. He handed me a note which, he explained, had been sent by Mr Andrew Crosse from Bristol with orders that it must be delivered with the utmost haste, and that the same courier was to return as quickly as he could with the package that I would give him. After reading my Master's note I took the man to the kitchens where the cook fed him while I prepared the required package. Poor fellow had ridden all the previous day from Bristol, but had failed to quite reach Broomfield by nightfall. He told me that, after all he'd heard about the terrible place, he had no intentions of calling here after dark, so he'd slept in a barn.

Recalling the real-life nightmare I'd endured the night before, I couldn't blame him, and it was with some apprehension that I went through to the laboratory. I need not have worried: the four dead mites were still corpses lying exactly as I had left them. Two of these I raked off into a tiny glass jar. Into another I placed two of their live brothers from the herd that was still marching around the volcanic slab. Then I wrote a note to Andrew Crosse describing all that I had discovered the night before. I wrapped the jars and the note in padding which I then placed in a leather pouch which I sealed.

"No one," I said to the courier, "is to open this package save for Mr Andrew Crosse. Is that understood? No-one, no matter how important or powerful they may be. It is quite safe while sealed, but I cannot vouch for what may happen if it is opened by anyone other than the Squire."

The courier looked alarmed – I was not exactly surprised to learn later that he'd made it to Bristol in record time. I knew it because, within two days, I had received another missive from my Master, but by then his new instructions were in vain.

I do not know how to convey the next part of my narrative, for I doubt anyone shall believe a word of it. But I must tell it, for I am determined to write down the life that was Johnny Walford, no matter how unbelievable some of the occurrences may seem. Reluctantly, I come to the most horrifying and unnerving thing that it has ever been visited upon me. Tom Poole was there, and he will either vouch for what I say, or he will not, depending on what he deems best. I have always trusted this dear man, and have looked to him for wisdom since I was a boy - however, in fairness, I must state that he is reluctant to verify certain details, though he was present during the following section of my tale. This denial of his does put a question mark over what I shall describe; indeed, it even causes me to question the sanity of my own mind. But, to continue in the spirit of this narrative, I must recall the events as I remember them.

The day after the courier called was as bad as the Atlantic Ocean has ever seen fit to throw at us. The heavens were in a bad mood and the clear, cold sunshine of the morning had quickly been obscured by a strange, freezing fog which, in turn, was blown away by a mighty gale. Mr Poole had turned up at lunchtime to find out if there had been any further developments. I, of course, did not inform him of my battle with the indestructible mites, instead I had told him of other worries concerning the staff. Since he had given them his reassuring speech, only Beale and his large commanding wife had the courage to stay in the house at night. The rest slept out in the stables: indeed, I'd been forced to give over my own little garret to three of the maids and so had taken myself to a guest room in the Court.

By the time Mr Poole had sorted out the servants and taken a look at the latest figures from the Estate, the lurid fog had given way to that atrocious gale I mentioned. It came as abruptly and as brutally as any storm I have ever seen. One minute the seething fog was there, the next a low dark wrack had taken its place, moving rapidly in from the west. We looked at it from the windows and saw how, strangely, the low clouds were scudding in one direction while much higher vapours were moving speedily in completely the other. There was something weird about that weather, but I must say, I was glad of it at the time – for it brought about the happy result that Mr Poole was forced to stay. No man would have travelled in those conditions unless it had been a matter of life and death.

After my old benefactor had decided he must stop the night, I built up the great fire in the main hall and I fetched a selection of smuggled beverages from my Master's cellar.

"Good man Johnny," smiled Mr Poole, much cheered by the sight of the bottles. "I do not think your Master could begrudge us a noggin or two in the circumstances."

He bade me sup with him and, although the butler obviously thought this amiss, I ate my dinner at the front of the house to keep our guest company. After the meal we settled in Mr Crosse's best chairs by the fireside and Tom Poole chatted about his businesses and his extraordinary number of influential friends. As a backdrop to his deep comforting voice, the wind howled in the chimney and beat about the eaves, but we were snug enough and for a while paid little heed to the maelstrom outside.

It was about ten o'clock that things started to occur. Memorable, alarming things that to this day make the hairs stand on end at the back of my neck. We were helping ourselves to yet another tipple in the great, gloomy room when a dazzling flash illuminated the place like broad daylight. For most folk such an occurrence would be, at most, mildly exciting or maybe even frightening – but in the house of Mr Andrew Crosse, lightning meant action. And lot's of it. With some four miles of copper cables stretching around the grounds collecting nature's aerial power, the occurrence of an electrical storm meant that the laboratory had to be disconnected before the charge built to an explosive degree.

I leapt out of the armchair the moment that first flicker lit the room and was at the door of the great hall by the time the thunder rumbled. I knew the gap between the light and the sound meant the lightning storm was not yet upon us. But there was not a moment to waste: although I believed I'd left the connecting switch open for the sake of safety, I had to make sure. It was one thing having nature's naked voltage blast into the laboratory when Master was in command, but I had no taste for such thrills myself. I ran down the long vestibule to the laboratory, grabbing a lantern as I went. As I swung the great oak door which seals the laboratory from the rest of the house, another bolt hit nearby and I was blinded by the flash that flared from the conductors inside the room. Indeed, I fell backwards because of the pure force of it and smashed my lantern against the wall. Plunged into darkness, I was alarmed to feel something grab at my arm, but it was only Tom Poole who had followed, wondering what I was up to.

"I have to check the main switch is disconnected from the lightning collectors," I shouted over the rumbling din. "Otherwise there is a danger the storm might blow the place to kingdom-come. Quick, there are lanterns over by the desks – we can light them from the fire."

In the darkness, with the old man still holding onto me, I made my way across the room. And it was then that we – or least, I – heard the unearthly sound and, for one horrible instant, saw the terrible scene that is forever etched upon my mind. It was the strange noise that first stopped me in my tracks. It was like the clattering of twigs in a breeze; like an eerie tapping on a window pane. And it was coming from the very centre of the laboratory. Looking back I recall we could hardly hear it above the racket of the storm, but that clattering was enough to freeze the blood in my veins. Why? Because it was the unmistakable resonance of movement – in a place where there should have been no activity whatsoever.

Then the lightning hit again and for perhaps two or three seconds the great room was lit brighter than the brightest day. That is when we - or at least, I - saw them. I think I know why Tom Poole claims he did not share that awful vision: he insists he was blinded by the flash, but I believe one way of coping with horror is to deny you ever laid eyes on it. Who knows? Was it some hallucination, some illusion brought on by the weird brilliance of the flash? Or was it real? I know not. I will go to my grave uncertain. I swear there were things moving in that great room. Large, unearthly things.

Suddenly the brilliance was gone and we were plunged back into pitch dark. I don't know what made me think of it but, out of habit I suppose, I counted until the roll of thunder clapped around the house. It was only three seconds, which meant the storm was almost upon us. Suddenly another flash... And this time I dived for the big leather gauntlets that we sometimes wore when working with hot cables or the like. I did not look at the creatures during that second flash, for I had urgent work to do. Taking one glove for myself I began my dash back toward Tom Poole when the lightning died again. This time it was just two seconds until the thunder boomed. So violent had this strike been though, that it had left the big capacitor cables glowing. There was enough flaming light for me to see that the great lever was indeed pushed to its safety position. And so the connection from the lightning conductors outside to the implements and instruments inside was open - yet, so violent were the surges that great yellow-blue sparks arced across the switching point. What I was about to do was dangerous, but I knew there was only one way to exterminate those awful creatures and that was to couple their huge metal bench to those fearsome incoming surges of electricity.

I handed a gauntlet to Tom Poole and shouted: "Put it on and take this clamp."

Thrusting a screw-clamp into his hand, I leapt onto a table over by the wall. From there I could just reach the main cable that came down from the big conductor in the organ loft. It was hot and my gauntlet immediately hissed so that I could smell the smoke burning from it as I jumped down.

"Clamp this cable end to the bench where the things are - and watch out, it's hot."

There was no time for social nicety now - I was giving Mr Poole his orders. And here is a thing that often I have mulled over since: "It's got to go on the bench where the things are," I had screamed, and Tom Poole reacted as if he knew exactly what I meant.

I could just about make out the shape of the big man bending to connect the cable end and with that I dived toward the big lever, which itself was burning hot.

"Is it done?" I shouted.

"I believe it is," he croaked back.

"Then get out of here as fast as you can, and shut the door behind you..."

From that moment I am unsure of any detail. I know that as soon as Tom Poole was clear I threw the switch and – not long after – the lightning hit again. I am talking in fractions of seconds here but, for me in those awful moments, time seemed to stand still. I believe that the next lightning bolt directly hit at least three of our collectors out in the trees. The resulting surge was beyond belief. The big room lit up as if it were some damned cell deep inside the sun itself. The organ wheezed and piped victoriously with the pure energy that filled its colossal bellows.

It was mad, it was insane: I was inside a flash, at the epicentre of an explosion. My eyes were blinded and my ears were deafened. And, from that touchstone of violence, from some terrible culmination of cosmic activity – I was hurled into the black, unstructured void of eternity. I thought, for one fleeting moment, that I was dead.

And then I thought nothing at all.

The next thing I saw was Anne Rice. It was a vague outline, a notion of her, but there she was – her face just a foot from my own. I could see her lips moving, but I could hear no sound. Then she faded and again I thought I must be dead. After what seemed like a long time in that black void, consciousness began to lurk again like a will o' the wisp and I fought to gain control of it. Again, there was Anne. This time for longer, and I heard her sweet voice speak my name.

I am told I was out of the world for more than three whole days, but at last I came back to the world. And there she was still, sitting by my bedside. I could only look at her for a moment before pain forced my eyes shut again. It took another four or five days for the agony to clear, which is not surprising as the explosion had stripped me of half my hair, eyebrows and eyelashes. I must have looked an awful sight. But Anne didn't seem to mind and she came everyday for a week to oversee my nursing. I was an invalid right enough, but gradually I began to mend. My hearing came back first and then, I thank God, my eyesight made a full recovery. Soon, even my hair began to seed itself again in those scorched areas and, after a month, I am told I looked more-or-less unscathed. The only thing that hurt for months after was my shoulder which was smashed when I'd been hurled across the laboratory.

There was one lasting moment I can recall from those black painful days. As I say, Anne came everyday to oversee to my recovery and, looking back, it is quite remarkable that we were allowed so much time together. But the doctor had proclaimed that her visits were helping me mend and so our private, intimate bedside meetings were allowed to continue. One day, though, we came close to shattering the trust that had been placed in us. It was the day the doctor finally took the bandages from my eyes for good. Anne looked so beautiful sitting there and, realising that I could see her properly, she got up from her chair and crossed to my bed. Without saying anything she bent down to kiss my lips. If, during that night of the explosion, my mind had been blasted through a helter-skelter of Hell; I was hurtling with much the same velocity through heaven. I pulled her slim body to mine and felt her cool hands on me. And there we were, suddenly, in some kind of passionate tangle, and goodness knows what would have happened had not Mr Poole's booming voice come echoing up the stairs.

"The invalid is still abed is he?" we heard him say to one of the servants. "I shall find my own way up."

In an instant Anne was back in her chair, but not for a moment did we take our eyes from one another until the old yeoman stepped into the room. Even then, we shot a thousand meaningful glances at each other as the old man spoke of this and that.

He came to see me most days and it was Mr Poole who'd told me what had occurred that frightful night. It seemed he had escaped the explosion by closing the laboratory door as I had instructed. That mighty piece of oak withstood the impact that shook the entire house. When he dared enter the room again he was confronted by nothing but wreckage and mayhem. The cables were still sparking and in their eerie light he was able to find me. It took him some time, for I was apparently covered in debris – and when he did come across my crumpled body, he was certain I was dead.

"What about the creatures?" was the first thing I asked him shortly after coming to: "Did it kill them or are they still there?"

"Which creatures Johnny?" said Mr Poole.

I muttered something, but he calmly replied: "The little mites? No, there is nothing left of them. In fact, there is nothing much recognisable left at all. The metal bench lies on the floor as if it had been turned to fluid, which I suppose it had. It is melted and the volcanic slab is shattered to a thousand pieces that have half sunk and set into the cold metal. I must tell you Johnny," he concluded with some gravity, "that the laboratory is ruined. We were most fortunate indeed that the house did not burn down, for it took Beale and myself several hours to douse all the small fires that had caught."

But this wasn't enough for me. Those creatures had haunted my nightmares during those long black hours of unconsciousness. Had we seen them? Had it just been me? From some deep black pool of memory I could envisage their great form. What I had seen were mites that had grown as big as goats. "You saw them didn't you?" I gasped at old Tom Poole. "Those monstrous things. You understand why I had to destroy them..."

He shook his head and said: "I do not know what I saw Johnny, it is all a terrible blur. My memory is unclear, but my wisdom tells me that you were a paragon of courage that night. You threw that master switch and if you had not I think we should have all perished. I will never comprehend what I saw in the mad light that blinded us in that awful room. It is all best forgotten Johnny. Anything that was there has gone. Forget what ever it was you think you saw, and remember how you saved the day."

I was confused by what he said: "But I connected the current, don't you see? I threw that lever and caused the explosion. I had to. It was the only way of killing them."

"Then forget it. It will do no good." he whispered laying a hand upon my sore arm, "Listen to your old friend and pay heed to the wisdom of my words."

I had many hours in that bed of pain in which to think of it. Were those creatures merely a figment of my damaged mind? Had the great blow I'd suffered caused me to hallucinate in the long dark hours of unconsciousness? In the end I decided to follow my friend's wise council. Speaking of the things I'd seen would have taken me down an unhappy road, of that I'm sure. I'd have been the laughing stock of the Quantocks. Deep inside, though, it went against the grain, for I'd been trained by Mr Crosse to let nothing stand in the way of seeking the truth. However, that dilemma was eclipsed by the loveliness of my darling Anne. I could hardly think of anything but those passionate moments that we had stolen together. She had always been fair as a child, now she had grown to be a beautiful woman. Her golden locks dripped down over her shoulders and her small, delicate face was bronzed by the Quantock sun and wind. Her perfect skin seemed almost translucent in its unblemished quality and her eyes were lit as if by some ethereal lantern. The next day, after Tom Poole's afternoon visit had interrupted us, we spoke haltingly and perhaps embarrassed about the intimacy that had occurred between us.

"I have been thinking of nothing else too Johnny," she said after I had told her of my own thoughts. "I loved what happened. I loved it more than I can possibly describe. And yet, it was wrong wasn't it? We are to have our whole lives together some day soon, but we must save ourselves for that happy time."

Never did I love her more than in those days when she nursed me for an hour or two each afternoon. At first, as I have said, she would come to the room where I was installed in a huge four-poster in the main house, but after a week or so we would sit, and then later walk, in the grounds. I was glad to be outside again - in the garden we laughed and talked glowing in the pure happiness of one another's company. Just once during that period I can recall an unwelcome shadow passing over me, and that was when I took Anne to see the wreckage of the laboratory. I had not found the courage to enter the place until that day and, when she said she would like to see it, I had shuddered at the thought. But I knew I must face it sooner or later, and so took her reluctantly to the big oak door. It was locked and Anne had to find Beale to get the key. Neither of us could believe what we saw. It was obvious at first glance where the centre of the explosion had been and there on the floor, just as Mr Poole described, was the melted mess of the giant bench. It looked like some tormented sea in miniature. Great waves of frozen metal rippled this way and that and among them small islands of rock appeared. These pieces were all that was left of our volcanic slab - what a jolt it must have been to blast it into a thousand shards. I hardly dared look, but there was no sign of the creatures – either the tiny ones I know existed or the giant horrors which perhaps I'd dreamed. No leg or claw had survived the blast. There was no trace.

Around us was the petrified detritus of a maelstrom. You could see how the explosion had fanned out across the room: around the big bench nothing had survived, but out against the far walls instruments, though damaged, were more-or-less intact. The lever, which I had wrestled with, was bent by some great force away from the blast and in that direction I could see a pool of blood which must have been my own. It was strange for me, standing there with my beautiful girl in the middle of all that mayhem. My emotions were tangled, to say the least. There was the sadness - seeing all our years of work undone. But there was joy. Joy at having miraculously survived the explosion. As for those ghastly creatures, Mr Poole was right, they were better forgotten.

Mr Crosse had been informed of the disaster and apparently his first instinct was to return to Fyne Court as soon as he could. But in the letter containing the news his brother Richard had begged him to travel to London in a bid to clear the family name from the avalanche of recent criticism.

"The doctor from Taunton assures us that Walford will survive more-or-less unscathed," wrote Mr Richard. "As for the laboratory, I can tell you that very little in the way of your work remains intact. Looking at the wreckage, it is a wonder that your assistant survived at all. Fortunately Mr Poole, who was with him at the time, managed to escape before the explosion and, at Walford's bidding, sealed the area by closing the oak door. Had he not done so, much of the house would have undoubtedly suffered."

"My advice to you is to proceed to London immediately. From what we read in the papers, you will have your work cut out in making good the honour of our family name. Speaking as your brother, and also for Mr Thomas Poole who is with me at this time, I must enjoin you to do everything you can to deny the damaging rumours concerning your work. We are with you in spirit, dear brother, and wish you every success in correcting the damage this propaganda has done."

In a few days I received a letter from the Squire. In it he thanked me for my fast action in saving his home. He said that both Mr Poole and his brother had written to inform him of my bravery.

"I do not pretend to understand all of what went on Johnny. There are some questions I would like to ask. For instance, I cannot fathom how the explosion occurred after you had switched the isolating lever to the open position. However, the answers to these mysteries will have to wait as I am bound to go to London to clear my name of the unfortunate and scurrilous accusations that have been heaped upon it. So it will be some weeks before I am able to make my return. In the meantime I pray to God that you will make a full recovery. Rest as long as you wish, do not think of setting yourself any tasks. Take fresh air when you are well enough and only when you feel quite strong are you to think of the laboratory. Even then, do not worry over much, for I am thinking of retiring from the world of experimental science, at least for a while."

When I felt well enough I wrote back to Mr Crosse sketching in barest outline my memories of the great storm. Putting it down on paper aroused some reactions in me that I'd not expected. For the first time since the ruinous night I realised I was really explaining how I had deliberately destroyed the laboratory and years of work. As for explaining the reason why, it seemed far-fetched to say the least - and I wondered if my Master might think that I'd gone insane. However, with great reluctance, I did mention the things I'd seen so fleetingly in the lightning and briefly sketched in the fact that, in my memory at least, they were those hellish mites grown in size more than a hundredfold. A few days later I received a reply.

"Dear Johnny, I have read your missive and understood it. As far as anyone could possibly comprehend such a thing. After reading your note I destroyed the two living mites which you sent earlier. I did this successfully, by-the-way, using a high voltage of electricity as you prescribed. Fortunately, I was able to use Mr Singer's laboratory, having first attempted various other methods, all of which were unsuccessful. As I have said, I do not comprehend it, but I will tell you this for your own peace of mind: I believe you had only one course of action that night and will say that your deed was nothing less than heroic. You knew the risks involved during such a storm and yet you did what you plainly had to do, despite the fact that it was bound to put your life in danger. For this courageous action, I shall forever be indebted to you."

Mr Crosse eventually returned home in the New Year, and I was appalled by the look of him. He had aged ten years. The only time I saw him smile during those first weeks after his return was when he first caught sight of me, standing alone in the wreckage that had been our workplace. He smiled as if glad to see me - then, looking about him, shook his head for a long time without speaking.

"You should have seen it before Walford set to work," said his brother, who had entered with him. "The place is unrecognisable compared to the mayhem it was in."

I had indeed worked long and hard. The blacksmith had helped me erect new benches and I'd spent hours piecing together Voltaic

Piles and other bits and pieces. The small sea of molten metal that had been the bench hit by the bolt, I had removed with the help of ten men. Mr Crosse immediately demanded to see it and nothing would do but to tramp out in the rain to where it lay in a yard. We went alone and he crawled about it with his magnifying glass looking at each and every one of the little volcanic stone islands petrified into the melted metal.

At last he spoke: "So, Johnny, they have gone."

"No trace remains," said I. "You can be sure that I searched every cranny and never a mite or any part of one have I seen."

"When I passed by Mr Poole's house last night, he recounted the dreadful night but would not speak of mites in any way," said Mr Crosse, and then turning to me he asked: "How big were they?"

I showed him with my hands, but added: "I am ready to believe it was an illusion. I was unconscious for half a week and the doctor told me a person in that state can suffer all kinds of visions and hallucinations."

"Are you saying that you did not actually see those things?"

"No Sir. But I am wondering if what I saw could have been altered in some way, highlighted, magnified, whatever - by the blinding flash. There is one thing more," and here I pulled from my coat pocket a brass implement which I thought I had seen in the claws of one of the creatures. "In my apparition, if you can call it that, one of the mites had hold of this. I saw it - in those blinding seconds - bend the thing as if it were a blade of grass. Later I found it lying on the other side of the room where the explosion had thrown it. But look, if you examine it closely, you will see that it is lined with small indentations. I have studied the dead mites that I killed previously - you know, whose brothers I sent to you - and, with the help of the microscope, have been able to make out that the two front claws have a sharp serrated edge. Enlarge that and you have the marks left on this shaft.... That is my only proof."

Mr Crosse sat down on a log and thought deeply for some time. At last he said: "That is the end of it Johnny. Keep that broken tube if you wish, but my advice to you is to forget that you have seen these things. What they were, and where they came from, we shall never know. There is a part of me that would throw caution to the wind and repeat the experiment under far more controlled and guarded conditions, but I have my other responsibilities now. You know of the battles I've had in attempting to clear my name. It has cost me dear. Not so much in money, although I have spent a good deal of that too, but my standing both publicly and among fellow scientists. I was not built to be out there in front of the crowd. I loathe it. This debacle almost upset my plans for marriage, and it has only been through the good offices of Mr Poole that such a sad development was avoided. The marriage has been saved on the condition that I now give up scientific research and look after my estate."

"To this end I have made some arrangements. The first occurs tomorrow when the editor of a newspaper is due to come here so that I can put the record straight with him. The mites, I shall say – and this is what I have been saying in London – occurred in a naturally forming residue and could happen anywhere given the circumstances, quite as nature would intend."

"And then, Johnny, there is the question of your future. The experimental work is finished, for the time being at least, and that means you will not be working in the laboratory. Instead I want you to take up a position as assistant factotum on the estate. I promised you once that I would never let you down and that I would back you all the way. I stand by my word. Take up this new post and before too long you'll be able to go to the father of that sweetheart of yours and ask him for her hand. There will be a cottage on the estate and good opportunities for you. What do you think of that?"

I was overjoyed of course and that night made my way to Anne's school so that I could tell her the news. Seeing her was never easy – I had to throw a pebble at her window – but she joined me in the grounds soon after. There was a big old cedar tree and under this we sat. But my news did not have quite the effect I'd expected. Anne grew silent and it was only after much cajoling and pleading on my part that she at last bade me not to do anything rash for a day or two. She said she needed time to think. Of course, I was distraught, this was the very opposite reaction to the one I'd so merrily expected. Was it that she no longer loved me, I asked. Eventually she told me she was worried about her father.

"You must not approach him yet, Johnny," she implored. "I think it is more difficult now than ever. Why did you have to get Mr Buncombe into trouble like you did? He is my father's closest friend and, because of his dismissal from your master's estate, he has now gone to live at our mill. You won't be surprised to hear that since he has been there he's been busy poisoning my father even further against you. You know my father was always inclined to say unkind things about you – I have never been able to understand quite why - but now he dislikes you with a vengeance almost as violent as Mr Buncombe's."

I groaned. There I'd been, so proud to be the undoing of the grasping thieving Buncombe. But really it had been none of my business. Mr Crosse would have caught him sooner or later. Instead, I had played a role too big for my boots - and where had it got me?

"I did not remove Giles Buncombe from his job," I groaned. "The fool did that himself. And here's an irony – as Mr Crosse would call it - your father has always been against me because of my lowly standing, and yet now I am about to take up respectable position once filled by his own best friend!"

I went home a dejected figure that night, with no clue as to the events that were soon to change the course of my life forever. The first was not so much a single event, but something more vague. I duly entered the role of assistant factotum - Mr Richard Crosse and Mr Poole had agreed to keep an eye on me, and it all seemed to fall into place without hitch. However, I am afraid to say that at once I found it dull work and in a short time I grew to hate the sight of rows of figures and entries. Where the laboratory work had been tactile and challenging, this book-keeping was monotonous and wearisome. Where I had worked late into the night with the Squire, now I couldn't wait to leave the little bureau at the corner of the stables and escape into the fresh Quantock air.

Even visits around the Estate were lacklustre affairs, for I do not like being at odds with people and often these journeys necessitated my calling on folk to harry them for rent or payment of some kind. Often there were disputes. It was while I was on one of these excursions that a singular episode occurred. I was striding down over Lydeard Hill towards the lovely hamlet of Aisholt and had just emerged from Muchcare Wood when I spied a distant figure. It was Green, the rabbit-catcher, and he was way away over to my left, running and leaping like a demented hind down over Aisholt Common. The deep coombe lay between us, but I could catch his shouts of "Johnny Walford" riding upon the breeze. So I ran towards him until, with the coombe still between us, we stood facing one another across the void.

"Tis yer father Johnny," shouted Green. "Er be taken bad."

That was enough for me. My business at Aisholt could wait. Using the contours around Middle Hill, it wasn't long before I had caught up with the rabbit-catcher who was catching his breath up by Black Knap.

"Tis yer father boy," he panted. "Er be terr'ble hurt in Slaughterhouse. 'Er wuz still there when I left 'un to come fur you. Yer mother's up there carin' fur 'un, while 'Nilla 'ave gone to Williton fur the doctor."

I asked what had happened and this was his reply: "Some begger's 'ad a go at 'un, Johnny. 'Ee ain't a-speakin' much, but 'er be there on the side o' the path in Slaughter'ouse Combe wi' a face like mashed tetties..."

I took to my heels and left old Green loping far behind. I reckon I made that journey across to Slaughterhouse Combe in under half-an-hour. Flighty Chidgey was there with my mother and between them lay the body of my father. At first I thought he must be dead but, hearing my voice, the old man rolled his eyes slowly toward my own.

As gently as I could I picked him up we descended Slaughterhouse Coombe to the woods where they had the family camp. We had often settled there, just under Willoughby Cleave in Hodder's Combe, so it was but a short distance for father to suffer the discomfort of the journey. He moaned all the way, and I was glad to put him down upon his bed. All this while my mother was in a flurry and fuss and she kept asking: "Who could have done such a thing?"

It was obvious that father had been dealt some kind of violent blow. He was a strong man for his age and few fellows from the villages would have dared tussle with him. Yet it immediately occurred to me this was the work of a human hand or boot. This was no accident or fall. Even if he had gone head over heels, there were no rocks or boulders up in that cup of the hills that could have harmed him so. Mother and I pulled his tunic off to reveal his wounds and discovered his whole body was covered in red wheals and bruises.

"Could 'ave been one of they nasty gurt stags," sobbed Petronilla.

Flighty Chidgey shrugged: "Tis the wrong time o' year, October's when a big stag might charge a man, though I tell 'e, I've never yeard o' it been done."

"Who has done this to you father?" I asked, to no avail, for it would be a few days before the old man would speak again – and then he either did not remember, or would not say.

All I could glean was that he was on his way back over the hill from Bicknoller where there was an inn. He'd left towards the end of the evening, merry with drink no doubt – and had been escorted up Bicknoller Combe by Green, who had left him at the place where father had to cut across Black Ball Hill in order to drop down into Slaughterhouse Combe. So he had descended into the blackness of this loneliest of Quantock valleys alone and, shortly after reaching the stream, had been attacked. The poor old fellow must have been lying there all night.

Leaving mother to fuss over the invalid, I went back to where he'd been found, and cast about for some evidence that would throw light upon this mystery. Close to the top of the coombe, a small side valley that we call a goyal enters from the north. In daylight, let alone at night, a man or several men could hide behind the spur of hill that's created by this junction. Their victim would have no chance of spying them until he passed within a few feet. In the soft peat at the spot, I could see signs of a struggle. By my reckoning, there were four different footmarks in that ground other than my father's, and I vowed as I stood there in the drizzle, that every one of them should be made to pay – whoever they were.

Old Dr Phillick came at last and, after a minute or two, pronounced that father should live. "Tis what we do call concussion and there is nothing much to be worrying about in the case of your father, Johnny, for I believe that he is a man with a dense enough skull. However, his jaw is broken in at least two places and then there are some cracked ribs. But, most serious for him, is the broken arm. I have set it, but how long it'll be before he can work with it again, I cannot say."

So now we were in a fix. Spring was on its way, which was when my father would make more than half his annual income in just a couple of months, what with the collection of the broom and the making of the brushes. Mother and Petronilla could do a bit, especially in the manufacture, but collection of the broom was always father's work. There was nothing for it, I felt, but to ask my Master for payment of some wages which were owing to me and this, at least, would help the family to survive the crisis for a time.

It was, of course, my duty to stand by them while father got over the worst of his pains. Having made the decision I sent word to Mr Crosse via Flighty Chidgey who was to beg his indulgence upon my behalf and request that I may be absent for a few days. I could take Eskie the pony up onto the moors and collect some of the broom that my father had earmarked for the business. Also I might be able to glean something of the facts that lay behind his beating.

He seemed a little better the following morning, so I left mother to nurse him while I went to the hill. My plans though, went immediately amiss when I found that Eskie had dropped a shoe; there was nothing for it but to head off down the coombe for the village where I knew old Theodore Treble would don his farrier's apron and deal with the thing there and then. I do believe that I must have forgotten that my brother William had been working at the forge for several years so, when I arrived at the low thatched building, I was surprised to see him in the gloom. I told Theo what I was after and straight away he set to work hewing a new shoe for my father's faithful pony, leaving me with little to do but attempt to engage my sullen brother in conversation. William was working furiously at the anvil and neither greeted me nor ceased his hammering.

"Have you heard what has befallen father?" I shouted.

For a while he did not answer but kept beating at the red hot metal until it had lost its heat. Plunging it back into the flames of the forge he turned at last and said: "I 'eard he have taken a beatin', which comes as no surprise to me..."

"What do you mean, no surprise to you?" I cried. "How many times has our father been beaten to within an inch of his life? Never. So how can you be so calm about it?"

William turned and fiddled with his burning rod. "Tis a wonder he have never had it afore. What wi' his smugglin' and the like. He is no saint brother, though you may think so. I knows of his dark goin's on see - and you, the Squire's lad, do not."

He sneered at me, the same old sneer I had seen crumpling his face many times before. He sneered, and I gazed back at him with the contempt I'd always felt for him. God only knows what was passing through that clouded, unhappy mind of his - but I knew sure enough what was going through mine. A thought had occurred to me as we stood there: a dark and menacing thought that had me suspecting William might know more of the crime than he was willing to admit. There was my brother claiming to know of our father's murky dealings, and just behind where he stood was Eskie, the little pony who could find her way by a whistle. Only a handful of people knew of Eskie's night-time skills, and William was one of them.

Could it have been him who sold his own father to the Revenue-men for a guinea? Surely, no son would do such a thing? It was quite beyond belief. And yet there was something about this brother of mine – something angry and disturbed. I pushed the thoughts from me and tried a different line instead: "Well then William, if you do know so much about father's comings and goings, then perhaps you have some inkling as to who may have tried to kill him? For that's what it was, believe me, father is fortunate to be alive."

He toyed with the hot mettle again, and I could see that sneer come back across his face: "Why should I care – tell me that? What did father ever do for me? Never once have I ever had as much as a kind word out of him. Not since I was a babe in mother's arms. He 'ave hated me just as much as he 'ave loved you. Johnny – apple of his rotten eye!" William scoffed with derision, turning to face me with the hot blade swinging in his big leather gauntlet. "Johnny-bloody-perfect. Johnny this, Johnny that. You're 'is precious son – you sort out the old fool's woes!"

For a moment I thought he was going to take a swipe at me with the red hot metal. And in the same moment I wanted to crush him backwards into the flames. The two of us stood there glaring, and such was the atmosphere between us that old Theo somehow picked up on it and ceased working on Eskie's shoe.

At last I spoke. Haltingly, and trying to control my passion, I said: "I never thought I'd hear a brother – any brother – say that about his own father. If we do not love our fathers, who can we love? If we cannot fight their fights, who can we stand by? I tell you William, I always knew you detested him, but I had no idea 'twas as bad as this."

"You had no idea," he spat with contempt. "Course you did not! Why should you? You were always well set up with him – what mattered it to you that he treated his dogs better than he treated me? And now 'is little golden boy is about to find the old broomsquire's foes and wreak vengeance 'pon 'em. You make me laugh John Walford. The Squire's errand-boy seeks revenge! Twill be like watchin' a year old pricket take on a Royal Stag if I knows anything about it."

He put the metal down on the anvil and somehow seemed to sink under the weight of his own melancholy. "You little fool. I 'eard 'ow you was down Kilve Pill savin' the old beggar from the Revenue. Thought yerself so 'igh-and-mighty didn't you. For all yer cleverness you can't see the wood for the trees though. Don't you realise father's bin messin' with powerful folk. Dangerous folk. Money men who'd think nothin' of takin' anyone down a peg or two. The old broomsquire and 'is 'alf-wit friend Montague are just the little pieces in their game - daft-witted dunderheads who takes the risk for a firkin of French. And when a little man steps on the toes of a big man, then watch out. Everyone knows that - 'cept for you of course. You've been too long mixing wi' the gentry."

He sneered one last time before stooping to pick his hammer - and I marched past him saying: "Thank you brother. You have told me all I need to know."

Collecting Eskie I left my unhappy sibling looking bewildered and annoyed, but I cared not what mood he was in, for I had a good deal of thinking to do. I couldn't get the thought from my mind that William had been the one to inform the Revenue of the goings on at Kilve, and I had an uncomfortable feeling Messrs Rice and Buncombe had been behind my father's beating. They knew it was the Walfords who'd landed Buncombe in trouble - Anne had told me so! I'd been too innocent about all this - it should have come as no surprise that they'd be after some kind of revenge. There was a part of me that wanted to go to the mill there and then to confront the fat miller and his mate. But, although I was certain they had been instrumental in my father's beating, whether or not they had actually dirtied their hands in Slaughterhouse Combe was another thing. Not that it would have made any difference to me the mood I was in that morning - my problem was, of course, my darling Anne. A youth wishing to impress a belligerent father hardly did so at the end of a fist...

For two or three days I worked hard on the high hill collecting broom so that mother and Petronilla had a goodly supply for the making of their brushes. Fortunately, it was cold, clear, sunlit weather in which Quantock can look so handsome as the light paints the curves of the coombes. The pale yellow light seemed to caress the lovely flanks and, at times, I would lay down on the sward to watch the small white clouds pass silently over my Quantock world. Or was it, like I imagined when I was a boy, that we were moving fast forever westward while the clouds remained still? A silent hurtling. Like my life. Events hadn't so much overtaken me, they had always been in front, as if some great scribe had designed my story long before I wept and crawled and laughed upon these hills. The plot I'd written for myself was an ineffectual thing pouring fast through my fingers like the sand on Monty's beach. Anne had told me that she could never marry without her father's consent. And he, I was ever more certain, had been the man who had been behind my own father's thrashing. How could I be civil to him, let alone ask for his blessing? It was impossible to think that he would look favourably on it even if I were to go cap in hand which, of course, I couldn't.

For all the long hours of these days spent up in the clear crystal light of the hill did I ponder upon such imponderables. But again, events overtook me, or drew me - like the passing clouds - inevitably toward my fate.

Father remained poorly. When I returned from collecting broom during those few days, I would nurse him in my arms and attempt to amuse him with stories and talk of all that I had learned during my years at the Court. Sometimes a trickle of blood would escape from the corner of his lips. Sometimes he would try to croak some sort of reply. But gradually he improved and by the end of the week was swallowing down some solid food and stringing a few words together. Venison seemed to do him powerful good and by the Saturday I returned from the hill to find him sitting up and demanding cider. It happened that there was none in our camp (a rarity at normal times), but he insisted there was nothing for it: he must wet his lips.

"Tis the only thing that shall 'elp Johnny," says he. "You must put some straw in the cart and harness Eskie. Then we shall go to the Castle of Comfort and I shall drink a quart or two of that medicine."

Mother and I protested, but there was nothing for it. The old man wanted his cider and told us he wouldn't live the night out unless he were to put some of its fortifying essence into his veins. In the end I came to thinking that if he were to lie in the cart and then sit snug in some corner of the inn, then no harm could come of it. I knew about his love of cider and the way it always seemed to cheer him to the roots of his soul. If there was any single thing he needed now, it was something to warm the cockles of his battered heart.

So I took him to the Castle of Comfort, an ironic name for inn in the circumstances, for I think the journey must have pained him even though I led Eskie gently so the cart wouldn't not founder and shake in the ruts of the lane. But we got there soon enough and I helped the sore old fellow through the door. A hush descended on the place as we came into the saloon. Everyone present - and there were quite a few that night - had heard of what had befallen old man Walford up in Slaughterhouse Combe, and none thought they should see him for some time to come. A couple of his friends had dropped in to visit and none who'd seen him during the week could ever have believed he'd be at the inn on Saturday night. But there he was, slowly, painfully, crossing the room to where I helped him rest his broken bones on the settle by the fire.

"Cider Jeremiah," he shouted. "And be quick about it."

That broke the ice and the fellows of the hills gathered about us to make a fuss over their old confidant. A great talk ensued concerning the incident that had almost robbed father of his life and, not unnaturally, the main thrust of it was over who had perpetrated the attack. Green was there and, as the evening drew on, he pulled me to one side for a private word.

"I don't want to make a thing o' it," he whispers. "If it got out it were me that said it, 'twould be my turn next. But atween you and me Johnny, what I've yeard is that your master's old factotum Buncombe was be'ind it. They reckons 'twas 'e and the three Nurcott's."

I knew the Nurcotts. Daft, lumbering great oafs, all odd in some way. Nobby with his squint eye, brother Derry with his air of vacancy, and old man Nurcott the dangerous, sullen father who had never been known to be civil to a living soul. What had happened to the mother, for I suppose there must have been one, I knew not. The three men lived alone on their small-holding down by the copper-mine below the inn. They never came out to socialise, and all but the bravest avoided them. There was one exception, and that was the miller. They were his tenants, he owned their farm and he employed them to mend his fences and see to the donkey work around his own estate.

Of course it was the Nurcotts, I thought to myself. They'd do anything Rice told them, and they would have enjoyed kicking a man into his grave, of that I had no doubt. And of course if was Buncombe. He must have somehow suspected my father of indiscretion during the smuggling business. The indiscretion that cost him a powerful and profitable job. Just thinking of him had me in a rage. If he had walked into the inn right then, I would have strangled the life out of him.

As it happens, I did not have long to wait. What I am about to write I have never whispered to a soul, for I would have been hanged long before now had it got out. Only my father knew, and he took the secret with him to his grave.

We were travelling back up the coombe, father in a much

improved state of mind, lying in the straw-filled cart with a flagon of Jeremiah's best to keep him company. He didn't seem to notice, but it was most certainly a more lumpy journey back than the one we'd had down to the inn. The reason for that was my own state of mind. The moon was out bright, so I had no excuse for misleading Eskie, but I was drunk with both cider and with anger. I had sipped far more than I ought and being a young man I was not used to the devil that lies within the drink. All I could see in my hazy mind were the Nurcotts and Buncombe waiting at the corner of Slaughterhouse Combe. Waiting, then attacking, cruelly and viciously, without giving my father a single chance. I swore over and again that I should do the same to each and every one of them. For I had the strength and the manhood to best each one of them.

Then, as if my thoughts had wished him there, I saw Buncombe far down through the trees. We had clattered past the mill and had taken the left hand track up through the woods to cross the ridge into the coombe where the camp was. The main track continues up the bottom of the main valley alongside the run of Rice's meadows. On the far side of these small fields runs the mill leat, and at the very topmost pasture there is the place where this race is divided from the main stream. A giant sluice controls the amount of water that flows down to turn the wheel and it has to be turned by a crank to lift it up or down. I have already mentioned that it had been a week of cold clear weather, but on this Saturday the heavens had made up for the unseasonable dryness by hurling great sheets of rain down on the hills. I had come home early from the broom, and it was only because the rain had stopped and the sky had cleared that I'd agreed to take father to the inn. This torrential rain had obviously swollen the stream and was pushing far too much water down the leat.

As soon as I saw the figure hunched over the winding gear at the sluice I knew what he was about: he was shutting off the race from the main river, so that no damage would come to the water wheel. I also knew, instantly, who it was that was winding the crank, through the trees some two or three hundred feet below were I stood. Buncombe was a stocky, burly man with such immense shoulders that it looked as if there had been a mistake when he was put together. He had the torso of a much bigger fellow, but the legs of someone small. But despite his size, I knew this was my moment. If I didn't do it now, I would never have the courage to face him. In that drunken instant I told myself that, if I were truly a man, I would seize this moment to revenge my father.

"Stay there," I whispers to the invalid.

I do not know if he realised what was going on or not, for within a second I had leapt off the edge of the track and was jumping like a goat down the near vertical slope of the wood. Buncombe never heard me. He was having troubles with the winding handle and the roar of the water passing through the sluice was enough to drown any other sound.

"Buncombe!" I shouted not once but twice to make him hear. My rage was boiling but nevertheless I felt a fool when he did not hear first time. "Buncombe" I shouted, and now at last he turned and in an instant his expression changed from one of surprise to undiluted malice. He straightened up from where he was hunched over the wheel, and only then did I notice that the big metal crank was detachable and he held it in his hand. A dreadful doubt shot into my mind. Buncombe, standing there grim and hating in the moonlight, looked a daunting prospect. If he were to catch me with that crank, then it would go very badly for me. Whether it was because of the roar of the swollen stream that we never exchanged a single word, I do not know, but we stood there silently glaring at one another for what seemed like a minute or two. He knew that I had come for him. I knew that his hatred of me meant he wanted it this way. He was a rough man with a reputation for bullying and physical abuse. I was not twenty years of age and, although big in frame and muscular, had not fought since I was a boy in Mr Baker's school.

This inexperience came to the fore when Buncombe hurled himself at me. I had never experienced anything like it. Boys rarely give their all in a fight, there is usually some reticence in a lad's desire to cause real harm to another. That was the only sort of fighting I had done. A tap here, a kick there, a wrestle and a tear. But there was no reticence in the way Buncombe came at me. He meant to smash my skull with that iron cranking bar, and he would certainly have done so had I not had the strength and agility to dodge the blow. But, no sooner had I felt the wind of the bar pass my ear, than I felt the agony of Buncombe's boot being buried into the depths of my gut. In a moment I was doubled in pain with my lungs seized in a cramp from being winded. There was nothing for it but dive to one side and roll away over the wet grass, for I knew that bar was coming down again. Buncombe missed and lashed out with his boot for a second time. He caught me in the small of the back and I yelped, but I kept rolling and, by doing so, gave myself a few vital seconds to catch my breath.

Never before, or since, have a faced such violence. Buncombe knew this work. He was confident and cool. Each time he moved a limb it was with a precision aimed at inflicting pain. Blow upon blow fell down and I found myself whimpering with panic and fear. I had but one thought and it was simply to keep avoiding that cranking bar. If he managed to land that on me, then it would be over. It was so heavy it would maim me, of that I was sure - but also, it was so heavy that even the burly Buncombe could not parry with it and aim it rapidly and accurately. So I squirmed and wriggled and writhed - more than once it thudded into the sodden ground within an inch of my head. But in the end, that bar was to give me my opportunity...

Thud. It buried itself into the turf again, but this time I grabbed it with both hands and, with all my might, I used it as a fulcrum to find the balance that allowed me to kick at Buncombe's ugly head. My boot caught him on the side of the neck and for the first time he took a blow from me. It seemed to surprise him and his moment of uncertainty gave me the chance to leap to my feet. But I kept hold of the bar, and so now he had one end and I had the other. He wrenched and pulled, and so did I.

I think we were just about matched strength for strength for though he was of a larger frame, there was no doubt that I was younger and more fit. Neither he nor I would yield - and so we embarked upon a crazy dance in that moonlit field. Pushing and pulling we circled this way and that. Wrenching and ripping we gazed fierce into each other's eyes. Still not a single word was said.

After a time my fear began to subside and the logical side of my brain began to gain some control. Kick him, it thought. You can kick him with your long legs, but he cannot reach you with his. And so I did and saw pain etched upon that ugly face. Again I kicked, and again. Each time I caught him, and each time it hurt.

I suppose he must have realised after a minute of this that he could only lose at this game. We both needed our hands to be gripped firmly to the bar, or it would be ripped free - but as it was some three feet in length there was no way his small legs were long enough to reach across the gap. He must have realised there was no alternative but to wrest the bar from me.

With a sudden violence that - even in the circumstances - took me by surprise, he lowered his head and charged at me. At the same time he kept hold of the bar and so did I. Only just though. The force of his charge was extraordinary and I could do nothing but fall backwards a pace or two. But then I found my feet and some sixth sense caused me to jump to one side. The effect of this was to put us into a spin. Round and round we went with no idea in either of our heads, I am sure, but to keep hold of that wretched bar.

That was when we tipped into the race and, in an instant, the piece of metal was forgotten. However, our battle was not - although surprised to find ourselves in ice cold water, blow upon blow was struck between us as we hurtled down that leat. It seemed like minutes but was more probably an instant - it matters not: one thing was beginning to dawn upon me: I was now getting the better of Buncombe, which was just as well for we would soon be in a greater danger.

I had better explain about the mill race. It is only four or five feet across and, at normal times, just two or three feet deep, ample to turn the big waterwheel. But this night - because of the heavy rain of the day, and because Buncombe had failed to close the sluice - the water was some five feet in depth and it was travelling down the smooth, stone-lined race far too fast for a man to stand against. Even I, with my large six foot frame, had no chance of slowing myself for a single second as we hurtled ever onwards toward the mill. But, where I could occasionally reach the bottom with my feet, the much shorter Buncombe never had a chance. This gave me the advantage as we carried on with our grim contest. With something to push against, my blows on him were delivered with far more force than he could muster. Buncombe was beginning to disappear under the water with increasing frequency as I lashed at his head. Soon he was coughing and spluttering from having swallowed too much water. I knew I had him then and showed no mercy as I pummelled him with all my might.

We were coming to the mill and both of us, I'm sure, could hear the roar of water from where the leat flowed out across its launder chute to tumble over the wheel. Now at last, our fight was forgotten. Suddenly it seemed a ridiculous thing to be doing in the face of this extreme danger. No man could survive being thrown out onto the great wheel, for he would undoubtedly be crushed as it turned and took him down to the depths of its underside.

Buncombe tried to grab me in a panic as we hurtled ever onwards. Then he began to struggle and grasp the side of the leat, but he had no luck as the banks were kept clean and smooth. My mind raced with the possibilities of the thing. All I could come up with was some vague plan to make a well-timed leap clear of the chute. What would have become of me had I been forced to take this option, I do not know, but I most certainly would have been killed.

It didn't come to that. As the leat approaches the mill it passes through one last field; the same orchard that Anne and I had played in all those years ago when we first met. At this point the leat is raised above the level of the orchard and runs along its own sizeable bank. Because of this the boughs of some of the trees overhang the race and, in one or two cases, dangle just a foot or two above the water. Seeing these branches in the moonlight, I knew they provided our only chance. So did Buncombe, and I watched him lunging at some of the lower boughs as we passed. I did the same, but for the most part we found ourselves grabbing at twigs which broke instantly under the weight.

Then both of us managed to clutch at more substantial boughs. If I could choose any wood to wager my life on, apple would be that last I'd pick. As anyone who has ever climbed an apple tree will know, it has worrying knack of suddenly giving-way under weight – and that is what happened now. Buncombe was stopped for just three or four seconds before his branch snapped and he was once again submerged in the race. It bore him directly down to me and, grasping at my legs, his extra weight proved too much for my fragile bough. Now we were both back in the stream and travelling fast towards what seemed like a certain death.

I had gone under the icy water after the branch had snapped and when I re-emerged gasping for air I saw, in the light of the moon, that we had but one final chance. A bough, bigger than the others we'd passed so far, crossed the stream and it looked substantial enough to bear any weight that we should put upon it. But it was higher than the rest. To reach it I would have to time my leap with precision. Buncombe would have no chance though, this high branch was no option for him. However, he saw it coming and planned his own escape. He kept close to me in the water and watched as I made to jump. I caught the branch all right, but instantly felt Buncombe grab my legs.

So there we were in the moonlight. Two men dangling from a tree, one up to his neck in a racing stream, the other half submerged and hanging from a branch that was straining under the combined weight. Two men in an icy mill-race, struggling with their final reserves of strength for this one last chance. At first my thoughts were to kick Buncombe free. I knew I could haul my own weight to safety, but was unsure that I had the power to pull us both to safety. Only my legs were in the water, but most of Buncombe was and the drag was ripping my arms from their sockets. However - and this is the truth - I did not kick. A thought occurred to me as I dangled there on the very edge of oblivion. How it came to me at such a time, I cannot imagine - but come it did, and for the next minute I tried my utmost to rescue the two of us. My idea was simply this: if I saved Buncombe's life then he would be indebted to me. He would undo the harm he done me, and the miller would allow me to marry his daughter. It was as simple as that, and I think it shows just how much in love I was with Anne Rice because for that minute my shoulders, arms and clutching fingers were in dire agony.

But the plan, whether it was noble or whether it was self-seeking, did not work. I had been collecting broom that day, as I've said, and in the gorse and furze it is necessary to wear thick leather chaps. I was still wearing these now, and they offered mighty little in the way of grip for the disgraced factotum. His fingers slipped and, with a horrible cry, he was gone.

Heaving myself to the side of the leat took every bit of strength I had left, and I have wondered since if I could have pulled us both clear anyway. But his grip had failed and I heard his awful scream as he went the few yards down to the chute. Then there was silence - an awful silence in which even the roar of the wheel seemed to subside for a moment leaving a void that marked the passing of a soul. For that was the result of his slipping from my legs. They found his mangled body in the morning, trapped in one of the great buckets of the wheel. Going around and around as if he had been enjoying a ride on a macabre merry-go-round in some mad fair of death. The spirit of the wheel had his supper that night and it must have been a gruesome scene that greeted early risers at the mill in the morning. No-one but my father and myself ever knew how Buncombe came to be rotating, crushed to death on that waterwheel.

But for the grace of God, I should have been there with him, for I only just managed to save myself. After the arm-wrenching traverse along the apple bough I hurled myself onto the bank where I lay exhausted. After a minute or two I slinked off through the shadows of the trees and was gone from that terrible scene. Later, I considered the commotion that there would be in the morning when they discovered his body, but at least I knew that I was departing without leaving a single trace of evidence behind me. Buncombe had gone out in the night to close the mill sluice and somehow had fallen into the race: it would have been easy enough to do while struggling with the great crank. It was a two-handled affair with a central spigot - I had often times seen two men working at it - and Buncombe had been trying to turn it alone, heaving at just one end. It was easy to see how the imbalance could cause the handle to spring out of its central bedding - if it did, then whoever was doing the pulling would be sent reeling.

All this seemed logical enough to me some thirty minutes later as I lay in my bed shivering and worrying over what had occurred. It is not every day that a young man causes someone's death and, to tell the truth, I do not know whether I was shivering with cold or remorse. I kept telling myself it had been a case of survival. I had confronted Buncombe, sure enough. I had run down there through the trees, hot-headed with cider - hoping, I suppose, that the meeting should end in blows. But if I had wanted to kill the man, then I should have crept up on him and dealt him an unsuspecting blow. Instead I had hailed him and he had turned on me with all the malice of the Devil. There could be no doubt that he hated the sight of me and I was certain he would have killed me with his iron bar.

Eventually I slept, but it was not easy. Dreams and nightmares fell over one another in a confusion that had me waking and sweating in fear. Always the waterwheel was there, spinning and groaning and grinding - pulling me into its blackened, mesmerising maul. And there in those dreams, somewhere in the imperceptible distance - Anne skipped and laughed and taunted just like she had done all those years ago.

PART 4

THE MAKING OF BROOMSQUIRE

A sore head. Dogs barking. It was a bad start to a worrying day. Someone had come to our camp and I heard mother talking. There was a mention of my name, indeed, I recognised the man's voice. It was Tom Poole and he was asking for me. I put on some fresh clothes and tidied myself up, though my poor head was banging thanks to the cider I had drunk and I was aching badly here and there from the blows that Buncombe had flung at me. Outside I found Mr Poole who had climbed down from his old cob while several village men remained mounted on their ponies at the edge of the clearing. My old friend told me that, as local magistrate, he had been hauled out of bed just after dawn by a servant from Rice's Mill. There had been a great to do, he said, since the girl who lit the fires in the house had been first to rise and had raised the alarm. Coming out of the woodshed she had seen the remains of Giles Buncombe spinning on the waterwheel. By the time Mr Poole arrived they had stopped the leat and taken the body down so that the corpse lay under a blanket. Tom said he could see by the shape of it that the man had been horribly mutilated.

Harold Rice told him how Buncombe had last been seen marching off to the sluice the night before while he and some other men carried on with their game of cards. Buncombe, having run out of funds, had volunteered to close the sluice after the miller had voiced his concerns about the heavy rain. At first, after the discovery of Buncombe's body, Rice had blamed himself and wept and groaned at the loss of his friend. He said he should have ensured that two men had gone for the job but, being in his cups and with a strong hand in the game, he hadn't given the matter another thought. It had occurred to none of the card-players that the man failed to return and they all assumed he had gone to his bed after dealing with the sluice.

"But what he doesn't understand is how the wretched man managed to fall into the race," says Mr Poole to me. "He cannot believe a fellow like Buncombe should slip. Or, at least, he did believe it at first, but now he does not."

"What do you mean," says I. "And why are you telling me all this?"

"Because, Johnny, Rice now believes that Buncombe's death maybe related to the fact that you were passing at about the time he must have died." He held his hand up to prevent me from remonstrating. "You see, we were all congregated in the front parlour at the mill and Rice was blubbering and saying Buncombe would never slip. 'There's more to this than meets the eye, I'll be bound,' he was moaning. 'I'll wager a hundred guineas that someone or something put paid to poor old Giles...'

"With that, one of the mill workers pipes up and says: 'What about the Walfords? There was no love lost 'tween they and Mr Buncombe and they must 'ave bin passin' at the time...'"

"Well, that was enough for Rice. It did not take him long to find out that you and father were at the Castle of Comfort and that you'd have been passing the mill on your way home at about exactly the same time as Buncombe was out on the sluice. That is why I am here: because Mr Rice has demanded an investigation. I do not believe there is a shred of evidence to go on, but he is openly accusing you of murder!"

Now, all this time my mind had been racing over the events of the previous night. I had, I believe, displayed the appropriate show of shock upon hearing of the death, but underneath this exterior I was thinking how to react when and if such an accusation came my way. Perhaps it was due to my thick head, but I could conceive of nothing better to do than stutter and stammer with incredulity.

"I never saw Buncombe," I managed to say. "I have not seen him since the day he left my Master's employ. A day which I am sure you remember Mr Poole. You know that I have taken Buncombe's old billet at the estate, so I cannot see why I should want to murder him. Had it been the other way around – had Buncombe murdered me – then you could understand it. But I had no reason to wish him harm. And anyway, you know, we all know; the track up here leaves the valley road close to the mill. If you say Giles Buncombe had gone up to the sluice, then you will know that we could not possibly have passed him."

"Hmmm," mumbles Mr Poole. "You are aware, are you not, that there's a suspicion in the villages that Buncombe was responsible for your father's beating the other day?"

I shrugged: "I have been busy on the hills trying to catch up with father's work. I have talked to him about that accident and he has not mentioned any names, indeed, he cannot recall anything that happened. But Mr Poole, you know me well enough: are you suggesting that I would stalk Giles Buncombe and somehow have him dumped onto that wheel? I would have hoped, and believed, that you'd think better of me than that..."

Tom Poole looked into my eyes and nodded. "You are right," he said. "I do think a good deal more of you than that. Moreover, Giles Buncombe was not a man who would let himself be harmed without fighting back and you appear unscathed. No, I shall inform Rice that I am satisfied you had nothing to do with the death. You did not pass him on your way home and anyway, you had no motive."

"Mind you," he adds, bending forward and lowering his voice so that no-one else could hear. "I happen to know of your attachment to Miss Rice. I cannot imagine, given her father's suspicions, that he will ever sanction such a liaison now. Believe me Johnny, he seems to have some deep hatred of you - and if I were you I would be careful. He is a dangerous enemy to have."

After he had gone I went in to see father who seemed somewhat recovered after his night on the 'medicine'. He was immune from the sore head that cider can cause, indeed he was positively cheerful and, being an ungodly rogue who believed in what he called 'the old ways', he was greatly pleased to hear of Buncombe's death.

"Ee were a blackguard if ever I knew one," he chuckled. "None shall mourn 'is passin' but old Ricey - and only ee 'cos there's no-one else'll who'll join un wi' 'is knavery. As for you havin' ort to do wi' it - wull, us did come 'ome direct. You 'ad a sick man to look after. I tell thee what though Johnny," he said quietly, reaching over to touch my arm. "No father ever 'ad a son so good as you. There ain't many folk that'd stand up to Buncombe in a fight. I knows what you did and it must 'ave taken a fair bit o' courage. Now you must tell me about it, for I was loathe to bother ee last night."

So I told father the grim truth and he smirked with glee proclaiming it was nothing more than natural justice. "Don't ever get to feelin' guilty 'bout it boy," he said. "Giles Buncombe wouldn't have tried to save you if 'tad of bin t'other way around..."

I made father swear that he would never mention it to a soul - either in or out of his cups - and I do believe he kept his word. Only one other person was to find out, as you shall hear shortly. Later that morning I went to the hill to work and to think. Mother wanted me to stay at home to look after father while she and Petronilla attended church. She said they needed to pray after such an awful thing had happened here in the hills. But I needed the fresh air and the solitude of the moor to help me contemplate the vagaries of my rapidly changing fate. As I climbed through the woods I could almost feel my spirit shedding its cares, like lumps of mud that fall from a cart in sunshine that follows a storm. It has always been the same with me. The wide open space of the hill conjures a deep sense of aloneness and privacy and a man feels as though he can breathe and be free. Sometimes I have wondered if it is the intensity of light that you get on our southern hills, for up on the commons and high heaths, all is bathed in light some days. When I have spent too long charcoal-burning in the woods and have felt moody and depressed, all I needed to wipe away this ennui was a walk to the high tops.

Such was the case on this Sunday, the day after the nightmare of Buncombe's death. It was a difficult thing for me to comprehend and my nerves felt shaken. I found myself wishing time and again that he had managed to cling on and that somehow I had been able to save us both. But then, would he have thanked me? I doubt it. More like, he would have had me arrested for attacking him and used the whole affair to prove what an unwholesome scoundrel I was. Brooding, I set about my work, chopping at the broom with the enthusiasm of a real murderer. It was late afternoon when I saw Anne - the weak, misty sun was beginning to dip over the great rain-veiled shoulder of Exmoor and the iron-grey ocean beyond - and from the corner of my eye I spied her issue from the woods on that handsome little mare of hers. She must have been two miles away when I first spotted her, but she came cantering over the heath and I think she was still half-a-mile off when I spied some difference in her normally cheerful demeanour. Anne's face was fixed with angst, as became increasingly plain as she came clattering up side-saddle and slipped straight down into my arms...

"Oh Johnny," she gushes, holding me. "What is happening to us? What is going on? Father is in a terrible temper flinging oaths at anyone who should utter a word. He says he is sure that you had something to do with poor Mr Buncombe's death and he has thrown dear Mr Poole out of the house calling him a fool."

I tried to calm her, but she began to sob - I had never seen her cry before and was overcome by her despair. "It was horrible Johnny. Horrible, horrible. Mr Buncombe going around and around with his head floundering this way and that. No-one has ever seen anything so horrible. And to think, we used to joke and make stories about the spirit of the wheel. It made me shudder to recall I should ever have believed in such a thing. But there he was broken to pieces and white and dead. And the wheel kept spinning regardless, as if it had been waiting for someone all these years. It was our secret - that was how we used to think about that horrible ogre of the wheel, do you remember? And now father's insisting you are implicated in Mr Buncombe's death. Tell me you are not Johnny! Just tell me!"

Her sweet, tiny, angular face was streaked in tears and I could feel her slim body quivering with emotion. I had never lied to Anne before - nor anyone else that I could recall - but now I had no choice. For a fleeting moment I thought of telling her everything, but so horrified was she by what she had witnessed that morning, I knew I could never admit to having been a part of it. I simply wanted to protect her from the horror of the thing. And anyway, how does a young man tell his sweetheart that he has just murdered her father's best friend? I said her father must have lost some of his reason through being so upset. That I was completely innocent of such a charge. That I could not possibly have encountered the dead man on his way to or from the sluice as I had taken the left hand track up over the spur.

After a while she began to calm down and, as the rain was now falling heavily, I suggested we take shelter in the little hut on the edge of a nearby goyal. The Walfords had used it for centuries as far as I knew; it was our shelter on the top of the hills. Inside there was a bed of dry bracken, and we both fell upon it once we had crawled through the low opening. Close to her, I could smell the sweetness that emanated from her hair and clothes. So close that I could see the moisture on her lips - felt myself falling into the deep pools of her eyes. Then we were embracing passionately and I could feel all the emotions of the past few days seeping, rushing, away from my weary flustered soul. What cared I for anything, as long as I had Anne Rice in my arms?

"My darling Johnny," she whispers. "I have treated you so churlishly. With regards to my father, I mean. You must understand - he lost his wife while she was giving birth to me, and that I have always known it was my place, my role in life, not to be a disappointment to him. But now it has gone too far. I know that he will always stand in the way of our happiness, and I will not have it. I cannot live without you. We will marry Johnny, despite my father. I will tell him this very day, and he must make up his own mind in his own time. Likely I will be disinherited, but what care I when I can have my lover and best friend?"

I told her that I could provide for her and that Squire Crosse would see us situated comfortably on his estate. I told her that I loved and her and worshipped her more than anything that ever lived or breathed since the beginning to the end of time. For years we had wanted this. We had waited patiently and dreamed impossible dreams. Now it was happening. At first in a passionate struggle, and then slowly, as I came to know her in the way such love dictates. The sun came out and sent a shaft of pale light through the entrance and into the darkness of the hut. Her immaculate being caused me to catch my breath. I remember the delicious luxuriance of it all. Some part of me wanted to hasten into the wells of pleasure, but some ancient wisdom took over and our falling into the crucible of love was slow, and measured, and life-changing.

During these moments I lost all sense of who or where I was - but then there came a jolt. Somehow in that heavenly tussling we had lost most of our garment and I recall feeling a trifle embarrassed watching her eyes flitting across my body. But this self-consciousness of mine did not last for long. Neither did my ecstasy. Everything, every emotion of joy and love I had ever fostered, was shattered within the next few seconds.

"Johnny," gasped Anne raising herself to her elbows. "What are those marks?"

Idiot! Fool! I still curse myself for not thinking - my miserable lack of sense cost me so dear it is still almost impossible for me to imagine the implosion it would cause. The excited, headlong, rush to be with Anne in this intimate way had completely overridden any memories of the punishing fight. So wonderful were these moments with Anne, even killing a man paled to insignificance. Although I had suffered aches and pains all day from Buncombe's kicks and blows, I had forgotten the nightmare while basking in the loveliness of her embrace.

But there were the bruises, the welts and wheals, so plain to see in the beam of evening sunlight. Buncombe's boot had never come near my head so that, clothed, I looked unscathed. Unclothed, I was like a man who had been run over by half-a-dozen horses. I was looking down at my body, desperately thinking of something to say, and when I looked up Anne was pulling her clothes around her and peering at me in a way I'd never seen before.

Under her breath, as if she were trying her utmost to control violent emotion, she whispered hoarsely: "You have lied to me. To think that I was going to side with you against my own father. Deny it Johnny! Tell me that you have not been fighting. Tell me Giles Buncombe did not make those awful marks upon you. Say that you did not kill him - prove it to me!"

All my life I have been quick to find an easy answer. My tongue has come to my rescue a thousand times. Yet now, at this crucial juncture, it remained immobile. Not a word could I think to say. In a flurry Anne was pulling on her clothes and, slowly, I did the same. As she began to climb out of the hut I grabbed her shoulder, but she span away and said: "Never. Never will you touch me again John Walford."

"But I must to tell you how it happened," I cried. "I didn't really kill him - I tried to save him. You know me Anne, I am not the kind of man who has cruelty in his heart. That man died in the wheel, it was the Spirit of the Wheel that we used to speak of as children that did for him."

I whined and pleaded, but it was too late. The damage was done.

"Do you really think I could have anything to do with the man who murdered my father's best friend?" she raged. "And, if killing someone isn't bad enough - do you think I could remain in love with a man who lied to me and - worse still - was happy to see his lies cause a breach between me and my father?"

Now Anne was out of the hut and pacing toward her horse.

"I just wanted to protect you from the horrible truth." I entreated. "Your father and Buncombe were the men behind my own father's beating. They nearly did him to death. That is why I approached Buncombe - to speak with him - but he was having none of it. It was Buncombe who attacked me..."

But it was too late.

"You are a liar," she screamed as she mounted the mare. "You lie to turn me against my father. You lied about those stupid mites to cover your own inept tracks when you destroyed half the Squire's house. You are a liar and a murderer - if there is anything to be glad of - it is that I discovered it before I became your wife."

With that she was gone. All I could do was stand there in the thin drizzle watching the love of my life gallop away. There was no point chasing after her, I knew that. What she had said had blown me apart as surely as if I had been struck down by lightning. My mind raced, but no thoughts came out of it. Only overwhelming despair. I stood there on the hill bathed in the evening light and washed by a fine mist of rain. There seemed no point in bothering to take the next breath. But breathe I did. The will for survival is within us all, despite the calamities that tear us apart. And calamity this was. Is it worth describing my misery? I do not think so. I have not set out in this narrative with the purpose of gleaning sympathy. Moreover, I do not wish to relive those unhappy days or weeks when I kept to the hill and sulked morning until night and struggled fruitlessly to find the haven of sleep upon that bracken bed. I swear I could smell the scent of her in that tiny hut a month afterwards.

For a few days I was sure the militia would come marching across the heath with a warrant for my arrest. But Anne obviously did not speak of her discovery, I have never known why. There were times when I liked to think she still loved me, but more likely, I knew she could not possibly admit to the way in which she came about her knowledge. How could she talk to others of the bruises on my naked body?

I will ask this: has anyone heard of another man who has, at one moment, been so very close to heaven - only to find himself plummeting to hell within a single heartbeat? I think not. Fate is most often a long, grey, drawn-out affair. Perhaps my misfortune has something to do with my being a broomsquire - being a descendant of one of the ancient now almost extinguished peoples. Maybe we old hill folk were born under different stars. The fate of the Dumnonii was a different thing to a modern fate. Certainly, my own destiny has always flickered violently, cruelly, this way and that, like a candle guttering in a Quantock breeze. I cannot describe my grief during those days, but somehow I stuck it out there upon the empty heath which eventually began to sooth the burning sorrow which had completely and entirely overtaken me.

My unique form of broomsquire fate flickered and fluctuated again within a couple of days. For some time since my father's beating I had been intending to return to Fyne Court to arrange my affairs with Squire Crosse. But day by day I had put it off, for I was beginning to be unsure of my future. I was profoundly unhappy with the job of assistant factotum. It was dull and meant interminable hours spent indoors. Of course I had been enthusiastic when I thought I could convince Anne's father of my respectability, but there was no reason for that now. In some strange way I was resigned to my destiny and now it seemed to me that this lay in what had perhaps always been my real path: I was a broomsquire. I could not - could never - escape it. It was if every ounce of me was made for the life - I felt most real up there amid the heather and broom, as if God had somehow moulded me to it. Perhaps there was also a youthful anger smouldering deep within me. Why should I not stay there and at least breathe the pure air of Quantock rather than stifle under the weight of dockets and accounts?

My poor parents needed help, so I had been putting off the visit to Squire Crosse, but I believe, in those weeks of misery, I had made up my mind to ask him for a release. However, this visit to Fyne Court was not to materialise, for one grey afternoon the Squire came to me. I was working hard cutting and stacking the broom and didn't notice that he was standing just a couple of dozen feet away. I nearly jumped out of my skin when all of a sudden he moved and I saw him leaning with his chin perched upon that long stick of his. How long he had been in the spot I do not know, he was just standing there watching me at my work, and he looked quite content to go on doing so. I knew not what to say or do - no doubt because I was exhausted by the work and the sorry state of my nerves - so I simply sat down on the sward where I was. With this, the Squire comes striding across and he swings his bag over to land at my feet.

"Bread and cheese in there Johnny," he says cheerfully. "You look as if you could do with something inside you."

"I'm sorry Sir, not to have..." I began to say, but Mr Crosse cut me off: "No, no, no Johnny, do not concern yourself about either your Master or his Estate. It looked after itself all these years - it even survived the attentions of the unfortunate Buncombe. You have had to do what any loving son would wish to do - you must take as long as you like to put your family's affairs in order."

I opened the bag he'd thrown me and helped myself to the food inside - I was ravenous having not eaten for what seemed like days. Somehow, the Master's sudden unexpected appearance had brought about a feeling of reassurance in me, and my nervousness ebbed away.

"Have it all," he laughed. "You look quite a sight you know. I would have brought a sack of food had I known that you were starving yourself to death up here."

We sat in silence while I devoured great lumps of bread and cheese, but eventually the Squire spoke: "What think you Johnny? Do you feel at home up here in the remoteness of this place, or do you miss the Leyden Jars and Voltaic Piles of our beloved laboratory?"

"I do miss working with you Sir. You gave me the best education any country boy could ever have working with the experiments. But I cannot say that I miss the ledgers of the Estate Office – I am beginning to doubt that I was built for such work."

"Ah do you not? Do you not?" he repeated. "It is, in fact, why I have come to see you Johnny. I have heard certain things from Mr Poole apropos the miller's daughter Miss Rice. He met her yesterday, it seems, and she was in a most agitated state. You know don't you, that her father is going about the place accusing you of Buncombe's murder? Of course I know it is ludicrous nonsense, but the whole affair seems to have upset Miss Rice enormously and apparently she is going away to Bath for a rest-cure.

"When Mr Poole pressed her, Johnny," said the Squire nervously, "she seemed to infer that her friendship with you was over. She would not say why and Tom Poole can only conjecture that her father has had some influence over her. To tell you the truth, both Mr Poole and I had high hopes for this proposed marriage of yours. And so – well – I made up my mind to find you today to see how things are with you..."

I suppose I sat there looking morose. There was a long period of silence before he spoke again: "You see, I regard you as a friend Johnny, and have not come up here to pry. But I am concerned about you. I have been concerned since that wretched accident in the laboratory."

Again I said nothing, and so he continued: "I know you were pinning your hopes upon a marriage with Anne Rice. And I know that you were keen to take the job on the estate – if nothing else, but to impress that loutish father of hers. But where does this leave us now? You see, I must ask because my own intended has kindly consented to marry me – with a few set conditions that have been put in place by her father. One of them is that I should take on a fellow, known and trusted by them, as factotum of my estate. Her father has looked through the books and claims I have almost run Fyne Court into the ground and he, quite fairly I suppose, demands that from now on it must be managed properly. Now, I could be firm over this and insist that you must stay on, but it comes down to this: if you want the post then you must tell me now, for I shall have to put up a fight."

I looked around at the big grey hills. The sun had broken through somewhere far out over the ocean and its beams were spilling down upon the sea like angel's wings. Far to the north I could see a small herd of deer moving cautiously from one coombe to the next. A buzzard wheeled high overhead and mewed its sad cry across an empty world.

"The fact is Sir, I am sorely heartbroken," is how I began. "Since I was a boy I dreamed and planned to spend my life with Anne, and for all those years she seemed to feel the same of me. But now it is over, and I am cast adrift. Much though I loved the work in the laboratory, and all the science I have learned from you - and though I have truly admired you, Sir, and been glad of your many kindnesses to me - I must ask you to release me from my position on the Estate. My father's health has been badly set back and my family have need of me. I know that I could bring them with me to Broomfield, but living in a cottage would kill my father. He is a broomsquire through and through. And that, of course, is what I am. The last of the broomsquires. It has been my fate, and in some strange way, I feel as though I must follow this destiny, whether I should wish to or not. Perhaps you will feel I am letting you down - certainly no other youth in the county would behave in this way. But they are not broomsquires - and I, Sir, I am lured inexplicably to the hill."

I turned to look at him and was struck by the sadness on his face. I concluded my little speech: "I could never feel comfortable at that indoor work, Sir, though I thank you from the bottom of my heart. My lot - I think - is to be out here where my ancestors have dwelt since time began."

Now it was the Squire's turn to be silent. At last though, he looked at me and said: "Since I first set eyes upon you Johnny, I knew I was beholding something apart from the normal run of man. There is indeed a wildness about you. And - I will say though perhaps I shouldn't - a majesty. Something alluring - and yet in some strange way, almost wild - even dangerous, perhaps. You know, do you not, that you have a remarkable natural intelligence and aptitude - indeed, it has never ceased to startle me. But the way you are - they way you move and speak - has some substance to it that is unlike the stuff of ordinary folk. In a way, I have sometimes wondered if you don't have the pure blood of some nobler aristocracy."

For the first time during our conversation he smiled the warm grin that I knew and loved so well: "I know of no-one else who would make the decision you have today. To give up a sought-after position, the security of it - the respectability - power over your fellow men. And all for what? A furzey hut upon a furzey down. A hard life eking out a subsistence living. Most men would say that you are not quite right in the head. But I am not so sure."

Now he caught me by the arm and I was surprised to see tears welling in his eyes: "Let me say this my friend," he murmured gently. "I have loved you in the same way that an elder brother might be fond of his young sibling. I will even say to you that I have never felt more close to another man, and doubt if I ever shall. I shall miss our adventures together – until, perhaps, the day arrives when I must return to the old life of science and research. Then I will come to the hill looking for you Johnny. Do you hear me? One day I shall come for you and once again we shall collect the thunder and the lightning and seek the questions and answers that lurk at the heart of our universe..."

I told him, most solemnly, that I would look forward to that time. We shook hands and I watched him disappear across the heath until he was a mere dot moving along the side of Lydeard Hill. We may have hailed from entirely different backgrounds – he was of the gentry while I was not even an agricultural labourer – and yet I can say that, apart from Tom Poole, Andrew Crosse was probably the best friend I ever had. Had certain events not occurred, then I believe the two of us may still be working with conductors and capacitors to this very day.

Now began a curiously joyful period of my life. That may seem difficult to believe given the misery of my parting with Anne, but once I had come to the decision with Mr Crosse, it seemed that many old tethers drifted away and were dissolved. My desire for respectability no longer overshadowed me and, reviewing my lot, I was glad that I had not been forced to spend my life with ledgers and accounts. Of course I was miserable about Anne, but would I ever have been truly happy trapped in the furnishings of dismal propriety?

As I believe I may have mentioned, it has been my good fortune to inherit a naturally joyous frame of mind. Some people take each and every turn of their existence with a pinch of suspicion and negativity; some merely shrug with the acceptance of it all; and yet others laugh and see the ridiculous side to life. I am of the latter clan. To me our existence is but a thread woven of beauty and tears. He who stumbles and falls in the mud may go forth feeling sorry for himself – he may have broken an arm or a leg, he may even have lost some precious jewel in the swamp – but he is alive. To my way of thinking, if you are alive then everything is well with your world. An obvious thing for a condemned man to say, I suppose; but I have always thought like it.

By the time I had collected enough broom for the annual tour of the villages, the hard work and fresh air, mixed with my natural disposition had allowed me to bury my sorrows and lock them away somewhere in the deepest parts of my soul. It was a fine Spring, and an even finer early Summer, and by the time the brooms were ready for selling there were few shadows left to haunt me. Anne, as I had heard, had taken herself to the city of Bath on the other side of the county and so my deep wounds were never opened by our accidentally meeting in the lane. Her father, no doubt, still bore his hatred of me and this was proved one night at the Castle of Comfort Inn. Fortunately, on this occasion, I had no need to lift a finger to protect myself – though it was obviously an attempt to lure me into danger...

We had been visited by the gypsy folk who travel up and down to goodness knows where across our peninsula. Most village folk were afraid of these dark people and blamed them for all sorts that they did not do, but my father loved them and so they called upon us two or three times a year. He said they were of a very different ancestry, but in some ways their lot was similar to that of the broomsquires. They too, he said, had always been forced to live on the edge of things. He liked them also because of a mutual love of horses and ponies. My father was a genius with hooved creatures and he could train a pony to do just about anything he wished. He would buy them from the gypsies, school them for harness or whatever, then sell them on to the village folk. Except for Eskie, of course. She was special and father would not have parted with her for all the oak groves on Quantock.

This night Britannia French – the woman they called The Queen of the Gypsies – had come by and set up camp next to our own in order to do some horse dealing. It was more than that: word had reached her – God knows how – that my father had been attacked and might die. She was most pleased to find him alive. He was in fact in rude health compared with the way he had been. Nothing cheered father more than the sudden and unexpected appearance of the gypsies. Britannia French travelled the world with a small tribe of her people – perhaps a dozen or so men and their assorted wives and offspring – and so it was quite an occasion when she turned up with her caravanserai. From the tiniest tot to the oldest wrinkled fellow, they were a motley looking crew. Dark and fiery-eyed, some people thought they were intolerably shifty, but when you looked at them and forgot the layers of wood-smoke, you saw as handsome a bunch of people as you could wish to meet. In fact Britannia was forever trying to marry me off to one of her lithe and comely daughters, but although I had all sorts of jovial times with them, I was never quite persuaded to fall for one. In the same way, I heard later, father had never become involved with the mother – with the Queen of the Gypsies herself – though I suspect there may once have been something between them.

He told me once: "Can thee think o' it – a mix o' their wild blood and ours? I should not like to father such a creature, and if I 'ad a done so, I should 'ave left for the Indies or some far place."

The night of their arrival we went to the Castle of Comfort, and I saw at first hand what he meant by this curious statement. I had not been out in what passed for society for a long while, and had arranged to meet one or two of my friends from the village so that I could do some business or other. Because of this I went on down to the Inn early leaving father and Britannia talking horses, promising that they would follow on later, for the Gypsy Queen liked her cider well and could drink it down like a man. Anyhow, I was strolling down through the woods and, as usual, had to walk right past the mill. As I did so Mr Rice came up the lane bouncing around on his trap with his two horses going at a rapid trot, and I had to stand aside to let him pass. Normally a man of my lowly position would have been expected to doff his cap, but I was blowed if I would greet that old devil in any way at all. Instead I looked directly at him with an angry look in my eye, and he did not like it, that was for sure. He quickly looked away and gee'd his pair into a canter. As he passed I could see two emotions mixing themselves up in his pallid, twitching face. Hatred and fear. If I recall right enough, the latter was getting the better of the former. Old Rice was scared of me when it was just a case of man to man. I knew that, in that instant in the lane. Perhaps he thought I'd chuck him in the leat so he could end his days spinning on the wheel like his friend. And maybe one day, I thought to myself, I would. Once safely inside his gate he turned to look at me again, and this time the fear had gone from his face and loathing had taken its place fair and square.

Now, to my knowledge the Nurcotts, who had been implicated in my father's beating, had never darkened the doors of any hostelry. Indeed they never mixed socially with anyone at all. But they did that night. Much to everyone's surprise the door of the Castle of Comfort saloon bar opened, and in walked the three mooncalves. They made no pretence as to why they were there. After paying for cider they simply stood in the middle of that dark and dusky room and stared at me with all the menace they could muster. Which was a lot, because this was a family that dined on malice and very little else. I had no doubts that the miller had sent them to deal with me. Having seen me in the lane in the evening, he would have been pretty sure of my destination.

The aggression and sheer hostility sat on Old Man Nurcott's face as if it were a metal helmet. His look reminded me of the expression worn by Buncombe just before he died, but this ugly show of anger was not there for long. The door opened again and this time my father hobbled in, followed by Britannia French and four or five of the gypsy men. Their entrance caused an electricity to flow around the room – there was no doubt of that – you could have heard a harvest mouse in the wainscoting. Britannia, who had been in a thousand fights and scenes from Dorchester to Penzance, immediately seized upon the frozen atmosphere that held the place in its grip.

The Queen of the Gypsies was a big woman. She was as tall as me and I dare say as strong. I have arm-wrestled with her once and her colossal strength cost me dear. Her face was almost as lined as Mud-Horse-Montague's and her hands were huge brown things that looked as if they were made of leather. Her eyes were dark, gleaming orbs that were set far too deep in her head. When those twin orbs looked at you in a certain way, you could not help but to feel some fear. She ordered cider for herself and drank a quart of it back like a man who has been harvesting all day. Beads of the apple juice ran down her jowls and onto the black shawls and overcoats that she habitually wore. The Nurcotts began to look distinctly uncomfortable and, as my father approached them, their discomfiture turned to ghastly alarm...

"Last time we met," father said, as he sidled up to Old Man Nurcott. "I reckons the odds wuz ass over tit."

As I say, Britannia French seemed somehow acutely aware of the tension in the place and suddenly she was at father's side. "What be you'm sayin' old friend?"

"What do you think I be saying Nurcott?" asks my father, putting his face an inch or two from the agitated man.

The old curmudgeon looked apoplectic with fear while his sons, who had no idea of the danger they were in, were a very portrait of wrath. They did not know the Queen of the Gypsies. Derry, the idiot, brought out a knife and, in a flash, lunged it at my father's throat. I jumped, but I need not have been concerned. It never got anywhere near to him. A great leathery hand reached out and I heard Derry's arm go snap. Then another leather hand struck out and chopped his brother in the throat, lifting him off his feet and sending him flying towards the door. Britannia French then placed both of her giant hands on the jacket of Old Man Nurcott. She lifted him from the stone-flags and carried him to the wall where he remained aloft, shaking and spluttering.

"Take your boys 'ome and think yerself lucky I be in a good frame o' mind," she said. "Next time I hear's of you botherin' any o' my friends, I shall 'ave yer throats out. All three of ee..."

Mother and Petronilla worked hard getting the brooms ready and with father's help I prepared for the annual rounds that would take us across hill and dale to the villages and hamlets of West Somerset. I had enjoyed a few of these trips when I was a boy, but thanks to my employment at the Court, had given our family's commercial activities no thought for years. Soon I was to learn that commerce was the least of it. Father used these rounds of his, selling the brooms to the housewives and servants of the farms and larger homes, to augment his social life. It was as if the loneliness of his calling compelled him to spend a month or two each year upon a whirl of human intercourse. He chatted to everyone we met. He flirted outrageously and boozed long into the night with old friends he had not seen since the year before. He had a way with women, though perhaps I shouldn't say it. Although he was now quite crippled and confined over long distances to riding on the cart, he still insisted on passing the time of day with the good wives wherever we went. Whether they were young or old he would flirt with them. Maidens indeed, of all shapes and sizes seemed enamoured by his attentions. From pale faced parlour girls to ruddy cheeked milkmaids, from the churners of butter to buxom cooks, from weary looking woodlanders to shy and winsome widows; all responded to his easy charm and the suggestive glint in his eye. I was embarrassed by this unashamed womanising, but said nothing for I sometimes wondered how long he was destined to last upon this earth and thought the old rogue probably deserved his portion of good cheer.

He had been elated by the news that I was to quit Fyne Court.

He claimed he knew the broomsquire in me would out in the end, and for weeks busied himself organising our summer tour around that region of the shire where we would sell the brooms.

"T'as been my desire to 'ave my boy wi' me on the rounds since thee were a tiny child. And now at last ye shall come along and learn the byeways of the country we do hold."

Father talked as if these rounds were ours by some God-given right which had passed down to the Walfords, but as we were the last broomsquires operating from the hill, I doubted it really mattered where we went. At first I objected to the idea that he should accompany me thinking he was too frail, but mother took me to one side and told me it was for the best.

"It will mean so much to him Johnny. He is so proud of you and would like nothing more than to show you the rounds."

Later I would wonder how much she knew of the wanton side of his life. Later still I learned that she simply blocked all knowledge of it from her mind. Gentle, home-loving mother did not want to hear of his rovings, and she must have sealed herself from it well because I was soon to find that father had an astonishing reputation.

"Lock up yer wives - here comes the Broomsquire!" was a cry I often heard. But it generally seemed to be spoken in jest because the fellows would always laugh and shake my father's hand. How he managed it I do not know, but the old rascal seemed to have a woman at every port of call. I would sleep under the cart during these travels of ours, while he would fix himself up in a sort of tent that he'd devised from the sails of some long lost ship that had wrecked on the coast. Many a time in the middle of the night I awoke to hear sounds emanating from that den of his. I have seen the most respectable women sidle into that flapping little home. In the morning he would show no shame, he cared not a fig whether I had witnessed his debauchery or not. How he got away with it, I do not know, but I was soon to find out why he remained so popular with the men...

The basic way the rounds worked went like this: we would set out with Eskie pulling our little cart full of brooms, and we would take a route through a particular corner of the shire – say from Brompton Ralph to Dulverton. We would spend half a day getting there and half a day selling before setting up our camp on the outskirts of some hamlet or village. We would then cook supper having bought, or been given, some morsel at a farm, or having poached a rabbit or a bird or two – then we would inevitably repair to the local inn. Here father would come into his own. Everyone seemed to know him, but to break the ice he would take along the battered old violin he was so adept at playing. His fingers literally danced up and down the neck of this woeful instrument and within seconds you could watch people's feet begin to tap upon the floor. The sound of father's remarkable playing could transform the mood of a village in an instant. Many a surly crew have I seen cast under the spell and it was a remarkable metamorphosis to watch: from mono-syllabic, bucolic, wretchedness to wild, dancing, jollity in the space of a minute or two - that was the form it took. His music ranged from a crazed rhythmic wildness that inspired in every person who heard it a craving to dance - to sombre, beautiful, dirge-like, ethereal airs and melodies that brought tears and sensations of distant, gracious, sad, bitter-sweet, joy to all but the stony deaf.

He also told stories. I soon discovered that he was famed for it - indeed I do not recall entering an inn where, sooner or later, some old associate of his would not call for one of father's yarns. I have watched mean-hearted tradesmen reduced to tears by the softness of his voice. I have seen rough, unimaginative yokels jump with fear as they listened to some tale of ghastly horror unfold. I have witnessed him silence a saloon bar packed with some hundred souls - just a few moments after having spurred them to dance like mad things to the music of his old violin.

In short, he was an entertainer. When the folk of a village got to hear the broomsquire was at large, they crowded the place where they knew he would be - which was more often than not the local inn. I don't believe I ever saw the old man purchase a drink of his own, for his arrival seemed to prompt some sort of unofficial, unheralded, annual party. The same would apply whether we were visiting a small, remote hill-top hamlet or one of the larger market villages. As we went from cottage to cottage, from farm to farm, the question was always asked: would he be in the village that night? I do not know why they bothered to ask for he was always bound for an inn. But not before selling the questioner a broom or two. Indeed, he rarely failed to make a trade at the door of a cottage or a house.

The arrival of the broomsquire was something like Christmas in the lonely country places; woman and children would use the occasion as an excuse to come to the inn where at normal times they were rarely to be seen. There were occasions, when a place was too small or crowded, when father would lead an entire community out onto the village green or some such place for dancing and merry-making. It was as if, for some of those people, he were a kind of soothsayer, necromancer or charmer. One who came but once a year. Word would go around and all the men of the village who played a musical instrument would turn up with their piece freshly polished, eager to join father in the minstrelsy, as they had done year in year out since any of them could remember.

He loved it. He knew each and every one of them and he knew their strengths and weaknesses, their passions and their favourites. He would bow courteously, for instance, to Wilfie Westlake the viola-playing butcher and – with a sweeping gesticulation of his hand – set the rotund red-faced man off into some ecstatic solo that he had been practising all year. The crowd would cheer and eventually, back my father would come at twice the pace. Then there'd be an even bigger hurrah. So it would go on – a man with a serpent-pipe would leap to his feet and play that resonant horn as if his life depended on it. Young fellows would try to outdo the old broomsquire for speed on their violins and he would let them catch up a while before accelerating unrelentingly onwards into some mad musical region of his own. This he would often punctuate with odd yelps and outlandish utterances that seemed to add an inexplicable spice of danger and barbarism to the proceedings. But none of it was so mad that he would leave his listeners and dancers behind or in any way alienate them; somehow they seemed caught up in the magic and mystery of it.

I recall one evening when I stood on a church wall between two huge dark yews and looked down upon the village green that was filled with folk dancing in the gloaming. A distant storm was brewing somewhere up by Exmoor's coast and I could see the sheet lightning and hear the deep rumbles of distant thunder. Not a soul in the crowd seemed to take any notice of this as they were transfixed by the man who stood in a single lantern's light in their midst. It was father, contorting and twisting his much bruised body as he sent that bow flying across those venerable strings. The faster he went the faster they danced. The more complex and aberrant his scales and rhythms, the more they cheered him on.

A learned gentleman friend of Mr Crosse's who saw it once said to me: "In the far countries they would call your father a shaman. He is a magician who knows of things that others do not. That music he is playing: it is the music of the mountains, the euphony of the streams, the diapason of the forest. I have never heard anything more beautiful."

I have to say that the gentleman had taken a good deal of laudanum at the time, but I had a feeling I knew what he meant.

To end these hypnotic and sensational gushings of harmony and song, father would cease playing at, what at times, seemed like an annoyingly inappropriate moment. Suddenly, when you were least expecting it, he would whirl about and stamp his foot and stop. In time I began to see his trick. The music of the jig is a wonderful thing but it must surely end. I have seen musicians, carried away with themselves, play until they drop, or at least until their fingers are so weary they begin to make mistakes. Father never did this, he believed in the abrupt termination of his melody – and in the dramatic effect that it always seemed to have. There would be a moment's silence as the crowd accustomed itself to having its very lifeblood so instantaneously withdrawn. And then there would be a roar of applause, peppered with shouts for more – or sometimes with demands for one of father's famous tales.

As for these, word would get around and, before we reached a village, folk would know if there were some new anecdote worth hearing, or whether they should ask for an old favourite that they'd heard before. On this first trip of ours, I was amazed to hear father's account of the death of dear old Marmaduke, our friend who made it his curious business to wander across the hills with a herd of phantom cows. I can tell the story hastily enough now, but to hear father's rendition of it would have even the most unimaginative spirit in tears and, I am told, cause sleepless nights among the most dull of folk.

Poor old Marmaduke suffered a sorry end. He would, each and every Sunday afternoon, cross over to the distant village of Monksilver where his ancient mother had lived forever and a day at a broken-down farm. Why he did not live there with her and help look after the place I do not know – there was no reason for him to be on Quantock save to look after that ghost herd of his. I imagine he could have done that anywhere. On this particular Sunday some youths from Monksilver had bated the cowherd, telling him that Old Nick himself had been seen on the lonely path that they knew he must return along that night. On that path to Bicknoller, they said, the Evil One manifested himself in the form of an indistinct white cloud of floating venom, and that Marmaduke was sure to see him. Poor fellow knew no better but to take the threat seriously. Soberly enough indeed to fetch a scythe from his mother's outbuildings and spend the afternoon sharpening it on a stone. That night he crossed the hill and, by a stile on the common by Capton, he was duly startled by an awful apparition. A great white shape came out of the dusk at him, making a noise dreadful enough to turn blood to water – awful enough for Marmy to take a swipe at it with his sharpened scythe. The thing staggered and shrank to the ground and slowly turned from white to red. Two youths came out from behind the hedge and, seeing what had happened, took to weeping and a-wailing as they ran off across that lonely moor. Marmaduke had taken the head clean off their friend. It was only a prank, but it had gone very badly wrong – that was what the judge said at the inquest. Marmaduke was free to go home and see to his troublesome cows, but instead he went straight to the place by Capton where he had killed the boy and was found next morning, slumped across the stile, stone cold dead.

Now, I have told this story straight enough, but you would hardly recognise the tale the way father told it that summer. Listening to him you could hear the noise the scythe made as it cut through the sheet and decapitated the luckless youth. You could see the phantom cows and you could imagine Marmy's horror as he realised what he had done. Father even added the dubious fact that the cow-herd had now turned into a phantom himself and was to be seen forever scurrying this way and that on the desolate heath behind Capton. There are always plenty of hares up there, but to hear father tell it, the one that you would see was bound to be Marmy. The cow-herd would haunt the place with his sorrows forever.

"I 'ave seen un dancin' on the old stone circle that the ancient ones put there long afore Christ came to Earth. Up on 'is back feet ee were – dancin' for the sadness of lost youth."

For some time father would have been sending his bow slowly across the strings as he spoke, and the music had, in its own enchanting way, described fearful, solitary, barren places; it had depicted fear and trepidation, apprehension and dread. But now, as he spoke of the dancing hare, so the bow would leap into a jig and father would be off. So too would the crowd, glad to be dancing again after the terrible places they had been.

That summer I became a man in more ways than one. And the one way I'm thinking about right now was in a hay-rick on top of one the little hillocks that circle the village of Luccombe, in Porlock Vale. The girl was as fresh an apple as any youth has ever plucked from the well-laden branch of life. We knew each other's nakedness deep in that warm, sweet hay and for the first time I felt the luxuriant fervour and intensity of a woman wrapped against my own flesh. It was incomparable to anything that I had imagined. More vigorous and ardent. I was surprised and delighted by the unearthly noises she cried out into the night. She crept away to return to her father's cottage just before dawn and when, much later I awoke in that sweet-smelling hay, a rush of contradictory emotions swept through me. There was a glowing delight and pride, and there was deep regret that the girl had not been Anne Rice.

The lass from Luccombe was not the only girl that summer. Until then I had assumed that women were shy creatures likely only to bestow their favours on a man with great reluctance. I had been wrong. I'm ashamed to say it now, but there were married women and fair young maidens alike. Indeed, seeing that I am about to die for my sins I may as well admit that I preferred the former. With a married woman there were few complications. They wanted something from you – for a reason I could never quite comprehend – and they would go about it with no strings attached. No question of becoming a sweetheart, no question of marriage, no question of love. I preferred it like that. Why? Because, of course, I was still in love. Perhaps I was angry too – maybe still trying to show something, I know not exactly what – to the distant unseen Anne Rice. For I have always been in love with her – and when other girls sought to take or win my heart with words of love I was always left with feelings of guilt or remorse. There is no doubt that I used those happy maidens for my own selfish ends, but in my defence – such that it is – I will say that I never once promised any one of them anything more than a fleeting bout of... Something. Joy maybe. Excitement probably. But only ever fleeting. I am sure there are many who will be appalled by what I have said. But it could not have been a plainer truth: I never had to go out of my way to seduce an innocent damsel or a married woman; the act was usually of their making. As for adultery, I talked to my father about it one red-faced day and he simply laughed and told me that it was the wildness of our blood that these women liked. He said they lived dull lives and that they were married to dull, unimaginative men. What mattered it, in the greater scheme of things, if a rogue broomsquire spread a little excitement and sensuality among the woman of the countryside? I suppose that with this fatherly blessing, I continued upon my merry way unchecked by moral reticence. I have little else in the way of excuses to offer.

These escapades, along with the drunken revels lasting late into the summer nights, became the flavour of that happy season. Not since I was a small boy did I ever feel closer to my father. I certainly learned more about him than I had ever known, and I believe that we became more than father and son: we became firm friends and I rejoice to think I was given this last opportunity to know him truly. He told me tales of his youth and gave me lessons on the violin, so that we would sit for hours in the midday heat in some shady nook - with me making a wretched noise upon the strings. It must have been an abuse to his ears, but he persevered and made me do the same. Through that perseverance I can play, but my prowess on the instrument is nothing to his genius. Mine is the crude sawing of a country-boy - his was the lively, moving flight of a virtuoso.

As I say, I am glad that we had these many happy hours together that summer before he passed away. Looking back, I believe he knew that he was soon to die, for he spent every single minute living his life to the absolute full. And, once we had returned from our travels, he treated mother with more kindness and gentility than I'd ever seen in him before. As August turned into September he would insist that she, Petronilla and I would sit around the evening fire with him and listen to his yarns about the broomsquires of old. Constantly he would praise mother whenever he could. As for Petronilla, it was his usual habit to tease her relentlessly, but now he spoke only in the most kindly terms to her, and I know the poor girl could barely comprehend how to take his new found affection.

Then one morning father went for a walk on the hill while the rest of us were about our early chores, and no person ever saw him alive again. It was the end of September and it had been one of those golden autumn days when the temperature is cool but the sky is of an unblemished blue from horizon to horizon. Father had been particularly quiet during the early morning and, eventually had come to each one of us to mention he was off for a walk on the hill. I remember now that he stood watching me as I prepared some wood for the charcoal-burning. For ten minutes he just stood there without saying a word. I regret that I did not take more notice of him for I know now that he was saying his goodbye. He turned and the last I saw of him he was flitting through the dark wood in that effortless way of his. Even so close to his end, father had more grace in his broken old body than most do in the prime of their youth.

By evening he had not returned and the three of us were in alarm. I told Petronilla to go to the inn to see if he was there and, if not, to collect some friends to help search for him. I was sure he would be on the hill and went there telling mother to stay at home in case he returned. I do not know what drew me toward Staple Plain. It is the high hill situated at the seaward end of the Quantocks – from it you can look west toward the Atlantic Ocean and the setting sun. Near the top a few old remains are strewn about the place; they are the graves of the ancient ones. It was on the side of one of these barrows that I found him. At first I thought he was merely sitting there wrapped in the big blue cape which is worn by all broomsquires, watching the glorious sunset, but as I drew closer I realised that there was something wrong from the way he was slumped and the awkward position of his head. He was quite cold, but his eyes were open and there was what looked like a smile upon his face. I sat down next to him and wept as the great red orb dipped slowly into the sea, and the vastness of West Somerset far below grew dark in the shadows of the coming night. The West alone was bathed in light. The West, the last refuge, the last home of the ancient folk. My father had come up here to die, of that I was sure.

I wept for him, and I wept for the void that his passing had left. I wept for me. Inside there was a boy who was not ready to be a man. This great man, this cold dead thing by my side, he had been that for me. But now he was gone and I would have to carry on along the great journey alone. I would have to be the last broomsquire. That is what he had said at supper the night before. He said: "My son, I feel sorry for thee, for I shall be leavin' this mantle for you when I be dead and gone. The last broomsquire. But when 'tis your turn to go, who will thee turn to? I worry 'bout that my boy, for there must always be one o' us on Quantock's furzey heath."

Had I stayed with Squire Crosse then my father would have been the last broomsquire. But now it was me. Sitting there watching the sun go over the edge of the sea, I wondered if I too would have someone to carry on the tradition. Only in such a way is life fully bearable: to see one's own seed come to fruit and to know that fruit shall go forth. I was this dead man's seed and, in me, he still had life beyond the grave.

I sat there until Flighty Chidgey came cantering up on his big bony old nag, and I asked him if he'd kindly fetch a spade from his brother in Weacombe which is a hamlet in the coombe far below that lonely height. He had returned by the time mother arrived with Petronilla and the rest of them. Poor little Nilla wept, but mother remained quite placid as she gently closed her husband's eyes. I said that someone should ride home to collect his violin as I thought it should be buried alongside him, but mother told me she had just found it placed inside my bed. He had put it there in the morning for me to have. Father knew many strange things, and he knew he would die that day.

Some of them tried to stop me burying him, and one or two said he should be put in the graveyard. But father never went to church in his life and did not believe in the Christian God. Instead he believed in the ancient things and was closer to the Dumnonii who were now just piles of dust in the barrows at our feet. And so I buried him there among them that night – and the last time I set eyes on him he was in that shallow grave, at peace in his blue cape, under old Green's lantern-light. I wrenched up a big stone and erected it above my father, and there it stands to this day should anyone wish to see it and pay their complements to the old rogue. What was it Squire Crosse's friend called him? A shaman. A necromancer. A womaniser and a charmer would be equal truth. I loved the man and, if I have any solace concerning my own demise, it is that I shall be joining him sooner than I would have liked.

Mr Poole came to us twice in the next couple of weeks. Once to commiserate and see if there was anything he could do to aid my grieving mother, and once to bring me a letter. It was from Anne and I still have it somewhere. It was a sympathetic missive, formally expressing her regrets over father's death. She said that she had always liked him: no matter how miserable her mood, he had always been able to make her smile.

She ended the letter thus: "I suppose we are all sent our crosses to bear. I know that you loved your father dearly and that you will be missing him sorely from the bottom of your heart. Life and death are outside of our control, as I grow older I realise that with more certainty, and with an increasing sense of apprehension. Our own destiny was cast asunder by a man's passing, was it not? Although I could never forgive you for what you did, my anger mellows - as time must surely mellow everything. My life is here in Bath now, where I have been most fortunate to find employment as governess in the house of a great family. But often I think of you as I go about this busy town, and have my own images of you wandering free out there on the empty hills. When those thoughts come to me Johnny, they bring with them great sadness over what may have been. Now, with the passing of your father, such thoughts are sadder still and all

I can pray is that God will send you fortitude and courage to face the coming days, and that he will eventually bring you some happiness in your life.

Yours in deepest sympathy

Anne Rice."

I didn't know what to make of the letter - for a while I felt great joy that Anne appeared to have in some way forgiven me. But after a day or two I was left feeling very barren indeed. It did nothing more than underline the fact that I had lost her. I had lost my dear father. I had lost the woman that I loved. And I was not yet twenty years of age.

The winter that followed was a long hard one. Snow came early at the end of October and often I rued the day that I'd left Mr Crosse's employ - especially when I heaved my way out of a warm bed to see to the charcoal kilns in the middle of a freezing night. By January the hot pleasures of the previous summer seemed less real than a distant dream. Sometime during the middle of that month came a colossal dump of snow and our huts were almost covered with the stuff. Great drifts made even short journeys almost impossible. There was one giant drift just under the ridge by Dowsborough that was a high as a house. Our normal work was out of the question, it was merely a matter of survival up there on the hill. More than one wild deer found its way into our pot, and there was no difficulty in keeping the meat: hung up in a sack outside it simply froze into a solid block. We were warm enough with our fire and ready supply of chopped wood. If we wanted extra heat when the blizzards blew in from the frozen east, then I'd chuck on a shovel or two or charcoal which raised the temperature inside the hut quickly enough.

But as we came into February the situation worsened. By Candlemass it was so cold that you could walk over the great drifts without sinking an inch. Everything was coated in ice. By then I was weary of my mother's company and constantly exasperated by my sister - so one freezing morning when there was not a cloud in the sky, I decided to strike out for the beach where perhaps Monty might have some fish. Not only was I bored, but I was wholeheartedly weary of the diet of meat, for we had run out of just about all other supplies save for a firkin or two of cider. Our flour had long gone, but we knew there was no good in us going to the mill - Rice would never have sold us an ounce.

The journey down to Kilve was easier than I had supposed,

thanks to the icy crust which now capped the soft snow. Where once I would have had to find a gate or a stile to pass through a hedge, I now simply walked directly across the top of it as if it wasn't there. In the village I managed to purchase a few supplies, though in truth they were all badly short of necessities. It was the worst winter anyone had known for years and the road through to Bridgwater had been closed for weeks. It was the same on the other side of the hills. Only the high ridge road was in any way open, and that only to the hardiest and most desperate of men. Up there the great winds had whipped the snow off the exposed ridge, except in places where it built up into impassable drifts.

The people of Kilve may have been happy to welcome a new face, for none had seen a stranger for more than twenty days, but you could tell the mood of the place in a trice. The folk were gloomy and worried. There would have to be a thaw soon otherwise things looked as if they might get desperate. Winter crops were ruined and there was going to be a late start to sowing that spring. Even Montague was more forlorn than usual, which was saying something as his natural disposition was one of sorrow. It was the first time he could remember the sea freezing, and he took me down the shore to where great slabs of ice creaked and groaned among the rocks. The main body of sea, of course, was free of this ice, but it was where the water met the rocks and mud that large sheets had formed.

"Ruined me nets," wailed the strange old man. "I were lucky to get most of 'em in afore it took on too bad. What I caught lately 'as come from lines and even then I lost a few o' they."

But he seemed cheered at my arrival as he had a scheme which he said should see us laden with fresh fish. About halfway between high and low tide marks Monty kept a boat. He once told me that the Quantock shore was the only place in the world where such boats existed: as there were no harbours you had to allow these hardy vessels to sink under the waves for their own protection. Monty called his boat a "flatty" because of its thick, flat bottom. In this was a bung which you pulled out before filling the hull with rocks. The tide would come in and the craft would stay firmly, and safely, where it was until the tide receded again.

Monty rarely used this boat of his as he proclaimed a hearty dislike of the sea, but he kept it, he said, as a matter of honour. All longshore fishermen in these parts had a "flatty" – but Monty's vessel was only put to sea when someone else was willing to take the oars. And there it was - full of rocks, until we emptied it. The old man shoved in the bung, and with much heaving on my part (and much cursing on Monty's) we dragged the heavy vessel across the mud and ice to the sea. We could have waited for the tide to rise, but Monty showed me an ominous looking build-up of cloud far to the West, saying the job was best done before that lot came home to roost. Once in the boat I headed for a gut of water between two pavements of rock which had not been frozen thanks to the input of a stream. The water coming from some nearby underground spring must have been just warm enough to escape the ice, and it was Monty's conjecture that this wide gut would be full of fish. My job was to row out and lay the net across its mouth, conveying one end to him where he'd be waiting on one of the promontories. His scheme was a simple one: having sealed this channel we would both march slowly land-ward on either side of the gut, heaving the net with us until we had scooped everything onto the little mud beach at the end. It was a great success. So many fish were there that it took four trips on the mud horse to bring them all to Monty's hut. I left him up to his elbows in fish-guts as he prepared fillet after fillet for the smoking chimney. Not that you needed to preserve them in those low temperatures - even an oily fish would have lasted weeks in that big freeze.

But now the temperature had risen just slightly, and that was a bad sign. The huge black clouds we'd seen building far on the horizon were now close by and both Monty and I knew it meant more snow. It looked bad, which is why I found myself scampering back up the track towards the village as fast as I could go under the great weight of fish I was carrying in my sack. I was nearly at the top of Pardlestone Lane and just turning left to cross over by Alfoxden Park when I saw her.

I curse that day. I curse Montague for his fishing. I curse the villagers who waylaid me as I passed through Kilve on the way home. I curse the snow and the darkening sky. Two minutes either way, and I should have missed her. But there, on the track that skirts the lower slope of Pardlestone Hill, I saw two women hauling themselves along as best they could. I could hear one of them moaning with pain, while the other snivelled with misery. The older one, hunched with her back to the wind, was swathed from head to foot in a pile of rags. The other, the younger one, was tall and straight, though covered from head to foot in scarves and coats so that you cold not see what shape she was under it all. The snow had just started to fall and they were hurrying along the lane as best they could. As I closed upon them I realised who they were, though I had not seen Jane, the daughter, since childhood days. She was Jane Shorney of Hunter's Moon.

I knew her, but I did not know her half as well as other men and youths in North Quantock. Jane had a bad name. What she and her foul-tongued old mother got up to in their cottage in that lonely hamlet of Hunter's Moon, is best left unsaid. It is only hearsay after all, and I can write only as I have found. As I say, I had not seen her for years, and few people from the hill sought the company of her mother who, rumour had it, was a witch. But there they were struggling along the track under Pardlestone with the snow thickening by the minute. Great thick flakes were falling now - each half as big as the back of your hand and in amongst them the two women were struggling with the bags that they were hauling along.

"Mercy young Sir, have mercy upon us," says the old harridan as I drew abreast of them. "Will you be of assistance to two poor ladies who'll be certain to perish in this blizzard afore long...?"

Something about the woman's appeal halted me. I would have helped them anyway, but there was something in her voice that had some hint of masterliness. She peered at me from under the rags that covered her head, and I could feel rather than see the piercing eyes that glinted there. She pulled her ragged cape back an inch and I noticed the look of anger and consternation etched across her mouth. The difference in their appearance could not have been more pronounced. When I turned my eyes to the daughter she was smiling. She had smooth, brown, attractive cheeks and deep set eyes that seemed to search and to find. Again, I could feel - rather than see - those eyes running up and down me, observing, calculating, discerning.

"Tis Johnny Walford, mother." she said loudly to the woman at her side. And then to me, smiling: "I hasn't seen you since I come to school. You have changed, I must say."

All this time my heart was sinking, for I could see what lay in store for me. Hunter's Moon was close to the village of Holford, about a mile and a half away to the east. My track veered south in the next few hundred yards, up the little coombe to New Ground and beyond over Long Stone so that I could drop down over Lady's Edge to our camp. I groaned, because struggling via Hunter's Moon would more than double my journey. But there was nothing for it: I offered to carry their bags and they were certainly not too proud to refuse. It was hard going that mile-and-a-half, for I carried a sack of chopped wood, a bag of food and my own heavy sack of fish. They explained on the way that they had run out of provisions in their cottage and had, like many folk on what had been a rare clear morning, made their way out for supplies. In their case this meant visiting East Quantoxhead some two miles to the north where they said there was a fellow who owed them some favours. What the favours were I did not ask, but stumbled along my weary way listening to their gossip and chat. It seemed that they knew my brother William, which hardly endeared me to them, and they sang his praises long and loud. It was almost enough to make me cast aside their load - though after a while I was able to reflect that here, at least, were two people in the world who had a good word to say about that strange brother of mine. I refused their invitations to sup once we had arrived and, leaving them with their load and some fish, explained that I must return to the hill before the snow became too bad.

"I owes you Johnny Walford," said Jane softly as I made to go. "I won't forget it either. I shall return the favour one day soon - for we believe in that don't we mother. One good turn deserves another."

I thought no more of it as I struggled up through Shervage Wood to Knacker's Hole and down through Holford Coombe to Hare Knap. By then the snow was bad and I reckon no-one save for a broomsquire could have found their way through that world of white.

That ill-fated meeting, that good deed of mine, was to have so many consequences. Indeed, I should not be sitting in this cell had I not stumbled upon Jane Shorney that bitter afternoon.

The snow stayed with us until the end of March - and as it began to thaw, and as the flowers and catkins began their belated show - so Jane came a-courting. I was an easy enough target on that lonely hill. That long, dark, frozen winter had wrought in me a fever of loneliness. I yearned for company and I yearned for the touch of a woman. And she had all the qualifications necessary to make polite courtship a mere formality.

One day I returned from the heath where I had been collecting broom to find Petronilla chuckling at some joke of her own. "You got a present in your hut," she laughed, and then followed me in so as not to miss a moment of further glee.

There on my bed was a gallon jar of what turned out to be cider

- the finest cider, in fact, that it has ever been my downfall to taste. Tied to the neck of it was a bunch of spring flowers and the words "From JANE" were written, or rather scrawled, on some paper which I found in their midst. My sister thought this a fantastic revelation. My mother was not so sure.

A few days later the weather had turned warm and I was collecting broom up on the hill. And suddenly there she was saying: "Johnny Walford - trust you to be in some lonely spot like this. 'Tas taken I all day to climb up yer!"

With that she slumped onto the grass and made a show of huffing and puffing as if to prove her weariness.

"What brings you up here?" I shrugged. Even then I was in two minds about Jane Shorney. Not only my mother's warnings, but some inner sense of self-protection seemed to come into play where she was concerned.

"Well," she replied with an indignant tone. "I seem to remember bringing a present all the way up to your camp the other day - and what thanks 'ave I 'ad for me troubles? None at all..."

I stammered a bit at this. "I... I thought that was a gift," I protested. "A thank you for my helping you and your mother in the snow. I didn't realise I was expected to come a-calling. Course, I might have done sooner or later..."

"Would you now," she says, smiling at me. "Well, that don't surprise me at all, from what I 'ear of your goin's-on Johnny Walford."

She pulled off her woollen shawl and lay it down behind her on the grass. Slowly she reclined so that she was leaning on both her elbows. She cut a fine figure lying there in the sunshine. Her dark brown hair swirled in great ringlets down over her brown face and further down across her well formed bosom. Don't think I didn't notice that. Never in any of these writings shall I claim to be a saint, nor even to be a well behaved country boy. I was what I was — perhaps it was something to do with spending so much of my time alone on the hill — but I could never ignore the delights offered by the female of our species. Jane Shorney was a handsome figure of a woman, no one could ever deny that. The curve of her hips was exactly the shape that I, in my own humble judgement, would wish a woman to have. Where her ragged skirt came down to her boots as she lay there on the heath, you could just see an area of smooth, muscular, brown leg. Whether it was her own natural comeliness, or whether it was a mixture of my loneliness and a young man's natural longing and desire – I was mightily attracted to the girl before me.

She opened the bag beside her and brought out a small pitcher of cider and offered me a drink: "See," she said. "I brought you this to show there's no hard feelin's. Next time you gets a present from a girl though, you ought to 'ave the manners to come a-callin'. There's many a lad in Stowey and Holford who'd be right glad if Jane Shorney were to bring them a pitcher and a posy."

"I've no doubt there are," I replied. "For I don't mind saying Jane, that you are as handsome a girl as I have met in all the cups and coombes of the hills."

She said something about not being used to pretty speeches and motioned for me to sit there with her in the warm sunlight and drink the sweet strong cider she had brought. Her mother was famous not only for her cider, but for the various liquors and potions which she brewed in their small cottage at Hunter's Moon – and it always struck me as ironic that such a foul and bitter old lady could manufacture something so sweet.

We flirted as we lay there on the sward, and eventually Jane went home with a noticeable spring in her stride. As I worked through the afternoon I could not get the girl out of my mind. Sure, there was something odd about her – argumentative and easy to offend – but these were not the aspects of her that I was musing on as I collected the broom. More is the pity. I was thinking of her in other ways. Those hips, for example, and the way they swung with such grace and balance as she marched off on those fine long legs of hers. I was thinking about the shape of her breasts and the way her blouse had been open at the top. Throughout her visit there had been a sense of something latent between us – so strong you could have cut it with a bill-hook. You could have grabbed it and bagged it like fronds of broom.

Jane Shorney was nothing if she was not crafty and cunning. In the coming weeks she befriended my sister – an easy task as poor Petronilla was a simple and lonely soul. On several occasions, returning from the hill, I'd find her at our camp in league with Nilla as if they had been friends all their lives. As soon as I arrived Jane's dark eyes would be upon me and my sister would giggle and my mother would tut and sulk. Then one day the Walford women-folk were away visiting sister Avice down at Nether Stowey. Jane knew they would not be at home – I have no doubt about that. She came a-calling anyway, and the moment I saw her I knew how things would be. She smiled, and I smiled back. She sat with me for a while by the fire talking of this and that and then she went to where she had put down her sack, and from it she took her usual offering of her mother's cider.

"I brought some of our better stuff today. Tis the apple brandy mother do make and tis just right for a man who've been workin' hard." She brought me a pewter cup and slowly, very slowly, poured some of the golden liquid into it. To do so she had to bend slightly to reach where my hand held out the drinking vessel, and as she did so my eyes were drawn toward that opening in her blouse. The opening to which my mind had so often returned during the past days – it is strange how a mere inch or two of flesh can obsess a man. This time Jane had left a good deal more of it undone and, as she bent, so I could see the pale curve of her breast inside. Without thinking what I was doing I reached up with my free hand until my fingers had found her thick brown hair, and once they were around the back of her neck I drew her towards me so that within a moment our lips were together. Jane's lips were soft and warm and the way she kissed was far, far more erotic than anything I had experienced before. Yes, more erotic and sensuous even, than my darling Anne's. I do not know what her secret was, for she had a small mouth and lips were not in anyway noticeable to the eye. Without saying a word we crossed to my hut. I recall knocking back the liquor she had given me as we walked, and feeling the fire of it seep down into my inner self.

Jane Shorney knew more than kissing. She knew how to do things to a man which I had certainly not experienced or even imagined before. She could take you to the very edge, to the summit of excitement, and then keep you there until you were in a state of ecstasy. She had a kind of genius for it.

It was only as time went on over the ensuing months that I was to realise just how one-sided this love-making was. She gave, but she never took. She knew how to pleasure a man, but did not know how to glean pleasure from him. She was keenly aware of the power of her sexuality, but was innocent of the enjoyment that it could provide for her. Whether this was something to do with my own shortcomings, I shall never know. I doubt it, for I have given satisfaction elsewhere. It was, I think, just her way. At first of course, it was impossible for an inexperienced youngster like me to realise such a thing, but as time went on it dawned upon me that as we rolled about in our passion – in those moments of pure lust on my part - that she, the inner Jane, was removed from it all in some strange way. In the months to come this would begin to irritate me - I would catch the look of distant absorption in her eyes as she took me to the brink of physical pleasure, and I would fail to understand why she could never catch the fires that were overtaking me. But then, during those months, a good deal more than that would irritate me when it came to this curious girl. In time I no longer even found her beautiful. Shallow it may seem now, but I began to find even her features aggravating. Her nose was too hooked. That mouth that kissed so well, too small. That sensuous chin, too frail and weak. Those curves.... Well, those curves remained. Indeed they grew. Within a few months of our first passionate, post-winter, love-making, she announced that she was with child. My mother groaned. My sister was overjoyed. My brother told me he would kill me.

Why should William react so? Because, it turned out, he regarded Jane Shorney has his property. Needless to say, this came as a bad surprise to me, for she had never mentioned it. It turned out that he was the fellow at East Quantoxhead where the mother and daughter had been that snowy day to "collect their favours". William, it transpired, had been seeing Jane for several years. So too (I later learned) had several other men, but William did not seem so angered by them. And anyway, they were not being named as the child's father; that honour was reserved for Johnny Walford. If the Castle of Comfort had not been crowded the night William came for me, I do believe he would have carried out his threat there and then. Instead it took a dozen men to hold him off me. He was a strong man, William - built with much the same solid frame as me, only older and probably wiser when it came to using his fists. They say he'd often had to resort to them over the years. But the look of bleak hatred in his eye that night in the Castle of Comfort was enough to tell me that I would be no match for him. He had never liked me, for some reason best known to himself, but now the dislike had turned to hatred.

This is how it all came about. Jane remained in my hut that fateful afternoon until long after mother and Petronilla had returned from Stowey. I walked her home to Hunter's Moon in the night, after they had gone to their beds, and I kissed her at the gate and whispered a few pretty words into her ear. All women seem to like such attentions, but Jane loved these dainty speeches more than most. She said no-one had ever spoken to her so before. Indeed, I do not believe the poor girl had ever received much in the way of kindness. No doubt men had been pleasant enough so as to have their way with her, but it's true to say none sought her company outside the lusting. I learned her long-dead father had beat her, and worse, when she was a child. Her mother was a viperous old hag who, I believe, used the girl for her own material ends. When the men of the villages heard that I was seeing her they laughed and jeered and nudged each other. As far as the world of Quantock was concerned, Jane Shorney was nothing more than a loose woman who took her chances and opportunities when she could.

As for my early days with her? I have never been one to abuse another - and I say that knowing that I am soon to meet my Maker who will know the truth of it. I have believed, all my life long, that kindness and love are far better swords in the armoury of man than bitterness and abuse. But the amorous attention I paid Jane in those first few weeks was certainly not done through any high ideal of mine. I had but one thing in mind and it was that warm brown body of hers, and to get more of it I left no stone unturned. Gushing courtesy. Fervent pursuance. Such were the arrows in my bow. It was like using a fusillade of canons to kill a deer. A surfeit of words. An overabundance of adoration. I became quite addicted to the physical relationship and it led me to play out this charade of love. But, of course, I was not in love. Oh yes, I loved her ripe, sensuous body, but only in the way that I can say that I love the crispness of a fresh cool apple. Jane though, in her own strange and even malicious way, fell very much in love with me. Looking back I realise that she fell, not for the real Johnny Walford, but for some ideal she had of me. It was probably the very fantasy that I had manufactured for her, so I have no-one but myself to blame. What she thought she saw was a kindly knight sweeping a girl into a dream. But I was no knight. Just a man of ordinary lusts and passions. It suited me to have Jane come by during that late spring – which was selfish, I know, for I was aware that I should soon be on my broomsquire's travels, sewing my wild oats, as they say - happy and content to be young and free.

As spring turned to early summer and I began to prepare for these perambulations, so Jane attempted to tighten the slender hold she had over me. I have to admit that I was confused by her adherence. As I've said: she had a name in the area for being loose, and that suited me fine. Or did it? Had I not wooed her so that she would love me? Perhaps I had seen the capturing of her love as a challenge – but now I had won it, I soon began to lose the desire for it. Yes, I am sure I am to blame every bit as much as she for the way things went between us. Perhaps even more so in those early days.

When I told her of my plans for travelling around the county, Jane promptly demanded that she come with me, or that I should not go at all. I laughed at this and told her it was the way of the broomsquires and that if she didn't like it then she should fall back on one of her old sweethearts for succour. This was our first, but by no means our last, quarrel. I still feel sick in the pit of my stomach thinking of it now – what a woman Jane Shorney was when she was roused. She came at me with nails and fists and I suffered many a bruise and scratch before she went running off down the coombe. Poor old mother was a witness to all this – in fact, anybody who had been passing for miles around would have heard the row, so tumultuous was Jane's assault. Anyway, mother reminded me of her warnings: "She means to have you my son, by hook or by crook. She'll have you where she wants you unless you're man enough to stand up to her."

With mother's persuasion, I set about the age-old business of loading the cart and set off on my travels the very next day and did not return for several weeks. It was odd being on the road without father, but I took the old violin and found that the village musicians were just as keen to play with me as they had been that dear departed genius. Indeed, I believe they were in some ways more keen, given that they were not to be eclipsed by anything I could do with a bow. And so the broomsquire's annual round of merrymaking still went on – and a wonderful time I had of it. Within a month I had forgotten all about Jane Shorney and, on the few occasions when I had to return to Quantock, I shamelessly avoided the route by Holford or Hunter's Moon. What about the lure of her body? Well, my sorry tale gets worse: I began to make a point of travelling via Crowcombe where an ancient farmer had a young wife who was a particular friend of mine. Many was the night I slept in the hayrick in the fields behind their farm – and never alone did I rest my weary head in that sweet summer hay.

Then an incident occurred which took me by surprise. It was towards the end of July and I was attending to business far off on the Brendon Hills. It was the usual thing: I had done the rounds calling on the far-flung cottages and farms and had sold most of my stock by the time I entered the village of Luxborough. There is a pleasant inn by a stream at the bottom of the village, and near to this is a sort of public field – a narrow meadow where the village folk hold their few festivities. For years, when he was in this distant neck of the woods, this field played host to my father's camp, and I presumed to do the same. As the shadows lengthened in that deep valley I could see people already making their way to the hostelry and knew that a night of revelry was assured. There was a particularly fine village ensemble at Luxborough and I was looking forward to an evening of gigs and reels, and more besides if my luck was in... But there, walking towards my camp in the gloaming, was Jane Shorney. I knew her instantly even though she was some way off, for the way she walked. The way she moved her hips – everything about Jane stopped the breath in me and caused my heart to beat. It was her physical presence. It reached deep into me and grasped the longings that lurked in there. She came to my fireside silently and not once did she take her eyes from mine.

"So, Johnny Walford," she uttered at last. "The boy with so many pretty words and speeches. A boy, but not a man. No man would treat his girl the way you have. Not once this moon have you been to see me. I hear there's others who 'ave been takin' up yer time – like a cheating vixen over Crowcombe way for one..."

"I have been about my business Jane," says I. "And anyway, last time we met, you stormed off saying you hated the sight of me."

I could see her clenching her fists, and I wondered when my pan of stew would be kicked from its perch – as it was the nearest thing to her. But somehow Jane mastered that terrible temper of hers and eventually she sat down on the shaft of my cart and said: "Well – I've 'ad to come to find you, seeing that you has been too busy to find me. Now, ain't you goin' to offer a young lady somethin' to eat or drink? Or must I go down to the inn where I sees they're a-gathrin' for some sort of do..."

When I handed her a bowl of the stew, she grasped my hand and pulled me to her – just as I had done to her a couple of months before. Her kiss was as hot and erotic as it had ever been. Within a minute we were inside my tent. I am a man of weak resolve, and that weakness has led me to my doom. I should have said no – should have sent her packing there and then. I did not love her. As we fell on the rough old blankets, I knew that. But I could not resist her. And so there we were, locked in each other's arms, until some youths from the village came into the meadow to find the broomsquire.

"Are you there Johnny Walford?" said a girl's voice. "Everyone in the village is waitin' for ee..."

I knew who that girl was, and I had looked forward to seeing her later that night - but the mere sound of her voice had Jane coiling up with jealousy. So we had another of our quarrels and I left her there in the tent and took my violin to the inn. Within the hour she was there too - and the way she moved, the way she danced with the men... Oh Jane. My poor lost Jane. Did the Devil carve and render thee from the very crucible of temptation? Did he give you those lithe limbs and that tortured soul? Oh Jane - I can see thee dancing now. The mesmerising, entrancing dance that has led me to my death.

She was like a cat among badgers, like a sparrow-hawk among crows, like a hunter-mare among cart-horses. Jane could move those lithesome limbs of hers in a way that somehow emphasised her womanhood. She was beautiful. And, I am afraid, she was quite amoral and utterly evil.

But I had yet to discover the full extent of these remarkable qualities of hers. In the meantime life continued to unroll its uncertain folds of fate across my happy horizons. For I was happy, there can be no doubt about that. The next day at Luxborough I decamped and returned home with Jane riding alongside me. I had to return to replenish my stock of brooms and, as we went, so I told her of my love and all sorts of other ridiculous artifices which I thought she wanted to hear. A night with her was enough to recharge my physical adoration. Jane went home to Hunter's Moon a happy girl that afternoon, but by that same evening my veneration of her had worn off. By the next morning I was gone again.

It was not until September-time that I was to hear news of her. I was, as I believe I've mentioned, to become a father. All summer I had put this to the back of my mind, I daresay I had even forgotten it completely - I was young and, as I have already said, selfish. Since the life I had wanted for so long had been turned upside down - since my dream of marrying Anne Rice had been thwarted - I had given up on the idea of taking life soberly. I found it hard to imagine what this news of a child would mean to me and I am afraid I did not display sufficient gravitas. Once again she took flight down the coombe that September's eve when – with a large round belly, she had come to see me. Such scenes were public property in our camp. It is not like living in a house where thick walls can muffle raised words. My mother listened with her usual despair and when the girl had gone took it upon herself to instruct me in what she called the truth of the matter. The basis of this was that Jane Shorney was not to be trusted, that she was lying, that she would do anything to get her claws into me - and that if I didn't watch out I should be trussed up like a chicken for the pot before I could say the words Will's Neck.

"And to think that Squire Crosse and Mr Poole should believe you to be clever," she jeered. "Can't you see it Johnny? Don't you know what the girl is up to - wi' her wicked old mother behind it I shouldn't wonder? Oh I've no doubts that she's wi' child all right. Tis a wonder tas ne'er 'appened afore. But as for the babe bein' yours - well, tis common knowledge what she's been up to whilst you been away this summer."

Perhaps some inner pride made me argue with that − I told mother there was every reason I should be the father.

"Tush!" she shrieked, waving the suggestion aside. "One night - from a whole summer...You don't think she's spent the warm nights darning stockings do you? I knows very well what Jane Shorney 'ave been up to - and so do every man and woman from Stowey to Quantoxhead."

She wouldn't enlarge upon this gossip any further. But I was to hear something of the story later that night. It was when brother William accosted me with all his black rage in the Castle of Comfort Inn that I was able to glean something of the truth of Jane's nocturnal journeyings. Once William had been dragged outside and told to go home, some of my friends guffawed at my show of innocence.

"Didn't you know she's been seein' William," said Flighty Chidgey. "I cannot see 'ow. Every feller in Somerset do know. And ee ain't the only one, that be for sure. I reckons there's two or three in yer who've 'ad the pleasure of Jane Shorney since Midsummer's Night."

I couldn't believe my ears. I'm sure I reddened while trying to brush it all aside saying none of it meant a jot to me. But, in truth, I was hurt. In some vainglorious way I had believed that I alone had captured Jane's heart. That night I sulked inwardly at the news, and drank heavily. As I staggered home I told myself I would never speak to Jane Shorney again, but within twelve hours the promise was gone. We humans are fickle, witless, things - I do believe - unless some mantle of greatness is placed upon us. Such folk are few and far between, though it has been my honour to know one or two. Not Johnny Walford though. I join the masses: fickle and witless. The next day, hurt and confused and nursing a sore head, I went to

Hunter's Moon. Jane and her mother hard at work with their cider making. You could smell the sweet, sour vapours of it a mile away as the manufacture of the golden fluid was in full swing at the back of their cottage. I wondered what they did for the rest of the year, for the cider-making only goes on a month or so in autumn. One thing was for sure - when they worked, they worked hard. I sat on the wall of the orchard watching them - and so intent were they upon their toil, they did not notice me. Which suited me as I had no wish to speak with the sharp-tongued old crone who was the mother. After the pressing of the cheese it was apparently Jane's job to haul away the old apple mash to feed to the orchard pigs. Her mother remained in the outhouse to set up the new cheese on the press, so this was my chance to have words with the girl. She was taken aback to see me sitting there and hurried me to one side so that we should be out of view and then she began to kiss me and tell me how glad she was I had come. But I cut her short and came directly to the point.

"My brother wishes to kill me," I said. "It seems that you are his sweetheart. Oh, and then there's a few other fellows at the Castle of Comfort who I've heard also claim to have lain with you. So what I want to know is this: how is it that I am honoured with fathering your child when I have only been with you so little?"

I have never seen a person's face change from happiness to wrath in so short a time. Not only wrath, but fear creased that smooth brown handsome face of hers. Her small mouth puckered as she began to cry, and I knew that some arrow had found its target. At that moment I didn't like her, nor did I like myself, or any other person on God's earth. I just wanted to leave and to be alone – so, turning on my heel, I began to walk away. She came after me, screaming, pleading, wailing, punching, kicking - until eventually I was forced to break into a run to avoid her blows.

Later I was at the wrong end of another attack - this time from my sister Petronilla. She called me a brute and said she couldn't understand how I could turn my back on the girl who was to be the mother of my child. "Of course tis yours," she shouted. "You only got to see poor Jane lyin' down there ill as if to die - and you should know that tis yours all right. No woman 'ould get 'erself in such a state if t'weren't the case. She don't love William - never 'as. And she only saw they other men cos you 'ould take no notice of 'er..."

Mother and Petronilla fought like cats and dogs over this. And I left, silently without them noticing, and went to spend a few days over on Robin Upright's Hill where I had a small hut and some trees to coppice. That was where Tom Poole found me.

"I have heard something of a scandal concerning you," he shrugged as he pulled up on that old cob of his. "You seem to court a dramatic fate Johnny, my boy. I cannot help but wonder what will become of you. I have heard your name mentioned from Dulverton to Goathurst. There's a lot of idle chatter concerning you doing the rounds in a particular quarter of the Crowcombe parish. But none of that amounts to a mole-hill compared with what I hear coming out of Hunter's Moon. None of the former surprises me – you are obviously an attractive fellow to women – but I do worry about the latter, namely the case of young Miss Shorney. Jane Shorney is not for you – mark my words, boy – only the worst will come of it."

It was my turn to shrug. "I am still young Mr Poole, and an ungodly fool to boot. I admit there are many errors to my ways, but I have never set out to make mischief. There are times when I certainly miss the ordered life of Fyne Court."

"Ah well, it might be that I have some good news for you," says he, climbing down from the saddle. "If Mr Crosse was able to give you some intellectual guidance, then so might Mr Samuel Coleridge. I believe you met him when he was here with Robert Southey. Well, such an impression did Quantock have upon him that he has now made up his mind to come here to live."

Coleridge. I can see him now, loping up over Robin Upright's Hill with his long, unkempt, black hair blowing in the wind, I can hear him wheezing as he collapses, enveloping my shoulders in a great hug. Poor Sam always had trouble passing a good lungful of breath. I wonder where he is now, and what he would think of these awful straits of mine? But I must not be gloomy, for some of the best days of my life were spent traversing the hills with poet Coleridge. They arrived a few days after Christmas, and a few days later he came to find me.

"Johnny Walford!" was the cry I heard piercing those frost-bound wastes above Holford Coombe, and I knew at once whose voice it was. Coleridge had a thing that they call gusto, and it was this that carried that great voice of his across the hill.

"So the mites had the better of you and Squire Crosse," he laughed as he embraced me like some bosom friend. I had met him just that one peculiar night on the path from Blue Anchor to Watchet, but if a stranger had witnessed this embrace he would've been forgiven for assuming we were long lost comrades in arms. Indeed, a stranger did soon appear, but not before Coleridge was slapping me on the back once more...

"Johnny Walford," he cried looking me up and down. "You are the finest example of mankind that it has been my pleasure to observe. And with luck this Quantock air will soon have me following in your giant tracks. Talking of fine fellows - meet Charles: he is a fellow poet and has come to live with us in Stowey."

I looked up to see a pale youth huddled deep in overcoats, standing watching us with a nervous, forlorn expression upon his face.

"This is Charles Lloyd - a poet of excellence who is soon to have work published in conjunction with none other than the great Charles Lamb," said Coleridge, gesticulating to his friend that he should come and shake me by the hand. "Meet Johnny Walford, Charles. Experimenter, creator of life, technician and broomsquire... Do not think I haven't been following your doings with interest Johnny, and a fine story it makes. I hear God eventually saw fit to destroy the laboratory with one of his lightning strikes. I imagine he was jealous of your discoveries."

He laughed, but did not stop in his verbal outpourings. Nothing could stay the poet when he was in full flow. It was his habit to broach the most intimate subjects with no hint of embarrassment and, when it came to stamping upon a fellow's sensibilities, he seemed to have no shame - yet he was one of the most kind-hearted men I have ever known. "I also hear tell of your remarkable adventures with the female kind, dear boy.

Indeed, it is the gossip of the village. Our scandalised Nanny informs us that you have been having your way with young ladies all over hill and dale."

I must have blushed because within a moment the poet was once again smothering me with embraces and roughing my hair. "Never mind that old friend. We are all envious of fellows who find such favour with the ladies, are we not Charles? Anyhow, I have not sought you out to tease you Johnny, I have come to ask a favour. The reason I have returned to Quantock is that I seek the simple, wholesome country life and the purity of its air. I believe that being close to the glories of nature will be conducive to my work and help bolster my indifferent health. I am making a garden you know: I shall raise my own vegetables and live an exceedingly healthy life. But as part of this pastoral regime of mine, I intend exploring this small portion of paradise from one beautiful end to the other. I shall

166

have great walks far and wide and it is my hope that you shall join me on some of these. You see, I need a helmsman who knows the byways and dear Tom Poole tells me none could be better fitted as a guide than you. Which cheered me no end, as I recall the great pace that you set that night from Watchet to Fyne Court - and I would prefer a fellow who can stride. But it is more than that. I would far rather wander with someone of your acumen, for I cannot put up with an associate who is dull."

I told him I should be honoured to escort him on his adventures, as long as the charcoal burning did not have me in its smoky grasp. I too could recall the night we marched to Fyne Court from the port of Watchet, but for me the memory was due to the far-reaching effect the young poet and his friend Southey had wrought on my outlook. Many, many times I had mulled over the things they spoke of that night. So when Coleridge mentioned that he intended to pay me for my services as a guide, I told him I would not accept a penny. In the end we agreed to walk as friends and I am proud to say that we were companions and equals out there on the hill. Not once did the poet make an issue of the difference in our standing.

He had married Sara Fricker in Bristol, and they had produced a child called David Hartley, but he wasn't happy and nothing would do that he should move his family to the countryside. Thomas Poole had shown me the letter Coleridge had written to him, I can still recall what it said:

"When am I to find rest?" he wrote after pleading Mr Poole to make the necessary arrangements for the move. "Disappointment follows disappointment, and Hope seems given me merely to prevent my becoming callous to Misery. Now I know not where to turn myself.... I have been poring into a book as a show for not looking at my Wife and the Baby. By God, I dare not look at them.... If any circumstances have occurred that have lessened your Love, or Esteem, or Confidence; or if there be any objections to my settling in Stowey on your own account, or any other objections that what you have urged, I doubt not that you will declare them openly and unreservedly to me in your answer to this, which I shall expect with a total incapability of doing, or thinking of, anything, till I have received it. I shall have six companions: my Sara, my babe, my own shaping and disquisitive mind, my books, my beloved friend Thomas Poole, and lastly, Nature, looking at me in a thousand melodies of love..."

Now here he was in front of me waxing lyrical in his unstoppable way: "I have been telling Charles here that Poetic Feelings are like the stretching boughs of mighty oaks," said Coleridge walking by my side to the hut where I kept a broth warm by the fire. "To feel the best of them one must pay homage to the gales, toss in the strong winds and go forth before the gust."

That was the way he would talk, and that was why I loved him – for all his wayward moods. These mental tides of his would lead him from the very heights of vigorous enthusiasm and delight, to the pits of unreasonable despair:

"Like one that on a lonesome road
Doth walk in fear and dread,
And having once turned round, walks on,
And turns no more his head
Because he knows, a frightful fiend
Doth close behind him tread."

That was the way he put it, and I know what he meant. My own wraith has followed me and, indeed, has brought me to the pretty pass I find myself in today. Coleridge and I would oft times speak of the inordinate pursuance of our fate. However, what he saw in me, what he found in my rustic company to nourish that mercurial intellect of his, I was never to fully understand. If pressed I would have to say that he had some unearthly fancy concerning my life upon the hills. To him Quantock was a rural idyll and I was a denizen of it – just as a faery-being might flit through some imagined paradise of sunshine and antediluvian prayers.

Indeed Coleridge once told me that he had written the following words about me:

"He on honey-dew had fed,
And drank the milk of Paradise."

He would ask me of this faery-world of mine as if it were really separated from the plainer and more mundane kingdom of mere mortals, and I would tell him what a shame it was he never had the pleasure of my father's company. The old man knew of such things. For instance, he would sometimes tell of a youth he knew who picked fruit in the light of the moon, and Coleridge became fascinated by this story. He was a beauteous boy – my father used to say – who lingered alone, at night, silent and wild. Father knew him, and said he was a remnant of an older Earth. I have seen that lonesome, singular youth – just once – and that, alas, was with the help of laudanum. But the tale of the nocturnal boy who picked fruit was enough to get Sam Coleridge in a fervour of delight. I also mentioned to him the long Walford lineage from the Dumnonii tribes and by this he was also transfixed, especially when I played the strange dirge my father had taught me on the violin. Sometimes, when he spoke of such ephemera as the fruit-boy or the ancient peoples, father would play a special piece, and it was a veil of loveliness – there seems to be no other way to put it. A spectral thing of few notes, but almost oppressively beautiful. The strains of it would, perhaps, enshrine images of the little fellow picking fruit under the moon or speak of an ancient people walking slowly through a golden light. I would play it to Coleridge and he would weep for the fairness of it, especially when he had taken opium. The silken, sumptuous, grip of laudanum.

"And all put on a gentle hue,
Hanging in the shadowy air
Like a picture rich and rare.
It was a climate where they say
The night is more belov'd than day."

He wrote that. And I felt it. At least, I did if I swigged laudanum with him. So esteemed and cherished did that fluid, flitting, sensation-fuelled world become, that for a time after Coleridge's eventual withdrawal from Quantock, I had the pains, the desolation, of missing the drug. So strong was the opiate's effect on me, I even began to believe in my poet friend's far-fetched image of life on the hill.

"Sea and hill and wood
With all the numberless goings on of life
Inaudible as dreams."

And so Samuel Taylor Coleridge walked into my world and soon I was a regular visitor at his cottage on the main street at Nether Stowey. From there he and I would find our way along the little footpath which led through the gardens at the rear to Tom Poole's bower where, so long ago, my father and I had stood before my benefactor to ask for his support in the matter of the poor old Greenslades in their lonely tower. But now I would drink the flip our gracious host was always happy to supply, and I would listen to the talk of great men.

Coleridge's wife Sara was not at all as I had imagined she would be. I thought none but some delectable Amazon, fleet and lithe of limb and mind, would have appealed to this sensuous man. But that was not Sara Coleridge. She was rather a plain woman, who looked as if she spent a good deal too much time indoors. Which I believe she did with little Hartley, for certainly she never joined her husband on his far-ranging perambulations. I had the feeling that this life in Stowey was not for her, but that she was putting up with it for his great art. Not that there was much of that in evidence for a time: Coleridge's writing, I mean. He had inaugurated a periodical over which he enthused for a while, but The Watchman, as it was called, died an unsung death. I recall him gently scrutinising his maid's exorbitant use of paper one morning as she stooped to light the fire.

"La Sir," she rejoined. "'Tis only The Watchman."

If the country life did not suit Sara, then it has to be said that some elements of it did not agree with the great poet either. For instance, the cottage was plagued by mice, but kind-hearted Sam Coleridge was loathe to set a trap for them: "'Tis telling a lie," he explained to me when I chaffed him for it. "'Tis as if you said, 'Here is a bit of toasted cheese: come little fellows I invite you!' when I mean to assassinate my too credulous guests. O foul breach of the rites of hospitality..."

He was aghast when I let him into the secret of my taking deer, though not so aghast that he would not enjoy a bowl of stew from my pot. He claimed it was the food of the Gods, but asked me to remind him not from whence it came. His own labours in producing food ended in naught. He was determined to eat less meat and feed his family on the vegetables he grew, but as the summer rolled by, he was forever having to explain to his guests why the garden was full of weeds: "It is only because it has not yet come to its age of discretion and choice," he would say. "The weeds, you see, have taken the liberty to grow, and I thought it unfair in me to prejudice the soil towards roses and strawberries."

For the country folk, of course, this was all part of Sam Coleridge's rich vein of foolishness and aberration. In the whole of Quantock, only Tom Poole and I took him seriously, or were able to laugh along with him. As for poetry: like gardening, it was often put aside for the joy of the hills. I do believe however, that I was present during the compilation, or at the moment of outset, of two of his great works and these occasions I shall mention with pride. But first I feel I must keep up with the chronology of this tale and stay faithful to the order of events that have affected my life.

During the early part of that year I rarely had reason to visit our family encampment in Hodder's Combe for I had a good deal to do on Robin Upright's Hill. When I wasn't coppicing I was off a-roving with Coleridge and his strange companion Charles Lloyd. Consequently, during the month of March I did not see my mother or my sister once. And I was in for a very great surprise indeed when I at last called there again. The first thing that greeted me as I descended down over Hare Knap was the sound of a baby crying. I suppose I should have known what it meant, but it was left to my mother to inform me of the details. I always took a couple of our dogs with me on my travels and on this occasion my father's old lurcher Wisp ran down over the hill to the camp she knew and loved so well. On seeing her, mother came out to greet me – and to stop me in my tracks with her news.

"Tis Jane's baby," she said hurriedly. "We've taken both mother and child in. We had no choice in the matter Johnny. When you sees what your brother have done to her, you will know that. And we cannot trust that old witch to have her at Hunter's Moon."

"What do you mean – what William has done to her?"

"You best see for yourself. You know I never liked the girl – but not she or anyone else deserve what he have done."

I found Jane half sitting, half lying in the gloom of one of the huts, with Petronilla fussing about the baby. As I stooped to enter, Jane tried to hide herself under a blanket – which was not like her at all. For once in my life I was utterly confused as to what to do or say, but mother took control and told Nilla to show me the child. It was the first tiny babe I had ever seen, let alone held – a boy, not yet a week old. Nilla pushed the bundle into my arms and I had that unparalleled sensation you get when you see your own flesh and blood for the very first time. The little fellow squirmed and held his minute hands slowly up to me. His eyes were closed, but the little hands moved so slowly and gently. It was as if the child was reacting to events in some other space and time. Later, much later, I began to believe that this small being was not from any seed of mine. But in that hut that late March morning, as the showers of spring marched east across our warming hills on their way from the great ocean beyond, I felt the human alchemy that causes men and women of our kind to feel. That improbable mix of fierce protectiveness and unutterable warmth.

Jane was peering up from beneath blanket. "That is your son," she said.

It was then, for the first time, I noticed that one of her eyes was swollen and bruised. I gave the child back to my sister and bent down to pull back the material from her face. She tried to stop me, but it was only a weak protest. Down went the blanket, past wheals and bruises on her now pale face, past great red marks on her neck to more sizeable bruises on the tops of her arms. I stopped there.

"Did William do this to you?"

She started to cry.

"Why did he do it?"

Eventually she sobbed: "Because I told him it was your child."

Mother told the story: "T'was fixed a-tween him and that mother of hers that Jane and he should wed. She was not agin it at first, but she would not agree the child was his. And so those two devils kept her under lock and key at Hunter's Moon and a-times William went round there to talk wi' her and it usually ended wi' him beatin' her black and blue. All he wanted was for her to say it was not your'n, but she would not. How she can be so sure I do not know – but they say sometimes a mother can. Anyhow, one day at the beginning of the month she could take no more o' it and she escaped when the old mother were out sellin' the cider. Nilla found her lyin' by the side o' the road just under Willoughby Cleeve and brought her home and I agreed we 'ad to take her in. If one o' my sons has put her in the family way, the other is tryin' his best to kill her dead – so we Walford womenfolk 'as no choice but to stand by her. And that be the end o' it. You and William can says what you like."

I was surprised by mother's turn-around, for I knew she detested the girl. But she was a woman of high principle, my mother, and I could see Jane Shorney was now a member of the household whether I had any say in it or not. My emotions, as I have said, were ones of confusion. The effect the babe had upon me. The wickedness of that bullying brother of mine. How could he have raised a hand against a woman? Perhaps it seems me, of all people, saying that. But at that moment I knew once and for all that William had some incarnate evil within him. I had always feared him, but now I knew that I must one day stand up to this malicious dangerous brother of mine or he would surely do for me and this hapless girl. Poor Jane. She did not appear the alluring siren any longer as she lay there in the blankets of our gloomy hut. Indeed she looked half-dead. The beatings and the childbirth had almost finished her. For the first and, perhaps, only time my heart reached out to her. Mother caught my arm and led me outside.

"What you do is your concern," she muttered. "I do not expect you, nay, I do not want you to marry her unless you feel tis right. But I am mother of this family and I say the girl and the babe stay with us. William came you know, just afore the child were born, and he raged about the place. But if there is one person that lad is afeared of tis his mother, and I hit him wi' a broom and told 'un never to darken this place again until he could mend his ways. I sent my eldest away 'cos of her in there, but what else could I do? The babe looks enough like one o' us and William is a danger to un, I tell ee that Johnny. William is a danger..."

I went to look for my brother later that day, for I had a rage upon me and had no fear of him. But he was away, according to the smith. He had gone to the flatlands beyond Bridgwater where they had work making the hinges for drainage gates on the rheins. What would have happened had he been there at the forge I know not, but I believe the life of one of us would have ended that day. On the way back I called at Hunter's Moon and took the trouble to pinion the old harridan to her kitchen wall.

"You should be ashamed," says I. "Your daughter and your grandchild could have died thanks to the treatment you and my brother meted out. Had it gone that far, I promise you, I should have snapped your withered neck."

She had no fear of me, I'll give her that.

"You're a fine one to make pretty speeches Johnny Walford," spits she. "You take a girl and dump her wi'out a by-yer-leave. You've bin the cause of all this and no-one else. And to thank ee for it I 'ave put a curse on thee. Ye shall be dead afore the child reaches two years of age. And that, Sir, I promise ee by all the powers vested in me...."

Black. Black, dark, powers. I did not believe her then. Now I am not so certain.

Over the days that followed a sort of truce developed between Jane and myself. Looking back I can see how she wheedled her way around my sister and my mother. Indeed the old woman began to take her side after a while, and when I would go off roving with Sam Coleridge and his friends, she would treat me to gales of rebuke. I suppose I deserved it. And yet there was something about Jane that caused my hackles to rise at every touch and turn. I did not want her as a wife and, increasingly, I became beset by the notion that the child was not mine. In my sober hours I would try to think of a way out of the corner I had been backed into. Sometimes I would repair to Robin Upright's Hill for days on end and then, at least, the womenfolk could not complain, as I was working hard to provide for them. But when I went a-roving with Samuel Coleridge there was always a scene.

Drink and opiates are a powerful mix and often I would return with my mind occupying a different planet up a different plain. Jane wanted me. She was encompassed by her own vision of me. I could have her any time I wished. That was the way of it, and often, when I returned from my wanderings fuelled by stimulants, I was very quick to want her. She soon recovered her alluring physical attractions after her terrible ordeal. As I have said: all men – and perhaps Johnny Walford in particular – are weak-willed creatures, especially when the lure of passion is set before them. Time and again, when I swore to myself that I would not touch Jane again, I would break my promise and lie with her. The next morning, with a painful head from drink and often laudanum, I would groan out loud because of my deceit. I still wanted Anne Rice, but failing that dream, I wanted to set out and find someone who could at least go some long way to replacing her. Jane Shorney I knew for sure, could never play that role. It was as simple, and on my part as selfish, as that.

And having once turned round, walks on,
And turns no more his head
Because he knows, a frightful fiend
Doth close behind him tread.

That was how Coleridge put it, and that was the way it was: thanks to my weak-will and probably also because of the drug and the drink, Jane was with child once more by the end of the summer. This time it was mine, of that I could be sure, for she never left the coombe in those days without the Walford womenfolk escorting her. It is no good my attempting to justify myself: there were extenuating circumstances – not least was the fact that Jane was ever-keen to seduce me to her bed. Her lustrous eyes were always piercing and suggesting. Her easy, erotic, nakedness was always there when I entered the hut we slept in. There were two main habitations at the encampment and I was free to go to the one where mother slept, or to the one where Petronilla, Jane and the baby were. If I chose the latter, Nilla would sneak away without a word. When you are young and full of hot blood and manly desires – and a beautiful woman is lying on her own and you are welcome to lie beside of her – there is little in the way of choice. Thomas Poole beseeched me to marry the girl – indeed the parish began moves to force us to marry because they were worried we'd end up going on the poor - for it was well known that she and I shared that humble home in the woods. But I would not. I could scarcely admit to myself that I had developed an affinity with her. Our lovemaking only ever occurred after I returned much the worse for wear, it had nothing to do with love. It had more to do with a heady mix of Rich's cider and laudanum.

It was Coleridge who first gave me a taste of the drug. I recall the occasion well, for it led to him penning what I understand is one of his most acclaimed poems. It was in May-time and I was up in the hut on Robin Upright's Hill so that I could be closer to the high heaths and the broom. Also, I was once again attempting to withdraw myself from the tangled web being spun by Jane down in the coombe, for every time I slept with her I felt I further sealed my fate.

"Tis high time you and I went a-wandering Johnny," said Coleridge who had arrived at an uncommonly early hour for him. "We have had modest strolls all spring, but the weather looks set to be fine and I yearn for a longer more sustaining venture. Do you recall when you first met Southey and I - we were en-route from Lynmouth and the Valley of the Stones. I would go there again Johnny - and, if you have the time and the mood for it, I should be most pleased of your company."

I needed no persuasion, as I have already stated - I cherished the poet's fraternity. Thinking back I believe there were three or four elements of my fellowship that suited him. I know he relied on me, to some extent, as a guide - though not completely - Coleridge was so filled with enthusiasm for the nature he saw around him, he'd think nothing of diving off down this valley, or ascending that hill. It mattered not if the detour took us from our route. However, to some extent it suited him to call upon my knowledge of the highways and byways for our meanderings. Then there was the fact that I could relate tales and legends from the past, not to mention a good deal of gossip and chat from the present. Then again, I think he felt comfortable being silent with me, just as Mr Crosse had. For an hour or more we would walk without a single word passing our lips. This, in some companions, can enkindle a perception of discomfort so that one or the other finds themselves forced to speak. This never occurred between us. When he was talking ten-to-the-dozen I was content; when I was relating some anecdote of old he would enthuse - but if we both walked on in silence, the two of us were just as comfortable.

Lastly, Coleridge was a nervous man. As brave as a lion in many ways, but strangely nervous nevertheless. I am sure this was a product of his perceptive mind. His eyes were forever darting this way and that as he took in all around him. If a dog were to bark suddenly, or at night an owl hoot, it would be enough to make him jump. After he had been on the laudanum this state of nerves grew noticeably worse. And so, I have a suspicion Coleridge liked the companionship of a fellow he could trust. He told me himself that he had wearied of the company of Charles Lloyd who was more nervous even than he, and certainly at the other end of the scale when it came to jollity. Poor Lloyd had recently left Nether Stowey to pursue his apprehensive and troubled life elsewhere. For the time being Coleridge had only myself and Tom Poole as companions, although this was soon to change.

So it was that morning I was soon striding out over Robin Upright's Hill with the man who should be regarded as one of the nation's greatest poets. I believe he was a little shocked when I ducked into my hut to wrap a badger ham in a cloth, for as I have said, he did not hold with the eating of meat. Only after eight solid hours of striding did he weaken and sink his teeth into it, and then he did not complain. He'd had a hard day of it. He was fit enough, but he was not used to the pace of a broomsquire.

"I want to reach Porlock afore dark," says he.

"Then we shall have to strike out fast enough," I replies. "For the place must be the best part of twenty miles from Robin Upright's Hill."

Late afternoon found us sitting high above Hurlestone Point which is the great rocky bastion that protects Porlock Bay from the east. Few places in the world can be as awesome and beautiful as this great bay, with its high grey shingle ridge bordered by meadows which are bordered, in turn, by the massive hills of Exmoor. All around the Porlock Vale do those mighty hills stand guard, shielding the place from every direction save the sea. Hurlestone is at the westernmost end of a mighty rampart they call North Hill, which runs six miles along the coast from the port of Minehead. Along here we had marched in the warmth of the late afternoon, for Coleridge refused to stop until he was in sight of the village of Porlock. Now we could see it nestled under the hills across the bay, and the eater of vegetables was right glad of the badger ham and cider that I carried in my bag. After we had eaten, he lay back and I could see the strong cool drink had mollified his mood. The poet would often recline on a grassy sward to watch the clouds passing by, or gaze for an hour or so at a pleasing view. When he was in one of these reveries, I knew better than to disturb him, and so sat there happily stroking my father's old lurcher waiting for nothing in particular to pass our way. The hypnotic sound of the waves crashing on the shingle hundreds of feet below somehow added a pleasant, almost stupefying ennui to the hour we spent there. Down in the great curve of the bay I could spy several smacks and yawls riding at anchor waiting for the tide to allow them into the harbour at the Weir on the far side of the bay. It is a pretty little port, no more than a hook-shaped dent in the shingle really, situated under the great shoulder of Exmoor where the big hills begin their coastal march off westward in a vertical forest punctuated with landslides and crags. That wonderful land is the haunt of the peregrine and very little else, save the smuggler who is brave enough to land there at night. The sight of the boats at anchor made me think of father's smuggling days and the elusive, enigmatic Laversha I'd saved from the law all that time ago. Laversha: I often wondered what had become of him; on which high seas, in which wild lands he ventured while I toiled in England's kind and gentle hills. But recently I had heard tell of him and his Cornish skipper Abraham Hicks. Rumour had it they had been up to their old tricks again - for certain Quantock had more brandy, rum and Hollands swashing about in its cellars than was usual. I had not seen the big dark skinned man since the morning he left Squire Crosse's impromptu court of law, though I often wished our paths would cross once more. I had taken to him - indeed, I had been greatly impressed by him, and liked to think that he had been struck by the cut of my own jib. One boat, far down in the bay, reminded me of the "Mavis" which I'd seen at a distance once - but, though her graceful lines were undoubtedly similar, I was no boatman so could not really tell. I dosed off and slept until Sam Coleridge awakened me.

"Come along young broomsquire," he yelled over his shoulder as he ran down the steep slope among the scree. "Let a poet show you the way to Porlock..."

We had our supper in the Ship Inn at the western end of the fore street. It is a fine old hostelry where a fire always burns and the ale is unfailingly good. An excellent meal it was too, a pie of local oysters and beef, and the ale was good enough to delay the poet in his plans. Consequently we stayed longer than we should, for we had yet to find lodgings. This was going to mean a further walk as Coleridge had something against staying in the village itself.

"We must be high, at altitude, where quiet sounds from hidden rills float here and there, like things astray, and high o'erhead the sky-lark shrills," proclaimed Sam loudly, much to the surprise and delight of the locals who were drinking in the crowded saloon. I knew the poet was enjoying the ale perhaps more than he should, as he always became more verbose when he was in his cups. But the Porlock fellows were not used to the eloquent ways of folk like Sam Coleridge and the landlord, who was a pleasant man, pushed a couple of glasses of best French over the bar for us.

"There y'go Johnny Walford (he knew me, as did every hosteler in the area) ask your friend there if the finest brandy will help fuel a few more of his fine words."

Coleridge lifted the glass to his lips and, savouring the wondrous essences of the drink, walked to the window to gaze upon the last redness of the evening:

"Ah slowly sink," said he,
"Behind the western ridge, thou glorious Sun!
Shine in the slant beams of the sinking orb,
Ye purple heath-flowers! richlier burn, ye clouds!
Live in the yellow light, ye distant groves!
And kindle, thou blue Ocean."

I do not think he heard the cheers and jeers when he stopped speaking, but for all their coarse merriment I know the men in that saloon has been held silent by the power of Sam's dreamy, sensual voice. One young jester though, began to taunt the poet by making a poor mimicry of his speech, and I was about to have words with the lad, but a farmer I knew called Richardson had him by the scruff of the neck.

"Don't you go upsetting the poet," I heard him say. "Or the broomsquire will knock every last jest out of you."

The youth looked over at me and decided he'd be better off having his amusement in some other place. Barnaby Richardson came over and I asked him if he would like to try the landlord's brandy.

"'Tis the best I have tasted in a long time," I said turning to the man behind the bar. "Last time I had the likes was when the 'Mavis' came a-calling at Kilve."

The man's finger went to his lips and he looked around nervously. "Have a care Master Walford," he whispered. "The men o' the 'Mavis' don't like their presence heralded."

"If you see the mate Laversha, give him my best regards," I

whispered back with a grin. "I should like to meet him again, if only to tell him of my father's passing, for they were friends some years ago."

He poured Barnaby Richardson a drink and the farmer was kind enough to invite Sam Coleridge and me to his house for the night.

"I y'eard un on about wantin' to stop somewhere high up, and they don't come much 'igher than Ash," he laughed, offering us a ride in his cart. And so to Ash Farm we went - a thousand feet or more above the sea. The poet had fallen into one of his reveries and was lying in the straw in the back of the cart while Barnaby and I sat up-front and talked of the latest events to have occurred at Porlock. Eventually Coleridge, a little brusquely perhaps - if you didn't know the man - asked us if we would be silent for a while as he wanted to concentrate on the moon that was coming up huge and full above the massive rampart of North Hill.

"Play that dirge of yours on the violin Johnny - the mood of it is upon me..."

So I took a swig from Coleridge's little flask of laudanum and played that godforsaken, outlandish tune."

"In Nature there is nothing melancholy," murmured Coleridge at one point. "Nothing, but some night-wandering man whose heart was pierced with remembrance of some grievous wrong. And many a poet echoes the conceit; a poet who hath been building up a rhyme when he had better far have stretched his limbs beside a brook in mossy forest-dell. Hark - the nightingale begins its song!"

We heard the bird, and for the first time I understood the mystery of my father's music. It was nearer to nature than to man.

Ash is an ancient and handsome farm tucked into a groove high on a shoulder of hill - but not so high that you can't hear the great ocean rollers breaking upon the beach a thousand feet below. It is as vertiginous a place as any in England. All about it is on the perpendicular save for the vast grey sea, which held a luminance of its own the night we were there. Mrs Richardson made a great fuss and put together a cold collation which we were made to eat, despite our recent supper at The Ship. Coleridge couldn't touch a thing and so it fell to me to wade into the ham and cheese. The poor old maid looked worried that a man who had walked from Quantock should have no appetite, but I explained that he was slightly out of sorts. Coleridge, indeed, made his excuses and left the big, homely kitchen and went on up to bed, and it was left to me to amuse the old couple with a yarn or two concerning people and places they knew. After an hour of this I made my own way up the old black twisting stairs by candlelight. We had been given a large room, complete with a couple of comfortable beds and - rare for Exmoor - its own small balustraded balcony that overlooked the great panorama of Porlock Vale. That is where I found the poet, sitting in a chair with his feet up on the low parapet enjoying the warmth of the night. I joined him and in silence we sat there, gazing at the stars and their sprinkling of earthly cousins - the few village lights far below in Porlock and Bossington, and the riding lights of boats in the bay. Coleridge had been at his laudanum and I could see by the look in his eyes that he was inhabiting some far off demesne of his own. There can be no doubt though, that the great vista, issuing forth beneath us in the light of the full moon, held the man riveted and I knew it was best if I did not utter a word.

At last he whispered, but not to me or any other living thing: "That deep romantic chasm - a savage place as holy and enchanted as e'er beneath a waning moon. And here were gardens bright with sinuous rills and here were forests ancient as the hills."

What he was talking about I had no idea, but sat back content to leave him in his reverie. For in truth I was in my own; the drink and opiates had reached far into my soul that strange, bewitched, night. So deep, that I heard not the clattering of stones upon the balcony. The first thing I knew was hearing a heavy rap on our door and turning to see the comical nightcapped personage of Barnaby entering our room with a lamp flickering in his hand.

"'Tis a person up from Porlock to see thee," he said to me with a distinctly nervous look upon his face. And with that, Laversha slid silently from the shadows into the pool of light.

So taken aback was I that I did not move from my seat, wondering if I were still occupying a dream, but the big dark mate strode across and took my hand. The grip of him convinced me he was no phantom of the opiates. The mate explained that the landlord of the Ship had told him where I was. "I came up to find you and pass on my sympathies. I loved your father well. I knew him and trusted him, which is a rare thing for me in this turbulent world."

Then he pulled a bottle of French from one of his ornate pockets and we set to drinking just inside from the balcony where Coleridge sat. Barnaby muttered something about the late hour and withdrew, leaving us with nothing but the light of the moon. In a while the stranger's voice must have, to some degree at least, brought the poet out of his musings, for he asked us to join him. When we did, he seemed altogether taken aback by the appearance of Laversha, which was not exactly surprising. You do not often set eyes upon a person like him in the West Country - indeed, the likes of the giant Laversha do not cross most people's paths in a lifetime. Where I could see every feature on Coleridge's face in the moonlight, nothing but the eyes of the mate stood out from that dusky visage of his. My companion bade the smuggler continue his conversation with me, which had moved on to tales of his recent adventures in foreign lands. The more the mate spoke, the more attentive the poet became. Indeed, Laversha weaved a splendid tale, something about an African bride and how he had lost her in some caves.

"As e'er beneath a waning moon was haunted
By woman wailing for her demon-lover!
And from this chasm, with ceaseless turmoil seething,
As if this earth in fast thick pants were breathing,
A mighty fountain momentarily was forced,
Amid whose swift half-intermitted burst
Huge fragments vaulted like rebounding hail,
Or chaffy grain beneath the thresher's flail:
And 'mid these dancing rocks at once and ever
It flung up momently the sacred river."

I read these words now in my dripping cell, and dream of Xanadu and Kubla Khan and his stately pleasure dome where Alph, the sacred river, ran through caverns measureless to man, down to a sunless sea. I see the damsel with a dulcimer. And to me she was, and ever will be, Laversha's Abyssinian bride:

"And on her dulcimer she played,
Singing of Mount Abora.
Could I revive within me,
her symphony and song,
To such a deep delight 'twould win me,
That with music loud and long,
I would build that dome in air,
That sunny dome! those caves of ice!"

Coleridge wrote those words that night, long after Laversha had gone to his ship and I had turned to my bed. He sat up and dreamed his dreams and penned those words until the dawn came streaking over the great vale. Whether it was the effort, or the laudanum, I do not know, but the high-strung poet made himself unwell so that we could not continue to Lynton for two more days. We stayed at Ash and while Coleridge rested, I took the opportunity to arrange some Quantock coastal business with Laversha whom I saw just once again when I plunged down a desolate coombe near Culbone on the coast. He had told me he would be there at a certain hour and I recognised the skiff pulled up on the boulder-shore. He was only too pleased to do business with me, and I with him, for I was sorely in need of funds with a growing family at home.

When the poet stirred, it was to spend an hour or two writing and rewriting his Kubla Khan on the balcony at Ash. He said he was cross with me for entertaining a guest so late that night, claiming he had been on the brink of a great work based on the nature of the sublime amphitheatre that lay before us under the moon. Laversha's tales had spoiled his designs. Nevertheless, he bade me read the poem on the eve of the second day and when I had finished I told him how I liked it and how the work reminded me of the smuggler's yarn, suggesting it was fortunate we were disturbed by a person up from Porlock that sepulchral night. There was only one part of the poem I had difficulty with, and that was in the final lines where he said:

"Beware! Beware!
His flashing eyes, his floating hair!
Weave a circle round him thrice,
And close your eyes with holy dread,
For he on honey-dew hath fed,
And drunk the milk of Paradise."

"I did not expect you to comprehend the ending my friend: part of it is indeed friend Laversha. But part of it is you."

"Why beware of me?" I asked with consternation.

"I have this notion that your blood is older than even these ancient forests above the Exmoor shore. I fancy that your stock was born in the first, original, place; an Eden long since lost down caverns measureless to man. Far down some sacred river. You are, as you have told me, the last of your kind and, but for some fortunate accident of time and place, the blood that is within you should have disappeared from Earth centuries ago. But you are here. Somehow you have survived. And there is something about you Johnny, something wild and different: to a modern mortal you would indeed be a demon-lover. Laversha has flashing eyes, and a great mop of floating hair. But in your own way, you have a greater essence of wildness than even he. Tis only a fancy of mine, of course, and one fuelled by laudanum, but if you do not mind, I shall keep my theory as it suits an ideal I have of things."

We went on to Lynmouth when Coleridge felt up to it and spent a day there wandering around the cliffs and beaches and visiting the Valley of the Stones, before returning across the hills into West Somerset. It was to be our only long excursion together because, in the following month, the poet William Wordsworth and his sister Dorothy were to call upon the poet, and shortly after that Mr Poole managed to secure them Alfoxden Park.

At first they came for a just a two week stay with Coleridge, and horribly cramped they must have been in that small cottage. I called one day in that month of June and found an uncomfortable domesticity haunting every corner of that crowded home. It was fortunate that Charles Lloyd had recently quit the place, as there would have been no room for the Wordsworths had he been there, and I am sure the poor fellow's awkwardness would have further disturbed the party. Sara Coleridge was, as usual, devoting her time to her baby, but I noticed that she also hung her arms around Sam's shoulders, or held his hand, whenever he was near to her. I have no doubt she loved him very much, but the truth of it was that I'd never seen this kind of outward display of affection before. It did not take long to realise what she was about: the poet was going out of his way to impress Miss Dorothy Wordsworth and these public affections could hardly pass unnoticed. I thought the girl was rather plain, at least upon the eye, though she improved greatly when she smiled. Which she did often in the company of Coleridge, indeed, she laughed at his every jest. When she wasn't laughing, she was gazing at him with large, adoring, grey eyes. So uncomfortable did I find all this that I made my excuses and left as soon as I could. There was another reason for my exit: I had the feeling that William Wordsworth had no fondness whatsoever for me. Later I learned that he did not welcome familiarity with the lower classes. The first I really saw of him he was sitting in Tom Poole's bower, dressed in an old fustian jacket under which were curious striped pantaloons. When I arrived his gaunt, unfriendly face peered into my own. He had a large nose which lent him an imperious expression even when he smiled which, unlike his sister, was most infrequently. He spoke with a northern burr, the likes of which I had never heard before. Sam introduced me and flew off upon his usual enthusiastic lyricisms concerning the lot of the broomsquires. But, unlike the other writers and poets I have met with Coleridge - like Robert Southey, Charles Lamb, Thomas de Quincy and William Hazlitt who all welcomed me into their company - William Wordsworth looked me up and down and then cast me from his sphere of interest.

I was mildly disappointed when I heard that the brother and sister had taken Alfoxden - which is a small estate not far from the series of coombes that provide the Walfords with their home. I realised their arrival would mean that I would see less of my friend Coleridge – but no matter, this was balanced by the fact that it was the time of year when I must be busy with the broom. Occasionally I would see the three of them - Coleridge, Dorothy and William Wordsworth - walking across the hills, but I think Sam realised there was some discomfiture on the part of Mr Wordsworth when it came to fraternising with local folk. So he would wave and perhaps come across for a quick word, but would never stop for a drink or a bowl of something as he used to when in the company of Charles Lloyd. As I say, this suited me at the time as I had plenty to be getting on with. After all, the frugal monies earned by me were not only feeding mother and Petronilla now, but also Jane and little Tom. The boy had been given the name after my mother told Jane that our family held Mr Thomas Poole in higher esteem than any other man in the world. During this early summer period, things did not pass so badly between Jane Shorney and myself. Perhaps it was the warm, balmy weather, or the fact she seemed to have mellowed with the novelty of motherhood - whatever the reason, she no longer seemed quite so sharp and ready to be cross. There were things, though, that still seemed to stir dark, angry currents in her. And those currents carried suspicion and distrust. If I came home late from a day's work she would ask where I had been - for me, it wasn't so much that she inquired, but the way in which she did it. Reviewing the life we had, I can see now there was insecurity in everything she did. I have known others to have suffered such self-doubt and fear, but they never did act so testily as she. It was if the entire world was out to catch her or trick her.

One day something occurred that made her indignant beyond belief. It was an insignificant affair, but it illuminated in her an entire spectrum of questioning and doubt. For reasons which I need not go into, we no longer bought our flour from Rice's Mill. No one though, had thought to inform Jane of this as she rarely left the camp, still being much afeared of meeting William and even her own mother. But as summer drew on Jane began to enjoy more confidence and one day she thought she would be doing my mother a favour by purchasing flour, as she knew we had run low. The Walford women were busy making brooms so, without thinking any more of it, Jane put young Tom on her back and walked down to the mill. She was just being handed the flour when old man Rice walked into the room.

"Ain't you living up wi' the Walfords?" he said. When she nodded she was, he had her thrown off the premises saying that no gypsy was welcome anywhere near his place. Even Petronilla had the sense not to tell Jane the full story behind the miller's wrath. That dear simple minded soul realised that one whiff of Anne Rice would have Jane grinding her green axe forever more. Of course, she plagued Nilla, and mother, and me, demanding to know what we'd done to cause such an attitude in Harold Rice who, in the normal run of things, would be only too pleased to take anyone's money. No-one ever mentioned Anne's name and eventually, to put her mind at ease, I mentioned it all concerned my father's penchant for smuggling. She had, of course, heard of the death of Buncombe the factotum and remembered the rumours that I was in some way involved. So that mollified her for a while, but it wasn't long before another occurrence was to set her off again. This time it was much worse. Indeed, it was to be the beginning of her journey to oblivion. And mine too, I fear.

Thanks to my trip to North Devon with Coleridge I had been late with the collection of the broom and mother and Petronilla had to work their fingers to the bone to get things ready for my summer tour of the villages. Added to this it was an exceptionally early whortleberry season and that meant the two of them were off just after dawn, bending double for hours on end picking trug-fulls of the tiny fruits off the low bushes. The berry picking was a good business for us, and Walfords for generations had enjoyed a reputation for selling the finest wurts. We knew the best places, and those goyals and raps remain a secret tightly held within the family. So all of us were working morning, noon 'til night - except for Jane, who would laze around the camp all day. She would not even keep the fires in, or cook, which would cause mother to grind her two remaining teeth.

Whether it was the strain of having Jane live with us, or simply the hard work in unusually hot weather, I do not know; but it proved too much for the poor old woman. She collapsed in the woods and Petronilla fetched me to carry her home. We called the doctor, but all he would say when he came that evening was that she was old and needed plenty of rest. The wurts had more-or-less come to an end, and it was only a matter of days before I set off on my annual journeyings, so it was decided that my sisters Avice and Sylvestra - who were both now married and living in nearby villages - should take turns in looking after her until my return.

The next Sunday we transported mother down to Sylvestra's cottage. I shall always remember that day: it was hot and the sun burned down upon us so that we put a small awning over the cart to protect poor mother. She did not look well at all. The sight of her put me in a turbulent frame of mind for I was deeply worried about her and wondered if I should be going off to sell brooms when she was in such a state. But she bade me go, giving me a look I shall not forget.

"There's things I haven't told ee Johnny - haven't known how to," she croaked as she embraced me when it came time to leave. "But when you do return in a week or two, come and take me back to the hill. Tis where I belongs and, afore I dies, I wish to make my peace with you and your sisters."

I told her not to speak of dying, but I should have known better. Mother had what I once heard Coleridge describe as a "native intelligence" – she knew about things or folks did not. Like the coming of her own death. One of the many heavy regrets I take to my own grave with me is that I did not stay with her. She died within the week.

It has been minutes since I wrote those last words and I have fair drenched my cheeks with tears, for I loved that uncomplaining, stalwart woman and believe the world will not see her like again. Word of her passing reached me on my travels and I wasted no time in hastening home. It was hot and I knew they would not delay in burying her and I knew that she wanted to lie beside her husband, not to be alone in some faceless grave beside the church. And that, I am glad to say, is where she rests now; high on Beacon Hill near the graves of the ancients, beside the bones of the man she loved.

Recounting the passing of my dear mother has thrown me off my track, for I was about to relate what else happened that Sunday. As I have said, I was in a turbulent state of mind; not only was I concerned for my mother but also, that morning, Jane had told me she was once again with child. I have mentioned this already, but it came as a shock to me that day, for this time I knew full well that the child would be my own.

"I doesn't mind you goin' off on yer travels now Johnny," she said to me that morning as we lay together. "Not so much anyhow. This time I knows you love me and you will be working for your family."

She pulled my hand down to her soft bare stomach which, I could feel, was already larger than it had been. I had feigned some degree of happiness, for I really was quite taken aback. But this only shows how dull I was between the ears - what else could I have expected from all the nights we'd spent together since she had come to live with us? If you lie with a woman, night after night, something is likely to come of it. Of course, being Jane, she was complaining within hours that I was not making a fuss of her, and I told her she must understand that I had other worries - not the least of which was mother being ill.

And so it was that the four of us, Jane, Petronilla (in floods of tears), little Tom and myself, said goodbye to mother at Sylvestra's house and returned to the hill that baking Sunday afternoon. I walked alongside the pony with the dogs, while the other three rode in the cart under the awning. I preferred it that way, both for Eskie's sake, and for my own. Up front I could at least have some peace in which to think. But my reflective mood was not to last for long...

Past Holford we turned into Hodder's Combe and were glad of the cool shade under the trees. That is where we came face-to-face with Anne Rice. She had, I learned, come to spend a week with her father and was on her way to see Mr Poole before church. There she was, suddenly before us, astride her little hunter mare; and me, standing there with my womenfolk and the child behind me in the cart. Jane Shorney was no fool; she saw the look upon Anne's face and watched me halt in my steps. My sister later told me that even from where she sat in the cart, she could see I had gone quite white and that my hand shook upon Eskie's bridle. Those moments seemed like an hour to me, but could have only have been a few seconds.

"Hello Johnny," said the woman that I loved.

"Good day to you Anne," I replied in a voice that I could not stop from quavering. I could hear a heartbeat punctuate each and every vowel.

"Is your family well?" she asked.

"No, I am afraid mother has taken sick. We have just run her down to my sister's cottage. She will be more comfortable there while I go to sell the brooms."

"Then, if I may, I shall call on her during the week before I return to Bath?"

"I am sure she would appreciate that, Anne. It is kind of you."

There was a short silence and then she said: "Goodbye then Johnny. Goodbye Petronilla. Ma'am..." She added to Jane as she passed the cart.

I have recorded this mundane conversation verbatim, because I can recall every word and nuance of it. Though it may seem mundane on paper, it most certainly did not seem that way to me. As I say, my heart beat so furiously from the moment I saw her, until half-an-hour after she had gone, I thought my chest might explode. I had one overwhelming desire and that was to ask her to walk with me on the hill. I'd have told her of the madness and mayhem of life that had led me to make so many desperate mistakes. And I'd have told her I loved her more than ever.

Instead, as we plodded on up the valley, I heard Jane's rasping voice, spiking, probing - and remembered the news she had given me that day. I was to be a father. Even if poor little Tom was not mine, as I suspected, I was to be a father – this time for certain. It was too late now. Far too late for Anne and I.

"Hello Johnny. Oh hello Anne. I never saw you like that afore Johnny Walford. Anyone 'ould think there was sommat a'tween you two. How is your family Johnny? I shall go an' see your mother then. Oh how kind of you Anne... Do you think I am a fool? Do you think I could not see what was going on? That's why that old miller would not sell me flour! You better tell me Johnny Walford - or I shall make you pay..."

That is how Jane went on far into the night. Quick as a sparrow-hawk she'd turned her course and picked out the unsuspecting moment. When a sparrow-hawk does that, it costs a thrush or a blackbird its life. And right then I felt like one of those hapless, helpless birds.

"There was always word, when we was younger," she continued distraught, "that you and she was sweet'earts. But I never went to school so I never knew the truth o' it. But I 'ad thought it was just a thing when you was children. I thought it must 'ave ended when you went away to Broomfield.... But now I ain't so sure."

She was saying all this much later as we sat by the fire - and she dug her nails deep into my arm with pure primordial hate. She claimed she had always suspected there was someone else lurking in the background, and now she knew what – or who - it was. Not once did I gainsay her, nor did I stop her pestering Petronilla until the girl was in tears and blabbing how I had always been in love with the miller's daughter. So that was that. Jane knew my secret – and maybe, I told myself, it wasn't such a bad thing. Perhaps she would go away and find one of her men friends to take her in and I should be rid of her. Child or no child, I knew I could never live out the rest of my life with her. There was something crooked and twisted inside Jane, and when I got too close to it, I wanted to be away as fast as the hill could swallow me.

And so once again I escaped on my travels. I was gone the very next dawn, but as I have said, I was back within the week.

They were all there when mother died. Sylvestra of course, Petronilla, Avice and even William who had been called home from the Levels. Understandably, they had difficulty in finding me. It was Flighty Chidgey, who had a knack for tracking people down, who caught up with me over Dunster way – but he only located me by accident as he was on his way to Timberscombe to look at some hounds. By then it was too late. Mother had gone to another place. What hurt me so is that they said she wept bitter tears wanting to see her Johnny one last time.

The funeral service was being held in the little church at the foot of the hills, and I could hear the Parson's plaintive voice ringing from the pulpit when I arrived outside. I left Eskie with a friend in Dunster and had run to Holford in just three hours – and so exhausted was I that I collapsed by the churchyard wall to catch my breath. That is where I realised that the fresh-dug grave I could see was for my mother. I suppose I cannot imagine what else I expected, but I was overcome by emotion at the sight of it. I could hear the sweet simple music of a hymn emanating from the church, and I wept and wept until a sense of calm washed over me. Standing up I entered the church and walked to the pew where my family stood, and looked across at the little cheap planked coffin bedecked in a haze of wondrous wildflowers.

After the service we filed out and, after being hugged and wept upon by my sisters, I announced to the congregation that mother was to be buried next to father up on the hill. At this there occurred a disgraceful scene: William flew into a passion and said it was not to be: that he, the eldest would decide upon our mother's burial. The Parson agreed and said he would have nothing to do with a burial outside sacred ground. But now Sylvestra spoke and said she knew it was mother's wish to lie beside our late father. You have never seen such a commotion at a funeral. Tom Poole put his hand up and asked if anyone else knew of mother's wishes – and all three sisters pitched in to say she had made her intentions clear several times during her last week.

And so it was. We borrowed a cart and conveyed her to Beacon Hill on Staple Plain where the two of them rest in peace to this day. William led the cortege. He somehow maintained his dignity and declared that, although he was much against it; he was eldest and it was his duty to bury his mother. On the way we passed Rice's Mill and I was surprised to see the curtains drawn and the employees come out and doff their caps as a mark of respect. Anne was there in the gardens, dressed in formal black, and when she saw me, she sank her eyes to the ground. I supposed she had not attended the funeral because her father had forbidden it, but I was to learn more of this later. In the heat of the afternoon we proceeded up to the ridge and two or three of us dug the grave next to father's bones. William would not have anything to do with the work, but retained his place as chief mourner with a look or murderous grief upon his face. Mr Poole, as churchwarden, read a prayer, and that was the last rite of the old broomsquire's wife. Our loving, hard-working, uncomplaining, soft and gentle mother was laid to rest.

The girls wept and William came to me and spoke so quietly that for a moment I thought he was going to be civil. It was, after all, the sort of occasion when most brothers would forget their differences. But this is what he said: "You 'as thwarted me yet again. Think not that I shall ever speak with ee, or 'ave anything to do with ee, a'tween now and the grave. The next time we meet, it will be in hell."

With that he span on his heel and was gone. I had a few words with Mr Poole and thanked him for supporting me in the matter of mother's burial and that dear man looked at me with a face lined deep by sadness and concern. Then it was all over and we were making our way down Sheppard's Combe and along Lady's Edge. Even though these places are central to our ancient home, a great weight of loneliness descended upon me, just as it had when father died, and I was in no mood for company. It was only much later, when my sisters and their husbands and families had eventually left the camp long after nightfall, that I mentioned to Petronilla the fact we had seen Anne Rice dressed in mourning clothes. Nilla looked nervous and I could see something was troubling her. She said she was tired and tried to pass me to go to her bed, but I caught her by the arm.

"Is there something I should know?" I asked.

Poor Nilla, she could never cope with being put on the spot. Within a moment or two she was gushing her story and a moment or two after that I was marching into the hut where Jane was putting the boy to bed. I wrenched her away... "What right did you have to send Anne Rice away from the church today?" I growled clutching her arms so tightly with my fingers that she gasped in pain.

"I didn't want her causin' no distress," said Jane, frightened, and yet with some aggression of her own. "She was not family - 'er father would not even sell yer mother flour or bread. Why should she come and weep tears over your dear mother when 'er own father once cast the poor woman from his house?"

"What do you mean? Anne had nothing to do with her father's arguments with my family. But this is typical of you. You have to make trouble, and for what? So that you can have your own way of things. You had no right to turn Anne away. Mother loved her and would have wanted her there. You can be jealous of it if you like, but that is the way things were!"

She pulled herself away from me and sneered. That look made me shudder inside. It was the very epitome of disdain. "You fool Johnny Walford," she hissed. "You poor fool. You think you're so clever with all yer long fancy words and yer fancy friends. You think I ain't good enough for the likes of you. And yet your blood was never good enough for others - I know that for sure. The Rice family for one. The very folk you would so like to sidle up to."

I thought she had somehow discovered how the miller had condemned the link between me and his daughter. But Jane continued, warming to her theme: "Just like you, ain't it? To forget that old man Rice cast your mother out because she was not good enough! Threw a servant girl out of house and home for having his child. Makes I laugh it does - that evil old man always denied that William was his own, just like you deny Tom!"

It took several moments for this to sink in. I slumped back onto a bench and just sat there gawping at her as if she's ripped the very stuffing out of me. "What lies are you spouting now?" I groaned. "How dare you say such things..."

She looked at me and, slowly, a baneful smile began to flicker across her lips: "You didn't know did ee? You didn't even know! Why did ee think William left as soon as ee could? Why do you think ee despises the broomsquires? As for you marryin' the miller's daughter - you never 'ad no chance at all. Not Johnny Walford the bright broomsquire boy – the one who goes round thinkin' ee's so damn clever. And all along, you knew nothin' at all..."

By now Jane was enjoying herself and her taunts and rasping, probing voice were beginning to choke me with anger and confusion. I did the best thing I could. I swept up my hat and walked out into the night. I did not stop until an hour or so later when I found myself banging on Thomas Poole's door, lucky to catch him just before he retired to bed.

"T'was never my place to tell you," he shrugged, pouring me a large glass of his French. I had asked him why no-one had ever thought to inform me of this incredible truth about my own family. "If your father did not, and your mother did not, what business was it of mine to disclose it? But there it is, and I suppose you are thinking it explains a lot about that brother of yours. Poor lad. He never belonged on the hill and, in truth, your father did not take to him. William was only a babe when he went there."

He sat down in his shabby old leather chair and looked me in the eye: "Jane has it right: your mother was once a maid at Rice's house. He lived there alone with his wicked old father; the mother having died from misery and grief – at least, that's what most people assumed – some years before. A more arrogant and selfish lout than the young Rice was in those days, it is hard to imagine. His father had only one small vein of kindness and that was all directed at his son. He spoiled him rotten, and the youth grew up doing whatever he pleased. By the time he was seventeen or eighteen he was forever drinking too much and losing at cards. Not that he cared a jot, for the old man would always bale him out.

"If I recall, he did not even bother to deny putting a servant girl in the family way. When she had the child though, she made the mistake of making some claim on its behalf to her master, and was thrown out for her troubles. I heard from your father how she lay in that bower of beeches, just down from the mill, for hours in the freezing rain. With a few shawls she made some attempt to protect her infant son, but so stricken with grief and fear was she, that she could not find the strength to move. Indeed, she had nowhere to go. No kinfolk, no friends. I believe if your father had not happened along when he did; young William at least – and maybe your mother too – would have been no more. But he did pass by, and he did put her in his trap and he did take her to his camp. And there, with your father, she stayed. I'll say this: your father and mother may have been thrown together, but I have never seen a man and a woman love each other more. You may be interested to know that, soon after taking her in, your father once came face-to-face with Rice in the hills and beat him half to death for what he had done. Later, Rice played clever and got your father involved with the smuggling – and in some way I have never fully understood – had some hold over him. It was his way of paying him back for the beating. There was something else: Rice married a while afterwards and his new wife died giving birth to Anne. Shortly after that, I have heard, the miller sought your mother out and begged her to move back to the mill to help him with the child. For a time he seemed obsessed by the idea, but your mother was in love with her broomsquire and happy raising her own family. Rice never forgave her, although he had no earthly grounds for acting so."

Tom rose to pour us both another brandy: "It is a little ironic," he mused, "That you have discovered all this from the woman who claims to have borne your child. A child that you deny is yours. So you see Johnny, how life repeats itself? We are caught up in some awful circle, it seems to me. Rice has his money and his mill; but I know for a fact that he has not enjoyed a single day of his life since the moment he cast your mother out. It was common knowledge he did not love that wife of his, and some say that – just like his own mother – she died of grief rather than the childbirth. And then Rice – miserable wretch that he is – goes crashing on through his sorry life exacerbating the misery of it all. He denies the only thing he loves her own road to happiness. I have no doubt he blocked the marriage twixt Anne and yourself as some sort of revenge. To get back at your mother in some twisted way of his own. You see, when the young drunken Rice was abusing a servant girl, it never once occurred to him he might be in love with her. But first love is a strange and awesome thing. Rice thought nothing of casting your mother out, only later did the selfish fool realise that he loved her."

With that I thanked him for his counsel and bade him goodnight. Outside in the cool night air, I turned to walk up and up the flanks of Quantock until I was surrounded by nought but the multitude of stars. I was a weary man by the time I reached Robin Upright's Hill. Weary, but older, wiser, sadder and, perhaps strangely in the circumstances, feeling more free than any other man this side of Laversha's wild ocean.

The next day I was off on my travels once again. Many was the village haunted by disappointed faces during the weeks that followed for, with the best will in the world, I could not bring myself to play upon my father's old violin. Merrymaking was the last thing on my mind, such is the respect for death, though, that none complained when they learned I was in mourning. One thing brightened the greyness and sadness of my days and that was a brief meeting with Anne Rice. She was down from Bath towards the end of the summer, and she sought me out and found me selling brooms in the strange wild hinterland known as Crowcombe Heathfield. It is as remote and lonely a place as any in Somersetshire, and it was only by luck that she stumbled across Eskie and the cart. I could hardly believe my eyes when I saw her standing there petting the old pony. We walked together for a while out onto the wild furzey heath that gives the place its name, and it was some time before we spoke.

"I wanted to say how sorry I was over your mother's death," she said. "But there is something else. The day before yesterday I met Petronilla and she told me what had occurred between you and Jane Shorney and how she told you about my father and your mother and William and everything. You may as well know that I have renounced father once and for all. When I think of the damage he has done! I spent last night at my old school at Bagborough and today, when I heard from someone that you were not too far away, I decided to come and find you before I return to Bath. I wanted to apologise. For everything. For my father, though goodness knows why I should make any excuses for him. And anyhow, I wanted to apologise on my own behalf for the way I would not listen to you. For the way I flew off without investigating any of the facts. Because of that, what has – or rather, what has not – occurred between us, is a tragedy. That is how I see it. I grew to love you after we met all those years ago by the waterwheel – and I want you to know that I love you still."

I could hardly believe my ears. In my wildest dreams I would never have dared pray that one day I should hear such words utter from Anne's sweet lips. My legs shook beneath me and I looked into her lovely eyes. She saw the expression on my face and, before I could speak of my joy, she went on and shattered my ecstasy in an instant... "It is too late Johnny. You have your Jane and she is growing large with your child. We must not make the same mistakes as our parents did before us. You must see that!"

"But do you not see how hopeless it is?" I cried. "That I should be content with that woman while you are in this world... It is unthinkable. There has only ever been one person for me, both of us know that. I know temptation got the better of me in months of desperation after you went galloping off to Bath. But believe me, I cannot live with her as man and wife - not if we were the last two people upon God's Earth. Not once, for a fleeting second, have I loved her since the day I met her. It is an awful truth I know, God shall punish me, but truth it is."

She looked away and I could see her exquisite eyes roving the great wide horizons of the heath. There was desperation in them as she gazed across the scorched, yellowing, dazzling landscape where the summers-play flickered in a shimmering mirage. At last she said: "I must atone for my father's wickedness. How think you a Christian God would regard a family that - not once - but twice saw an innocent child cast into the world without its rightful parentage? I will not do it Johnny. I will not stand between you and the child that Jane Shorney is carrying. We will meet, and God-willing, we will be friends. But from now on anything further between us would be against God's will and against all that is naturally right and good - and that I will not contemplate."

"But you are throwing away the best, the only chance we have," I wailed. "Jane will be tormented and miserable wherever she is. She was born under that star. She is marked by it and she will cast anyone close to her down under the same blanket of distress and suffering. But we...We have a chance of lasting happiness. At least the child will have one parent who has the sanity of being content."

She would have none of it and when I tried to reach out to her, to pull her into my embrace, she hauled herself away and climbed upon her horse. I begged her, with tears flowing down my face, I wept for her to stay - but, for the second time in our lives, she wheeled around and galloped away from me. I have never seen her since and now will go to my death with just a memory of the woman I loved.

PART 5

FINAL DAYS OF DISCONTENT

At the end of the summer I returned to Quantock and moved the camp to where I had been given a great deal of coppicing to do just under Robin Upright's Hill. With few words spoken, the truce between Jane and myself returned, although we did have one sour dispute when I told her she and little Tom could have the hut with Petronilla. I liked to get away from the place when I wasn't cutting wood or making charcoal, and took to wandering seawards to visit Montague. It was more than escape or pleasure; I had one or two arrangements to make concerning a nocturnal visit from a certain vessel. The mudhorse fisherman was all for the business, and said it had been far too long since liquor of quality had come Quantock way.

The route to Kilve Pill took me directly past Alfoxden Park and it was on one of my sea-borne journeys that Coleridge caught sight of me. He hailed and waved for me to tarry a while, and with that ran over to where a group of folk were sitting on a rug under a cedar. I could make out William Wordsworth, but I knew none of the others – his sister was not there as far as I could see. Then Coleridge came bounding over the grassy park to where I stood. "Johnny," he cries, "It has been far too long. Whither do you wander? For I should dearly like to join you for an hour or so."

I told him I was off to the beach where the mudhorse fisherman would fill me a basket with his catch, and the poet was delighted: "Nothing could be better," he enthused. "You know how I detest the taste of red meat. Nothing I can think of would suit me better than fresh sea-fish for supper."

So off we went, down over the shortcut to Crooked Copse and on into Pardlestone Lane. "I am glad I spied you passing Johnny," said Coleridge. "For there is a delicate matter in which I would value your advice... It concerns politics, something – I know – which you so wisely avoid. So you should, in this rural paradise of yours. However, politics is a Methuselah that will rear its ugly heads the world over, from the remotest islet in the widest ocean to the grimy back-streets of our frightful cities. Politics: the vicissitudes of man. Even Quantock must taste the poison of the thing, and I am rather uncertain as to what to do about one particular manifestation of it. Have you heard anything? Concerning Wordsworth and myself, I mean? Well, allow me to put you in the picture before anyone else paints you a different, less salubrious version of events. It seems that we are no longer as popular as we once were in these parts. Indeed, I have a suspicion that someone is bent upon procuring our removal from the place. It is no-one's fault but our own - my own, I should say - for Wordsworth is far more circumspect in these matters than I. It concerns my good friend John Thelwall. Did you meet him? He is a splendid fellow right enough, but he is - how shall I say - rather notorious. A free-thinking, republican. Not the thing to be, especially now that we are having this trouble with the French. Thelwall is an honest, warm-hearted man to be sure, but he does have an unfortunate appetite for expressing his sympathies concerning the French Revolutionaries. Often in public. Far too public, it seems. Now, I am not so foolish as to think the country folk were ever likely to take a verbose fellow such as myself directly to their bosom, but I was inclined to believe they had begun to soften in the case of one daft poet. However, friend Thelwall has proved to be one thinker too far. Only the other day he was spouting some of his more outlandish views in the Castle of Comfort Inn."

It was what Coleridge said next that caught my attention, for up until then I had not held much interest. I had seen what politics had done to Andrew Crosse, and I wanted no more to do with it.

"This dangerous talk of Thelwall's silenced the place – if, that is, you do not count the undercurrent of angry mutterings. However, reports of his outburst have reached the ears of Tom Poole and such talk has caused even that stalwart to become nervous of our standing. So, let me get down to the bones of what I have to say. It is this, and you may laugh: but both William Wordsworth and I believe that we are being spied upon. That is right - followed, shadowed. By whom, we are not sure. But several times we have been out on the hills - in places normally empty of a single sheep, let alone another man - and there has been a figure, darting behind a tree, slipping into a wood, ducking out of sight. We must have caught sight of him a dozen times now, if we have seen him once."

I was amused that such an unlikely thing could occur here in our empty hills and thought laudanum might have more to do with it that anything in actual flesh and blood, but said. "I can see why you are concerned, but why are you telling me?"

"Well, no-one else can move across the hills like you can. Can't you see? We must know if we are being followed or not. It may be some nervous caprice that we have manufactured for ourselves. Perhaps no-one has been on our tracks at all. But we must know, for it is worrying both of us and putting us off our work. And Johnny, if anyone can follow the follower, it is you."

I shrugged, and agreed to help any time he should ask for it. Shortly after that we reached the wide open space of the foreshore at Kilve and there, down by the edge of the great limestone pavements, was the bent outline of Montague.

Coleridge was much taken with him. "I have never seen such a fellow before," he whispered to me later as we made our way along the nets with the old fisherman. "Nor would I ever have believed there could be such a man, had I not seen him with my own eyes."

The poet was riding on the mudhorse, just as I had done as a boy all those years ago. He looked like some ridiculous figurehead standing there on the front of the sledge with his mop of black hair wafting back off his large pale face in the autumn wind. He could not take his eyes off the fisherman as he untied the nets and scooped out the shrimps and fish. It is odd, seeing someone you have know all your life, being watched through stranger's eyes. Monty had always cut a most singular figure, but looking at him now and seeing him, perhaps as the poet saw him, I was not surprised at Coleridge's interest. Monty's brown, craggy face was now almost entirely covered by the thin white wisps of a lengthy beard, and his mad eyes – which had always glinted more than most – seemed to have small fires burning deep within them. His clothes were far more ragged than usual, and he reeked of mud, eels, smoke, fish and sea.

Back in his cavernous hut we boiled the shrimps in the great vat and its steam filled the unseen corners of that black room with the salty smells of the shore. You could hear the crashing of the waves not far beyond and I believe no place in the kingdom spoke more of ocean than that dark hovel. I could see that Coleridge continued to be enchanted. He started to ask Montague about his life and at first the old man was taciturn and would hardly reply to a single one of his petitions. To help the conversation on its way I said: "Here's a strange conundrum for you Sam: ask Monty why he refuses to step foot into a boat. He has one you know, but you will never see him in it..."

Coleridge was fascinated and pecked away at the fisherman until the old man turned around, his eyes now ablaze in the reflected light of the fire. "I will tell thee a tale thou shalt ne'er be able to write down - no matter 'ow clever you be, for t'will mean unrest for thee and every other soul that reads it..."

With that Montague set off on a remarkable narrative that, at times, though hard to follow, was so dreamlike and bizarre that, at times I felt almost seasick, at other times a sense of profound loss and ruin washed over me so that when I say 'dreamlike' I most likely mean nightmare. It was the stuff of nightmares. He told of vast empty oceans and of heat and cold and of life sinking irresistibly toward death. He spoke of his own mortal fear and his feeling of devastation; of the way in which the ocean held him in hopeless, despairing, vassalage. He spoke of his desolate loneliness and isolation and of his overwhelming sense of guilt. There was something about a seabird that they killed. Not they: he. Montague had killed it and the spirit of this awful bird had led them to years of endless drifting upon a vast and empty ocean. One by one his fellow crewmen died until at last he was the only one.

How did Coleridge put it in his own words much later?

"The many men, so beautiful!

And they all dead did lie:

And a thousand thousand slimy things

Lived on; and so did I."

The tale went on and on. I had never heard it before - nor anything like it - nor do I wish to hear it again, for it froze the blood in my veins. It certainly explained why old Monty would never again step foot in a boat. It was the tale of when he was a deep-ocean mariner sailing in distant places far from any land. And the tale went on until the shadows of night overtook us and the moon and Venus came up between the islands of the channel. A church bell struck and seemed to awaken Coleridge from his trance, and he made to leave, but the old man gripped him about the arm.

"I really must go, I am late for an appointment," shouted Sam, as if suddenly afeared of the ancient savant. But the old man's long brown fingers would not release him from their bony grip. And on went Montague again, until the moon was high overhead and we heard the church bell once more issue its chime across the moonlit flatlands of the coast. Only after that did Monty release us, and we hurried out like fellows in a trance. Not a single fish did Sam Coleridge take home with him that night, but I believe he had caught himself a more substantial catch. I have read the rhyme and have seen how he dealt with the ancient mariner and his albatross.

It was December time when I saw him again and when I did he told me he'd been busy making something of Montague's extraordinary yarn. I never talked to the fisherman about it - and never again did I mention his awesome tale - I had heard it once and never needed to be told it again, for I still sometimes wake at night trembling with the nightmarish quality of it. But I returned often to his hovel on the beach in preparation for the 'Mavis'. When she came she fetched in west, past Quantock's Head, at a place they call David's Way. It is by far the most remote part of our coast, though the big house at East Quantoxhead is not far off and almost overlooks the shore where we imported our wares. The man who lives there is none other than the High Sheriff of the county.

Monty was against this landing place, and when I pressed him he said; "Cos thic brother of your'n do live in East Quantoxhead."

"What of it?" I asked.

"T'was thic Devil that 'ad the Revenue on us last time round," he spat.

William again. In truth he hated us. He had hated the man that raised him. And now father had gone, he had no-one left to hate but me. William though, was still working out on the Levels, so the appointed December night came and went without a hitch. We used the mudhorse at low tide, with barely a moon to see by, and we hauled the stuff up to where Eskie was waiting with her cart on David's Way. From there the track leads inland past a pixie mound and along a small ridge up into Herridge Combe. It took all our might to push the heavy load up from the bottom of this valley to the old Greenway Path on the ridge, and then it was easy enough down to Slaughterhouse where I'd tidied a small cave under a secret cliff by the side of the brook where it enters a thick clump of furze. From this modest hideaway I distributed the stuff all over Christmastide, and made a handsome profit to keep the hungriness of winter at bay.

It was the first of several such excursions and, always, Laversha turned up when he said he would and, always, I paid him on the nail thanks to the backing I received from various contacts in both hill and vale. We became good friends - that wild, reckless exotic mate and me. Once, after the Revenue had nearly caught us out on the cliffs when the 'Mavis' had gone aground, and he and I pushed the ship, half-afloat, back into the waves – and burst half the blood vessels in our bodies. It was a feat of strength I doubt a dozen average men could manage. Laversha said to me: "I never had such a friend as you Johnny Walford. Why not come a-roving with me and see life beyond these grey shores? You know I would do anything for you - I have sworn an oath - one that would take me to the ends of the Earth to protect you...."

It was after the December cargo had arrived that Coleridge came to visit me with more talk of his mysterious follower. I remember that because I was able to give him a bottle of Laversha's finest to help with his festive celebrations. The poet was always in penury and could not afford such luxuries for himself. But this time he was worried about more than the emptiness of his purse. I must say, I thought all the talk of silent followers was nothing more than s product of his rich imagination, and let it go at that. But shortly after New Year I saw him again and once more he voiced his concerns, though I could not go with him because Jane, who was large enough to burst, was suffering pains and we thought she must be near to giving birth. As it happens, she did not have the child for another two weeks - and that is a day I shall remember 'til the end.

Thank God Avice came up to our camp under the slopes of Robin Upright's Hill and took charge of the whole affair. I was there though, when the child came into this life; awkward and afraid I stood there watching the miracle of birth. They wanted me out, Petronilla and Avice - Jane was thrashing about too much to care, but I stayed gripped by this greatest of all life's mysteries: life where there was no life before. I was the first one to cradle her in my arms, choked with emotion at the sight of her. My own daughter. The little girl looked about with damp, unseeing eyes and she, like her brother had done more than a year before, waved her tiny arms and moved as if to the beat of another heart in another time and space. That tiny delicate being, naked and new in my great rough arms - with all the wilderness of my beloved hills soughing and sighing in the Quantock breeze around us. A broomsquire's child was born. I may have had differences with her mother, but I was the proudest man in Somersetshire that day and for a long time after. The child came too late for Jane and me; our detestation of one another was already fully complete. As if to make things worse, where I loved the little girl with all my heart, Jane seemed to shun it. She stuck to Tom, but with the girl she was always maintained a disturbing, unnatural, coldness.

Why we called my daughter Mercy, I cannot recall, but it seemed like a righteous name to me. Mercy Walford. What shall become of her? That is one of things that concerns me most as I pen these words. She was – she is - the most beautiful thing I have ever seen, and I would like to think she goes forth into her life under a lucky star and with God's Grace upon her side. I am of sure of it. Her unfortunate beginnings shall not sully the golden prospect that Mercy holds within her little hands.

Coleridge came one day and showered fine words over my beautiful girl. He also showed me a letter that he had written to Thelwall, who had been so taken with Quantock he was proclaiming his intention to move to the area:

"Very great odium Tom Poole incurred by bringing me here," wrote Coleridge. "My peaceable manners and known attachment to Christianity had almost worn it away when Wordsworth came, and he, likewise by T. Poole's agency, settled here. You cannot conceive the tumult, calumnies and apparatus of threatened persecutions which the event has occasioned round about us. If you too, should come, I am afraid that even riots, and dangerous riots, might be the consequence. Either of us separately would perhaps be tolerated; but all three together - what can it be, less than plot and damned conspiracy? - a school for the propagation of Demagogy and Atheism?"

"That should put him off," says I. "But why, Samuel, do you show me the letter?"

"Because word of Thelwall's intention has got about the place, I do not know how, but already we hear dark murmurings down in the village. I would appreciate it greatly if you could help counter these rumours next time you are at the inn, for Wordsworth is becoming so nervous he is threatening to move away. Moreover, the family which owns Alfoxden is saying his lease will not be renewed after his first year is up. I cannot tell you how disastrous it would be for me if the brother and sister were to leave. I have come to rely heavily upon them in any number of ways. But there is something else, the follower is with us now more than ever. For the past three days we have been haunted by him. Will you do that favour for us Johnny? Will you help us to find out who he is and what he is about?"

There is little I would not have done for my friend Sam Coleridge and that very afternoon, with the rain falling in sheets, we set about hunting the hunter. I do not believe Wordsworth liked the matter at all, and he certainly did not like taking orders from a broomsquire, but if the thing was to be done, it was to be worked to my design. Coleridge had told him that I could stalk a young stag in the brightness of midday and so the spy should be easy game for me. So the northerner acquiesced and, once we had discussed the machinations of the hunt, the two poets and the sister Dorothy set off from Alfoxden Park, making their way up through Alfoxden Wood and around by Willoughby Cleave. I was waiting out of the rain in a thicket of oaks where the valley makes a curve past Short Combe, positioned so that anyone walking on the path must pass directly below my little nest. Sure enough the three friends went by close enough for me to hear every word of their chatter. Wordsworth, in that burr of his, was declaiming certain theories on the subject of metaphysics when Coleridge suddenly changed the subject altogether and began a hearty monologue on the different notes of the nightingale. I could see Miss Wordsworth hanging upon his every word, while her brother appeared to be rather irritated by Sam's fanciful flights of song. I thought to myself, seeing Dorothy's admiring smile, that Sara Coleridge, for one, would be glad to see the Alfoxden tenancy come to an end.

Their chatter faded as they went on up Hodder's Combe in the rain, and I stayed where I was; not a muscle moving and taking short shallow breaths, intent upon every single sound. A tiny goldfinch came close, pecking invisible insects off a mossy branch. I watched her hop from stump to stem to bough as she moved off towards the stream. Her chirrups, and the gurglings of the fast flowing water, were the only things that were audible in that deep, damp coombe. And then the little bird piped up her call of alarm and she, and along with a yellow wagtail, took flight from the water's edge. Something had disturbed them in their sylvan endeavours and it, I knew quite well, was the man I was waiting for. I will give him this, he moved with all the liquid grace of an experienced stalker. No stone or pebble rattled on that path, no twig or stem of foliage snapped with his passing, though he travelled at an impressive speed. He was a long, grey, fellow whose only remarkable feature was an enormous nose. But neither that remarkable organ, nor his attentive ears or flitting eyes had any idea that another man was within spitting distance of him. As he passed, so the hunter became the hunted.

Up Hodder's Combe we went, with plenty of tree cover for him, and for me. Up again into Somerton and then, higher still, to Stert Combe. I, of course, had one advantage over the spy – I knew the route of his prey, for we had discussed every step of it beforehand. There were two or three things to be established by the exercise: the first was just how far the man would go in his hunt –

would he be content to follow just along the wooded coombes where the cover made stalking easy, or would he attempt the more difficult task of following them across the moor? The plan was for them to walk all the way to Crowcombe, where they would call at the inn before making their return, and this route would certainly entail a good deal of difficult terrain on his part. Secondly, we wished to know how far his researches would take him. Would he, for instance, move in as close as possible to his prey so as to overhear their talk? And lastly, Coleridge and Wordsworth wanted information on the spy himself. Who was he and what was the meaning of his work?

By evening I had the answers. The first queries were simple enough: the spy was a determined fellow and it was obvious that he intended sticking to his prey no matter how far afield they should wander. Moreover, he was intent upon listening to their talk. All this became apparent to me as I had watched the man pass out of the trees at the top of Stert Combe - from that moment I suspected he was intending to stick with his quarry for the rest of the day. It is hard to stalk on the open moors but that did not put him off, though he was forced to wait in a goyal until the three friends had crossed the summit of Black Hill. Had he not done so he would have been spotted on that featureless plain. This delay of his made my work easy as all I had to do was jump the stream, climb the wooded side of the coombe and cross the spur by Hare Knap. For a minute or two I would be exposed up there, but from his goyal the spy would not see me and even if he moved and looked my way, he would have merely spotted a yokel crossing a neighbouring hill. My course then took me down into Frog Combe where I turned sharp right to follow the curve of it south-west and then south-east. This now brought me to the open moor close to Wilmott's Pool on the far side of Black Hill where it was just a matter of a five minute stroll around to a predetermined rendezvous at Crowcombe Park Gate. This is where the poets would take their ease for a moment or two on a seat which the Carew family have set just inside the trees. It is a covered bench positioned in such a way so as to allow the weary walker a fine view of the vale through a gap in the beeches that are part of a great hangar that stretches all the way down to the village. There is a thicket of holly just behind this seat, and there is a second thicket just a stone's throw behind that. It was in the latter that I hid and waited. In a short while my friends duly arrived and, as arranged, rested on the covered bench. Five minutes afterwards, the man with the nose turned up and entered the thicket just behind them just as we'd assumed he would. From that hiding place he'd have heard every word of their conversation, indeed, I could just about make out what those verbose poets were saying from my more distant hidey-hole.

After a while my friends continued on their way and, moments later, the spy was after them. There was, I realised, little point in following the hunted and their hunter down to the inn, for I did not want to enter the place and be seen at close quarters by the spy. I was to pick them up again on their return route which took them directly past my hut on Robin Upright's Hill. It was simply a matter of my sheltering from the rain in my hilltop home and waiting for them to pass. This they did in an hour or two and, from just inside the door, I nodded to the three of them as they walked by. A short while later the spy came loping by, but he did not see me lurking in the dark interior of the hut. From this moment I knew the poets' route would take them down beside Lady's Fountain close to my family camp (it is where we collect our water) and whither they went, of course, the spy was sure to follow. It was easy for me to sprint away across the hill and dive into Frog Combe which descends to join Lady's Combe at a ford. In other words, they were taking a triangular route around the hill while I was travelling directly to this point where the valleys meet. I planned it so I would be in a position to bring the afternoon's adventures to a close at this junction. It was simply a matter of my standing behind a large ash tree and waiting, first for the three friends to pass, and then for the spy.

As he came by I jumped out and startled him, so that he leapt backwards with surprise. "Stay friend, stay," I declared, raising a hand to halt him. "I wish to 'ave a word or two with thee..."

I could see his eyes glancing about in alarm, as if preparing a means of escape should this meeting with a stranger warrant such a thing. For my part, I had decided to play the role of the simple rustic who is suspicious of all who pass his way.

"What is it man?" he asked. "How can I help? Quickly now, for I am in a hurry."

"Just you wait on a minute," I replied; my Somersetshire burr thickened like cream pouring from a jug. "Just you hold on. For I wants a word concernin' what you'm about."

"What the Devil do you mean - what I am about?" he said indignantly. "It is no business of yours, my man, and I would ask you to be out of my way!"

"Ah, but tis my business, see!" says I, warming to the theme. "For there's bin funny business 'ereabouts o' late. There's talk o' spies and Frenchmen and the like - and you Sir - 'as bin actin' suspiciously in my book."

"Look, I have no idea what you are talking about, but I am here on important business at the behest of some very important folk who live in this neighbourhood. And I shall tell thee this my good fellow, if I have to go to these people to complain of being accosted by you, then you shall be the one who is harmed by it - not I!"

With that he made to bustle past me. But not for a moment was I daunted by him, for I knew I could match him with one hand tied behind my back in a show of strength. As for his worthies, I gave not a hoot. So I grabbed him by the arm and said again: "Stay friend, do not think to pass me by until you 'as splained what you be about up yer on such a rainy day."

He tried to wrench himself free but was unable to and I do believe the first sniff of fear began to overtake him.

"The thing is," says I, "I 'as bin watchin' thee since you passed my little 'ouse up there on the 'ill. Bless me, I thinks to meself as I see they poet folk go prancin' by in the rain: they'll catch 'emselves a death. But I'm used to they and their strange ways. Good people they be. Good, God-fearin' folk, ne'er mind if they do walk in the 'ills composin' their poems while others is 'ard at work. Anyways, I'm thinkin' all these thoughts o' mine when what do I see? I sees you urnin' past like a man who is a-stalkin' a prey. What the devil can thickee there stranger be after thinks I? 'Er be after sommat, but there's nothin' up yer save they poet folk. And then I thinks this: they be gentry - the poets - and they be ideal folk to rob on a wet lonesome a'ternoon such as this when most folks is off the hill. Johnny, I says to meself, you better follow thic feller wi' the big nose, for ee's out to rob they poets."

"Don't be ridiculous man," says he. "I just happen to be passing this way because I am on my way to see - well, if you must know - I am on my way to see the miller Mr Rice who will be most put-out to learn that I have been accosted in this way. Now, unhand me and we shall say no more of it, for I can see you're a good fellow who is doing his duty as he sees fit."

"Not so fast, Mister. If you wuz walkin' to the miller's place - why stop when the poets stopped? Why duck yer 'ead down under the furze so's they couldn't see thee hidin' there? Oh, I saw thee all right. I wuz watchin' the watcher, though thee didn't see me do it."

He looked me keenly in the eye. "Look you bumpkin," he snarled. "If you do not unhand me now it will be the worse for you. You are dabbling in something more important than you can know and unless you stand aside I shall make sure charges are brought against you."

As he said it I noticed his free hand was reaching slowly into his great-coat pocket. It was a knife that came flashing out, but no sooner did it emerge I grabbed his wrist and bent it with such violence that the weapon clattered to the path.

"Now lookee 'ere," I growled pushing him back against a tree. "I do not take to fellers pullin' knives. I spect that's what you wuz goin' to use on the poets when you robbed 'em. I thinks my best plan is to knock ee unconscious, tie thee up, and then go down the village fer 'elp. There's a lock-up in Stowey and we'll get ee o'er there and the law can deal wi' ee..."

"No you are making a mistake, I give you my word," he hissed under the pressure of my hand at his throat. "Look, we will go to the mill together and Mr Rice will vouch for who I am. Please. Let us do that for then you will know that I am a government agent, brought here at the request of several important folk to spy upon those poets of yours. Do you not know we are at war with France? The word is that the fellows Coleridge and Wordsworth are both revolutionaries..."

"Ha," I laughs relaxing my grip slightly. "Then you 'ave bin made a fool of Mister. No two fellers in Somerset could be more be'ind King and Country than they. Tis the miller who you do needs to watch out for. Ee be a desperate Republican in secret – everyone do know that. You ask 'im 'bout 'is smugglin' and 'is connections wi' France – tis well known 'ere on Quantock what a slimy toad he be. Why, I do believe the snake 'ave deliberately put you on the wrong tack to cover 'is own goin's on!"

I laughed again and was about to let him go, but turned the grip vice-like around his throat once more and said: "Now look ee 'ere Mister Long Nose. I don't know who you really be, nor do I partic'lar care. But they poets is good people and I won't 'ave they bein' stalked an' terrorised in these yer 'ills o' mine – do ee understand? If I sees thee a-spyin' on 'em agin you shall a've me to deal wi' – and next time I'll break yer neck – not hang on to it while we 'as a little chat!"

And that was the end of our interview. The spy scuttled off down the valley and I never saw him again. Whether he believed my ludicrous tale about old man Rice I neither knew nor cared, but it would be pleasant to think the government agent saw fit to make the miller's life uncomfortable for a week or two. Our talk certainly put an end to his spying on my friends. Not only did he realise that his work was becoming common knowledge, and therefore useless, but the conversation he had overheard at Crowcombe Park Gate must have sent contrary signals to the great powers. Aware that the spy was probably listening, Coleridge and Wordsworth had both spoken warmly of their patriotism and of their loathing of all that was Revolutionary and French.

Nevertheless, Wordsworth believed his position on Quantock had become untenable and anyway, the great man was unable to renew his lease despite the protestations made by Tom Poole to the St Albyn family which owned Alfoxden. By June the brother and the sister were gone and, one month after that, my good friend Samuel Taylor Coleridge went after them. In such a hurry was he, that he left Sara behind for Tom Poole to look after until she was able to join him some months later. And so one of the most pleasant interludes of my life came to an end. My friendship with Sam Coleridge meant a good deal to me and I dearly loved the man for his bright, enthusiastic company.

Now I must enter the dark days. The final passage of this short life of mine. I will make it brief, for I am not proud of what has occurred. Indeed, I am ashamed by it. A woman has died, and because of it her husband must also go to meet his Maker, leaving two children without a parent or a home.

Shortly after the birth of Mercy and my adventure with the spy, Tom Poole came to me and, for once, was harsh and exacting with his words. "It will not do Johnny," he declared. "The girl is your own if the boy is not, and the parish insists that you shall marry. We are God-fearing people, you know that, and your continued presence in the parish will not be tolerated if you fail to make your position a legal one before God. Before you argue with me, think this: your right of coppicing can easily be withdrawn, as can your right to collect broom. Should these be taken away you will no longer be able to live on your beloved hills my friend. Think of that before you gainsay the Church. And one more thing. I know that these threats not will mean a jot to you if you are of a determined mind, but there is something else that might sway your judgement in the matter: you ought to be aware that Anne Rice has been proposed to by a gentleman, and I hear she is set upon the marriage."

They had me over a barrel of course, but as Mr Poole had said, their threats alone would not have altered my resolve. It was the news of Anne that took the wind from my already sagging sails. I behaved abominably. I sulked like a child before the absurd ceremony of my own wretched marriage took place. I sulked even more after it. If ever I have done a thing that has made the local folk dislike me, a thing that I am publicly ashamed of, it was the way I stormed out of the little church that forlorn afternoon when the showers and the sun chased each other across the countryside.

"There! I hope you are satisfied!" is what I said to my unhappy bride as I marched off between the graves after the service.

I have no excuses to offer. Jane had evil ways and a temper that could curdle blood – but she did not deserve that. What an appalling fellow I have been, I am quite willing to admit to it, but it took two of us to turn the paradise of Quantock into Hell. We were like two labourers demolishing a house. With great hammers we took it in turns to knock down each and every stone that supported whatever there was, whatever there had been, between us. Soon there was nothing left. I should have been content to leave it there, for I was always able to escape and rove the hills and embark upon my travels. But Jane was stuck there in the coombe, and she picked at the scars of our life like a child picks at a scab that has formed upon its knee. She picked until the blood poured.

The central symbol of her loathing seemed to manifest itself in the name of Anne Rice. Not a day would ever pass without her bringing up that sacred name. It was as if Anne was some devil-creature who had been sent to cast our lives to ruin. The more Jane picked away at the thought that I had been in love with the miller's daughter, the more she despised the thought of Anne. The spiral continued of course, for this caused me to loathe and abhor Jane more and more. Eventually the merest breath of her rasping voice was enough to send me loping off to the hill, where at least I had the larks and breeze to soothe my troubled soul.

A year passed after Coleridge left Quantock, and another year after that. I missed his company and I may also during those miserable months have missed the laudanum that he and his friends like de Quincey always seem to have about them. I could have procured my own, but it would not have been the same, I liked the effects of it in company with my poet friends because, I suppose, of the total sense of escape it seemed to afford. So wretched did life become, I do believe I should have been thoroughly addicted to the stuff had he stayed on. As it was I took to drinking more heavily than I should. That was easy enough, given that I was importing a good deal of contraband along the Quantock coast. Such was the pressure of the illegal work that it finished poor old Monty. I do believe he died of anxiety. One winter's dawn I found him frozen to his mud-horse, awaiting a shipment from Laversha that never came. What happened to our foreign friend I have never learned, though now, in my prison cell, I hear rumours that he has been seen of late along the loneliest stretches of the shore. Monty was frozen to that sledge of his, and as he sat there, quite dead, his eyes were wide open gazing at the great ocean that had so haunted his life. Laversha and the 'Mavis' never came again, which perhaps was just as well as my old friend Squire Crosse had ridden all the way from Broomfield to see me some weeks before Monty's passing. He warned me that Harold Rice was petitioning for my arrest.

"Everyone from Taunton to Porlock knows that you are smuggling Johnny. With your astute intelligence I have no doubt you can get away with it for some time yet. But you know, and I know, that your day will come. And when it does it may well be that I will have to sit in judgement over you. I have come to ask you not to bring that on me, indeed I implore you never to put me in that impossible position. For I love you like a young brother and you know that you are always welcome to return to my employ, so that you have no excuse as to money..."

After the smuggling finished I became wild. There were drinking bouts that would go on for days and I slept with more women than I care to admit to. During these dark days only one thing brought me back to my senses and that was beautiful Mercy. Her ringlety locks and her great grey eyes. I weep to think of her.

One night, returning home after a particularly lengthy drinking session, I came across the man I hated most: Harold Rice, bouncing down the lane in that governess cart of his. Some crazed mood overtook me and I ran and leapt up by his side. In the darkness I could feel his fear, and when he spoke I could hear the panic in his voice.

"What do ee think yer doin'?" he screamed.

"Don't you worry miller. You'll not die tonight," I snarled. "One dark dismal day though - just like I finished Buncombe - I shall come for you. Remember that old man. Every time you lay down to sleep, remember that Johnny Walford is coming - who knows when - and when he does your life will be at an end and they will find you spinning on that waterwheel of yours."

With that I leapt off and was gone into the night, though I could hear the miller sobbing to himself as his cart clattered and bounced him home. They say that for months he looked ashen and ill, and I am glad I have caused him such discomfiture.

As for my other enemy, William, I hardly caught sight of him during this time. On the one or two occasions we did meet, the old icy coldness stood between us and we did not pay heed to one another's existence, let alone speak. In the midst of my drinking bouts I recall hearing rumours about Jane being seen with him – and this neither surprised nor concerned me. So life went on in this wholly unsatisfactory vein until the terrible night befell us. The night. The night Jane died.

Let me say now that, though I do not claim innocence, I am still at a loss as to exactly what did occur up there on the hill. Yes, I was drunk. Badly drunk. Nevertheless, I am utterly perplexed as to some of the essential details.

Here is the tale as I know it: I had been drinking at the Castle of Comfort Inn and was well into my cups when Jane came in. Her arrival was a surprise as she had not darkened the door of the place for some while. We immediately fell into a dispute and she started to shout about how both brothers were alike and how we were as evil as one another. There must have been a dozen men in that saloon bar, and they all stood around witnessing this undignified row of ours. I asked her what she meant by bringing my brother into it.

"Have you been seeing him again?" I remember shouting.

"What if I 'ave?" she sneered "You Walfords is all alike. If you thinks I'm carryin' on wi' 'im you're wrong, see! You'd like it though, wouldn't you – if I was to run off wi' 'im. You could set up 'ouse wi' that little sister of 'is if she ain't married her Bath gentleman already."

Though there was such loathing between us, I had never raised a fist against my wife. Nor did I do so now but, feeling thick with drink, I brushed past her and announced to no-one in particular that I was off home. I was tired. Wearied by the alcohol, wearied by Jane, and wearied by life. All I wanted in those moments was my bed and sleep and peace.

From the Castle of Comfort it is not much of a climb up through the woods to a place called Five Lords where we turn right to ascend along the rim of Bin Combe and over Dowsborough to drop into Lady's Combe. Jane came out of the inn with me – I was too tired to protest – and all the way up the path she ranted so much I began to wonder if she might not be ill in some way.

"Don't think I can't see it!" she was yelling in her demented way. "Don't you think I don't know why you've been mopin' and drinkin' these past few months. Tis all about 'er gettin' wed ain't it? Can't you see I be a better woman than ten of she? That's right! Your own brother do say so. This very day ee 'ave bin on 'is knees to me again, beggin fer me to leave the stinkin' broomsquire's camp and move in with 'im down Quantox'ead. But I 'as turned him down again because I'll not let ee off that easily Johnny Walford. You 'ave turned my life to into Hell, and I am goin' to do the same to thee..."

At last I span around and faced her.

"Do you really want that?" I shouted. "Do you really want us both to live out our lives in misery? You have the Devil in you – and I would do anything to be rid of you!"

This stung her deep and she snatched out the most hurtful thing she could find to say: "Your brother don't think so – ee do think I be an angel."

"Then why don't you go to him? Take his child with you and leave me with mine. Petronilla and I will have Mercy and you and I shall be rid of one another for ever."

"If I goes," says Jane, with a distinct note of triumph in her voice. "Then they both come wi' me. After all – they'm both William's."

I was stunned. Shattered. There was only one thing I had left to truly love in this world and it was my little Mercy. And she is mine: to this day I am sure of that, you only have to look at her. Anyway, I was more filled with grief and rage than I've ever been in all my tumultuous life. For the first and only time in that life, I struck out and hit a woman. I can still hear the thud of it as my fist hit the side of her head. There was a gasp of pain, and then she was rolling over and over down the steep slope in the dark. It took a moment or two for me to collect my thoughts, for the violence had made me feel sick inside. Then I jumped down through the wurt bushes after her. It took me a while to find her, lying next to one of the dwarf oaks that grow on the higher flanks of Dowsborough, but find her I did and I held her in my arms sobbing with grief and shame for what I had done. She lay there unconscious. I tried to wake her, but eventually picked her up with thoughts of carrying her home. She was breathing still, I remember noticing that as I struggled back up the steep slope to the path. But she did not wake. So I turned and headed along towards Robin Upright's Hill thinking, I suppose, that at least I'd get her under shelter of my hut there, as a fine rain was beginning to fall.

I came to the point where the path splits and I halted here with indecision. My drunken mind could no longer make its mind up upon anything and I stood there in the rain unable to move. Whether to carry on to the hill hut, or drop down into Lady's Combe where our main camp was situated just a little further away - the simple choice was suddenly beyond me. Somehow my inability to think caused a weariness to overtake me, and I lay Jane down on the bracken and sat there by the side of the path to catch my breath.

The next thing I knew the first grey streaks of dawn were beginning to extend across the eastern sky. I wondered where I was for a moment as I lay there shivering with damp, and then I began to remember and looked around for Jane. There she was, lying in the bracken close by, just where I had left her. Only there was something that disturbed me about the way she lay there in the damp half light. Something was wrong. There was a darkness about her neck and chest - I reached out and touched her blouse, and my fingers sensed a cloying wetness there. My hand went up to her neck and those wet fingers continued their probing search until they leapt away with horror. It was when they felt the great hole where her throat had been. I lifted her limp body so I could see the throat in a better light. Her head fell back lifelessly at a horrible angle and that graceful neck of hers lay bare in the growing light of day. Across it, in the place where my lips had so often wandered, I could see a great gash running from ear to ear. She was cold. She was not breathing. The boundless and horrible truth dawned on me as the sun clawed its red and golden way above the eastern rim of the hills. Jane was dead. She had been murdered.

Whether the drink was still upon me, or whether the plain horror of the thing got the better of me, I do not know. All I could was sob and the sobs got longer and more uncontrolled until I could hardly breathe. In panic I thrust her body into a ditch which descended off to one side of the track, and then I took to my heels and did not stop running until I reached my hilltop hut. There I sat for an hour or more until the blind panic subsided and I realised that my clothes were covered in Jane's blood. There was a spare tunic stuffed in the corner of the hut and, without thinking, I changed into it. As I did so my big clasp knife fell from my pocket and I looked at it with dismay and dread. Slowly, I picked it up and pulled open the blade. It too was red with Jane's blood. This knife - the one my loving father had given me, the one I had used all my working life to cut the broom - had been the thing that had cut Jane's throat. There could be no doubt about it, for blood would never otherwise have found its way onto that closed blade.

Had I really done that terrible deed? Had I killed Jane in cold blood? Could I have taken out this blade and ripped it through the softness of her throat? Did I have that amount of malice within me, that I could do such a thing in my drunken sleep?

I had struck out, certainly, and perhaps I had knocked the life from her in doing so. There was not much life in Jane when I carried her from where she fell, though the last I remember she was breathing still. But I have no recollection of doing this thing with the knife. I cannot explain how it came to be.

Still in wild confusion I lit a fire and burned the blood-drenched shirt, then ran off to wash in Lady's Fountain. The cold water brought me back to some degree of sense and I walked quietly down to our main camp where I could hear Petronilla seeing to the children who were just stirring from their night's sleep. I sneaked into my hut and pretended I had been there all the night. I am not sure if I drifted into sleep through pure exhaustion, but it did not seem long before there was a great commotion going on outside. The dark shape of men filled the doorway of my hut and suddenly a voice was shouting: "Find his knife!"

I recognised that voice. It belonged to William, my brother.

That knife. I had gazed upon it with so much horror up on Robin Upright's Hill. I had burned the clothes, I had run home and managed to enter the place without attracting the attentions of my sister. But that knife. I knew, as William said it, that it was still lying on the floor of the hut up there. I knew also, that I had dropped the thing in horror and had not picked it up again, let alone wiped it clean. From that moment everything became chaotic. What William was doing there I did not know. But some men held me and tied my hands and Petronilla was shouting and crying and the children were screaming with fear. Some other men came into the camp and one of them held aloft my knife. They had been to the hut.

"He has murdered his wife," they cried.

At the Assizes William gave evidence against me. It was he who had found Jane's body. He later testified that she had been with him that day and the two of them had planned she should come to live with him. She was being forced to do it because of my drinking and violence at home. She had told him she would return to his cottage at East Quantoxhead that very night, and when she did not arrive he had gone to bed in disappointment. But during the night his suspicions turned to fear and concern. He said it was well known how drunk I could get, but what wasn't generally known was how violent I could become with my wife. At dawn William came out onto the hill looking for Jane and that is when he found her body in the ditch. He had run down to the village to raise the alarm and he had wailed that it must have been his own brother that had done her in.

I will not go into the full details of the case, for it has been well documented in the broadsheet newspapers. Suffice to say I had a number of character witnesses who said they believed I could never have committed such a crime. Petronilla's testimony that I had not been violent at home seemed to go unnoticed. Eventually, though, my undoing was wrought by William's story that Jane was to leave me, followed by the finding of the blood-drenched knife in the hut on Robin Upright's Hill, along with the blood stained remains of some charred clothes that were identified as mine.

A great groan went up at the judgement and, as Lord Kenyon donned his black cap, he wept which is a thing the inmates of that jail say has never happened before. I was numbed. I still cannot conceive my awful end. It is some small comfort to think the people of the hills have said they do not want me dead. That I admitted to striking Jane sealed the day, for she was as good as dead by the time she rolled down through the wurt bushes.

And so at last I come to the end of Johnny Walford's story. This is my final full day upon this Earth, for tomorrow I am to be taken to the gallows. My dear friend Thomas Poole is calling to see me later and to him I shall hand over this narrative for safe keeping. My corpse is to be taken down from the gibbet after a year and a day, and at that time he is to hand this manuscript to Anne Rice. I would not distress her with it beforehand, while I am hanging there: she must read it as if it were all some distant memory. But at least she will know the whole truth of my story.

For myself, I am ready to meet my Maker, though I shall miss the high hills and the fresh breeze that forever blows across Quantock's airy ridge. I shall miss the wild things and the lonely moon, the raging sea and the cool softness of the streams, the heaths and coombes, woods and cliffs and tracks and the redness of the soil – and all things that were the physical companions of my life. Most of all I lament that I shall not see my little Mercy again. Of course, I am also burdened with regrets regarding my dear Anne. Why fate should have cast us so cruelly asunder, I still cannot fully understand. But I am about to go forever from this ill fate to the place where I hope my dear father and mother await me. Perhaps the place where the ancient peoples are already gathered in some great new universe beyond the mountains of the west. I am the last broomsquire, and when I die at the noose, we shall be no more. God have mercy upon us.

POSTSCRIPT
BY THOMAS POOLE

It is one year to the day since they hanged Johnny Walford and tomorrow they will be cutting him down as ordered by the sentencing judge. Since the execution I have not had the heart to pass by what they now call Walford's Gibbet, for I could not bear to see him swinging there. However, no matter how painful it is for me, it is my duty to write down the events of the day that Johnny died as it was a promise I made to him on the eve of his death.

I must begin by saying that there were incidents which occurred on that day that I still do not understand, even though I have had a year to think them over. I have kept these small doubts to myself for one good reason: it reminds me in some ways of my position concerning the strange creature's in Andrew Crosse's laboratory, mentioned in the preceding narrative - there are things that I cannot bring myself to believe - let alone convince another party of the truth of what I may, or may not, have seen. In other words, there is some small seed of doubt in the back of my mind as to whether or not that disintegrating corpse that swings this one last night is really the body of Johnny Walford. It has been estimated that two thousand people attended the execution: one thousand nine hundred and ninety nine of them went home thinking the broomsquire had been despatched to meet his Maker. I am the one person who is not so sure of it.

Most probable is the explanation that I loved the boy, and that my poor old mind cannot bear the thought of him dead. Wishful thinking has caused me to reach out and grasp at any straw, and in doing so I have clutched at one or two areas of uncertainty that I have, perhaps, magnified and promoted in some way. A while ago Samuel Taylor Coleridge wrote to me asking me to pen a report of the execution so that he could publish the thing in a new journal of his. In that narrative I gave the official line. Now, because this is a private document, I give my true thoughts and, in so doing, leave it to some future reader to make up his or her own mind as to what really did occur at Walford's Oak.

These then, are the events as I witnessed them.

Johnny Walford was brought west to Quantock from the gaol at Bridgwater one fine summer's morning. They had prepared a caged cart for the journey, and this was escorted by a guard of a dozen men and a captain. All went smoothly until they reached my own village of Nether Stowey, where events began to occur which would make this no ordinary country hanging.

I travelled to Bridgwater on the eve of the execution to say goodbye to my young friend, and to collect from him the manuscript that lies before us. Upon returning to my village in the evening, I found the place in a state of uncommon tumult. I have never seen so many drunkards in the streets, and the din from the local inns would allow no-one in the village any sleep until the early hours. Johnny Walford was a popular man and there was, I knew, a feeling of anger abroad that he should die for the death of the woman who made his life hell. For weeks there had been rumours circulating that he did not carry out the murderous act. Certainly, the brutal cutting of a defenceless woman's throat was not in his nature - there was and is a commonly held belief that someone else carried out the deed while Johnny lay there in a drunken sleep. Some were pointing fingers at his unpopular brother William, for it was well known that the man hated his half-sibling and had good reason to be jealous of him. However, I was surprised at the unrest in Stowey that night. There seemed to be some agency at work whipping up the emotions of the villagers. I entered The George and, in the snug where some of the more respectable citizens gather, learned that an uncommon amount of contraband had found its way - not only into Stowey - but into villages and hamlets all along the slopes of the hills. There were rumours that the notorious smuggler Laversha had been seen about the place and that he was threatening to seek revenge for Johnny's death.

By the next morning the mood of the community had, if anything, worsened. Men were drinking heavily to dispel the thick heads inherited from the night before and, sometime around midday, a great cheer went up as a youth loped up our main street announcing the prisoner was on his way. I have never seen anything like it: within a minute or two the street was full and the mob began to move towards the Bridgwater end of the village to greet the condemned man. By the time they reached the last houses there were so many folk crowded into the street, they completely blocked it. The captain took a rather high-handed view of this and ordered them to clear the way, but I think even that haughty fellow was somewhat surprised by the spirit of the gathering. An angry jeering filled the place and the soldiers began to look nervous as they stood before the cart. On board Johnny Walford sat sullen behind the bars of his cage.

I had no chance of winning through to the front to use my influence on the crowd, so I climbed the wall of one of my properties in order gain a better view and hear what was being said. Several of the men at the front were telling the captain that the village was against the hanging and folk were determined they should not be allowed to proceed. It was futile, of course, they would have only made trouble for themselves, but they were drunk and boisterous and seemed set upon a fight. The captain was obviously an experienced officer and he saw that the situation required a diplomatic solution rather than one drawn out at the end of a musket. I heard him ask what they would wish for so that he could settle the situation.

"What do you say Johnny?" I heard them shouting...

"They'll hang me one way or t'other boys," he yelled back. "All I ask for is a quart of cider to steady my nerve, and then I shall be ready for it."

A great cheer went up for that popular young man, and a deal was struck by the ringleaders and the captain. It was that Johnny should be allowed to enter The George for refreshment before proceeding on his way.

"One thing, though," shouted the captain. "No-one shall enter there save Walford and a couple of my men. I'll not have the village ghosting him away - you shall all remain outside."

So the throng turned and swarmed back into the village, surrounding the troop and the cart up to the inn. As he passed my vantage point, Johnny gave me a desolate smile, and already I could feel the great sadness welling in my weary, sorry soul. I saw him again a few minutes later, and it was a sight I shall never forget until the day I join him in the Life Hereafter...

The horde was pressing against the walls of The George and the militiamen who stood guard at the door were having a job to keep them back. Scuffles were breaking out as people scrambled to get a peep through one of the windows of the place and it was all I could do to push my way towards the front. Being village magistrate I was eventually able to reach the door and demand entry, for I would speak with my young friend one last time, given the opportunity this surprising turn of events had provided. The captain recognised me and I entered the cool, dark, saloon where Johnny sat alone. There he was, with a lone sunbeam filtering through an upper window, illuminating him in all its golden glory. We could hear the commotion going outside and see the faces clamouring at the windows, but in the room there was silence and an uncanny sense of peace.

"So Thomas Poole," smiled Johnny, putting down his tankard, "I do believe if they were to hold a popular vote like the one Coleridge speaks of concerning his democracy - then I might be elected mayor."

I smiled and shouted through to the landlord to bring me a glass of flip.

Sitting down opposite him I asked: "Are you ready for the ordeal? Is there anything I can do or say?"

He took another long draught of his cider and looked across at me: "Don't you worry Mr Poole. I am as ready for death as I ever shall be, by which I mean - not at all. But, what will be, will be - and there is nothing I can do about it now. All I can do is repeat what I said yesterday: there is something wrong about the way Jane died. I have thought it over a thousand times a day, and from the bottom of my heart do not believe t'was my hand that did it."

"Do you know who did?" I asked.

"Not for sure. But it is my belief it could have been William. That very night she had refused him when he begged her to leave the hill and live with him. It was just the opposite of the tale he told the court. There was a running sore between us, as you know, and I believe he came that night to have it out with me once and for all. When he stumbled upon us lying there by the side of the road, me drunk and asleep, Jane unconscious from the blow I had struck her, a blow I freely admit to - he took his revenge. He saw that, by killing her with my knife, he should kill us both. God forgive him for it, for I cannot. I daresay he will be there today - as he was in court - and the only smile in the whole of Quantock will be the one on his face."

"I am not so sure," I replied. "The mob is angry and I do believe he has made himself scarce. No-one has seen him for a day or two."

Soon after that Johnny took his last long draft and together we stood and embraced like father and son.

"Goodbye dear friend," I sobbed. "I do not think I have the courage to come there this afternoon."

There were tears in Johnny's eyes when he beseeched me: "Please come Sir. For I could do with a friend to stand by me to the last."

Then he turned and strode out of the place with that great loping gait of his. Another cheer went up as he climbed aboard his cart and entered his cage without waiting for the guard to put him there. It is some two miles to the corner of Bin Coombe where the gibbet stands. I am told that a team of men had been there all morning preparing the rope and the cart that would be used in the hanging, and an audible sigh went up as the crowd rounded the bend and saw the hangman standing there. He was a giant of a man, standing high on the cart with his legs apart and a hood upon his head. Leather gauntlets stretched halfway up his arms and the Stowey people shuddered as he shouted instructions to his men.

There was a short talk between him and the captain of the guard while the crowds gathered - each man and woman placed themselves as best they could to watch justice being wrought. At last Johnny was taken from his cage and manhandled up onto the gibbet cart. Now a hush descended on the coombe, which was a thing of note I thought, given the number of people gathered there. All that could be heard was the brook and a few birds chirping in the woodlands that stretch beyond the coombe into Johnny's beloved hills.

The captain of the guard was asking Johnny if he had any final wish and now there was an excited stirring as he replied: "I would speak with Anne Rice..."

I later learned that he had spotted her on the journey from Stowey, so he knew that she was there. But Anne had retreated over the brow of the hill, as the poor girl's courage had ebbed away. It took a few minutes to find her, but at last she was brought, half-fainting, through the crowd. The crowd was being held back a distance of a dozen or so feet by the militiamen while the cart itself was ringed by some burly looking fellows who were in the hangman's employ. Anne was brought through the first cordon, but was stopped by the side of the cart by the hangman who jumped down to speak with her. You could see she was terrified as his masked face drew near to hers so that he could whisper a few words into her ear. All this time Johnny was standing there with his arms tied behind his back, looking down with tremulous sadness at the girl he loved. After a moment or two the great masked man lifted her up with all the ease of a child lifting a kitten, and deposited on the cart beside the prisoner.

Now there was complete silence. Not a person in that crowd dared to breathe as each of them strained to hear what Johnny was saying to her. But he spoke quietly as she lay there at his feet looking quite white and ill, and several times I thought she must faint away.

However, the girl was courageous enough to keep her eyes locked onto his, and somehow she remained propped up on her elbows listening to his pitiable address. No scene so tragic as the sight of those two lovers could I ever have imagined in all my years of book reading. Tears flooded down my face, and I know that there were few dry eyes in Bin Combe during those last, dismal moments. Childhood lovers bidding their last farewell; it was almost too much to stand.

Then the moment was over - the hangman, who had climbed back up to inspect his ropes, turned and pronounced the time had come. With this he reached out in a swift movement and placed a sacking bag over Johnny's handsome head. No mortal, as far as I know, ever saw his face again.

He was stalwart, I must say that. His body did not flinch or move at being plunged into the blackness of that sack. But it was too much for Anne; she hurled herself upwards at her former lover screaming his name, and the weight of her sudden embrace knocked him off his feet. Down they went together onto the flat bed of the cart and then a great cry went up as they rolled off the back and fell out of sight. The big hangman was down there with them in a second, and in another instant the entire scene was filled with his assistants so that none of us could see what was going on. It was mayhem for a minute and then the hooded prisoner was returned, roughly, to the platform by a dozen strong hands.

The fall had obviously been a blow to the over-stretched nerves of the poor Johnny, because now, instead of standing patiently awaiting death, he writhed and kicked and squirmed. We could hear his muffled screaming under that awful hood. No fewer than four of the hangman's burly assistants were required to hold him steady enough for the noose to be put around his neck. The Lord forgive me, I can understand the fear of it, but I was surprised if not a little disappointed to see brave Johnny lose his fortitude at the very end. It was not what I would have expected of him.

The rope was tightened and the two horses attached to the cart were whipped. Off they shot and there was a crack as the rope went taught under the weight of the falling body. It was horrible. He writhed and kicked and struggled in some grim final, fatal fight for life. But at last the Quantock air that had fuelled his life, was taken from him, and Johnny Walford breathed no more.

It has been my dreary duty to attend several hangings over the years. At each and every one of them there has been a spontaneous roar from the crowd as the condemned man drops. If he is loathed for his crimes, it will be a cheer; if his death is regarded as being undeserved, then it will be greeted by an angry jeer. When Johnny dropped there was only a communal intake of breath. So quiet was it, that it was almost inaudible. You could hear just one thing above and beyond the struggling of the dying man: that was the beautiful fluted song of a skylark high above.

Once Johnny stopped kicking the hangman finished his grisly deed, by hauling the corpse high until its sad limp shape almost reached the bough some five and twenty feet above the ground. And that is where my young friend has remained bound by a metal cage, through sun and rain and sleet and snow, all this long year. Tomorrow they will cut him down and bury his remains beneath the tree: it will only be a few bones and weathered rags that are placed in that unmarked grave, though some of his old friends are saying that handsome Johnny Walford looks better dead after a year than most men do in their prime.

Now for the subsequent remarks I wish to make regarding the few doubts and questions which have been nagging at me. I will start at the point where my own reservations and qualms began. As one of the local magistrates it was my duty to go forward to sign the official witness document declaring the prisoner had been duly executed in accordance with the sentence of the court. There were three people required to make their mark, and one of them was the hangman himself. Now, a curious thing happened as I made my way towards the captain of the guard who held the document. The hangman, being closer, had reached him first and so was bending over to take up the quill as I arrived. What I am about to state next is, I must admit, as fanciful almost beyond belief – and I beg the reader to remember that my nerves were badly shaken by watching the death of my young friend. But here it is, for what it is worth: as the man bent forwards, so the back of the hood he wore rode up to the collar of his tunic – and in the little area beyond, for a fleeting moment, I could see the man's skin. It was quite dark. No man born north of the Mediterranean would have skin this colour.

I had but the merest glimpse of it, but that glimpse has been enough to get my suspicions galloping where they shouldn't. There is only one man of that hue who has ever come to these parishes to my knowledge, and that is the notorious mate they call Laversha. Johnny's narrative states the man had sworn to repay him in thanks extricating the three of them from the clutches of the Revenue. The mate is a legend in some parts of the West Country for his daring deeds and his absolute disregard for authority. He is supposed to have some sort of hideout on the island of Lundy not far down the coast off North Devon. What I am about to propose would not be beyond his resourceful abilities.

In the coming weeks I discovered the identity and whereabouts of the hangman on duty that day, and went to Taunton to speak with him. He was tight-lipped to say the least, and would only say the work of a hangman is not open to question by the likes of me.

"Have you got a complaint to make Sir?" he asked. When I said I did not, he would answer me no more. It did not escape my notice that, as a prison warder who spent most of his working life indoors, he was one of the palest men I have ever seen. The work of an executioner is unique – and it is not uncommon for a hangman to keep his hood firmly on his head during the process. It is an unpopular role and there must always be a danger of revenge. But in this instance, my mind cannot help but reflect on how just entirely covered Johnny's hangman remained. So there is this question of the skin colour. It is no exaggeration to say these thoughts have harried me each and every night from the night of the execution until this.

After I had signed my name by the gibbet and talked to the captain of the guard for a minute, I recall looking up to take one last look at what remained of my friend hanging high above us. I have to admit, it certainly looked like the young broomsquire, the clothes and boots were the same as the ones I had seen just an hour or so before in the saloon of The George. When I looked down again, the hangman had gone. I could just make out his cart careering off down the track scattering the crowds, but it was all a blur from where I stood and he was almost hidden from view by the dozen or so men who rode with him.

For nostalgia's sake, so that I could meditate upon the short and happy life of my lost friend, I rode up over Dowsborough and made my way home along the ridge of the hills. At a place where Johnny used to collect the broom I stopped and lay down on the sward for a while to collect my thoughts. It was from that lofty place that, after an hour, I was to spy the second thing that would stir some small degree of doubt within me. A boat, a yawl I think, was setting its sails just off Quantock's Head, an odd place for a ship to be anchored – there being no landing stage or quay anywhere near. It was as still a day as you could wish for in this breezy part of the world, so hardly a breath filled those sails. Most skippers would have remained at anchor and waited for a waft of wind, but this fellow was so determined to be away from the shore, that four men were out ahead in a pulling boat, rowing for all they were worth, towing the vessel from under the lee of the cliffs. I can see her now, slowly making for the centre of the channel where a few whiffs of breeze eventually filled her sails. Then off to the west and the Atlantic she went with every piece of cloth they could put on her raised to help them on the way.

Who was on that boat I wonder? It is a question that will haunt me until I die.

There is one other thing. William Walford has not been seen from that time until this. His disappearance is a mystery. His cottage was left intact, as if he intended returning to it, but there has been no sign or trace of the man from when he was last seen, two days before the execution, until now. Some say guilt overcame him and he finished his own life. Others say he had only remained in Quantock-country to see the downfall of his hated brother, and as soon as this was achieved he was off to foreign lands. I wonder. William loathed his brother to such an extent that I believe nothing would have kept him away from the hanging. I saw the evil smile upon his face when Judge Kenyon passed sentence and it sent a shiver down my spine.

So what is my fanciful, outlandish, contention? Well, as I say, it is only by believing in the incredible that one could possibly give credence to my suspected, and I will add highly private, version of events. Let us imagine that Laversha, the smuggler, took Johnny's plight to his heart; let us imagine that he used his rumoured wealth to corrupt the hangman from Taunton. I believe most men have their price, and having met the miserable gaoler, I would not imagine he placed his too high. Given that he went hooded and covered from head to toe, who could have known the colour of the hangman's skin? Save for just one poor deluded Nether Stowey businessman who may or may not have caught a glimpse of it...

Then let us suppose Laversha used his influence to whip up the emotions of the countryside. I heard talk that he had been seen and know for a fact that the place was suddenly awash with contraband liquor. The crew of the 'Mavis' were a rum lot, by all accounts, and there were others besides. I have since heard that Britannia French and her people turned up a few days before the execution. It would have been nothing for them to kidnap William Walford.

Then there were the scenes at Nether Stowey the morning Johnny was brought through. It is not in the nature of Stowey folk to join an angry mob, but something riled them to it that day. Why? In my fanciful version of events, how could that help Johnny's cause?

Well, what if Laversha needed a delay to prepare his own prisoner? He would require sight of Johnny's attire so that the same clothes could be found. I am talking here about a switch. William Walford was exactly the same height and build as his half-brother. It was generally known that Johnny believed it was his own brother who slit Jane's throat. Suppose Laversha dreamed up his own version of justice? Suppose he thought William should hang for the crime instead? Once the bag was on the head of the prisoner, there could be no telling any difference, as long as they were dressed in more-or-less the same attire. There can be no doubt that, when the doomed man was brought back onto the cart after toppling off under Anne's embrace, he acted in a very different way. I do not believe Johnny would writhe in such a panic, but the person under that hood most certainly did.

Here is another doubt that clouds my mind - looking back I believe Johnny Walford was too much at his ease when I had my final talk with him at The George. I had seen various people have words with him as cart passed through the throng - what if news of a switch reached his ears then?

"Ask for Anne Rice," is what I can imagine someone whispering up between the bars as the crowd crushed against the cart. "Laversha says make sure you fall when she embraces you."

That is all it would have needed. Anne herself could easily have been primed for it: been told that it would not take much to topple Johnny who was bound hand and foot. The fall. The ensuing confusion. No-one in the crowd, nor even the militia, could see what happened there behind the cart. The more I think of it, the more I believe - in the hands of daring, resourceful men - a switch would have been possible.

Nine tenths of me assumes that they will cut down Johnny Walford from the gibbet tomorrow morning. But I do have a shadow of doubt about it. A small part of me believes they exchanged him for his brother behind that cart. Same height and build. Hooded. Same or similar clothes. The dark patch of skin I swear I saw. The hangman's cart being driven away at speed surrounded by men so you could not see what lay within it. The boat desperately pulling off Quantock's airless shore. The fact William has never been seen since…

There is one final thing. I had undertaken to ensure Petronilla was kept in sufficient funds so that she could raise the children. She would come to me once a fortnight and I would give her alms: it was a private arrangement and we did not want the neighbourhood knowing of it. Six months ago Petronilla failed to appear. I went in search of her and found the Walford camp empty with a look of vacancy about it that led me to believe no-one had been there for several weeks. The only clue I had was from a Mr Chidgey whom I saw one day with the Walford pony. He told me Petronilla had given him the beast one night and said she was moving away to live. She would tell him no more, saying her destination was a secret.

"That is right," said Avice, the sister, when I called to question her. "She 'ave moved to Bath where she be workin' for 'er that used to be called Anne Rice. The lady 'as given Nilla a position so she can help with the child she had six months ago. Anne kindly said the Walford children can go with 'er and they will be looked after."

So I went to the miller to ask him what had become of his daughter, but the man was ill in bed and, apparently, was in so bad a way that he could no longer speak.

The housekeeper explained: "Tis the daughter see. They say she've had a child and left the country and ain't never likely to return. She were to get married to a gen'leman, but we hear's that 'ave fallen through."

Coleridge wrote a line once: "The joy within me dallied with distress."

In my case it is the other way around, my sadness and distress has been lightened by my dalliance with the version of events that I have construed, perhaps, to help bear the burden of my grief.

Either Johnny's bones are to be cut down tomorrow, or they are the remains of his unhappy brother. Some days I believe one thing, the next I am miserable and believe the other. But when I go down to take my ease in the lime bower I usually turn to the happier version of events. Coleridge left me an Aeolian harp which hangs there in the corner of my garden and sings in the breeze. When it does I am minded to recall the words that the poet wrote while listening to it one day:

"Such a soft floating witchery of sound
As twilight Elfins make, when they at eve
Voyage on gentle gales from Fairy-land,

Where melodies round honey-dripping flowers,
Footless and wild, like birds of Paradise.
Nor pause, nor perch, hovering on untamed wing...."

When I contemplate those words my mind inevitably portrays a vision of Johnny Walford and his lover and the children. They are together, laughing, in bright sunshine on the bows of a ship. And they are far, far away, passing through the isles of some Earthly paradise.